D1328374

Breathing Out the Ghost

To Carol—
Thank you so
much for your support.
I really appreciate you
buying it and your
kind words about it.

Best,
[signature]
4-21-08

breathing out the ghost

By
Kirk Curnutt

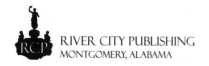

RIVER CITY PUBLISHING
MONTGOMERY, ALABAMA

© 2007 by Kirk Curnutt. All rights reserved.
All rights reserved under International and Pan-American Copyright Conventions. Without limiting the rights under copyright reserved, no part of this publication may be reproduced, stored in or introduced into a retrieval system, or transmitted, in any form, or by any means (electronic, mechanical, photocopying, recording, or otherwise), without the prior written permission of both the copyright owner and the publisher of the book.

Published in the United States by River City Publishing
1719 Mulberry Street
Montgomery, AL 36106.

Designed by Lissa Monroe

First Edition—2007
Printed in the United States of America
1 3 5 7 9 10 8 6 4 2

This is a work of fiction. Names, characters, places, and incidents either are the product of the author's imagination or are used fictitiously, and any resemblance to actual persons, living or dead, events, or locales is entirely coincidental.

Library of Congress Cataloging-in-Publication Data:

Curnutt, Kirk, 1964-
Breathing out the ghost / Kirk Curnutt. — 1st ed.
p. cm.
    Summary: "Colin is looking for his son and the man he believes responsible for the boy's disappearance. Assisting him is a PI who lost his license and whose warped sense of duty ties him to Colin. A noir thriller, a tale of the consequences of unchecked grief and painful truths"—Provided by publisher.
    ISBN 978-1-57966-070-3
    1. Missing children—Fiction. I. Title.
    PS3603.U76B73 2007
    813'.6—dc22
                        2007027722

For my mother
who cleared the land

And my son
who reaps the harvest

"Remember that my life is breath;
mine eye shall no more see good.
The eye of him that hath seen me shall
see me no more;
thine eyes are upon me, and I am not.
As the cloud is consumed and vanisheth away
so he that goeth down to the grave shall
come up no more;
he shall return no more to his house,
neither shall his place know him any
more."
—Job 7:7-10

"At this stage of the history I was disabled by any further search for my little boy. The incessant strain upon mind and body for the past months—the anxious pursuit—the weary labor by day, and the sleepless nights—were surely a heavy burden to carry, without the heartless slanders and infamous calumnies which were coined and circulated about Mrs. Ross and myself. All these coming on like a flood made serious inroads upon my reasonably strong constitution. For several weeks I had felt my strength yielding to the excessive tax upon my system, and for days was kept up only by longing for our lost darling. When the break came, it was sudden and overwhelming. . . ."

—Christian K. Ross, *The Father's Story of Charley Ross, the Kidnapped Child* (1876)

idiot wind

Let me tell you about the time your grandfather took a sledgehammer to the car.

It was the summer I told everyone I was sixteen, the summer I lost all sleep because the hourly boys at Dow walked out on management. Your grandfather worked the acid tankers back then, and he was beholden to the union, so that left seven of us—me, Mom and Dad, Robbie, and the girls, Cassie, Devlin, and Sally—to get by on three hundred dollars a month strike pay. Right away we were unable to meet the mortgage, and toward the end grocery money was scarce. With five children, my parents had no savings account. We did the best we could, of course. We learned to swallow powdered milk without making faces and not comment that we were dining on macaroni and cheese for the umpteenth day in a row. We knew to appreciate our mother for our one indulgent delicacy: the bread she baked with flour and eggs donated by the church auxiliary. Years later I realized she encouraged us to gorge on her endless loaves so we'd be too bloated to complain. She wasn't the only one who picked up tricks that summer. We kids learned not to ask for seconds or to speak too loud. We learned to stay outside long after dark and to keep the fan running in the bathroom. We did these things because we didn't want to set your grandfather off. Let me tell you, it wasn't easy. In that environment there wasn't a tiny sound that didn't ring loud as an explosion, not a move to be made that didn't make the claustrophobia all the more stifling.

Nights were the worst. You thought with silence would come sleep, only there wasn't ever any silence. As you lay in bed you became aware of all sorts of noises. The cedar beams popped and groaned, the drywall cracked as the foundation shifted. Outside, birch leaves slathered themselves creepy-crawly on the shingles. If you were lucky you might drift off for an hour or so, but then a pipe would clang, or an eighteen-wheeler somewhere would accelerate, and you'd be brought right back into a state of lucid, aching insomnia. What usually kept me bright-eyed and bushytailed was the sound of your grandfather pacing the house. He was doing his best to wear out his restlessness.

Your uncle was a little smarter than me in those days. He wore headphones so he didn't have to hear the racket. All night his spindle dropped records onto the turntable beside our bunks. I know your grandfather heard that sound, too, because he often came into our bedroom to set the needle back in its grip. Some nights I would hear him slip the headphones from around Robbie's ears, not gently at all, really, so I'd be wondering why Robbie never woke up. It never entered my mind he might be playing possum, like I was. Then other nights I'd feel your grandfather breathe all over me, hot and heavy. He didn't just inhale and exhale—he had this kind of anxious *humph* that burst all concentrated, like kettle steam. There were times he would hoist himself up and onto my covers, and he would try to relieve the deadweight by resting it on me. This would go on for hours until I'd imagine my spine cracking. This particular night, though, he just stood at my bedside and whispered, "If you're up, I need your help."

breathing out the ghost

He led me to the kitchen and handed me a bottle of sleeping pills he'd bought off his shop steward. "Hide them," he said. "And don't tell me where." Then he turned around and started counting out loud.

I didn't question. I slid a few drawers out. I shuffled the cracker and cookie boxes, opened cabinets and rearranged soup cans, all to throw him off the scent. Then I stuck the bottle behind an old jar of pickled something-or-other that had sat untouched for years in the lazy susan. When I went back to bed he'd taken to sitting crooked on the davenport, peeking out a bay window that looked past a flowerbox and some shrubs to the front yard. I didn't realize what a good job I'd done until, some time later, I heard him rifling the spice rack.

You see, son, the thing is, when you crave it most, sleep is like a ghost. The relief it brings evaporates from your memory, but the weight of wanting it remains. Sometimes as I drive now, thinking I can find you having to convince myself that I can find you& I imagine things crawling across the highway. Not dogs or raccoons or deer even, but shapeless things. What are they? Hard to say, exactly. They usually appear around the thirteenth or fourteenth hour when I have a hundred miles to go before I can rest. But that's phony of me, I know. There's nowhere I'm expected. It's not about getting anywhere now; it's just about getting on.

I like to think that's the feeling he faced as he grabbed hold of that sledgehammer. He wasn't attacking the burden of his expectations, but something altogether more formidable: their loss. I can't tell you what he thought his life should have been. I only saw the resentment he felt for what it had become. I do know what my intentions for my life were: you, plain and simple. And the joke is that now I, too, must live with what I don't have. Back then I couldn't begin to imagine what kind of indignation could shove a man to such extremes, but now it's as clear to me as the yellow lane lines in front of my face. You can't start a fire without a spark, and my hiding those pills was the flint he needed to strike out against.

Lucky guy. I'm still waiting for my turn to go off.

Here's how the rest of that night played out:

By the third crack of the sledgehammer your grandmother was slapping the walls, feeling for the light switch. Then came another concrete smack as the hall trembled into brightness and Robbie audibly stirred. I felt responsible, knowing as I did that I'd buried your grandfather's treasure without leaving him any kind of map, without leaving him so much as an X to mark the spot. So I slipped down to the bottom bunk and put my toes on Robbie's chest, rousing him. The turntable was playing the second song on side two of *The White Album*, which, two days earlier, we'd shoplifted together.

By the time we made it to the living room your grandmother was already at the bay window. The T-shirt she slept in barely covered the fading blue butterfly tattooed to her thigh. She had to stand on her toes to see through the shrubbery, which needed pruning. It was one of the few bits of yard work we'd yet to complete as we tried to reassure your grandfather that, despite the past due notices piling up by the telephone, his world could still be tidied and orderly. I remember the smell of varnish on the trim as I joined her at the window. The evergreens and saplings outside shivering. A silhouette dancing in the driveway, reflections flashing off the mallet. The whole family joining us.

Cassie, Devlin, and Sally clung to Mom. They slept in your grandfather's old T-shirts, too, and each time the hammer sounded they seemed to shrink, swallowed alive in his stained cotton. Robbie and I, we were older, so we just stiffened and gawked. Soon we could see lights from other houses flip on, and the neighborhood became a constellation held together by the gravity of our disbelief. Your grandfather struck the windshield so hard a wiper flipped over the car's roof. After that, the girls covered their ears and hid their faces, but I was looking at that butterfly tattoo. You must understand: your grandparents were seventeen when they had me, so when I was younger I saw her more as a beautiful older sister than a mother. Once after church I spied the minister pointing at her, whispering to a parishioner, "Five kids, out of *that*," and I had to agree. Your grandfather had a butterfly tattoo as well, on his right bicep. They were matching jokes, a dare they'd carried out when they were too young to know better, before we happened. But by that night I'd already recognized that those tattoos had become sad graffiti on an earlier undercoat of life that the grit of getting on failed to cover up.

He didn't stop until he pounded the bumper clean off. For a time, he stared at it, and though darkness confined him to shadow, I imagined him looking at it remorsefully, as if it were a mutt he'd struck while speeding. He didn't seem concerned or even aware that he woke the neighborhood; he just carried the hammer into the carport and joined us in the living room.

"Now they're welcome to it," he said on his way to bed.

We didn't know what that meant until the next day when the repo men showed up. Robbie and I were in the yard, playing with an old chemistry set that, like everything in our lives that summer, somebody from church had given us out of pity. We watched as the men backed the tow truck into our drive, indifferent to the front tire that gouged our yard. When they finally caught sight of what they'd come to collect they scratched their heads and spit into the grass. Then they stared at us, waiting for an explanation. I stiffened my shoulders and said the only thing I knew to say. I was my father's son, after all.

"You're welcome to it," I told them.

After the car was hauled away, we went inside to make sure our sisters knew not to ask where it disappeared to. I don't know if my dad relaxed at all that night, but at least he didn't go digging in the lazy susan. Years later—I was in college, I think—I found his bottle of sleeping pills right where I left it, right there behind that jar of pickled something-or-other.

It's funny. Back then I would have given everything I owned—which, obviously, wasn't much–for a little peace of mind. Now I've lost all I ever wanted, and I'm afraid to sleep. I'm afraid to even rest my eyes for fear of what I might miss.

It's funny, too, how in the years since then I've come to admire what your grandfather did. At the time I hated him. He embarrassed me. That's why I told everyone who didn't know better that I was sixteen when I was really only fourteen. I was already shaving by then, and stashing the odd-job money I earned from neighbors thinking it would get me a life of my own. I didn't know yet that being a man doesn't mean you're always able to exact control. I didn't know that sometimes immolating yourself in anger is your only option. Now I can honestly say I love my father more than I'm capable of loving anyone else, including you. Why?

Because a man seeking his father seeks God, but a father reduced to searching for his son only chases after the man he thought he ought to be.

(*Laughter*).

Sorry. That's as profound as the philosophy gets when you've only got you and the life you should be leading left to entertain.

Maybe that's the real difference between your grandfather and me: he wasn't the kind to talk out of turn. There was more eloquence in that one act of beautiful ferocity than you'll ever hear in these rambling hours I've put to tape. I, meanwhile, am a blabbermouth. I can't shut up, I can't not talk, and I hate myself for it. Sometimes I have to say your name out loud, A.J., just to believe you ever really existed. It's almost a year since you've been gone. The milestones are becoming millstones. A whole year, and what's become of me?

I've become the Ahab of the interstates, mewling and puking, raging at the breath of a mist that recedes into nothing.

Raging about it, about you. If you were here, would you hide my pills for me?

Sometimes I get so tired sleep jumps in front of my wheels, a suicide.

But you, you're different. You're a vapor, a whiff, a movement, and all I have are the leftover vibrations to chase. You can ponder perpetual motion, sings the radio, and believe you me, I do. Perpetual motion's my spook.

The wind's steeper now, and it's not even tornado season. It rattles the truck, sucks hard at the windows. I have to strap the recorder to the dashboard with duct tape to keep both hands on the wheel. I have to. Wind is a sound without shape, another ghost, another claustrophobia. There are so many now, I run into them, headlong, all the time.

So many that sometimes I think that this truck is nothing but your grandfather's old house straddling four stupid, spinning tires.

philately

In the aftermath, Robert Heim would look back and recognize the paper cut as the pivot from which everything that was to happen from there on out had sprung. If the sting of the slice from the envelope hadn't been so distracting, he would've noticed the lack of a return address, the familiar eighth-grade-education slant of the handwriting, certainly the stamp, on which a watercolor rendering of a napping mother bathed in strokes of auburn and tan nestled a child alongside two ominous words: AMBER ALERT. That should've been impossible to overlook, but Heim was tired from his night shift and flustered by the number of bills choking his box, and so after he sucked the seeping blood off his index finger, he ripped the envelope open, irritated at the prospect of being obliged to attend whatever friend's child's birthday party he assumed this was an invitation to. Instead, he was greeted by a Halloween message (*Have a Spooktacular Day*) cute enough to give his four-year old a giggle. For a second Heim considered sharing the pun with Alex. Nothing cracked his son up like wordplay. He knew he wouldn't be able to repeat the joke, though—not without thinking of the note scribbled beneath it:

> *Hey ho Heimster-holster:*
> *I hope you are happy in your new life. I am in mine.*
> *Your friend, D. B. Johnson*

Anybody else might have crumpled the card or torn it in half, but Heim returned it to the envelope. He was careful that way. He believed in sequences and procedures but most of all in consequences, so as he sat on his stoop to settle his senses he imagined the trouble there'd be in his family if he simply threw the thing away. Stephie, his wife didn't wholly trust him anymore, was maybe even a little scared of what he was capable of; he suspected she went through the garbage now and then to make sure he hadn't drifted back to the business that had gotten him convicted, fined, damn near divorced. To persuade himself that hiding the card wasn't a misstep, Heim did what he always did in moments of uncertainty: he marshaled the numerical facts of his life and stood them in a line. He was thirty-three; over the past seventeen years he'd worked sixteen different jobs (exactly one of which he'd been passionate about); he was his wife's second husband, though she was his first and—unless he screwed up again—his last; he was dad to a stepdaughter and to a son of his own; he'd recently managed to cut his credit-card debt to under twelve thousand dollars, which meant at least a portion of the monthly three-hundred dollar check Stephie sent in finally went to principal instead of covering the interest; he was on probation for three years. Reciting these figures was a trick he'd learned in the Air Force, sort of like saying your name, rank, and serial number over and over.

What they didn't teach you in the Air Force was that some numbers unsettle as much as they square. Like the number of cards. This was the sixth one in ten months Dickie-Bird Johnson had sent him. It was only the second he'd opened, but still—six. That was more than five, and five was how many Heim had convinced himself it would take before Dickie lost interest and left him alone. Why five he couldn't say. It just seemed like the right number for making your point, especially when your only point was to taunt someone you'd managed to get the upper hand on. Now Heim knew it wouldn't end until he and Dickie and St. Claire all rode the circle to completion. He rose, sighed, wondered when that would happen, whether Stephie would still have him after it did. In the meantime, all he knew to do was focus and make sure he was never again too distracted to look over his mail before opening it.

THE PAPER CUT CONTINUED to bleed, so he went to the junk drawer in the kitchen for a bandage. He wrapped his fingertip until the pressure turned his skin red. The tightness was comforting; it gave him a sense of security. So did the To-Do list he found on the refrigerator when he reached for a glass of milk. Unlike other men he knew, he never complained about the errands his wife wrote up for him; Heim was a man of lists as well as procedures and sequences and consequences. Lists were steps, steps were patterns, patterns were forms, and forms ensured a shape to things. Today's list was disappointingly simple: a small grocery run (including paste and a new pair of baby scissors for Alex's daycare), then run Trace, his stepdaughter, to a piano lesson in the afternoon.

Simple, but perfect. He could exercise and then finish a couple of files on the freelance gig he'd picked up. He ran background checks on local contractors for a consumer referral service. It was his sixteenth job and relatively easy work—all computer—and he was as close to passionate about this job as he would probably be for some time to come, if ever.

He hadn't forgotten about the card, but he was trying to. It was tucked under his arm. He was fighting the temptation to look at the postmark. He didn't need to know where Dickie was. Then again, if Dickie was stalking him, maybe it was irresponsible not to look. His family might be at risk.

This was the sixth time Heim had wrestled with this dilemma. Except for the first card, he hadn't looked at any of the postmarks, and nothing bad had come of it. Dickie even managed to slip out of his thoughts from time to time. That was usually right before the next card showed up. Heim again considered that his family might be at risk. If not his family, maybe him—though it was unlikely. Attacking adults wasn't Dickie's standard M.O. How different life would be if it were, Heim thought. Maybe then somebody might've believed him when he claimed self-defense.

He went into his bedroom, tossed the card onto the rumpled duvet, and stripped off the uniform from his fifteenth job. Since summer he'd been the nightshift rent-a-cop for a chain of grocery stores. From midnight to eight he patrolled fluorescent aisles, making sure teenagers didn't five-finger snack pies and candy bars. It was by far the lamest of his many careers, but it was also the first money he'd been able to bring home since his legal problems, and it had allowed him to start making amends with the creditors who'd come after him while he was unemployed the previous winter. Heim hung his shirt and trousers in the closet and sat on the edge of the mattress in nothing but his underwear. For several minutes he turned the envelope over and over in his hands. He wasn't really looking; the postmark just sort of jumped out at him: Tippecanoe Indiana 46570, the stamp read. Tippecanoe Welcomes You!

Easy enough. No harm, no foul. Heim couldn't say where Tippecanoe was, but he knew the Indiana state line was two hundred miles away. Two hundred miles of Michigan between him and Dickie seemed a safe enough distance; Dickie was Indiana's problem.

He pulled on a pair of sweatpants and laced his tennis shoes, relieved. One of his few pleasures this past year had been running. He'd taken it up while on bail, to burn off the stress of waiting for his lawyer and the D.A. to hash out his case. Now he was so addicted, he'd started training for a marathon. Dickie could send all the cards he cared to; it wasn't going to interfere with his regimen. Heim was a man of routines as much as lists and sequences and procedures. This morning he planned to swim seventy-two laps at the Bay City Y, then do eight miles on Salzburg Road. The run would leave his calves quivering all the way up past the flanks of his thighs to the ilium ligaments lashing his oblique muscles to his pelvis. And that brand of exhausted tension would signal accomplishment, a goal achieved.

Hidden under a pile of winter sweaters on an out-of-reach shelf in his closet was a fireproof lockbox. He hadn't opened it in two months, not since Dickie's last love note. As he set the box on the bed he heard the familiar rattle of something he didn't want to see; he opened the lid and tossed the card inside without looking. He'd almost returned the lockbox to the shelf when he realized how silly it was to be this nervous.

He reopened the box and laid out the six cards on his mattress. Apparently, generic stamps weren't good enough for taunting a guy. Dickie had decorated each envelope with a commemorative one, complete with etched selvages. In addition

20

breathing out the ghost

to the Amber Alert, there was a Judy Garland, a chocolate kiss, a Jonas Salk, the tallest cactus in America, and a Christmas Madonna with child (with a June cancellation). On a whim Heim opened that one. It was a Father's Day card.

He threw it down and then arranged the six of them in chronological order. The postmarks told a story: the first one was from Cass City, which wasn't surprising since that's where the trouble with Dickie had occurred. Heim even recognized the date—only a few days after he signed his plea deal. The next ones were stamped Tecumseh, then Niles, both still in Michigan, then Tipton, Indiana. It was the fifth one that caught his attention: Mine La Monte, Missouri. So Dickie had wandered that far west over the summer and was now doubling back.

He returned the cards to the lockbox and the lockbox to the shelf. Lap swim at the Y didn't start until nine, so he had a half-hour to kill. He decided to knock out one of the background checks.

He booted up the computer in the den and logged into one of the records databases he subscribed to. Background checks were easy, but not easy money. No matter how many Heim ran they never seemed to add up to more than two hundred a month. Before his private detective's license was yanked he could make seventy bucks an hour hunting down deadbeat dads and runaway wives. Kids and mental cases were harder to track because they rarely used credit cards or social security numbers. They made the work harder, but Heim appreciated the challenge. The best part of his fourteenth job, the one his probation could get yanked for going back to, had been going on the road. He liked chasing down leads regardless of whether they led to conclusions. The road was order and discipline. On average it took him twenty hours to find someone. There were cases he hadn't closed, of course, though not many. Trails go cold fast if somebody's intent on not getting caught, but you sensed right away when you couldn't solve those so you saved the client his money and you your sympathy. Several PIs he knew mislead clients by pursuing dead-ends to rack up the bill. Heim had never done that. The only case he ever kept working when he wasn't one hundred percent sure he could close it was A.J. St. Claire. By the time things went sour on that one he wasn't even invoicing his time. No, sir. That case ended up costing him, and dearly, too. It had cost him just about everything he valued.

The first background check was a no-brainer. Two clicks of his computer mouse and Heim knew that a contractor in Midland County had been sued twice in small claims court for shoddy work. Heim doubted that the guy would get much work in Bay City once he faxed in his findings. He printed off the information, intending to do the paperwork later.

He let his mind wander back to the cards in the lockbox, to the canceled stamps that were the signposts of Dickie's vagabonding. What would take Dickie all the way to Missouri, what could wash him up in a place called Tippecanoe? It couldn't hurt to check. Stephie would be mad if she found out, but there were ways of making sure she didn't. All he had to do was erase it from the browser history. She'd told him in no uncertain terms she didn't want him looking at the website whose address he now typed. It was almost comical. Other wives snooped into their husbands' URLs to see if they were peeking at porn. His suspected him of surfing the National Center for Missing and Exploited Children.

Sure enough, there was an active Amber Alert in Indiana. Heim grabbed an atlas from his file cabinet. It had been issued in Franklin, twenty miles south of Indianapolis, but that was a long way from Tippecanoe in the north-central part of the state. The odds of it having anything to do with Dickie were slim. Probably a custody dispute gone bad. Even if it turned out to be an abduction—and less than one percent of them ever did—it was still Indiana's problem, not his. Heim clicked away from the list of ongoing alerts and out of curiosity typed MI into the search box. Twelve children had gone missing in his home state in the past year, including one, he discovered, just in the last week. Amanda Totch. She lived only forty miles away in Mt. Pleasant. Well, at least that wasn't Dickie's handiwork; Dickie didn't like girls.

Heim surfed through some of the other photos, the majority of them classified as runaways—the odds on that were even greater than on family abductions.

He changed the time parameter to twenty years and re-searched the database. He had an image of himself sitting at this same computer two decades down the road, wondering which faces had changed and which hadn't. At the moment the oldest of the now thirty-four thumbnail pictures that popped onto his screen had been missing since 1989. She was thirty-three if she was still alive. Thirty-three was his age, too.

Back when Heim didn't have to go behind his wife's back to get on this website he would log in and look up the oldest cases he could find. For hours he would stare at the computer-enhanced photos of what the missing were supposed to look like now, and he would invent lives for them. Invariably, the stories were all the same: the missing were alive, all healthy, married, clean and sober and unexploited, mothers and fathers every one of them, all content to live out whatever identity they'd assumed over the length of their disappearance. There was only one problem with imagining they were safe: you had to wonder what they thought about the families who never knew what happened to them, who might still be searching for them. It was the one place where his fiction-making powers seemed a little spotty. The only answer he could come up with was that they had their reasons for remaining unaccounted for. It was the weasel way out, but Heim didn't believe it reduced his stories to facile exercises in the power of positive thinking. They were exercises in narrative, rather, which he also believed in because narratives were sequences and sequences were patterns and patterns forms and forms gave sha—

He switched the computer off when he realized he was no longer looking at the girl his own age. He'd found himself staring at St. Claire's son. A year was too soon for a computer-enhanced photo of A.J., but Heim couldn't quite convince himself that twenty years from now when he next logged onto this website there wouldn't be one.

In the meantime, it was 8:45 in the morning, and he was already irritated at having to worry about cancelled stamps and postmarks and lockboxes. The circle was closing, but not today. In fifteen minutes, he would be immersed in an Olympic pool where in the elemental simplicity of cold water the chop of his stroke would re-steady the rhythm of his disrupted day.

Heim almost had himself convinced of that, but then the phone rang.

Season on the line

He'd fallen in love with maps.

It was odd because in his old life St. Claire had been a graphic artist—a typographer to his thinking, although designing scripts had never amounted to much professionally—and maps weren't much of an art form. Land was always green, water blue, the lettering Helvetica. Functional without flourish, Helvetica was a boneless sack of a font, a wooden leg without feet, much less toes. St. Claire had been taught to read left to right, top to bottom, line by line, straight edges all anchored by the good grace of a serif, but thinking this way had detoured him during the first nine months of his search for A.J. Then a gas station manager in Michigan City, embarrassed to have sold out his stock of Rand McNallys, donated a box of used maps, and St. Claire spent an entire night poring over them.

St. Claire spent an hour looking at a map of U. S. Highway 1 where south was printed at the top of the page. It made perverse sense. A map didn't document a world; it created one. And that made him realize he had two options: he could continue to allow the landscape to dictate his direction, reprimanding him when the wayward heresy of his own thought threatened to lead him astray . . . or imagination could overthrow all the learned and cultivated senses, all the aristocracies of precedent and popular opinion, and he could drive on instinct.

He chose the latter. He became his own mapmaker when he found the world he'd tried to trace in others' coordinates didn't exist. He ceased to believe in north, south, east, or west. *It won't be long*, he sometimes thought, *and I'll prove, really prove, that the world is flat.*

"You bring your own placemat today, sweetie?"

The waitress, *Rowena* according to her nametag, held a plate and a pot of coffee. She was nodding at the tracing paper spread out on the table. Pencil scratches marked its surface, lines and shades and shapes, along with the names of towns he'd visited—Kilmanagh, Cumber, Pinconning—plus the name of one he wouldn't, Bay City, because it was the place he'd left behind. This was his map, his story, a statement of where he'd been and what he'd done. (He would say "what I found," too, only there was no need for that: he'd found nothing). Some days his map seemed nothing more than a rambling doodle pad, yet he continued to add to it because a year after leaving home, after leaving his wife, Kimm, he still needed to believe that black marks on a piece of paper could be made to speak a truth.

Rowena was round and maternal, with an attractive face blemished only by a smile that exposed her hacksaw teeth, which were the dull color of flat beer. Otherwise, she hardly seemed worn by what St. Claire imagined was a life of two-dollar tips. She'd been his waitress for all three days he'd been coming to the diner, but she'd only ever served him coffee, never food, because he hadn't eaten in that time. "That was fast," he said.

"Yeah, well," she replied, "we aim to please. You going to let me put this plate down, or you expecting me to feed you?"

"Sorry." He took it and, because he wasn't ready to put away his map, laid the plate at his hip. The waitress scoffed a little. As she leaned forward to fill his coffee cup, he smelled her perfume, a crisp ginger that didn't exactly complement the salty sludge of the biscuits and gravy she was slinging.

"You didn't come in for the search this morning."

"My truck wouldn't start. I had to catch a tow."

"You didn't hear the news, then. They gathered everybody up at dawn just to tell them they weren't needed. Not going to be another search, 'parently. They took the stepdad in. Says he's refusing his lie-detector test. That says something, doesn't it?"

"Maybe, maybe not. My guess is they'll send parties out, regardless." As he drank from the cup the coffee steamed his face. "We can't not look for her, can we?"

Rowena eyed him, then his map. She was trying to read it. St. Claire liked her, but she was nosy. He'd told her as much as he thought she needed to know: he'd come to Mt. Pleasant to volunteer in the search for a four-year-old named Amanda Totch who'd disappeared five days earlier from her car seat while her stepfather took a leak at a gas station. His first afternoon in the diner they'd struck up a conversation about Amanda—everyone in Isabella County was talking about her—and she'd let him know she wasn't buying what the stepfather was selling. "Who the hell leaves a kid alone in a car these days?" she asked.

He supposed he could have embarrassed her by admitting that, the preceding November, he'd left his son alone in a car, in the parking lot of the Bay City Home Depot. He'd needed only a box of nails to square a piece of replacement window trim, so he told A.J. to lock the doors and read his comic book. When St. Claire returned not five minutes later, the comic book was blowing over the pavement along with homework from a discarded book bag, and A.J. was gone.

That was just the beginning of the story he wouldn't tell. There was a lot more to it.

"You eat that food," Rowena said on her way to serve other customers. "You'll hurt my feelings if you don't. You don't eat enough—I can tell."

"I will." To prove he meant it he cut off a wedge of biscuit and put it in his mouth. He knew he needed to eat. He'd walked thirty miles or more of field helping look for Amanda, and not once had his appetite stirred. That's what happened when he was lubed on speed: he lost all sense of time, distance, structure, and purpose. He lived a spin cycle of thirty-six hour mornings and fourteen-hour nights, driving by day, then dry-humping the sleeping bag in the camper at night, fending off bad dreams.

Then there was the talk to contend with. It was the other reason he'd missed this morning's search. When St. Claire was high, words flooded his head. He would turn on his tape recorder and lose himself in their torrent, talking until he lost consciousness. He might not listen to the tape for days, if he listened to it at all—it was too embarrassing. Yet he kept every one he made. He had boxfuls, boxfuls of blather, all addressed to his boy, his boy who'd stay disappeared if he ever heard two seconds' worth of that self-pity. But the tapes were as much a part of his story as his map.

He swallowed and began to chew a second bite, trying to urge his senses awake, to goad a craving out of his exhaustion. It was hell to come down, but he was almost there. Tonight he might sleep without a Nembutal, and maybe tomorrow he'd shit solid. That was how St. Claire knew he was okay, though it rarely comforted him. There was nothing comforting about being okay; it just left him stranded in the thick of his anger and grief.

breathing out the ghost

As he ate he stared at his map. It documented his Season on the Line, an old shipman's term he'd learned from a cartography book. The line was the meridian that whalers followed from feeding ground to feeding ground, allowing them to plot the perimeters of a meeting place, to mark off through space and time the most likely course for making their yearly catch. If he was going to think of himself as the Ahab of the interstates, St. Claire reasoned, he might as well live the metaphor to the full. Only now he knew that Isabella County wasn't the destination he'd hoped for, that it was less a sign of his ability to thread the maze of currents and eddies that had carried A.J. off than a confirmation of what he couldn't bear to admit: he was drifting. If Amanda Totch's stepfather was indeed refusing the lie detector test, this story was over—and St. Claire would enter Mt. Pleasant onto his chart as one more false chase, one more wasted week. Gazing into the tangle of lines he realized the cracks in the tabletop were visible through the tracing paper. They reminded him of all the interstates on all the abandoned maps he'd studied and then driven, the blue veins of I-75 running toward Saginaw and Flint, the red arterial highways, 46 and 52, carrying oxygen from the heart of the state, keeping his hope fed. Now he would need a new route, some new direction to pursue.

He continued to eat, a tiny bite at a time, feeling at home amid the grunge of the diner. This was his kind of place, or at least the kind of place that suited the person he felt he'd become: handwritten menus, initials carved in the tabletops, a health inspector's score posted nowhere in sight, coffee cups stained on the inside, just like him. Truckers gathered in twos and threes, trading road stories and playing cards. The row of old people at the counter drank in silence, glaring with bleared surliness at the napkin dispensers and condiment bottles. The air was anchored in dishevelment and languor, which made St. Claire feel weighed down as well. He finished his coffee and set it at the table edge, waiting for another refill.

The door swung open, and St. Claire recognized the grimy young man in work overalls who was supposed to be fixing his truck. He led a teenage girl to an empty seat at the counter, motioning for her to sit, then consulting the manager at the soda fountain. Their conversation was finished in a moment, then the mechanic nodded and made his way to the exit. St. Claire pushed himself out of his booth, nearly upsetting his plate, and caught the man by the cash register.

"My truck done yet?"

"I told you I'd need at least an hour to install a new starter and battery. That was just twenty minutes ago." He motioned over his shoulder through the greasy window to an auto-shop across the plaza. "Like I said, I'll come get you when it's ready." The whole time, the mechanic was watching the girl run her fingers through the blond stripes dyed into her black hair.

St. Claire returned to his seat and rolled up his map, sliding it into its cardboard carry tube. He picked at his biscuits and gravy but didn't eat any more. Several minutes passed before his waitress finally came around for his refill. She caught him looking the girl over.

"Boys pulled her out a drainage ditch, but she won't give over her keys, won't let them look at her car. They're deciding whether to call the police or not. They think she's on something."

"She's not."

"That's what I said." Conversations in the diner were easy to overhear, so she lowered her voice. "I know what's a trip and what's not. She won't call nobody, though. They said they put the phone right in her hand and she wouldn't have nothing to do with it."

Sure enough, the girl turned as if sensing somebody talked about her. She had the vacant, blasted look of a lot of kids St. Claire had run into on the road—eyes empty as rabbit holes, empty, inexpressive mouth. Kids liked to think that look made them untouchable even though they'd been touched by so many different hands you could practically spot the fingerprints on them.

"I'll take care of her." He looked at his food. The biscuits were soggy and the gravy thick and he felt responsible. "Tell them I'll take her off their hands if they start on my truck right now."

The waitress looked more curious than concerned. "How you plan on taking care of her?"

He answered by standing and walking to the counter. Up close, the girl smelled badly and her hair looked like a knot of seaweed, but something in her face made him think of yearbook pages and feathered hairdos and God-awful soy burgers in the school cafeteria. She didn't look older than sixteen or seventeen, despite the pierced eyebrow and tattooed wrist. St. Claire thought of an old girlfriend who once ran away. She had hitchhiked to Toledo before two troopers dragged her kicking and screaming from a truck full of boys too into their *Physical Graffiti* to remember to hide the hash pipe from passers-by. She was returned home and promptly became the joke of school because nobody could figure out why, if you bothered to run away, you'd run to Toledo.

"You want some coffee?"

The girl smeared her thumb along the formica. "I'm not thirsty."

"You want some lunch?"

"I'm not hungry."

"My food's over there. I'm killing time. As long as I eat and look busy I can stay the afternoon, no problem. But they're going to call the cops on you."

She shrugged. "I didn't do nothing." Like she was proud of it.

He leaned in a little and whispered. "You're too obvious. You want to evaporate."

She didn't answer, just breathed in a deep wheeze. Maybe she was asthmatic. A.J. was. He'd spent three days in the hospital once with pneumonia. St. Claire had just gone freelance after several years in a small ad agency, and he wasn't up to snuff on the insurance. There'd been a slipup in the paperwork, and suddenly the claims agent was telling him the family wasn't covered. That meant a two thousand dollar hospital bill, which he and Kimm agreed to pay off in monthly installments. But money was tight because the business was just getting going, and groceries, clothes, gas, they all came first. Before he knew it, a collection agency was on his back, and he'd had to borrow the balance due from his mom, which was a true kick to the nuts.

The memory drained him—it seemed like somebody else's life—and for one suspended second he thought he was falling asleep. He couldn't believe you could be this tired and still be alive. But then the girl's wheezing stopped, and he heard her voice, hollow. "You hear me?" she was asking. "Will you buy me some smokes?"

SO SHE PLAYED HER part and ate like a runaway, finishing what was left of his breakfast in a half-dozen bites. Sitting across from her in the booth, St. Claire closed his eyes and counted to three before opening them. It was a game he'd learned from the road that usually gained him an extra fifty miles before he'd give up for a night and pull into a rest stop.

"Don't ask my name," she kept saying. The tobacco of her Pall-Malls smelled as brown and offensive as her body odor. St. Claire realized that, except for the waitress and the manager, he was the only one in the diner not smoking.

"I don't want a name. Or a reason."

"You asleep?"

"The sooner you eat, the sooner we can go."

"Go? You mean together?"

"Don't try to putty up some fräulein face for me. You're not going anywhere alone." The underside of his eyelids itched, and he was aware, too, of a hollow molar he'd been trying to ignore. His saliva tasted metallic, the taste of tin foil on a tooth filling. He was going to have to see a dentist soon. "From here I can see a good thousand in damage. I'm guessing you don't have the money."

"Maybe, maybe not. You don't know what I got." She looked across the plaza. "What's the matter with your truck?"

He told her.

"Cost a lot?"

"More than I want to pay."

He stirred his coffee, making little whirlpools. When the waitress came and collected the bill, St. Claire asked how much the motel across the access road cost. The waitress didn't look concerned, only wise, as if she'd already guessed how this story would end.

"Wait a minute," the girl said. "You can buy me smokes and food, but no way am I *effing* you."

Every trucker in the place took a generous gawk, but St. Claire was thinking of the word. *Effing*—he liked it. He imagined it dressed in the scrolling letters of an old Gothic type, Gostich maybe, the droopy *f*s curling like Christmas ornaments testing the strength of an evergreen branch. Only occasionally anymore was he reminded of how he used to think in scripts.

"My truck won't be done until morning. We sit in a garage, people get suspicious. We sit here smoking up a storm, people get suspicious. We go rent a room, everybody saw it coming."

Her hair fell over her face. When she tugged it from her eyes he could tell she was a little scared. "What will you want me to do?"

It kicked on a burner in him. *Don't act like you don't care if you really do*, he wanted to say. "Go over there and try swapping yourself out for repairs. You'll be lucky to get two hundred, and that won't get you far, now will it? I can get the room tonight, so enjoy the generosity while it's offered."

That shut her up. He threw his satchel over his shoulder, the cardboard tube dangling at his back like a sword in a scabbard, and he led her outside. She walked a few steps behind him, cautiously, clutching a purse undoubtedly stuffed with eyeliner and lipsticks and little notes: *Dear Daddy, I wish I could tell you face to face how much I hate you for . . . for . . .* for contributing to the maturity of minors. As they came to the shoulder of the access road the low-sloped sun conjoined their shadows.

At the motel he asked the desk clerk what a room went for.

"Thirty-one ninety-five, plus tax." Then the clerk noticed the girl waiting outside. "Second person's five dollars additional."

St. Claire counted out the bills. "That enough?"

The clerk took it as a dare, and the two blinked at each other for several seconds. "It's your money, Jack." He gave St. Claire a key, pointing to the location of the room on a crude map of the building: a crooked rectangle with an arrow twisted around a stairway. St. Claire thought of his old maps and how they were as primitive as this scratchy hieroglyphic. He reminded himself to stop relying on others' directions or he'd remain permanently lost.

Back outside, he offered the girl the room key. But when she went to take it he gripped her fist as though it were a baseball, squeezing until she squinted and grimaced.

"I want to tell you about somebody you should know. His name's Dickie-Bird Johnson. I've never met him, not yet. He's my white whale, if you know that story. Three hundred and thirty pounds of pale avoirdupois with a conviction for molestation and a history of dodged accusations. He's a carpenter from Sinclair County, just north of here. His mother still lives there. Every morning she rocks herself in and out of lucidity on the porch of a dilapidated one-story that overlooks a playground, of all things. I know because I've driven by that house, many times." He yanked her toward him. They were close enough that he was breathing into her eyelids. "You could be talking to him right now."

He let go of her. She opened her hand. They both saw the key had left a deep impression in her palm. St. Claire told her to go to the room and wait. Then he went back to the diner.

On the way he scouted out her battered Hyundai in the auto-shop lot and memorized her license plate. Not until he reached the diner door did he look back. Sure enough, the girl was going up the motel stairs, dutifully.

Inside, Rowena looked surprised to see him. St. Claire asked for a pay phone, and she pointed him past a jukebox. From his satchel he pulled a Franklin planner, two years outdated, and flipped through the list of addresses Kimm had transcribed there; she was organized about those things. He should remember the number, one he'd dialed countless times those two months before he took to the road . . .

The phone rang seven times before anyone answered. He didn't wait for a hello.

"There's a girl in Room 101, Howard Johnsons. She's a runaway stranded from a car wreck. I want you to send somebody to get her."

"Colin." Heim's voice popped like a jar lid pried open. "Where are you?"

"She's in Mt. Pleasant."

"Mt. Pleasant? The Totch girl? You're there? Colin, you can't just call me up out of the blue. It's been nine months; things have changed . . ."

"The girl's not going anywhere, but you should come quick. I've got the license plate of her car. You got a pen?"

"Listen, I'm telling you, buddy, I changed jobs—"

"Get a pen."

"I'm saying—"

St. Claire started reciting the number.

"Wait," Heim said with exaggeration, as though it took the wind out of him. "Okay, I've got a pencil."

St. Claire rattled off the number. "I'm tired of seeing her kind out here," he added, but regretted saying it. He liked to think he was harder than that.

"I'll be there in an hour, but I'm in a different line of work. You want me to call Kimm?"

"Later."

"Cut the shit, desperado. You have to tell me what's up."

"You *know*," St. Claire whispered heavily. "I'm out here, I'm doing it, I didn't give up."

He looked over his shoulder. No one at the counter had moved a muscle.

Heim's voice on the other end of the line dropped, like he was telling a secret. "Just wait for me. I may have news—I think I know where Dickie is. There's a possible chickenhawk in Indiana, and Dickie's been in Indiana lately. It's not much, but it's something. You and me, we'll go get him. We know him better than he knows his sick self."

"Where in Indiana?"

"I'm not saying. You've got to wait for me. We'll go together and then you can come home. Will you wait?"

"I'll wait," St. Claire lied, and he hung up.

ACROSS THE PLAZA ST. Claire found the mechanic picking at the underbelly of his truck with a screwdriver.

"Where's the girl?"

"She'll be home by lunch. I need to get on the road. Can you put a rush on?"

"I'm putting a rush on already. If you want your battery falling out, I can hurry. You seen this here?" The mechanic pointed to the rusted floorboard on the passenger side. St. Claire slouched against a wall, nodding ambivalently. He wasn't worried about the rust. He hadn't had a passenger in over a year.

"We're not used to this, you know. Between you and that girl, this day couldn't get no stranger."

"What about Amanda Totch? She happen a lot?"

The mechanic stopped to size up St. Claire. There was a good ten years' difference between them, but St. Claire was smaller and slighter, gaunt and spooky, too, with circles under his eyes sturdy as highway cloverleafs. He hadn't bathed in four days. The mechanic tapped the screwdriver against his leg. "I'll get you on the road in twenty. How about waiting inside."

St. Claire browsed the maps on the sale rack and eavesdropped until the owner recognized him. "That's your truck, huh?" He had a part in his hair that looked like it'd been laid in with a blowtorch. "Battery and alternator's a big expense for an old hunker. The tow's another forty. Now if you had a motor-club card, that tow would've cost you nothing. But you don't."

"You don't have any maps of Indiana, do you?"

"Not unless you get an atlas, but they're only proper for interstates. Something tells me you've taken a lot of back roads." The old man peeled an orange, dropping the curls into an ashtray. "My boy says you got close to a hundred and thirty on your odometer. She'll nickel and dime you from here on out, I 'spect."

"How long from here to Indiana?"

"Depends where in Indiana. It's a big state. Not that I ever drove it. I don't like distances, never have."

"You get used to them. Sometimes whole days just evaporate and at night you shock yourself realizing just a morning ago you were seven hundred miles away."

"You a salesman?"

St. Claire was tired of questions. The easy way out was a lie. Just tell the old guy what he wanted to hear, settle his conscience

breathing out the ghost

so he could sleep well. St. Claire was no stranger to lies and excuses; explanations took too much time. "Vacation. Coming home from a cross-country trip."

It was a fib he'd never tried before and, judging by the station owner's expression, it needed more practice. St. Claire decided to wait in the garage again. His presence annoyed the mechanic, so he went and leaned on the outside wall next to the free air pump, closing his eyes and counting to three again. He'd done seventy-two sets when the mechanic tapped his shoulder with the screwdriver, saying, "You can pay inside."

The owner figured the tax and then, licking his forefinger, tore St. Claire's duplicate out from the bill. "You got yourself a twelve-month guarantee on parts and labor, but then again, you'd have to be around here to get any use out of a guarantee."

St. Claire pulled out enough bills to cover the tab. His cash reserve was low. The credit cards were worthless; two months earlier he'd pulled over in Cheboygan for gas and watched an attendant run his Visa through the machine once, twice, three times. "Your check probably just hadn't cleared," the kid had said as St. Claire paid in cash. But he knew Kimm had stopped the account.

The station owner handed him his keys. "The girl's taken care of?"

It was a funny euphemism. The old man wanted to know if St. Claire was getting what they all expected. What runaways were supposed to be too scared or too needy not to give away to the first idiot that took a shot—a good *effing*. St. Claire had an eerie feeling that, this time, if he really let the station owner believe what he wanted to, he would be some kind of hero. *Welcome to it*, he thought.

The truck gasped as if for breath, then knocked into a decent rumble. The mechanic hadn't tightened the belts, but their shriek sounded like good accompaniment for St. Claire's nerves, and besides, Heim was probably halfway to town by now. Dickie-Bird in Indiana was luck, pure fortune. He wasn't sure where in Indiana, but he'd find an internet café on the way to tell him. A straight southbound line would have him there by dinner. St. Claire locked his doors and eased onto the outer road until he came to the interstate. All in all Mt. Pleasant had cost him two hundred and forty-six dollars, not counting the loose change he'd thrown around for tips and newspapers. It might be a fair price. He held the wheel tight and concentrated on the long dividing line that drew him to his feeding ground.

After only a few miles he realized the distance wouldn't slip away quickly enough. He slid a baggie from the waistband of his underwear and dropped a blue tablet. It didn't matter how exhausting it was to clean up and slow down; it didn't matter how the words were going to hurt when they came raining through his brain. St. Claire was an expert sophist when it came to persuading himself that control, balance, dignity—all those nice emotional symmetries—were worthy sacrifices if he could just arrive somewhere that added up to something. And he would need his strength—he repeated this to himself a few thousand times over the next eight hours—because his season on the line would be coming to a head, shortly.

mother comforts

Twenty hours after Chance Birmage was last seen walking toward Sugar Creek east of Franklin, Indiana, breakfast was served on the lawn of the Shiloh Baptist Church. There were stacks of fresh-baked biscuits, crocks of scrambled eggs, bubbling pots of tomato gravy, jars of strawberry preserves freshly unsealed from the canning cupboard, even homemade cakes braided with thick epaulets of baby-blue frosting. Standing a few feet away on the Jefferson Street curb, Sis Pruitt couldn't get over the pageantry. Nobody ate as lavishly country as this anymore. For most folks a morning meal was a hash brown and a hot splash of coffee from a drive-through up on Highway 31. Anything short of a wedding—a baptism or a confirmation or a fish fry even— was grocery catered. The volunteers must've cooked straight through the night, Sis decided. It was as if, afraid of what the future held for them, they'd reached back to a past most gladly gave up in childhood in order to make this day seem no more threatening than a Sunday social.

"I could run to Kroger and pick up a sweet ham," Pete offered. Her husband seemed embarrassed to be holding the box of zeppoles they'd purchased on the way from their farm on Route 4.

"There's too much here already—it'd just go to waste. All this heavy food's going to make folks want to nap, not walk. Don't they remember what kind of hoofing they've got ahead of them?"

She led him across the graying fescue grass to the picnic tables where the food was laid out. Sis felt the crowd part for her. People didn't back away elaborately or even consciously, just enough to compound her self-consciousness and make her regret giving in when Pete insisted they help search for this boy. It would make the situation stranger for both the town and them alike if they didn't, he'd argued. The news reports, not content to focus solely on the current tragedy, wouldn't let anyone forget—Chance Birmage was not the first child to go missing in the Franklin area. The first had been Pete and Sis's daughter Patty, seventeen years ago. As it turned out, she hadn't really been missing. She had only been waiting for her body to be found two rows inside the cornfield off Greensburg Road where she was left to lie, garroted with her own brassiere.

"We owe folks a debt," Pete had said.

That wasn't the part Sis disagreed with. "You know what they really want, right? They want us to reassure them history isn't repeating itself."

She knew they wouldn't go any deeper into the subject. They didn't talk too deeply about much anymore. Pete simply squared his shoulder and set his chin: "I can live with owing the bank, but I can't live with owing a whole town."

So here they were with a box of zeppoles. A church woman greeted them with a hug and set their food next to a hot platter of black-pepper bacon. A loitering child immediately sniffed at the fried batter. Embarrassed, his nearby mother yelled at him to *git*, and he had to dodge the lunge she made for his arm.

The organizer smiled grimly at Pete and Sis. "We're asking everybody to wait to eat until the blessing, but Preacher's with the family. Miss Manners doesn't exactly cover occasions like this, does she? Folks aren't sure how to act. . . . I hope it's not imposing, but the grandmother would like to pray with the both of you sometime, if you're willing."

"The grandmother?" Sis asked.

"Chance lives with his daddy's momma. His real momma does, too, but not the daddy, not lately anyway. . . . Well, it's complicated. When Mrs. Birmage—the grandma—found out you farmed, she said Mr. Pruitt here must know her son from working Skelley's grain elevator."

"I knew him to see him," Pete admitted. "Everybody at the elevator knew By-God. He was there off and on until ADM bought in. Old Skelley kept him around because he felt sorry for him, but there was no way the corporate boys were going to tolerate him. He was the first to get let go, but that was a time ago. I didn't even know By-God had a boy."

The organizer's eyes dropped to the ground. Sis wasn't sure if it was blasphemous to nickname a man "By-God" as Bob Birmage had been throughout his adult life or if the woman simply thought it was inappropriate to use the name in these circumstances.

"We'll come sit with Mrs. Birmage after a while." Pete spoke up because Sis hadn't. "We're finding our sea legs right now. You understand."

The organizer tried to demonstrate that she did by giving Sis another sympathetic hug.

"You speaking for both of us today?" Sis asked after the woman left.

"It's bound to be my turn sometime in thirty-seven years of marriage." He meant it as a joke, but the joke fell flat. "Folks aren't going to understand your hesitation if you're not careful. They're going to think we're judging the Birmages. I have a feeling there's plenty of that already. The least we can do is meet the grandmother if we're asked to. It's no secret you've sat with other families over the duration."

She had, but this was different. A year or so after losing Patty, when it was clear the wound wouldn't heal on its own, Sis had helped start a chapter of a national support group for parents of murdered children. It was only the second one in Indiana, so most of the membership had to commute down from Indianapolis or Muncie or up from Evansville, and somehow the distance separating their tragedies softened the immediacy of Sis's own. The group met to talk, both amongst themselves and to schools and to various Rotary or Elk or Odd Fellows clubs around the state. Sheriffs and lawyers frequently asked them to counsel families of victims of violent crime.

That wasn't the case here. As everyone gathered still wanted—still needed—to believe, eight-year-old Chance was wandering the banks of Sugar Creek, so busy climbing sycamores and pulling mussels he wasn't aware he was lost. Wasn't even aware that anyone was looking for him. That was a big difference from Patty, but there was another one, too, and Sis couldn't help but resent Pete for not acknowledging it.

"Those other families weren't here in our backyard," she reminded him. "They weren't made to wait for news in the exact same churchyard they made you and me wait in."

BECAUSE PETE RESPONDED THE way he always did when Sis's hurt threatened to surface—which is to say, he didn't respond at all—she stalked off for coffee. She was skimming the excess creamer she'd spilled into her plastic cup when a school bus rolled up in front of the church. The bus doors gasped open and the Johnson county sheriff, Dub Ritterbush, hiked through the serving tables, not bothering to greet a single acquaintance.

"Okay folks, listen up." He clapped his hands, and the morning chatter subsided; except for one fussy baby, it sounded crisply silent for the first time that morning. "We want to thank the church folk for bringing food today. I want you to eat to your pleasure, but you got to be done in fifteen minutes. Once you finish, load on the bus so we can get out to your checkpoint as quick as possible. When we're all in our places, we'll let you know what we're going to use you for. Now—" He searched out one of his deputies. "Justin, what's your tally?"

"Sixty-seven at last count, sir."

"Okay. I'm taking four score of you with me. I need the rest to stay here in town to post fliers. We got the pictures done up?" Another deputy assured him that photocopies were ready to distribute. "Get the businesses to put the fliers in their windows, staple them to telephone poles. You are *not* to go to any private residence. The city police are going to be searching in town, and they don't want to be stepping around you. Now, who's my ten?"

When hands rose slowly at first, Sis stepped behind the coffee urn. She was relieved when Dub counted off more volunteers than he needed. "We've got a map I want everybody to look at. You'll start on the outskirts and work your way in. So you don't waste time tracing each other's footsteps, I'm asking that you call in every half-hour so your location can be tracked. For that job I'm putting you all in the very capable hands of Mr. Pete Pruitt here—"

He motioned toward Pete, who looked aghast to hear his own name.

"Now then, where's Pastor? We need to say grace and get down to brass tacks."

A deputy hustled inside and then returned accompanied by a stout man in crisp khakis who asked everyone to bow his head. Everyone did except Sis. She was eyeing Dub, whom she'd known since childhood. They were the same age, fifty-five, had graduated in the same high-school class at Southwestern and still attended the same church on Smithland Road they'd grown up in, so she had a half-century of memories of him to call upon. Fifty years felt like a boulder of time, but the memories gave Sis something to do other than pray. She tended to tune out whenever it was done communally; she hadn't met a minister in a long time to whom she was willing to cede the authority to speak to God. Only when she heard the crowd's collective amen did Sis think to close her eyes and drop her chin.

"That was a dirty trick," she whispered when she caught up to the sheriff at the head of the food line. "Just because you're making Pete stay here all day doesn't mean I'm going to. I can't, Dub. I need to walk this off."

The sheriff peeled the cupcake paper back on a sausage muffin. "I was half expecting a call from you last night. You and Pete are the only folks who know firsthand what it's like to wait through one of these searches. You could tell the Birmages what they ought to expect. Last night I asked Cinda if I ought to try calling you. She told me not to. Cinda said if you didn't call then it was your way of saying it was asking too much."

"This all brings back too many feelings. Once I heard the search was based from here, this same church, I was too upset. So many things were so suddenly fresh. I had to take Tillie and Joey to my mom and dad's so I could work it through."

"Sis, you know we'd be here if it was a tornado or any other kind of emergency. It's the same reason we were here seventeen years ago: the church is centrally located and it has the biggest congregation in town. I have to consider logistics, even at the cost of feelings."

"I'm not criticizing and I'm not asking for folks to dance around me. I'm only saying I'll be more help if you let Pete and me go out with the others instead of making us stay with the family."

"You don't think it'd be hard for you out there as well? We've got to follow the creek, Sis. That means we've got to cross Greensburg Road by Smiley's Mill, and that's not a hundred yards from the very spot."

"I drive past that spot all the time. I still shop at Smiley's. I probably see that cornfield more than I see Patty's grave, but I can do that because at some point it became routine. Maybe I could smile and dispense hugs and tell the Birmages everything will be okay if I'd been to this particular church even just once in the past seventeen years, but I haven't. Dub, the last thing this family needs is to see me walking backwards through a decade and a half. Shiloh Baptist has plenty of women who're better comfort givers. Look at how much comfort food they rounded up on such short notice."

"I know this isn't easy on you and Pete, but that doesn't mean it's easy on anybody else. A lot of folks are having flashbacks."

"I know that. Do you know Pete's way of keeping his head above his memories? He tilled soybeans until nine o'clock last night—way past dark. He'd be at the bottomland today except he knows it'd look odd if we weren't here."

She saw Dub's eyes widen a bit; she wondered if that was his reaction when a suspect ratted out a conspirator without any prodding.

"Now see, what you just said, that's why I needed you yesterday. There are things I'm supposed to look for, but the criteria for clues in situations like this has always struck me as faulty. I was trained to think that if somebody isn't grieving like I suppose they ought to, that's a sign to get suspicious about. I was never quite clear on what exactly 'ought to' means, though."

"There is no 'ought to.' 'Ought to' is what other people insist on to stable themselves."

"Probably so. Last night I was sitting with the grandmother when the mother comes waltzing into the parlor, drinking a beer. If I'd followed my instincts, I'd have said that wasn't the right way to behave when your boy is missing, that it might be an indicator even. Only I already knew there was nothing really wrong with it, other than it made me uncomfortable as hell. Awkward isn't illegal, and beer isn't evidence of anything, any more than tilling soybeans is. Especially when the mother's already passed her lie detector."

"What about the father? Have you tested By-God yet?"

Dub squeezed the empty cupcake wrapper in his fist. When he couldn't find a garbage can he tossed the wrapper next to a plate of crisp sausage links, his lips wrenched flat with a forced smile. "Here I am talking out of turn, damn near spilling secrets I shouldn't be, and all because of how your strength is disarming— it makes people want to confide in you. That's a gift, I reckon." He glanced at his watch. "You'll excuse me now. I'm looking down the barrel of a long day."

She saw him glance east, where State Road 44 led out of Franklin into the countryside. It was only then that Sis realized how much territory the search had to cover: Sugar Creek ran for forty miles.

"I'll do what I can for the Birmages, but there's something you need to know."

The sheriff's eyebrows warily shot up, and all forty of those creek miles seemed to be etched in the creases of his forehead. "And what should I know, Mrs. Pruitt?"

"You reckoned wrong. It's never felt like a gift. Not once."

SHE HAD MADE HER point but it didn't make her feel any better. The fact that Sis felt compelled to make a point at all embarrassed her. Dub had no sooner walked off than she wanted to pull him back and explain that grief to her wasn't always easy to distinguish from vanity: it led you to believe that you had a certain authority over other people, that you were special. It wasn't entirely your fault either—other people encouraged that attitude. They didn't know it, but they fed it by treating you as if you had some wisdom to impart, a lesson to teach. What had being the parent of a murdered child taught her? Nothing—nothing except the inexhaustibility of her own anger, anger at constantly being reminded of what she'd lived through, what she'd always *be* living through, and most of all anger at the presumption that she should be over it, that she should have proved that life goes on, if not for her sake then for the sake of those around her. That was never the hard part, Sis thought. Life went on anyway, whether you wanted it to or not. The hard part was being left behind to breathe out the ghost of the one who'd gone on.

Sis realized volunteers were stepping around her in the food line as if she were a statue or memorial that couldn't be disturbed. Embarrassed, she backed away, but she stepped on someone's foot. When she turned she discovered it belonged to the child she'd seen hovering over the black-pepper bacon. Before Sis could apologize, the boy pointed at her and said, "It's Rogue!"

His mother stepped in and took his hand. "It's your hair," she explained, embarrassed. "He's all into *X-Men*, and Rogue is the character he's taken a crush to. She has a streak of white coming out of her part just like yours. That's all he meant by it. Kenny, say you're sorry."

"No, no," Sis jumped in. "It's all right—I'm the one who almost trampled him."

The woman smiled and tugged the child off. Sis started to tuck away the swoop of gray framing her eyebrows, but she stopped when she couldn't decide whether hiding it was more ostentatious than having it. Pete liked to tease her by calling the streak a skunk stripe, but she didn't like that term at all. She preferred to think of it as her lightning bolt. It was her way of reminding folks how hard she'd been struck.

She joined the church women as they stacked plates and trays on a bussing cart, then began wadding up the disposable tablecloths, breaking down the tables, and stacking the folding chairs, to later be lugged through Shiloh Baptist's ornate archway to a storage room. Meanwhile, across the lawn, Pete's men stuck to themselves at a rolling bulletin board with a large white map pinned across the cork. Sis eavesdropped as he used a red marker to divide the county into more-or-less equal pie slices. The segregation reminded Sis of the family gatherings of her childhood, back when men would take to rockers and porch swings to debate the "real" work of farming—market prices, crop yields, government regulations, irrigation, fertilizer, combine maintenance. Meanwhile, the women crowded into kitchens where they reached around each other for tenderizers and rolling pins and graters. After the meals the men would joke about the frivolousness of women's work, how it was really an excuse to gossip, and then without a hint of irony they would head straight back to the porch to digest their food by chewing more fat with each other. Sis wondered if it was still like that. She assumed it was, though she didn't know—she and Pete hadn't entertained at their farm in ages. It didn't feel right to.

When the churchyard was cleared, the women relocated to the kitchen in the fellowship hall. They began sacking sandwiches and snacks to shuttle out to the volunteers for lunch. Spreading peanut butter on white bread, Sis found herself lulled by the rhythm of their small talk, which ran in synch to the pace of the work: trading recipes and family lore, regretting the creeping fall, how they were too busy to sew homemade Halloween costumes, reminiscing about old ways. Even though they often spoke at the same time, they weren't really interrupting each other. Rather, their words seemed to blend until the kitchen wasn't occupied by just a group of women but a common experience, a voice. Sis was grateful that nobody mentioned Chance or praying with the grandmother. She was happy to blend in and lose the peculiarity she felt doomed to shoulder. Her only mistake was to think she could partake of this community, not merely observe it.

"Oh, you're coming to Blue River?" she asked when in passing one of the women mentioned Bears of Blue River, the upcoming heritage festival in Shelbyville, the next town east of Franklin. "You should visit our booth. We're displaying a quilt we've made. You should all come see it."

"I didn't know you quilted," the eldest of the organizers answered. "I don't know how you'd have time with those two youngsters to chase after. My kids are long grown and gone, and I don't have time."

"It's like any other hobby. You make the time if you really want to do it. I can't claim I'm much of an expert. My mom was a great quilter before she got arthritis, but I wouldn't have known how to get going if it weren't for my POMC group. It's a collaboration. We each had a picture of our kids transferred to cloth, and then we pieced the squares together. It took us near six months of meetings."

"What's a POMC?" somebody else asked.

That was when Sis realized she'd singled herself out. She tried to invent a harmless name out of the abbreviation, but she wasn't fast enough.

"Parents of Murdered Children," one of her hosts whispered.

Sis watched the women's faces harden with sympathy. There was an awkward silence as she tried to go back to making the peanut butter sandwiches, but she had broken the chain. The assembly line fell apart; the worksong of small talk would not start anew. She felt a palm on her shoulder.

"I've got a picture of Patty you can use if you want." It was the organizer who'd hugged Sis and Pete in the churchyard. "For your quilt, I mean. It's her senior picture. You probably don't remember my nephew, Mike Sigmund, but he was a year behind Patty at Southwestern. I didn't know they knew each other, but I was helping my sister Vivie—Mike's momma—clean out a

breathing out the ghost

chesterdrawers a while back, and I came across the picture in an old tin of his. There's a note Patty wrote on the back. It's so sweet I almost cried to think that nobody had read it all this time since. I know it'd make you and Mr. Pruitt proud to see it."

"I never much liked her senior picture," Sis confessed. "She had big ungainly curls in that one. I always liked her hair straight, but that wasn't how girls wore it back then. Plus the backdrop—it was all aqua neon, like a laser-light show. That backdrop dates that picture too much for me."

The woman looked tongue-tied. She hadn't expected her gift to be refused. Sis wondered if it would muzzle her more to know that there weren't any pictures—period—of Patty in the Pruitts' home. Pete had boxed them up a few days after Patty's funeral, without a word. *But those are the things you don't get into because they're only good for unsettling. . . .*

"But, of course I'd love to see what she wrote your nephew," Sis corrected herself. "I only meant her senior picture isn't right for the quilt. My friends and I—my group—when we started talking about doing it, we made a decision that we didn't want to use any studio shots or formal portraits. There's just no life to those. You have to understand, most parents who lose their children, their last glimpse is already unnatural. I hope it's not wrong to talk about this now, but the way they're posed in the casket is so stagnant that it looks nothing like them in life. Pictures are all you have to blot that memory, the more candid the better because you want to remember your child in motion, spontaneous. . . . That's all I meant."

The organizers were looking back and forth amongst themselves. Finally, one of them—the eldest again—spoke up.

"I'm sure your quilt is beautiful, Mrs. Pruitt. . . ."

Sis gave the woman the word she hesitated to say: "But?"

"No *but*, just a concern. I—I wonder if now's the time to display that quilt. You know—" She nodded at the open doorway and the world outside of their conversation. "Given the circumstances. . . ."

"THEY DIDN'T COME OUT and say, 'It's not right,'" Sis told Pete, "but that's what they were thinking."

It was noon now, and the volunteers who'd remained at Shiloh Baptist were breaking to eat their peanut butter sandwiches. Most sat with each other in the fellowship hall, but the Pruitts had elected to stay outside in the churchyard. In case of what, they weren't sure. There had been no news from the creek.

"That's what got me the most. They tiptoed around it seven ways to Sunday. They wanted me to say I'd give up the booth so they didn't have to outright ask me to."

"Maybe you should sit out Blue River this year. If stepping aside for now gives folks relief, well, then maybe that sacrifice is worthwhile. Lots of townships throw heritage festivals this time of year. Maybe we can find one a little farther out—north of Indy, say—and we could hang the quilt there. Shelbyville's not but fifteen miles from the Birmages' land."

Sis pulled the arms of her sweater over her fists. The wind had steepened; she blamed it for the chill between her and her husband.

"*We'll* show it on the other side of Indianapolis? Does that mean you'll be in the booth with us if the POMC does take the quilt to Blue River? That would be a first."

He gave her a hard stare, but the only thing Sis could think was how unfair it was that her husband's grief had aged him so well. The first year of Patty being gone the shock stripped him gaunt and turned his hair white, giving him symbols of perseverance. Sis merely felt eroded by comparison. She suffered recurring bouts of eczema that forced her to wear more make-up than she liked, and her body hadn't recovered from the late-life wear and tear of birthing Tillie and Joey.

"Spite's not going to make you feel any better. It's just going to upset you more when you realize you're resenting folks who don't deserve it."

"I know you think I'm acting strange, but I'm not the only one. It's you, too—every one of you. You don't see it in yourselves because you're so busy looking for it in me. Listen to what you said if you don't believe me; listen to what they said in the kitchen. None of you want me to go to Blue River, but that's two whole days from now. And you know what that means, don't you?"

Pete bit into his sandwich instead of answering.

"It means you think they'll still be searching for the boy then. It means you and everybody else is assuming they won't find him."

"Let's go meet the grandmother right now," Pete said, his mouth still full. "We'll see her and then head home. This is too damn hard."

HE DIDN'T SO MUCH lead Sis into the church as he left it to her to follow. After thirty-seven years, only the opposite would've surprised her. She caught up to him in the maze of hallways that led to the preacher's office. Preacher wasn't at his desk, but the church secretary was at hers, and she recognized the Pruitts. Everybody knew Pete and Sis because of what had happened to Patty. "Mrs. Birmage is expecting you," the secretary said, pointing to the school wing across the courtyard.

Preacher waved to them from the doorway of a fourth-grade Sunday-school classroom. "Not the first place you'd look, I know," he whispered when they were in earshot. "Mrs. Birmage wasn't feeling well, so we brought her over here. This is where we keep our one recliner. You don't know how uncomfortable office furniture really is until you've got an elderly woman having back spasms. We didn't realize we'd had her on her feet all morning."

When he motioned them inside Sis realized why Preacher whispered: the grandmother was stretched out in the recliner, asleep. Her thick feet barely reached the leg rest.

"Don't wake her. Let her rest."

"Oh, it's all right. She told me to. She's been waiting to meet you."

He squatted by the old woman's elbow and gently shook her wrist. Mrs. Birmage opened her eyes with such a start Sis didn't know what else to do but introduce herself and blurt an apology. The grandmother struggled to raise herself from the chair. She shook Pete's hand, but she wanted a hug from Sis. "I'm not sure what all I should be doing," she mumbled into Sis's shoulder. "I hoped you could tell me if I forgot something."

Sis felt tackled, even though the woman's welted skin felt tender and pulpy as bruised fruit. "You haven't, I'm sure. Everything's being done that can be done."

"They'll find him," Pete added, gratuitously. "Soon, I'm sure."

Preacher, who had taken the only other adult chair besides the recliner for himself, suggested they pray. Pete and Sis had to perch on kiddie chairs. There was no place to hide and daydream this time; Sis bowed her head.

Dear Lord, we remember Rachel weeping for her children in the Book of Jeremiah. We honor the weight of her lamentation as we remember all the mothers left weeping for their children. But we also understand the lesson you insisted upon when Rachel refused the comforts that worship lends us: 'Keep your voice from weeping, and your eyes from tears, for there is a reward for your work, declares the Lord and they shall come back from the land of the enemy. . . There is hope for your future, declares the Lord, and your children shall come back to their own country. . . .

Those last words made Sis think of Greensburg Road. Patty never came back from the land of the enemy. The enemy was a day laborer who'd mistaken a smile at the Franklin ice-cream parlor as an invitation to rape. Fighting back was an invitation to be strangled, then pitched like trash into a cornfield. It was hard not to think of that field as Patty's only true country.

She felt a rush of relief when Preacher finally said his amen. It was breath. She'd been holding hers through the prayer.

"I'm going to leave you folks to talk in peace," the minister said, patting Sis's knee. "Chance's momma is coming back with her folks from their church shortly, so I'll be with them. If you need anything, please let me know."

That's going to be hard if you're gone, Sis wanted to say, but didn't. Nobody spoke, not for several seconds. When the grandmother finally did Sis wished she could go back to pretending to pray.

"They think Bobby done this. Nobody will say it outright, but I can tell. They think he took Chance so his momma can't have him. They only think that way 'cause him and the girl don't get along. Bobby only left 'cause he couldn't take the girl's nagging. He tried to make steady money, but that ain't easy these days. Chance's momma could work herself. I told her I'd watch the boy after school, but she wouldn't hear of it. She says I'm too old and that any work she did find wouldn't pay the gas it took her to get there."

Pete finally spoke, because Sis hadn't. "The sheriff has steps he's got to go through. He has to look at the family; that's always the case. It was that way for us even, all the way back when. All Bob's got to do is agree to a lie detector, and they'll leave him be."

"You're the first person today not to stutter calling him 'Bob,' Mr. Pruitt. Everybody starts to say 'By-God Bob' before catching themselves. I know that's how folks think of him. My husband and I tried to cure him of saying 'By-God' when he was growing up, but it was like a hiccup he couldn't lose. Ever since he was thirteen or so, it was 'By-God this,' 'By-God that.'"

"It's an easy test. They ask questions, and you just answer. You don't feel a thing."

"Oh, Bobby won't let them wire him up. That was the first thing the girl said when the sheriff's boys came: 'Give me my test right now so you know it's not me.' I told her nobody even knew for certain yet Chance didn't just wander off, but she told them deputies straight away that it's all Bobby's doing. 'Find him and see for yourself,' she said. 'That son of a bitch won't ask for a test like I am.' She said that right there in front of me, in the selfsame parlor she's been staying in rent-free for two years."

Pete was looking at Sis like a man begging for a lifeline. When she didn't throw him one, he stood up. "My wife's better at this part than I am. I better get out front. My flier-posters will be reporting in soon."

He was out the door before Sis thought to excuse herself and catch him in the hall. He looked offended when she asked what he thought he was doing. "You were leaving it to me," he said with the hiss of sizzled meat. "As many times as you've run off from me and the kids to sit with some other family, suddenly now you're talked out?"

Sis recognized how right Pete was: she hadn't spoken on purpose. She'd wanted him to carry the load for once. She couldn't quite admit it, though, so she scrambled for an excuse.

"I was listening. That's how you make people feel better: you listen and let them get it off their chest. . . . Please, don't make me do this by myself. We should do it together."

Her husband pulled her into an embrace and stroked her neck, but his touch felt foreign. Touching was like talking—the Pruitts hardly did it anymore, not even in bed. Most nights Sis kept her children tucked between her and Pete. It was the only way she could sleep.

"I've got to be doing something," Pete whispered, his voice unsteady. "I'm sorry. I can't take just sitting around talking. . . ."

He left her standing there, next to a bulletin board decorated with snowflake angels.

"YOUR HUSBAND'S A HANDSOME man," Mrs. Birmage said when Sis returned to the Sunday school room. "Bobby used to be, but he went too thick in the middle. Chance is already taking on his daddy's heft. He's going to be a big boy. . . . I know you're called Sis, Mrs. Pruitt, but that's not your Christian name, is it?"

"No, ma'am. My given name is Beverly. My father nicknamed me Sis. It was an odd choice because for a long time I wasn't a sister: I was twelve before my mom and dad had another baby. Neither of them can explain to me what was in their heads."

Mrs. Birmage was no longer idle in the recliner; the old woman's fingers were busy knotting thread around a spindle. She was tatting.

"Can I ask what you're making?"

"Just a cover for a throw pillow. Nothing too fancy. Do you tat?"

"No. I never even quilted until about six months ago. Did you go to bees when you were a girl?"

"Once in a while, but never as much as my momma and aunts." Mrs. Birmage pinched a bubbled picot into place. "It was all boys in my family except for me. None of my brothers were much for staying inside. I baled and milked twice a day just like them. We never had money enough to distinct between boys' and girls' things. All we had was work that needed doing. I never tatted nor stitched until Bobby was born. It seemed the smart thing to do—making these little bits was better than buying them secondhand."

Sis wondered how many nights Mrs. Birmage had sat in her farmhouse making "little bits," whether when she bored of doilies and decorative fripperies she turned to something more substantial like sewing sweaters or mitts. Perhaps she took as well to the household arts in which Sis's own mother had apprenticed—pressed flowers, candle making, repoussé and découpage. Sis wondered if relics from these country hobbies cluttered Mrs. Birmage's shelves and countertops as they did at Sis's folks' house. Maybe the old woman hoped Chance would grow bored with toy cars and plastic guns and ask his grandmother about crayon crafts and plaster of Paris. Or maybe not. Tillie and Joey weren't interested in the trinketry that once entertained farm wives; Patty hadn't been either. Truth be told, neither had Sis herself, despite her mother's best efforts. Even a half-century ago brocade and crotchet seemed impossibly old-fashioned pastimes, as pointless in an age of store-bought jewelry and clothes as milking a cow on a three-legged stool.

Watching the bumblebeeing convolutions of the old woman's wrists, Sis regretted her indifference, realizing these amusements weren't meant to be practical or even useful. Years down the road, once he broadened into manhood, Chance would probably do what Sis found herself doing in middle age: seeking out the remnants of her mother-want, her craving for maternal assurance. One evening he would rediscover the sun-catcher motif his grandmother made the day he couldn't be found, and he would recognize the deep ache of care wrought in the loops and frets, the patterned outpourings that were the sweet pap of love, the mother's milk of affection. These things were more substantial than words or embraces because knowledge of them was passed down in the unsentimental shape of work, work whose end product was always tangible, lasting. Sis understood now what Pete meant when he said he couldn't just sit and do nothing.

"You think Shiloh Baptist has any potatoes in that fancy kitchen of theirs?"

The grandmother's intricate lacing stopped mid-twist. "I heard said they were making sandwiches. Nothing fancy, I 'spect, but if you're hungry maybe they'll let you fry some—"

Sis smiled. "I'm not hungry. Not for food, anyway. Come help me make something for Chance. We can do it together."

She led the old woman out of the Sunday school wing and over to the kitchen. There they surprised the women organizers, who were cleaning up after the sack lunches. The women looked doubtful when Sis described what she wanted to do. The doubt hardened even after she sermonized on her husband's words:

"You've fed people all day. Now you need something else to do. None of us needs to sit around just waiting."

It irritated her that the women didn't accept the explanation as quickly as Sis had accepted it from Pete, so when she spotted a leftover paper tablecloth from this morning's breakfast still folded on a sideboard she snapped it open and set to work with the markers. As she and Mrs. Birmage began stenciling stars, the other women slowly joined in, contributing rockets, shrieking comets, planets with friendly faces. Over time the roomful of mothers started trading stories—the funny ones, not the serious. Sis described how Patty was filling the fuel tank of the riding lawnmower once when the gas squirted into her eyes and she ran perfect circles around the milk shed screaming she'd been blinded. Another woman recounted how the first time her son took the mower out he ran it straight over her tomato vines. Mrs. Birmage told how Chance, even at eight and in 4-H, still thought a cucumber was a *cute cumber*.

One of the women said her boy was so into superheroes he was forever borrowing bath towels for capes. He'd thrown a fit this morning when she hadn't let him come to church wearing one. Lately he'd been after her to sew his granddaddy's old high-school letter—he'd gone to Southwestern, so it was a big red S— onto a blue T-shirt. Sis realized the woman was talking about Kenny, the boy who'd mistaken her for one of the X-Men.

"That Rogue character your boy thought I looked like," Sis asked, "what superpowers does she have?"

"Oh, I can't keep them straight. There's too many. They either fly or turn invisible."

"My daughter was Rogue for Halloween last year," another woman piped up. "She's a kind of sponge. She absorbs other people—soaks the energy straight out of them. Sometimes it's a good superpower, because she can take away their pain and save them. Sometimes it's a bad thing, though, because Rogue can't touch anybody without hurting them." The woman realized everyone in the room was staring at her, and let out an awkward laugh. "I watch too many cartoons, I know!"

When the background was colored, two volunteers scrubbed the dirt from a package of bloated baking potatoes. Others scavenged the church for a grab-bag assortment of acrylics and ink stamps. Sis cut the potatoes in lengthwise halves, counting the number of letters they needed: eleven. They were one potato short, so she sliced the last one in fat vertical chunks thick as sausage quarters. Then the women patted the moisture from the spuds' surfaces with paper towels and divided up carving duty.

"I'll do the E," Mrs. Birmage said. "We need it four times. Somebody else is going to have to take the W and M, if you don't mind. Too many arms and legs on them for my shaky hands."

They were unconcerned with whether the shapes or sizes of the script they whittled matched. When all the letters were completed, Sis stirred a small bottle of red acrylic paint with a toothpick and poured some onto a newspaper. There was only one color, and not much of it, so they decided to use a spongy inkpad as well, though it was half dry.

"I wish my daughter's toy bag was in the mini-van," Sis said. "I just got her a new stamp set with green, red, even purple pads. Our type'd be prettier with something more than black ink."

The others needed a moment to realize that by "daughter," Sis meant the living one, Tillie, and not Patty.

They dipped some potatoes into the paint, the rest into the pad, and then took turns pressing the halves onto the white space they'd left in the center of their design. For more color variation they used a green magic marker on the L and C. The ink didn't cling to the potato well, so the green came off as a pale peppermint, which was fine because it made for a good contrast to the denser, more durable pigments. When they finished spelling their message one of them suggested somebody run to Mrs. Birmage's for pictures of the boy. "There's lots of empty space still. We can Scotch tape them."

"Only not the same picture as what's on the flier," Sis insisted. "No school pictures. Get ones that show Chance doing something . . . things with lots of movement."

Mrs. Birmage explained that all her photos were stored in a toy chest in her bedroom. A couple of volunteers dutifully collected their purses and disappeared to fetch some. Everyone else settled into chairs, but they were all too excited to wait patiently.

"It doesn't have to be finished to hang," somebody said. "It's living art."

Living art: Sis wished she'd thought of that herself. With the help of the organizer who'd hugged her twice today, she strung their makeshift canvas to the transom. The woman gathered in a circle to admire their handiwork.

WELCOME HOME, CHANCE, the potato printing read.

the goner

Heim's right hand shook as he set the phone down. The buzz of St. Claire's disconnected line was fresh in his ear. He was trying to assure himself it was that noise, or maybe its vibrations—not some apprehension within him, at any rate—that made his fingers unsteady. Their trembling was slight, almost imperceptible, but the more he stared at their tips, the more removed he felt from his body, as if he were outside of himself and could only witness, not control, the surges and pulses that flashed along his nerves.

His eyes fell upon the scrap of paper that read *Room 101, Howard Johnsons*. The oils of his palm had stained the arched end of the grip where he'd held the phone to his ear; the damp impressions left by the creases in his skin were slowly evaporating. In a few moments, there'd be no trace of his ever having taken St. Claire's call. That spooked Heim even more. At least in Dickie's case he had cards to keep, but a voice was only breath, insubstantial.

He balled and unballed his fist, still trying to subdue the sensation that grew thicker and heavier now even as he tried to work out its kink. To do that he had to return to his computer and the website he wasn't supposed to look at, where he clicked back and forth between the pictures of A.J. St. Claire and the Michigan girl, Amanda Totch, and the Indiana boy, Chance Birmage. All three were profiled on the Center's alerts page, but so were fourteen other children. It would've been easy to write off the connections linking them as coincidence had Heim believed in

65

coincidences, but to him a coincidence was only a surface excuse for the deeper pattern you didn't want to see. This particular pattern was emerging through the emulsion. Heim knew he wouldn't swim today, wouldn't feel the quiver in his calves from his Salzburg Road run, maybe not for some time to come. Not until the circle closed. Already he was missing the burn of training, of the accomplishment, the goal that'd gotten done. The shake rattling his fingers could only remind him of loose ends that needed wrangling. He turned the computer off and went to pack.

Walking to his bedroom he counted steps—one each for the sixteen jobs he'd worked these past seventeen years. In the Air Force, he had been a communications journeyman, a vehicle dispatcher, a senior airman in accounting and finance, and a staff sergeant information manager in a classified-documents office. After his discharge he worked for UPS, built decks, laid shingles and linoleum flooring, and installed cabinets. He'd managed an apartment complex and for two seasons raised pigs for market on his grandfather's Kalkaska county farmstead. He tried his hand at selling office equipment and then cars, but they all were deadening compared to the only one he'd ever really liked: the fourteenth one, already two jobs removed.

In the bedroom he stuffed three days' worth of clean clothes in a travel bag. He made sure to include some heavy gloves and his Green Bay Packers ski cap in case he had to sleep in the car overnight. Then he showered and shaved. There was nothing hurried about his actions. In his mind he was making a list of everything he'd need to tend to before he could take off after St. Claire. He'd need cash, gas, a map to get him through Indiana. Heim believed in details. He kept credit-card receipts to double check his Visa bill at the beginning of every month, and he made sure to always have a hundred's worth of twenties in the house in case the ATM at his bank was down. He'd even started keeping spare keys taped under the bumpers of his cars after Stephie once paid forty bucks for a locksmith to retrieve hers from her Toyota.

Heim thought maybe he should call his supervisor at Kroger and give notice, but that was one detail he was content to leave undone. Back out in his living room he tucked the paper that said *Room 101, Howard Johnsons* in his wallet and erased the number of the truck stop St. Claire dialed from off the caller ID. That was two less things to worry about.

He was already out of the house and in the driveway, his bag tossed in the back of the used Suburban his in-laws had given him and Stephie as a wedding present, when he thought of one more thing. It wasn't a detail that'd slipped his mind; it was a step he wasn't sure he should take. But then an impulse led him to kick the Suburban out of reverse and cut the engine. He went back inside and dragged the stepstool back to the closet, and again retrieved the lockbox.

What he was looking for rested under a thick envelope stuffed with car titles and property deeds. It wasn't the same gun that had gotten him in so much trouble with Dickie. That one had been a .45 Glock he'd bought at a surplus store in Saginaw. This one was a .22, a mouse gun by comparison. Paps, his grandfather up in Kalkaska, had given him the snubnose. Heim had lost his Glock in the probation agreement, and he wasn't supposed to touch another handgun for three years. But Paps was a real second-amendment type, and he'd convinced Stephie to keep the .22 in her name. She only agreed to do so after Heim promised he wouldn't go near it, not even in an emergency.

He popped the cylinder to make sure the gun was unloaded. Then he sniffed the barrel. The thing hadn't been fired in years. He went to the kitchen and found the cleaning kit under the sink. He lubricated the cylinder to make sure it wouldn't jam upon rotating. Then he ran the wire-bristle brush through the barrel to remove any gum. When he'd wiped it down one last time, he pulled six bullets from a tobacco tin also stored in the lockbox and filled the chambers. He was careful to set the safety before he stuffed the pistol between his belt and the small of his back. He also made sure to return the lockbox to the shelf and straighten the sweater pile so there was no sign of him having been there. He reminded himself to fetch his cell phone from the battery charger and to put the gun in the Suburban's glove compartment when he got to the truck.

Now there was only one other obstacle to leaving, and it was a big one. He guided the Suburban out of his drive and followed a series of crooked streets until he came to the Methodist church where Stephie worked. He parked the truck and zipped his windbreaker to the middle of his chest. The church's narthex was ghostly quiet as he cut through it to the fellowship wing where his wife managed the nursery. She'd taken the job back when Heim was still trying to get out from under the law. As soon as he'd lost his detective's license, it was clear that the first thing that they couldn't afford was to keep Alex in preschool. The woman who ran the daycare center had felt sorry for Stephie—though not, she'd let it be known, for Heim. Rather than take Alex off the roster, she finagled Stephie a position there. A few weeks later, the college-aged girl who oversaw the nursery quit to follow an Air Force boyfriend to Kokomo, and Stephie was bumped up to running the baby room. Working for the church had proved a good deal even when she was just a regular staff member because employees didn't have to pay for their kids to attend. That meant the two hundred they'd been spending for Alex's tuition could go straight to household expenses; along with what she earned (it wasn't great money, but it was good enough) they'd been able to eke by. Since Stephie had been at the daycare, Heim had told himself that she would have started working even if he hadn't lost his cool with Dickie. His wife was the kind of woman who was big on being around babies—they allowed her to believe in innocence and simplicity.

As for Heim, he didn't know what he believed in anymore. Or, rather, he wasn't sure that his beliefs had a place in the world as he'd come to know it. When he first heard about A.J. St. Claire, he took the case because it spoke to the clarity of purpose that he sought for his life. *What is unbalanced can be evened; what is lost can be found.* It all seemed noble enough, but off the bat Stephie had resented the parents, Colin and Kimm. He tried to relate to her the almost desperate intensity with which St. Claire talked about his son, how he was teaching the boy to draw, to play guitar, to stencil letters in a straight line. Stephie had just stared at him coldly and asked, *What about your own kids? Did you know Trace is thinking about trying out for the pom-pom squad? Did you know Alex can get through* Horton Hears a Who *by himself now?*

The kicker was the night she caught him at three a.m. sitting on the corner of their bed staring at a St. Claire family photo. Heim tried to justify it by saying he couldn't sleep, that he didn't feel as though he *should* sleep anymore. Sleep seemed indulgent when he could be *doing something.* Stephie had shoved away the bedspread and stomped into the bathroom to brush her teeth, loudly. She'd returned not a minute later, the toothbrush clamped tight in her jaw, the sides of her mouth streaked with spearmint paste.

"You're a goner for this one, aren't you," she had said, more a statement than a question.

Not long after that night St. Claire started slipping off the deep end, disappearing for three or four days at a time. Kimm would call, crying and begging Heim to find him. What else could he do? He'd track Colin down to a county lockup in some hick burg where he'd been detained, sometimes for harassing people who knew Dickie-Bird, other times for bothering police working another missing child investigation. Heim never thought twice about jumping in the Suburban to race to Cheboygan, Glenn Arbor, Alpena, Pentwater—wherever St. Claire had washed up. He'd deliver Colin back to Kimm, usually putting him up for a night in a motel so she wouldn't have to see him coming off his latest amphetamine binge. Pretty soon Heim wasn't looking for A.J. or even Dickie-Bird Johnson anymore. As Stephie put it, he'd become a bodyguard, a glorified babysitter. *You won't save him from himself,* she kept saying.

Then, one weekend shortly after New Year's, St. Claire was gone for good. "He's not coming back," Kimm said. Heim tried to reassure her, but deep down, he had to admit that the conversation was a mutual con. By that time he knew Colin well enough to know that he was a goner.

The only part of it Heim didn't understand by then was the implication of what Stephie had said. What, in other words, happens to you when you're a goner. What you're capable of. Then, a few weeks later, a fluke lead came his way and he tracked Dickie-Bird Johnson down to a grubby motor lodge outside Cass City. There was a confrontation. A police complaint. Humiliated, Heim found himself calling his mom for money for a lawyer to save him from an assault charge. All because he'd gone out of his mind for a few minutes. And now here he was, with a police record that made it illegal for him to work the only job he'd ever liked.

He stood at the door to the nursery, watching Stephie through the glass inlay, wiping an undiapered infant who lay prone on a changing table. He told himself that lying was protecting her and that she needed that protection because she'd had a tough time of it. Knocked up when she was in her early twenties, she had to drop out of Saginaw Valley State before she was anywhere near finishing a degree. Trace wasn't even two when the father, some Midland County kid, ditched on the shotgun marriage. That was why, Heim believed, Stephie could never identify with St. Claire—she didn't much care for men who cut out on their families. For more years than she'd cared to, she'd had to live with her parents. When Heim first met her—he was twenty-five then, and just getting out of the military—she was at the end of a string of waitress jobs, trying to save up to get back into school. She was suspicious of him at first because she'd known a lot of guys his age to turn tail when they heard about her kid. But Heim had loved Trace, and he started to see himself as someone who could bring a little stability to both mother and daughter.

In retrospect, it turned out to be a pretty piece of self-delusion.

When Stephie had finished dressing the baby, he pushed his way into the room. "Hey," he said.

"What are you doing here?" Stephie asked, surprised. Her smile faded when she saw the windbreaker and the car keys dangling out his fist. "Where you off to?"

The odor of the room snuck up on him, and he winced. "I don't know how you can take this smell. Dirty diapers and Lysol—god damn."

"Don't swear. You're in a church." She buttoned a red jumper around the squirming infant's pudge. "But you really want to know why I like this? I like to watch the babies breathe. They don't take it for granted. They haven't gotten over the novelty." She laid the child in one of the many basinets lining the wall. "So like I asked: where you running away to?"

Heim exhaled through his mouth, trying to avoid the stink. "Paps called this morning. He's got a sow he needs help farrowing. A week, tops."

He said this, recognizing a certain cynicism he usually took for granted in Stephie, the way she steeled herself against whatever might happen next. It was a precaution that wouldn't allow her to ever feel fully secure with him. It came from her getting pregnant after only a few months of dating Heim. At first, she wouldn't marry him, believing he would evaporate on her one day. After she finally consented he tried to show her that she'd seen the worst that there was for her to see. For the most part, the promise had held true, at least up until this past winter.

Stephie turned her back as she checked the next baby's bottom. "What about Kroger?"

"Paps said he'd give me a thousand if I came up there. That's two weeks Kroger work. Plus, it's daytime work. I might be able to sleep a night finally."

Stephie set a second infant on the changing table, saying nothing. She had to wrestle to get its pants over the diaper.

"I won't be able to run those errands for you. Can you get Trace to her piano lesson this afternoon?"

"Do I have a choice?" She snatched the tape ends of the plastic diaper, wadded it, and tossed it into the trash.

"Where's Alex at? I want to say goodbye."

"In the gym, on his cot. It's nap time."

"Okay." He withdrew without kissing her, got halfway to the door before turning. "One other thing. Paps' phone is out. He didn't pay his bill this month, so if you need me you'll have to call the cell—all right?"

Stephie nodded disinterestedly, concentrating on the wriggling child, who whined at being wiped so roughly.

Heim went back into the stuffy hallway and followed the carpet to the darkened gymnasium. Cots stretched out in uneven rows, their canvas bowed by the weight of resting toddlers. A woman sat at a desk flipping through a fashion magazine. Heim smiled at her. She recognized him and went back to browsing. He stepped through the maze of cots looking for Alex. Only a few of the kids were actually sleeping. Most lay stiffly on their backs, staring bored at the ceiling; others lay on one side so an arm or leg dangled at the floor. That way they could whisper or make faces at each other. "Quiet, please," he heard the woman with the magazine say when a stray giggle broke out.

"Hey bud," he whispered as he squatted at the side of Alex's cot. The boy shot upright and started to throw his arms around his father's waist.

Reflexively, Heim caught him just below the shoulders and pinned him firmly back to the cot. The boy blinked vacantly, unsure why his embrace had been refused. Heim closed his eyes for a second, feeling a burn ripple along his rib cage, and cursed himself for letting details go unchecked. He reached around to yank the elastic waistband of his windbreaker below his belt to hide the .22 he forgot to stick in the glove compartment. Thankfully, the woman was too caught up in killing time to notice.

"I've got to go for a few days. You can handle that?" Alex didn't speak. "You won't even know I'm missing." He kissed the boy's forehead and then rose to leave before waiting for a response.

As soon as he was in the Suburban, Heim put the pistol behind a maintenance manual in the glove compartment and slapped the lid shut. He sat immobile for a few seconds before punching his fist into the passenger-side seat cushion. He felt a weight pressing down on his neck and chest and realized it wasn't just from the lies. It came, too, from knowing he couldn't take the lie he'd have to live if he let this last shot at finding St. Claire's son go.

As he drove away, he had the distinct impression of passing through time, not space, for he wanted nothing more than to get to the end of the next few days. He tried to ease his uncertainty by thinking *there is an order to things and not just an order but a design and if I am nothing else I am an instrument for bringing that design into relief.*

It was no good, though. Although he kept going, he couldn't outrun the contradiction that shadowed his actions. Robert Heim loved his family, and he was betraying his family, and no amount of thinking things through was going to reconcile those two facts.

breathing out the ghost

everywhere and nowhere at once

At dusk when the search for Chance was called off for the night and the doors of Shiloh Baptist were locked behind the last of the volunteers, Sis walked to her sister's craft shop up on Main Street. She would've rather been home with Tillie and Joey, but she and Martha were in charge of planning their grandmother's upcoming birthday party, and there were still a lot of details to be ironed out. Grandma Brandywine was turning one hundred and seven, and such a preposterous milestone couldn't be ignored; even with a missing boy haunting Franklin, it was too great a testament to strength and endurance and pluck and determination and all those virtues that all things human are supposed to embody. One hundred and seven years was different from a quilt riddled with dead faces. There was nothing to celebrate in that case, only stories to tell.

Still, she could not escape Chance. His first-grade picture was stapled to nearly every telephone pole she passed. Mrs. Birmage had told her that only days before the photo was taken the boy had lost two teeth falling off a three-wheeler, leaving him looking like a pale jack-o-lantern. Now his gummy smile hung in the coffee shop across from the courthouse square, in the Jim Dandy up the street, on both doors of the public library, on phone booths and on the public bulletin boards of Franklin College, each similar face surrounded by thick type spelling out an oddly first-person plea: HAVE YOU SEEN ME?

A block before Martha's, at a battery of newspaper dispensers, the same image was plastered on the front pages of the *Franklin Journal, the Shelbyville Daily News*, and the *Indianapolis Star*. Sis squatted down to study the pudgy face, wondering whether it would look any different wrenched wider on a billboard. HAVE YOU SEEN ME? She imagined where all she might encounter those words. No, not a milk carton—that was a cliché—but the odd, unexpected places: the roaring backside of a combine, a yard sign stuck unceremoniously at the edge of a cornfield, a flea-market, dusty and indistinguishable from antiques on the auction block. If they didn't find Chance, Sis thought, this face would become a permanent part of the landscape. A boy nowhere to be found would be seen everywhere.

"Who's on a fifty-dollar bill?"

It was Chris Stempel, an estate lawyer Sis knew from a few years back when a mild heart attack had pushed her father to get his estate in order. Sis was embarrassed that he'd snuck up on her. She stood quickly so he wasn't staring down at her scalp.

"Excuse me?"

"I was reading the papers this morning and thinking how I'd come to know that boy's face so well already. Like one of my own kids' pictures"—he was staring at the headlines behind the glass—"I was thinking how it was easier to call up his face than remember whose is on money. I don't mean George Washington or Abe Lincoln. But a fifty? Whose face is on a fifty?"

"I don't know that a fifty-dollar bill's ever passed through my hands, Chris. Not being a lawyer, you know."

He laughed, and he seemed his normal self for a second. "You're a quick one, Mrs. Pruitt. You'll be happy to know we're not all swimming in champagne. By the way, I saw your daddy last

breathing out the ghost

week. He says Grandma Brandywine's turning another over on the odometer pretty soon. Pretty amazing to make it to triple digits."

"I just hope we can have the party in peace. Not exactly the right atmosphere for a celebration."

"I don't suppose. Like I was saying, the boy's picture got me thinking. You know how they print those circulars, the ones with missing kids' faces on them? They usually come with the mail, or the Sunday paper, slipped in with the coupons, but sometimes you get them stuffed in sacks at the grocery and the drug store. I picked one up just a week or so ago, and for some reason I really looked at the faces. I mean, I never gave them that much thought. Just like money: you know there's a face there, so you don't bother to look at it, you take it for granted. This time I made myself look. Most of those kids are teenagers—runaways—and they've been missing five or six years in some cases, so you know they don't look like their pictures anymore. And then you start measuring the time they've been gone according to your own life. One poor boy had been missing eight years, and I was thinking of my girl Kenley, and how in that much time she'd moved from elementary to high school, from Bluebirds to band to varsity softball. Her room's been redone twice. I can look at two pictures of Kenley taken eight years apart, and it's like looking at two different people. And then I thought of that boy's parents, and how they had only one face to go on, and how they had to live knowing that the face they knew had dissolved into some other face, their child becoming not their child."

He spoke without pause, almost without breath. Sis knew he didn't expect an answer, that he wasn't even asking a question. This happened fairly often. People who lost a close family member or who suffered through a divorce—sometimes folks just caught in the throes of a passing depression—they presumed Sis's empathy. They believed that talking about Patty for so long now gave Sis the patience needed to listen to them stumble through feelings they'd only half reckoned.

Chris palmed the crown that peeked through his thinning hair, embarrassed. "I'm talking nonsense. I know you've got better things to do than listen to my jawing."

"It's all right."

But it wasn't. Moments like these left Sis feeling dishonest. She couldn't tell Chris that she didn't deserve others' trust or intimacy because she did what she did for selfish reasons. She didn't want people forgetting Patty. It was that simple. If the only price for keeping her daughter's ghost haunting them was listening to their stories—well, it was a small one she was willing to pay.

"I'll let you go. You give Grandma my best. Willard Scott come calling yet?"

Sis laughed a little. "You know, Mom used to send grandma's picture to the *Today* show and then make her watch all morning, waiting. They didn't announce her name until she turned one hundred and three. Then they ignored her one hundred and fourth. When we wrote asking why, a producer called to apologize. He said there are too many centenarians around nowadays to fit them all in a thirty-second bit. Did you know the oldest person in the world is one hundred and fourteen? That's only seven years older than grandma, but there are forty-four other people between them."

"I wouldn't be surprised if fifty years from now you're your own Grandma Brandywine. Your family's genes aren't just durable—they're indestructible."

She tried to smile politely at the compliment, but as she always did she thought of the one in her family who'd taught her how vulnerable they really were. "Honestly, I don't know I'd want to live past one hundred. It seems like a desert of time."

"How about I ask you when you're ninety-nine? Take care, Sis."

With Chris's leaving she remembered what she was doing on Main Street at this time of night without her children, so she went on to Martha's tiny shop. It was stocked mainly with home-cast dolls and crochet outfits her sister made and traded. The place was stuffy with the aroma of a single shelf of potpourri and grape candles. Martha was helping a customer, so Sis loitered at a consignment rack of hand-painted greeting cards by local artists. She was considering buying one just to support her sister when the doorbell rang and Chris stuck his head in the shop.

"Ulysses S. Grant," he called to her.

"Huh?"

"Grant's face is on a fifty dollar bill."

Sis smiled. "I'll take your word for it. Like I said, being a farmer not a lawyer, I've never seen one of those."

AFTER THE FINAL CUSTOMER left, Martha and Sis locked the door and closed out the register. The day's take was just shy of two hundred dollars. That didn't seem to bother Martha, whom money never bothered, but it flustered Sis. She and Pete had lent Martha money to help open the shop. They'd known full well the loan wasn't likely to be paid back, but they offered what little they could afford to lose because that's what you did for family. You helped out, even when the business plan seemed as flippant and improvised as its name: *All Dolled Up*, Martha insisted on calling her shop.

"What kind of husband you think Chris Stempel would make?" Martha asked, zipping up her deposit in the nightly bank bag.

"You taking applications?"

"I'm only saying men talk differently to the women they're not married to than the ones they are. Chris was all 'Yes, Mrs. Pruitt; No, Mrs. Pruitt' with you just now. It makes me wonder how polite he is at home."

Sis tried not to roll her eyes. It was hard sometimes to think of Martha as her sister and not her daughter, and not just because of their age difference. Martha was the only woman Sis knew who'd never had children, and that somehow made Martha seem a teenager still, even though she was in her forties.

"Chris was that polite because I'm fifty-five. I'm old enough to be his mother."

"That's not true. He's only two years younger than me. You'd'a have to been fourteen to birth him."

"I wasn't but nineteen when Patty came along. That's only about as far from fourteen as Grandma is from the oldest person in the world."

Martha wasn't interested in Sis's math. She was still thinking about Chris Stempel. "He reminds me of Max, the way Max used to talk. Men sound that kindly when they don't have enough emotion in them to run hot or cold. They're the sort whose tap runs dry—sort of like Pete."

"Don't drag Pete into this. He has all the feelings he needs, thank you very much."

"Honey, if Pete Pruitt was any less demonstrative he'd be mistaken for an end table. You'd have to wax the rings of his back from where folks set their coffee mugs." When Sis didn't laugh,

Martha stopped smiling. "Don't get mad; that was a joke. Did you ask Pete about Grandma's party yet?"

Sis's silence was answer enough.

"You know my position on this," Martha said, surly. "My place is too small. Mom and Dad's house needs more cleaning than you and I have time to give it. Now if you want to rent a banquet room, that's fine. Just don't complain when I can't kick into the kitty. You know how much money I don't have for hat-passing."

"And you know why we can't have Grandma's party at our place."

Martha sighed. "It's not Pete saying no that you're worried about. It's his saying yes what scares you. Because if you did host this party then you wouldn't have an excuse anymore for you two living on that farm like monks."

"I don't know too many monks raising seven- and five-year-olds."

Martha paperclipped the day's few credit card receipts. Sis decided she'd know when business was booming when Martha needed a rubber band to gather them.

"You know, if you were married to Rick instead of Pete not talking wouldn't be a problem. Talking would be. You'd have talked Grandma's party to death. Rick is the exact opposite of Pete: he feels everything a little too intensely. His tap doesn't just run—it gushes."

Rick was Martha's second husband, but her first ex. They'd met in a glazing class at the Shelbyville community center not long after Max, Martha's first husband, passed from cancer. Max had been a nice enough local farmer whose main attraction for Martha was that he let her walk all over him. Rick was flashier.

Sis remembered how upset she was when Martha confessed to falling in love with him less than six months after Max's death. Their romance fell just short of a local scandal, the first in Sis's family since Grandma Brandywine had taken up with a man named Horace without benefit of marriage way back in 1927.

"That's how crazy things have changed since Grandma," Martha rambled on. "If I'd have just shacked up with Rick, nobody'd have cared. But because I wanted him married, that's what bothered folks. People not approving because of Max affected our relationship a lot, you know."

Sis was looking at the porcelain doll heads that lined the walls. The shelf they sat on ran three-quarters of the way around the shop and was hung close to the ceiling where a wallpaper border should've been. "Maybe if you're in the market for a new husband you should just cast you a new one. You might be better off pouring your own mold."

Martha unlocked the door to let them out. A gust of wind swooped into the store.

"You shouldn't try to be mean, Sis. Face it: mean's not in your nature."

THEY WALKED THE DEPOSIT to the bank and then started for the little house on Depot Street that Martha had rented since Rick left her. Halfway there, amid a block of faltering houses that dated back a century, they began to hear the sound of playing children—wordless, bodiless whoops and shrieks that made Sis wonder if they had wandered into a goblin patch. It was a silly thing to imagine—the world was too real and too hard for spirits and sprites—but as the voices rose through the leafless trees, shrouding Sis and her sister in the eerie ether of disembodied fun, she couldn't help but imagine it as the sound of Chance Birmage calling to them, summoning them to wherever he was. Sis took a breath and reconciled herself to the likelihood that tonight when she tried not to dream, these whoops and shrieks would congeal into recognizable words from a recognizable face asking a question that after only a day already seemed freighted with judgment: HAVE YOU SEEN ME? Only that's not what a missing child would whisper to you in your sleep. More like WHY HAVEN'T YOU SEEN ME?, she thought.

Then they turned a corner and saw where the voices were coming from. Two children, a boy and a girl, sat in a swing facing each other under the anemic glow of a single yellow bulb. They were trying to coordinate their dangling arms and legs to get a smooth glide going, but they weren't having much luck—in part because the girl was much bigger than the boy, and her roller skates dragged in the dirt when the boy tried to back up and stand so they could gain some elevation when he kicked out his legs. "You're not doing it right," the girl complained when the boy launched them forward and their motion petered out after no more than a half-arc.

Sis flushed with embarrassment all over again for thinking of goblins. "They're spidering."

Martha repeated the word indifferently.

"Yeah, see, look at how their legs hang together—like a spider's legs. That's where the name comes from."

"I'm pretty sure the *Kama Sutra* calls it something else."

Sis shot her sister a frown. "Those kids are maybe five and six. They're innocent. Maybe you could try looking at what they're doing innocently and not project your own dirty thoughts onto them?"

"It was a joke, okay? No need to turn me in to Perverted Justice."

"I spidered all the time when I was a kid. All the way up to twelve, probably. Elaine Haskins and I were champs at it in fourth grade. . . . Good God, Elaine's a grandma now."

"Elaine Haskins is one thing. I bet you didn't spider with *Blain* Haskins, now did you?"

"Nobody thought to name a boy 'Blain' back then. Boys were still Charlie and Ross and Harold. Those were family names; 'Blain' sounds like some kind of grippe. But even if we had known 'Blains' teachers wouldn't have let us spider with them. That would've been more than halfway rude."

"My point exactly. Those kids may be innocent, but they're still feeling *something* sitting there that close together. You can't convince me they're not. And it's because you know they are that seeing them sitting in each other's lap is so disarming. You'd never let Tillie and Joey spider together—you know you wouldn't. It wouldn't look right. You'd throw a fit, they'd cry, and then the next time I babysat I'd have to explain why they're only allowed to do it when you and Pete aren't around."

"If that's your way of getting out of babysitting, congratulations. I'll call somebody else next time. What's disarming to me is that they're out here on their own. They shouldn't be."

"This is Franklin," Martha shrugged absentmindedly. Not a half-block away the un-taped edges of one of Chance's fliers flapped against a utility pole.

"I wouldn't let my kids out unaccompanied on the farm, and that's five miles from here."

"You've got reasons. Other folks don't." Martha noticed the crosspiece of the swing set bowing with the children's weight. "Is it just me or does that thing look like it's one bolt away from falling in on itself? It must be twenty years old. The parents are probably thinking lawsuit."

They watched the children kick and grope again for altitude. This time Sis and Martha heard the chains holding the rubber seat groaning.

"Do you ever wonder if you're denying Tillie and Joey this freedom? I'm not saying you are—I'm just asking if you ever doubt how much protecting you do."

"I doubt it all the time. I never felt safer for the kids than when they were in me. It was different with Patty; it was all different with her. I was so green I was clueless about what a loss of control you feel when your baby breathes its first. With Tillie, I was so terrified of losing her that I drove Pete and me both crazy. I'd stay four feet behind the Guernseys in case one got a notion to kick. How can you milk a cow from four feet back? But it wasn't just outdoor work. I couldn't round a counter for fear of a sharp edge puncturing my stomach."

"You had your reasons," Martha said again, only impatiently this time. Sis knew that was her cue to stop talking. Talking wasn't her job; hers was to listen. That's what people expected from her. She wished she had someone other than herself to listen, though. She would have liked to describe how, cradling Tillie seconds after the delivery, she had caught a glimpse of her own afterbirth as the hospital staff prepared its disposal. Severed from the child's stomach, the blue lifelines running through the pasty gray knots of the amniotic sac turned earthen red, asphyxiating on air. The baby had been born into the vulnerability of life, and Sis felt her power to protect that existence die away to the rhythm of the girl's inhalation. Two years later, with Joey, she went three days overdue, and on the way to the Caesarian section her doctor joked about her not wanting to give up the child. She laughed it off, but he had the right idea: sometime in the third trimester Sis grew so convinced of the sheltering calm of her belly that she decided she'd let the doc fetch this one.

Nobody wanted to hear that story from her, though.

"Hey, I almost forgot," Martha said, changing the subject. "Did you know you're nearly as famous as Grandma? I found a list online of the oldest birth mothers in Indiana. You're there because of Joey. You'd think that forty-nine is about the high end for a woman to get pregnant, but you're only like number twenty two or something. There's some lady in Evansville who had twins at fifty-seven, but she used in-vitro fertilization. You're one of the few on the list without that asterisk."

"Do they have a list of the longest spans between children?"

"What do you mean?"

"I mean that I had Patty at nineteen and Tillie at forty-seven. That's almost thirty years. That must be some kind of record, too, don't you think?"

Martha blinked as she pushed her glasses higher on her nose. "I'll have to look for that list. That one didn't enter my mind to look up."

"When you find it, make sure there's an asterisk on it explaining why I had Tillie and Joey so late. You know why, don't you?"

"No need saying it. I know why."

Sis said why anyway: "I was having my own grandchildren."

BEFORE MARTHA COULD RESPOND they were interrupted by the clap of a screen door and a rustle in the mulberry bushes that trimmed the back porch of the house. A border collie charged through the foliage and across the gray fescus grass to the fence where Sis and Martha stood, barking and stuffing its snout through the chain links, trying to bully them away. But Sis and Martha were instead watching the old woman who had rushed outside after it. She dashed more limberly than her stooped body would seem capable of, not stopping until she was off the porch and at the swing set, where she snatched the girl off the boy's lap. She did it with a violent jerk to the girl's arm that sent the girl spilling backwards, one roller skate knocking the boy's left elbow. Before they knew what had happened, Sis and Martha were watching the girl lie in the grass, one foot still caught in the swing seat, howling as the old woman stood over her shaking a finger. The boy was crying, too, rubbing the nub of his arm.

"If I told you once I told you a thousand times to leave that boy alone! You done disobeyed me for the last time. Now get up and get those skates off and into the garage because you're not playing with them again if I have anything to say about it! And when your daddy hauls his sorry behind back to town I'm getting him to take this swing set down!"

When the girl didn't respond quickly enough, the old woman yanked her to her feet and swatted her rear end. It didn't stop her crying. The woman was about to spank the child again when Sis yelled, "Don't!" The old woman froze, her open palm straight in the air.

Martha couldn't believe it. She didn't like feeling conspicuous. "We're not nosing. . . . There's a boy missing. My sister here's been over at Shiloh Baptist all day helping folks look for him. When she saw your little ones here in the yard alone she started thinking about hi—"

"They wasn't alone. I been sitting right there around the corner the 'tire time, and I can hear every word they say. I didn't raise five of my own to be told at seventy-seven what's doing right by a stranger, no matter if you're church-minded or not."

"They were only spidering," Sis insisted. "It's just a game. . . ."

"They're playing a game they been told plenty not to play. You want to make an issue of it then talk to their daddy. He'll be back next Tuesday. Until then, I got my hands full, and I don't have time for their disobeying."

"We don't mean offense," Martha said again. Now it was Sis's turn for disbelief: Martha was fighting back a laugh. The old woman's anger seemed so out of date it was almost funny. She grabbed Sis's arm and tugged her along before the woman could shout at them. "Sorry," she called over her shoulder. "My sister can't take people shouting and spanking. . . ."

She didn't speak again until they were safely down the block. "Boy oh boy. I would quote Dad and say that woman is mean enough to eat her young, but I'm not sure I'd be exaggerating. If that's what hardscrabble does to you, I'm glad I'm pampered."

"She reminded me of Grandma."

"What? Come on now. . . . Grandma's a hundred and seven. She threw one shoe at you once and you've been chewing that nut for forty-five years. It's not like you wouldn't have been upset if Tillie kept touching figurines she'd been told to keep away from."

breathing out the ghost

"I don't resent Grandma for that. Why do I ever tell you anything? You never understand what I'm saying. You don't remember the way Grandma was before she got old. She was already in her seventies before you were born."

"I'm sure she was an evil old witch who made you eat worm-ridden apples. How's that for sympathy? Next you'll tell me you were an abused child. Then you'll say that girl back there is, too."

"What I'm saying is that 'biddy' as you called her doesn't have a right to that kind of anger. Her meanness is all eccentricity; it's not earned. Did you see her? She's Mom and Dad's age. Have you ever seen them lose it like that, over something as silly as spidering? Her sort of vinegar is more akin to folks in Grandma Brandywine's time. Notice I said 'folks,' not just Grandma. I would never say she abused me for throwing that shoe at me. I deserved the licking I got. All I'm saying is that folks back then wore themselves out so bad by forty that if they made it to sixty or seventy they were entitled to be ornery. . . ."

"You don't know that woman. We can't say what she's entitled to and what she's not. You heard what she said about the dad. I bet the dad dumped those kids on her and then lit out for the territory. That's what men do, you know: they light out for parts unknown."

Sis was shaking a little. "It's not even meanness. People in Grandma's time were *hard*, not mean, and Grandma was the hardest of them all. She was that way because back then they didn't have time for feelings."

"What are you talking about? Jesus, Sis—you're losing it."

"Haven't you ever heard Dad talk about the beatings they used to get when he was a boy? They were the kind that'd land you in jail today. I'm sure that old lady had her share of them;

they're probably why she's the way she is. There wasn't a tool or implement on the farm that was too cruel for instilling discipline."

"It didn't make Dad hard or mean, though. That's how mean that biddy back there is: she's a bastard."

"Did you never hear the outhouse story? When Dad was nine he was helping clear this old homestead Grandpa Mercer bought for pasture. There was a rickety outhouse at the back of the property. Well, one afternoon Dad feels nature's call, so he sneaks in there. He has to sneak because the other hands mercilessly catcall anyone they know to be squatting in the bushes. Only Dad no more than drops his dungarees and hikes over the hole when the old wood gives way and he falls down five feet, bottom-first. It's all shit and shale down in that hole, of course. Too deep and slippery to climb out. The other men are pounding the homestead so hard they can't hear his yelling above their hammers. He had to spend the night down there. He might never have got out if another man out to relieve himself hadn't yanked open the door to find Dad staring up through the hole."

"Can't say I ever heard that one. What's it got to do with being hard and mean?"

"After Dad was hauled out of the outhouse, he goes running across the field to Grandpa Mercer, thinking a father's got to be grateful to know his son his safe. Only Mercer's not so affectionate. He slapped Dad's face so hard Dad went facedown down into the soil. For making everybody worry, you see."

"I'm not sure I quite believe that one. Slipping in a shitter is the ultimate tall tale of farm life. Everybody around here tells some version of it."

"Whenever I've heard Dad tell his version, he's always heightened the drama by clapping his hands to recreate the sound of that slap." Sis did it herself; her clap crackled through the chill of the night, sharp as a pistol report. "*Only it hurt lot more*, Dad would say. Then he'd laugh off the memory. Now, if that had happened to you or me, we'd never have laughed once. We'd be scarred for life and still resentful. We'd have had therapy or read self-help books to get over it. I mean, I can still remember how that shoe felt, and how hard I cried, and how I never wanted to go back to her farm until I was so much older. I used to wail when Mom and Dad said I had to stay with Grandma."

"Maybe Dad laughed because that slap was nothing compared to what else he had to get over next. If the outhouse thing really happened, it couldn't have been too long before Grandpa Mercer died. Then Dad had to contend with Horace."

"It couldn't have been easy being a boy back then with your mom shacking up with some guy. It's a surprise Dad was never more bitter about it. I've always wanted to ask him what it was like."

"You should ask him," Sis said. She felt out of breath from chasing down her thinking. "I have, plenty of times. He'll tell you what he's told me: 'I didn't think about it much at all. We didn't have time to introspect back then—we were working.'"

Sis stopped on the sidewalk. Martha couldn't figure out why; Depot Street was still two corners away.

That's the thing I like least about myself, Sis was thinking. *I'm too introspective. I wish I didn't have time to think. I mean, I don't really, but I do it, constantly. I think of Patty every single second. I wish I didn't, but I can't help it.* She turned to face Martha. "You want to know something really crazy? There's a part of me that's thinking right now how I'm not all that different from that old woman. *I envy that anger*—the ability to express it, I mean. I want to be a biddy who's made herself a bastard, too."

Martha shook her head. "You're so full of it. I saw your face when she spanked that kid. You wanted to hop the fence and handcuff the old bag."

"You just don't see it in me because you don't want to. Nobody does. One day I'll do something to make you recognize it. Then you won't be able to tell me mean's not in my nature."

"Stop talking silly already. Jesus, you're *Sis!*"

Martha spat out the nickname as if it were all the logic she needed to make her point persuasive. *But Sis isn't really me,* Sis wanted to say. *My Christian name is Beverly. 'Sis' is just something that was put on me before I was old enough to be able to tell anybody who bothered to ask that I wasn't okay with it. . . .*

A pair of headlights stopped her mid-breath, before she could get a single word out. It wasn't until she recognized Pete's truck that she was able to surface through the whirlpool of her thinking.

"Hop in," Pete told them. Over his shoulder, draped in shadows, Tillie and Joey looked like drowsy goblins as they strained against their seatbelts to see their mother.

"What's happened?" Sis asked, apprehensively.

"Dub's boys got them a drifter. Found him in a truck down by McCrea's Hill. Thought he was a dead man they had such a time getting him to wake."

how to act normal

The first thing they want you to do is account for yourself. Easy enough, you say. Laws of motion, distance, time, and space work in your favor. You can name the landmarks of specific interstate exits, the smell of diesel exhaust as the trucker with the nudie silhouette on his tire flaps passes you, even the splash of your piss as it hits the porcelain of the Texaco bathroom in Asthtabula, the one where the condom machine dispenses postage-stamp-sized porn. You can impress them with your ability to absorb the landscape at eighty miles an hour, to predict the evergreen groves where state troopers nestle as they lie in wait for speeders and the fern- and reed-lined gullies where deer stumble, confusedly drawn to death by the sound of the traffic. If that fails to awe your audience, you keep careful records. You save receipts, keep the log current, connect the dots on your homemade map. And if nothing else works, you tell your sob story. You spill the beans about the stifling presence of emptiness in your life, about the hole gored in your soul. You resort to this final measure in the belief that your motives are explicable, that others will excuse your actions because what you have been through deserves special consideration if not outright pity. But there you're seriously mistaken, and you make a fatal *faux pas*. You forget you have stepped off the scales, you don't register according to standard instrumentation. In your effort to make them understand, you overlook the warty truth of what happens when you refuse to give up and go along to get along:

You scare them.

You see, I had been in this place before, A.J. I sat in the same chair (although it was a different chair), facing the same mirror (only then it was smeared with the palm prints of some previous suspect who cupped his face to the glass trying to see to the other side), sweating under the same scrutiny (but a sheriff this time, not a team of detectives). On both occasions they wooed me with coffee and officiousness. But you decline the cigarettes because you don't smoke and smoking makes you look shifty anyway, and you don't drink anything that they offer because the caffeine brings out a nervous tic in your fingertips. They are looking for that tic. When you sit you don't sit straight back with your hands on your knees as in a job interview—too formal; they'll think you're hiding something. Don't lean forward with your arms crossed on the table. They take that as a dare. You're daring them to trick you into saying what they want to hear from you. Instead, you tuck the chair tight to the table so it touches just below your ribs and you fold your hands together. They will rock in their seats and then stand and pace behind you, but you do not move. You do not relax, nor do you stiffen up. You have to prove to them you are behaving just as someone in your position should. They will call that behavior normal but you won't. For you, there is no normal anymore.

This time, my second time "in the cage" as it's affectionately known, was actually easier. I had a good excuse. I'd driven eight hours straight on forty hours of insomnia, so by the time I hit the swatch of county blacktop known as Smithland Pike, I could barely keep my eyes open, even with the speed. So I pulled over on the shoulder in front of a fat pug of a hill and crawled in the back of the cab. I thought I'd slept forever when I heard the banging. Later I realized I'd only rested two hours. That made it harder, because I was feeling fuzzyheaded when I pushed my way outside into the arms of deputies who were demanding identification. I showed them my license and let them run my tags while I cooked up a good story.

Who was I?

I could have been visiting family members, but then they would want names. I could have been on a business trip, but I doubted that one would fly given how little like a traveling salesman I looked. I might have even claimed to be a Deadhead, but I was afraid they'd test me on the lyrics to "Saint of Circumstance." The best I could do on the spur of the moment was a quasi-truth: I was out vagabonding.

But why here, wherever here was?

I'd gotten off I-65, gotten turned around, gotten sleepy. I didn't blame the deputies for sniffing suspiciously at my scent. I pulled open the back hatch and showed them the lettering and sketches I practiced to put myself a-slumber. Here's Centaur, I said. Nicholas Jenson, 1470, one of the first typefaces to trim the black Gutenberg bulk into svelte seductiveness. And look at this one. Futura. Sharp Bauhausian right angles that put the *rrrr* in a*rrrr*t deco, the modernist's favorite script. Makes me think of John Held, Jr., and the Arrow Shirt Man. (*In the mean time, the in-between time, ain't we got fun?*) They scratched their necks and hocked loogies into the sumac while I rambled. I was grateful when they asked me to have a seat in the back of the squad car. Across the county road I could see the wet land and some still-blossoming beans and a sow snorting in her morning manure. Another man arrived, short, pot-bellied, looking like he'd rather be facedown in a plate of bacon. Would

I mind coming downtown? Only since he was a sheriff, I don't think he said downtown.

During the ride, I retraced my steps, trying to figure out where I'd gone wrong. I blame it on Bembo (Francesco Griffo, 1495). It looks too much like Roman inscription—foreign *and* decadent. I should've played it safe with Garamond. It's known as the "teetotaler of types."

THE LAST TIME I was hauled in the conversation went something like this:

"What was the boy doing when you left him?"

"I've told you already."

"Tell me again."

"He was buckled in the passenger seat. Reading a comic book."

"What comic?"

"*X-Men.* We always watched the cartoon together. Every afternoon at four. We would have watched it when we got home."

"Was he fussy?"

"He's too old to get fussy anymore."

"What does he get?"

"He doesn't get anything. He's a very calm child."

"He *never* got upset? He *never* made you mad or got on your nerves?"

"Never. He never did."

He reclined in his chair, his hands on his belt buckle, victorious, nodding his head, all-knowing.

"You did it first," I told him. "You know you did."

But he was as self-assured as an all-day sucker by that point.

"You crut," I said. "You feeb. You used the past tense first. You did. You."

YOU SEE, THEY HAVE a checklist, and all the time they promise you they're sweeping the streets for the usual suspects, they're giving your grief the stink test. They look for a wayward smile, check for the crock behind the crocodile tears. And you can understand why. The guilty are pretty bad actors. They don't stick to their story. They mumble over lies they themselves find preposterous. They confuse the chronologies they hastily string together. They even come up with cartoon villains to deflect blame. A black man stole my baby. An intruder strangled our girl. There's this guy—Dickie-Bird Johnson. Find him. Talk to him. I know he's the one.

Here are the symptoms they search for:

Inconsistency. Recite a story more than once and *you* see whether the song remains the same. It won't, trust me. Each telling is a narrative event tailored to the needs of that moment, that audience. They know this. The reason they have you tell your tale again and again is to measure how well you sweat out the changes. For example, you say you stopped at a Home Depot on the way to your house. Why? Maybe once you say you went for nails, and you even tell them for what: *I've been meaning to square this bit of window trim in the guest bedroom; it was water damaged over the years from the gable on the roof where water collects and seeps in under the tar paper.* They write this in their notes, thinking maybe next time they're at your house they'll sneak a ladder around back and check for weatherworn shingles. An hour later they ask the same question and this time instead of answering "nails" you mistakenly say "caulk." Aha! the detectives interrupt you. You told us you were there for nails! *But surely you understand that once you hang the trim you must run a caulk bead around the edges for a tight seal.* But the more you try to explain, the more it looks like you're inventing as you go along. So everywhere you are now, you memorize your movements. You make sure you can recite them as spontaneously as if they were the digits of your Social Security number. You are no longer allowed the luxury of not being letter perfect.

Background. This one's a little harder to prepare for since you never know whom they'll decide to question about you. They'll interview your wife first, of course, asking her to characterize your relationship with your son. Here it's good not to be too intimate with your spouse, especially when it comes to talking about your love for your child. You don't mention your own father—that's a definite no-no. You keep mum about all those hours you heard him creeping about the house, mumbling into his hand how he'd never hit the broadside of thirty. (And then it was forty and after that fifty, and by golly, by that time he got his wish. At forty-two). You don't mention how you saw him speak of himself as buggered by defeat, riddled with kids (five!), boarded up in an aluminum-sided shanty. There is a certain profile, understand, of a man so strangled by disappointment that he thinks the best he can do for his children is to relieve them of the burden of living. This inevitably comes up in the suicide note, usually to the tune of some Greek chorus that goes "the sins of the father are passed on to. . . ." But your mother, A.J., for all the books we'd read and talked about together, failed to make this connection, so it didn't seem odd to her that while she recited every private conversation we'd ever had about you the police scratched their notepads furiously and licked their lips with long bubbled tongues. Nor did your teachers, nor the peewee league coach, nor the guitar instructor they eventually tracked down.

What was it that was odd about you and me together? Well, let's see, I was a little intense, a little anxious for you to succeed. I made you learn your multiplication tables. How many parents actually sit down and write out index cards with 6x8 on the front and 48 on the back? Each afternoon after *X-Men* I sat you at a card table beside my desk and had you make collages and lunch-paper puppets while I worked. Strange indeed. Oh, and I drew out chord positions for you. Who does that? Okay, a father might teach his kid a G major or a G7, but a G *minor* 7 or a G major with a suspended 5th? What man shows his son how to play a G7^{add}9^{sus}4 so when the boy strikes that chord his father can burst out with *It's been a hard day's night, and I been working like a dog. . . .*

It's bound to be beyond somebody's pale.

So you take your children to the lessons and you pay. And when there's a student conference at school, you don't rearrange your schedule and ask impertinent questions about what standardized scores mean. You love your children, but you make it clear that you don't over-love them—or that you're not lording your love over them, trying to win some sort of approval your old man never bothered to beg from you. You don't want to give them anything to hold against you in a court of public opinion.

<u>Disposition</u>. Okay. The basic theory here is that if you're guilty you're 1) aching to confess because whatever happened wasn't premeditated or you're 2) boasting of your criminal deeds because in your psychopathic hubris you find taunting the authorities an enjoyable pastime—better than pachisi. Thus, they look for any cue

that you're not quite the sad sack you portray yourself as. A woman in Arkansas whose toddler was stabbed to death shoots a can of silly string over his tombstone. A *truly* heartbroken mother might blubber over a coffin, but she'd leave the party favors at home. Ergo, six months later, said Arkansas woman finds herself the recipient of a second-degree murder conviction. The jury weighing the evidence cites her strange comportment at the burial service as sure proof that she killed her own. Amanda Totch's father fails just as spectacularly when his actions are given the once over. He claimed his daughter disappeared at a filling station. The security cameras there catch him dialing 911 while asking the clerk if she saw someone mess with the little angel in his truck. When the befuddled employee turns to look outside, dear old dad is so pleased with his acting debut that he pockets a tin of chew for a prize. Later, at his mother's home, he breaks down when detectives show him the tape. They wait to do this after he pulls out the tin in plain sight and stuffs a wad behind his bottom lip.

I heard that story on the radio on the way down from Michigan.

And then there was me, public enemy number one. What aroused suspicions on my part?

The Sunday morning after you were gone, I mowed the lawn.

WHICH RAISES AN IMPORTANT question: just who is it who gets to cock the prop of propriety? What busy bee pollinates the bitter honey hive of inappropriate behavior?

They found your grandfather belly-down dead across a pair of train tracks that ran alongside the hydrochloric acid pump station on the west side of Bay City. The old man (*old—he was forty-two years old—seven more than me*) wore the same rubber suit he'd been wearing since he was seventeen (which is when I was born), the same rubber suit in which, when the tankers arrived on those zippered train tracks, he would chock the wheels, screw the pipe assemblies in place, check the fittings for gas leaks, and then twist the diodes to let the burning fog fill the galvanized bellies of those tankers. A conductor found his body (*seven years*, I keep saying to myself, and the shrinking age span sticks in the shallow pan of my craw). In the five a.m. moonlight the man thought a tarp had blown upon the gray rails.

When I think about it hard enough I can feel your grandfather's chest cavity gripped by the numbness of an eroded heart. I see myself as him, falling, his forehead—*mine*—snapping backward as the skin slashes across the lowest rung of the ladder welded to a tanker's flank, the hard plastic goggles cracking, my nostrils—*his*—stapled back as our chin hits the pavement. But the embarrassment of that fall can't compare to the indignity of our knowing that we die alone, of knowing we must lie there hours, invisible to the roving security patrols and the midnight-shift workmen who step outside the pump stations only to fetch the spare deck of cards they keep in the glove compartments of their cars. Blood in the head of a prone body drains down into the face where it coagulates, purpling the pores, so that in the morgue it looks as if our features have been stained by wine. (*And that image is forever linked in my mind homonymously with the whine of your aunts' crying as they wake from their Edgar Allan Poe dreams of premature burial. I could not dream, could never sleep, for the sound of dogs digging under the crawlspace, licking at the condensation on the pipes.*) Later, at the funeral parlor, the disfigurement means the mortician has to rouge up our face until it's as pink as a saloon floozy's.

SO THE MORNING AFTER they find the body on the railway tracks in front of the pump station the neighbors arrive with armfuls of meat, baked beans, cakes and pies. We're so sorry, they said. Here's a pot roast. What a sad way to go. Don't worry about the serving dish; we'll get it back at a better time. The dining table soon grew crowded as a refugee camp, so we piled the Pyrex and Tupperware containers on the kitchen counters, and when that space filled, we set up Dad's old poker table and made a montage out of mismatched hot pads so not to mar the green-felt surface. It was more food than our house had ever held. For once we didn't worry about asking for seconds. As each uncle, aunt, cousin, co-worker, and congregation member arrived we raced for a new paper plate, jostling for the spatulas and tongs. Eventually, the bolts of my jaws ached from chewing. I knew that once upon a time communities along the old range lines stuffed baskets with food, sometimes even butchering a spare shoat to save suffering families the burden of preparing meals. A lot of menial work went into making a dinner back then that a household in the grip of shock just couldn't shoulder. But more importantly, the very humdrumness of frying pork and peeling potatoes took away from the solemnity of the moment. A family was supposed to confront its anguish, to wail and moan so it might come to grips with the fact that life had irrevocably changed.

But now it was different. Eating was a welcome distraction, not for us but for *them*. However the piles on the plates clashed (macaroni cheese sauce oozing orangely under the spinach salad), however sour the mixtures they made (runaway grapes rolling in the gravy!), our guests chewed to prove that their existence hadn't been diverted. For the price of a quick casserole, they bribed us into agreeing that this was God's plan, life was going on. Their clichés were breath mints: they wanted us to suck away to sweeten the bad taste our misfortune left in their mouths. And so we did. For a week straight, we ate no less than five meals a day, not including impromptu nibbles at the open refrigerator and the fingerfuls of whip cream skimmed off the pie tops. The more we gorged the less we felt, and the less we felt the more we ate and slept and slept and ate again.

YOUR MOM WAS THERE. The night before the service we lay in the bottom of my old bunk bed. (My brother—your uncle—without a girlfriend then, had been exiled to a rollaway bed set up in the living room, its creaky accordion springs our only entertainment during those insomniac hours).

"You know what I'm thinking of?" she asked. She asked that a lot. She liked for me to guess her thoughts. "I'm thinking of that night, freshman year, when we made that pallet of New Mexico blankets on the dorm floor and we read *The Death of Ivan Ilych*."

How appropriate. The story begins with Ivan's funeral, attended by an array of colleagues who feel nothing but relief that the grim reaper got someone else. Oblivious to the reality of death, they go through the motions, genuflecting, praying, dispensing embraces, all the time thinking about the bridge game they could be having. As one gentleman phrases it, they're there because they're bound to "the tiresome demands of propriety."

"How did that one line go? You know the one I mean."

Of course I did.

Ivan Ilych's life was most simple and most ordinary, and therefore most terrible.

"You remember what we did after we read it?"

Of course I did. That winter semester the temperature had dipped to record lows, leaving heavy layers of frost gripping the windows and freezing the locks around campus. There was little more to do than wrap up and count the hours while the overworked radiators knocked and rattled. So your mom and I read together—*Notes from the Underground, The Trial, The Crack-Up*. Deep shit, I know. That afternoon she'd suggested Tolstoy, with whom she was already familiar. She said, "Let's read it and promise that our lives together will never be this way."

"So what did we do?" she whispered in the bed, rubbing backside against me.

I kissed her shoulder and reminded her: "We made love."

And so we did again, that night before the funeral. Your mother reached down between her legs and brought me into the buttery hollow of her thighs. Right there in my brother Robbie's old bottom bunk, with my mother's heaving sobs drifting through the duct vents and the rollaway creaking outside to your uncle's incessant tossing. I would like to tell you it was one of those life-affirming moments, our smothered grunts a defiant, fist-shaking *huzzah huzzah* to the hell hounds on our tail. (If this were a movie, you would have been conceived that night, but it isn't, and so you weren't). The truth is our lovemaking was inspired by very selfish motives. For your mom I think it was the secret thrill of knowing she could arouse my attention, however grim the circumstances (and what a poor prize my attention turned out to be—a minute's worth of furtive poking and the pipes, so to speak, were unplugged).

And what was my excuse?

Chalk it up to the tiresome demands of impropriety: I gave your mom that perfunctory fuck for no other reason than it was absolutely, one hundred percent wrong to do.

WRONG. JUST AS IT felt wrong to be relieved, rather than sad. But I was, undeniably, relieved. *You think you are God's lonely man,* I grew up thinking, *but you have no philosophy. No philosophy at all. Anger needs an aim: invent, create, act. Otherwise you are only scaring sparrows at random.*

In the days following the funeral I found myself wanting one of the other four to acknowledge what I knew—that they felt the same. No, not happy—*certainly not!*—but relieved, drained of tension and emptied, like your intestines after a hearty, heave-ho shit. But no one ever did. And no one ever will. To this day, nobody talks of it. *The broadside of thirty, forty, and after that fifty.* Nobody.

Well, I take that back. Someone dared speak of it once, sort of, and let me tell you, it was a doozy.

A month later, the phone rang. I was spending most nights at your grandmother's, trying to make sense of insurance actuaries and pension payments, making sure your auntie Sally, who was in seventh grade then, didn't cut swim practice and finished her homework. It was your great-grandmother on the line, your grandfather's mother. She hadn't shown up at the funeral. We weren't certain why, except for an ambiguous claim of illness. ("Of the mental variety," quipped another of your aunts, clever Cassie). But here she was now, wanting to know her son, your grandfather, had committed suicide.

The receiver trembled in my mother's hand. I watched that trembling cascade along her arm and into her body like a wave overtaking its own frothy rush. Then, she suddenly screamed into tears. Sally, who had been doodling on a tablet on the living room floor, leapt up at the noise, but your grandmother was already stepping into the kitchen and pulling the recessed door shut, a thin attempt to save us from the anxiety of seeing her humiliated. Sally and I tried to eavesdrop but all we could hear was "How can you ask me that?" and then a minute later: "If you think about it, there's damn easier ways to kill yourself than with a myocardial infarction."

As the oldest I was the only one later privileged with the story. That night after she went to bed I crept into her room where she lay huddled up and sobbing. Since the funeral she'd taken to letting a different daughter sleep with her each night, but now she was alone. I tried to brush the hair from her forehead but she seemed too fragile like that, so I stopped.

"Why does she think he killed himself?"

She wouldn't speak.

"Tell me."

Still nothing.

"Come on, Mom. Say something. You've got to."

"Does it matter why?" Her voice was thick with mucus so she seemed to speak in a mouthwash gargle. "She thinks it. That's the fucking problem."

Our intimacy ended with that one and only obscenity I ever heard her speak. She told me to get lost. Making sure Sally was bathed and in bed by ten—that was the only help she needed from me. *Go home to your wife. Go home and make a baby.* What she didn't comprehend then is what we hadn't comprehended while acquaintances tracked dirt through the foyer to park themselves consolingly upon our davenport. I wasn't there to make her feel better. She was supposed to do that for me. When she made it clear she wouldn't, that left only one person who could. So after I made sure Sally scrubbed behind her ears, I called lights out, and I borrowed my father's keys. To your great-grandmother's house I drove.

In those days I wasn't accustomed to long hauls. Two hundred plus miles was an eternity. But up I-75, the esophagus of Michigan, past Hartwick Pines, through Grayling and over the Mackinac Bridge to just short of the Sioux Locks I never once got sleepy. I was too busy imagining how the old woman would wither under the weight of my righteous indignation. When I got back home my mother would declare me crazy for rushing up there, half-cocked but without a bullet in the chamber, as she liked to say. *You've got book smarts but those aren't smarts at all.* But to me that trip seemed the most natural thing in the world, for I was rehearsing the big soliloquy.

You know what the big soliloquy is, don't you, A.J.? It's the grandiloquent speech you pass your life preparing to deliver, the life-summing Saint Crispin's Day rant that purges your soul of the impurities others plant there, the one that levels your enemies along with whole city blocks. It's Ahab at the flaming corposants: "Oh! thou spirit of clear fire, whom on these seas I as Persian once did worship, till in the sacramental act so burned by thee, that to this hour I bear the scar; I now know thee, thou clear spirit, and I now know that thy right worship is defiance. . . . I own thy speechless, placeless power!" It's Lear bearing dead Cordelia stage right, blazing furiously at the hope she might exhale one last ghost of life: "Howl, howl, howl, howl! Oh, you are men of stones: Had I your tongues and eyes, I'd use them so that Heaven's Vault would crack! She's gone forever! I know when one is dead; she's dead as earth! Lend me a looking glass; If that her breath will mist or stain the stone, Why, then she lives. . . ."

It's me, Colin St. Claire—*c'est moi*—at any given moment of my life.

You see, when push comes to shove, your grand soliloquy comes off more like a blast of hot air out of an anxious monkey's arse. Unless you're Gregory Peck in *To Kill a Mockingbird*, you can't pull it off. It's too theatrical, too scripted. When the actual moment arrives your words become a dog bone in your dog throat. You couldn't choke them out if you tried.

THAT'S HOW IT ENDED with me and your great-grandmother. It was two a.m., not exactly the best hour for a come-to-Jesus meeting with a seventy-year old. So I spent hours scalding my tongue at a local slop 'n' spoon, the caffeine screwing my pace even more. Then, come dawn, I got lost trying to find the Lovely Meadows trailer court. (Wait right there: I know what you're thinking. The trailer explains everything, right? But you're wrong. A lot of old people your great-grandmother's age rent out their residences and move into mobile homes, where there's less maintenance to fret over).

When I finally find her place she won't answer the door. I'm ringing the little tin-sounding doorbell and calling her name into the peep hole, all for *nada*. When I try the doorknob it turns freely in my hand. I take a step into her entryway, which smells like it's been misted in burnt rice. I hear someone: "Who is it? Arnie, is that you?" I couldn't tell you who Arnie is or was.

"It's me, Grandma. Colin."

"Colin? My boy Colin?"

I peek into her bedroom. She's sitting on the edge of her sheets in a full-length nightgown. The morning light is strong enough to burn limpid gold through her window shades, and dust particles swirl through the air, tumbling into each other, spinning and falling. And then I catch sight of her face. There's a gauze bandage taped across her left eye. Come to find out she had cataract surgery the previous day. Come to find out I haven't yet inherited my father's balls. I hadn't quite figured out the lesson of what his example was there to teach me: that real indignation requires you cut out the cancer of empathy, to snip the umbilical cords of fellow-feeling. All frumped up, hair died so black it's stained her skull, your great-grandmother looks so vulnerable—a parched chicken—that she brings out all the old needs and sentimentalities in me. I fall to her feet, burst into tears, drop my head in her lap, and weep into her kneecaps, all the while repulsed by my own weakness. In the end I'm emptied of emotion but not of duty, so while she dresses I play the selfless grandson *because that's what's normal and therefore what's expected* and bust eggs in a skillet. As punishment for my softness I let the white grease spatter my forearms. Then we spend a day together like we've never done before. Later that afternoon she gives me a box of my father's old Boy Scout handbooks. The inner cover of one reads *Never rest never lax never rot* in the skittish curls of a cursive scrawl. His name, his age (13), the date. And I think *only four years until me.*

Before I leave for home I run her to the dentist where she gets fitted for a new top plate of dentures. Her current ones cracked, she tells me, when she bit into a chunk of peanut brittle. The day is both banal and bizarre. I get lost in the gyres of her gossip, only to wonder if she even remembers asking what she asked, much less if she knows why. ("There's damn easier ways than with a myocardial infarction," my mother said). Somewhere south of Grayling I do what my family subsequently tells me they've done.

I forgive your great-grandmother for not acting normal.

SO WHEN THE DETECTIVES decide that my mowing the lawn that morning violated the laws of propriety my first thought was: *What goes around should come back around.* The joke of it all is that when I first pulled on my ratty sneakers and headed to the garage to gas up the Craftsman, I believed what I did was wholeheartedly rational. It seemed saner than sitting around, eating the mounds of food once more delivered in a never-ending stream by the neighbors (only they were different neighbors this time; *ours*, not your grandparents').

It was Sunday. We skipped church because attending didn't seem right. Your mother slept in. I awoke, turned on the television (but only the news, because anything else would seem odd), and I made coffee. I drank it as I always did: a third non-fat milk, one blue package of Equal. Was it somehow an indulgence to partake of a luxury like artificial sweetener? Should I sip it black? Should I pour my own pot? After all, if cooking our meals was out of the question, why was I capable of coffee? As you see, when you break things down, this business of what's normal gets pretty complicated.

I was on my third cup when I peeked out the window. There was a city police car parked in front of the mailbox. The officer inside was supposed to wait until nine to sit with us so we could have our privacy. Grass poked up along the sidewalks, and I noticed that most of the neighborhood had trimmed theirs the day before, on Saturday. I knew it had to be mowed sometime. I knew the rest of the day would be lost to the tedium of sitting out another round of phone calls, questions and answers. I knew I didn't want a fourth morning cup. I knew I wanted to do something. *Invent, create, act.*

I finished the front yard before they stopped me. Perfect perpendicular lines. When maintaining your yard it is best, you know, to rotate the direction of your mowing. Horizontal swaths first, then diagonal left, vertical, diagonal right. Guaranteed to give you that perfect checkerboard appearance. Like I said, I got the front done before detectives showed up and asked me to accompany them downtown. Since they were city cops, I know for a fact they said "downtown."

"What do you think you were doing?"

"I needed to get it done. I just needed something to do, to keep me from thinking."

"From thinking about what?"

"What do you think? All *this*."

"Is there something bothering you we should know about? If there is, maybe you'd feel better if you get it off your chest."

"Look, all I was doing was trying to retain some semblance of normalcy. Just for a while."

The detective reclined in his chair, his hands on his belt buckle, victorious, nodding his head, all-knowing. (Does this sound familiar?)

"I have to tell you, Mr. St. Claire. It doesn't look right. It doesn't feel right."

"Give me a lie detector test, and I'll show you."

"You want a lie detector test?" He seemed excited. "Do you have a lie we need to detect? You should think about it. Ninety percent of people who take lie detector tests fail them."

This is a lie, but it's perfectly legal for the police in this situation to lie to you. So you see what I was up against. When you're dealing with people who've decided you're not right, there's no proving them wrong.

"WELL, MR. ST. CLAIRE, here's the deal." So says the sheriff after giving me a night's hospitality in a holding cell. "We're letting you go."

"I guess I should thank you for that."

"Don't get smart with me or I'll find a reason to keep you another twenty-four hours. Now I have two choices. I can ask you to get out of Dodge, but with my luck you'd turn out to be a grade-A perp and I'd end up toting fertilizer for a living. Or I can tell you to stick around and hope to God you can keep out of trouble."

"I'll keep out of trouble."

"Around here, mister, trouble is sacking out on strangers' property. You know what McCrea's Hill's for? Every Easter morning the Mt. Gilead Baptist Church walks topside for the sunrise service. That's my home church. Fifty-five sunrise services and counting. I can remember a good forty-six or forty-seven of them, and I look forward to a whole bunch more. So next time you get drowsy, you get yourself a motel."

So I smile, gather my belongings, claim my truck. But I don't get a motel. For starters, I can't part with the cash right now. But more importantly, A.J., I don't want clean sheets and a shower.

I gave up on normal a long time ago.

kodachrome and calico

Heim was in his third hour of waiting at the Cow Palace Diner on Highway 9 just north of downtown Shelbyville. The Cow Palace was a greasy spoon and the melts and gravies and fried meat crusts clogging the menu wouldn't be good for his triathlon training, when and if he got back to it, so he wasn't eating. His server patiently refilled the unsweetened tea he sipped, and from time to time she brought a coffee or a dessert he ordered knowing full well he would slide it to the far corner of his table to cool and harden, untouched. As long as he kept ordering Heim figured the diner couldn't claim it was losing money on his loitering, even if management didn't seem particularly concerned about folks lounging. Most of the elderly clientele seemed to be doing exactly what Heim was—sitting, staring through the translucent letters stenciled on the street-front window, anticipating what the slow-rolling traffic outside would bring by. Only their stone faces suggested they had more practice riding out their wait.

To kill time he went through the local papers, circling names and underlining details. If the timeline of Birmage boy's disappearance was correct, Chance had descended onto the creek bank at the same time Heim had been enjoying his last run along Salzburg Road. He pondered if that was synchronicity or just a coincidence. There was always a lot to ponder, he decided, when you were expecting something to happen at any second.

As it turned out, Heim's something wouldn't happen until after the lunch rush as the kitchen crew broke down the salad bar.

"You lose more weight you're going to be the Invisible Man," he told St. Claire.

"You about got me arrested bringing me here."

"From the look of things, you could have used the jail time. To rest."

St. Claire slid into the booth and ordered a banana split, a Cow Palace specialty. Heim hardly recognized him. Forty pounds thinner, he looked like a stick figure. His hair was bushy long and his eyes were set deep in his head, like two boot prints stomped deep in snow.

"They only let me go because they couldn't charge me with anything, not even vagrancy. Twenty-four hours with nothing to do but think a single thought: *Dickie's not here.*"

"He could've been. If you'd have waited for me in Mt. Pleasant like I told you to, you might appreciate why that point is important. . . . I got our friend from Howard Johnson's home to her parents. They send their thanks."

"I don't care."

"If that were true, you wouldn't have called me. You know what it all boiled down to? Trigonometry. The kid failed an exam and was afraid she'd have to go to summer school. She said she'd had to go last year and her old man flipped his lid because it ruined the family vacation. She was afraid of how he would react this time around, so she just took the car and ran. That seems to be a common response these days: get in the car and go. It helps to have somewhere to go to, though, wouldn't you say?"

"It beats sitting at home doing nothing except not caring."

"Home is where we both belong. Kimm would tell you that if you would talk to her. My wife would appreciate you knowing it, too."

"You're the one who brought me to Indiana on a wild goose chase."

Heim shrugged. "You might've ended up here without me. Surely you've been outside of Michigan these past ninth months. We're not the only state where kids go missing, after all. And even if we were, you didn't think Dickie would keep between the Great Lakes just to make it easier for you to find him, do you? I know you haven't been thinking that way, Colin. Because if you were, it'd mean you haven't been doing anything but driving in circles this year."

They sat in silence until the banana split came. St. Claire stuck a spoonful of ice cream in his mouth and then let the spoon hang from between his lips. Heim was staring at him.

"You've made great theater out of all this, but you've got to be tired. How long since you ate a meal cooked by somebody you knew on a first-name basis? When's the last time you slept on a mattress?"

St. Claire pushed the banana split aside and laid his forehead on the rim of his water glass. His nose dangled an inch or two above the table. "Care to bet on this Birmage business? I can name the tune in three notes."

"So what are you on nowadays? Tell me you haven't graduated to meth."

"No, I keep clear of redneck cocaine. I dare to be drug-free."

"You're on the down cycle, I can tell. Saw it all the time in the service. Up for three days, down for one. But you better get yourself together. The bohemia stuff doesn't play well out here in the cornfields."

"It's not a stranger abduction; I'm the first stranger to come around here. Besides, the parents are separated. One of the deputies told me that. At first they thought it was the mother, but they were able to clear her. The dad's a different story. I put my money on him. He won't take the polygraph."

St. Claire raised his chin. The rim of the glass had formed the red outline of a Cyclops eye in the middle of his forehead.

"This is the fourth straight time now that either a dad or stepdad has refused the polygraph. It's starting to feel like an insult, like the joke is on me. I'm to the point where I'm ready to presume all dads guilty just to be done with it. If I could go back, I'd confess just to save myself from ending up going through this over and over and over. Unfortunately, I passed my test. That's another joke on me, I suppose."

"How about you try to say a sentence without 'me' in it? Contrary to what you think, you're not the only one this past year who has come close to wiping out. You're just the one who's made the biggest spectacle of it."

"I have a new theory: *Always lay your marker on the dad.* You know why? It's the dirty biological truth of genealogy. Ask any scientist who's ever scaled a double helix of DNA, and he'll tell you: a father is only a presumptive parent. It's the mother that seeds the genes."

"You're not the tragic hero you think you are. All you're doing is throwing a hissy fit. You remind me of the guy who wakes up one morning and finds his house has been egged or his trees toilet-papered. He's so indignant he decides to sleep on the porch, hoping the perpetrators will come back so he can catch them. I used to feel sorry for you, but now I don't. And I won't until—"

The ends of St. Claire's lips curled into a smile as Heim stopped himself. "Go ahead and finish that sentence. It's okay. I want to hear you say it. Say, 'Get over it, Colin.' Say, 'Move on.' Say, 'Let it go.' Why should you be any different?"

They stared at each other until Heim reached into his pocket and threw a refrigerator magnet between St. Claire's elbows. TIPPECANOE WELCOMES YOU! it read.

"You ever been? I don't recommend it. People go thinking that's where the Battle of Tippecanoe took place, but it's not. Same county, but to see where Harrison routed Tecumseh you have to head down to Lafayette. Tippecanoe itself doesn't have much to brag about except for its post office. The postmaster there remembers all of her customers, especially the stamp collectors." He threw the Halloween card envelope with the AMBER ALERT stamp on the table next to the magnet. "Dickie bought a sheet of these stamps last May. The postmaster remembered him to a T: *Big fat boy*, she described him. *Big fat boy with a little skinny boy at his side.* Look at the cancellation date and you might think Dickie was back in Tippecanoe last week. Not so. Only the little skinny boy was."

St. Claire's back stiffened. "How little of a little boy?"

"Not little enough, I'm afraid. This one's eighteen, a kid named J.P., from Cass City of all places. He spent the summer with Dickie until he got smart and ran. Stole a satchel of his stuff, too, including this card, pre-addressed and stamped by Memorial Day. Dickie's got such a sense of humor he apparently plans his jokes six months in advance—"

"Where is he?"

"I'm getting there. Yesterday the postmaster informed me that the skinny boy has been running around Tippecanoe with a white-haired girl with a dented face. They were the ones who mailed this card. They thought they'd have a laugh on Dickie mailing the unsent letters they stole from him. Now Tippecanoe's not so big of a town that there's not more than one white-haired girl with a dented face to find. Needless to say, J.P.'s been taking it out on her for what Dickie did to him all the way from Cass City. The police have pulled him in twice over it, but she won't press charges."

"I don't care about any of this. I want to know where he is."

"You'd care if you saw that dented face, the same way you cared enough to save the Mt. Pleasant girl. There's still something in you making you care. There's still something in me—that's why I'm here. Hopefully, J.P. will understand that by the time his wrists are out of the casts. Even if he does go back to denting faces, it won't be that girl's. I made sure she was safe. You see how busy my yesterday was."

Heim didn't bother to watch St. Claire's face pale. He didn't want to see it because it would confirm everything he thought: Colin had no clue what world he was trying to run in.

"The last thing J.P. told me before his wrists needed casts is that Dickie's in Missouri. The Mark Twain National Forest to be exact. It makes sense; I have another card Dickie mailed from Mine La Monte, which is right by there. He and J.P. camped at Mark Twain this summer with the Rainbow Family. You ever heard of them? They're these hippie deadhead types who throw huge tribal gatherings every year, like some bizarre Shriners convention. You wear tie-dye instead of a fez, and there's complimentary Ecstasy instead of *hors d'oeuvres*, but the community is structured and internally policed. The tribe even has its own security staff called the Shanti Sena."

"Last summer was last summer. He could be anywhere by now."

"He could, but he's not. It only took me two telephone calls to check out J.P.'s story. The Missouri state police put me in touch with a lieutenant in the Shanti Sena, a guy named Ray. Most of the Rainbow crowd left at the end of August, but the hardcore ones camp together year round. They're none too happy that our friend is still hanging with them. Ray is willing to meet us Tuesday and take us to him."

Heim could see the suspicion bring a milk cloud to St. Claire's yellowy complexion.

"You can go with me or you can tool around another year on your own, Colin. But *this is it*. If this whole Ramblin' Jack thing of yours has been genuine, if you've really been doing this for A.J.—then now's your chance. Dickie-Bird won't give you another one. I won't either."

The waitress arrived, nurse-like, on her rounds. She asked if something was wrong with the banana split. St. Claire said no; he'd decided he wasn't hungry. The waitress said she still had to charge him for it, and she ripped the check off her bill tablet.

"I'm at the Best Western." Heim slapped a keycard on the tabletop. "Up the road, room two-forty-six. We get a decent night's sleep and tomorrow afternoon we're on our way. We can know something definite by dusk."

St. Claire stared out the window. Heim took a money clip from his pocket and dropped bills next to the morning's untouched coffees and desserts.

"Your banana split is only two seventy-five, but I'm going to let you pay it yourself. It's time you understood what you cost the ones you leave behind."

THAT NIGHT IN SHELBYVILLE the Bears of Blue River festival began. It was a modest, Main-Street-long procession of snow-cone vendors and arts-and-crafts tents broken up by the occasional 4-H pen where toddlers fawned over a newborn calf testing its shaky legs. Up a side street a small Tilt-a-Whirl had been erected, but pinned in by the fading brick of the surrounding storefronts, it seemed laughably constrained, unable to extend its tentacles and give riders their money's worth. At one end of Harrison Street was a hip-high stage bathed in blue and pink gel lights. Onstage, a woman wore a lavender suit with spangles that shot their reflection back into the air, making the night surrounding her glisten like a planetarium ceiling. *I'm the pride of the double-wide*, she chirped, her perky yodel goading the drummer's beat to a gallop. *Do me right or I'll tan your hide. . . .*

At a picnic table a few yards from the stage's imposing black stack of speakers St. Claire absentmindedly tapped a foot to the thud of the bass drum. He was focused on the wet finger he rolled over an oily paper plate, cinnamon and sugar crumbs from the elephant ear he'd just eaten gathering on his skin. As he rubbed the sweetness into his gums, using his finger like a toothbrush, he wondered if any of the locals took offense at the singer's constant references to mobile homes and pickup trucks and county fairs. It was hard to say; they seemed as cowed as he was by the belligerent way she dug her spurs into the lyrics. It was more like parody, a world away from "Old Dan Tucker," "The Young Man Who Wouldn't Hoe His Corn," "Keemo-Kino," and other songs that he assumed were the true folk heritage of these parts. He wondered what locals knew of that heritage, if tonight were simply a diversion or if the festival was really their way of keeping connected to a time that grew more remote with each passing season.

The festival was attended mainly by families, fifty-year-old fathers with bellies thick but tight from a lifetime of ham and bacon, mothers stout but still self-conscious enough about their appearance to tidy themselves with make-up. St. Claire wanted to believe he was in the one place in the world where people still lived to the inherent syncopation of their labor, to the rhythm that once effortlessly gave form to folksongs and stories. But he knew this generation of farmers had grown up distanced from any real tactile contact with the medium of their work, cultivating the land from within enclosed tractor cabs outfitted with tape decks and air conditioning. It was healthier to be protected from the grain dust spit up in the harvesting, and, besides, who was St. Claire to judge? Until last year, he was no different, plying his trade on a computer because typefaces were quicker and cheaper to reproduce digitally than by stenciling and inking.

That was why this sort of gussied-up country music was bad. For all the talk of heartache and endurance, there was no real emotion or investment, nothing of the soil or the art of endeavor, just twang and technique. Aural wallpaper. No wonder nobody seemed to be paying attention.

He took advantage of the polite but indifferent applause that greeted the song's end to step away from the picnic table. He slipped past a series of sawhorses into a group dawdling around a folding table stacked with complimentary cups and lid grips, all bearing the indecipherable slogan of some local business. It felt good to stand in the heart of anonymity again. Eating the elephant ear, he'd felt exposed, an easy target for Heim or the sheriff who'd held him for a whole day. He was sure at least one of them was just a few paces back, tracking his every move. It was much safer to stay in the crowd, brushing along the backs of people to whom he was a nothing but a spill of wind, a ghost of a phantom.

He had looped around one side of Harrison Street, passing another series of unassuming booths piled with caps and T-shirts and brochures, when he was stopped by a wide broadcloth faintly rippling in the breeze. It was a quilt, he realized, decorated with photos of smiling faces. What struck him was their casualness— these weren't school photos or staged Olan Mills family poses, but random, candid shots. Only when St. Claire leaned forward, curious why these particular images and not more polished ones, did he notice the second odd thing: other than the small group manning the canopy, he was by himself. No one else was stopping.

"Maybe if we had freebies to give away," somebody was saying.

St. Claire squatted to study the pattern holding the squares together. Each photograph rested on a white strip of cloth, separated from the one beside it by checkered blocks of calico, chintz, gingham, and other fabrics. A different decorative stitching framed the pictures—thin curlicues of gloss blue, little waves of gold, red hearts and ivory crosses. Below the faces were names and dates, some sewn in straight hand, some cursive:

David Roger Chilton, 1963-1982

Steven Scott Rossnagle, 1986-2002

And a pig-tailed black girl:

Lateesha Lawanda Morris, 1990-1994

It took him a moment to calculate that the oldest face here was at most twenty-two or three. Eavesdropping on the low, solemn chatter around him, he figured out as well why these particular pictures. They were the last ones taken of a child before he or she was murdered. He knew this because a red-haired woman sipping a Coca-Cola was telling a fellow booth-worker the story of her daughter's photo: "Missy didn't like her hair this way, and she was fighting me tooth and nail over taking it, but I told her I didn't drive all the way to Vincennes to come home empty handed. I was so proud she was at college because she was the first in the family to go, too, and I said I don't care whether you like it or not I'm putting a picture of you in every Christmas card I send out."

The daughter wasn't hard to pick out—she had her mother's coloring. The more he examined the image the more St. Claire sympathized with her unwillingness to pose. Her hair indeed looked as though it had been recently cut. The ends were jagged and jutted awkwardly at her shoulders. She was sporting thick black rims that fell low on her nose.

Melissa June Tidewater, 1953-1974

Never Forgotten

The woman, this girl (she hadn't really lived long enough to become a woman) had been dead thirty-three years. Melissa Tidewater was a year older than St. Claire's own mother. He tried to gibe the girl's image with what his mom had looked like at fifty-two. Missy would be gray now, the Buddy Holly spectacles replaced by a sleeker, more contemporary style.

Meanwhile, the photo itself had aged even though the person in it remained the same: it had that unreal, early seventies' Kodachrome tint, the kind where the hues are so supercharged and irradiated that they border on gaudy. Missy's auburn hair was nearly orange, her skin sallow—even the wood paneling in the background glowed olive. He thought how hard it must be for this to be the last vision of a child one could have; he couldn't even name A.J.'s last picture. He didn't want to name it. He knew if he did he'd next wonder at what point this girl's parents not only accepted that she was gone but that the things memorializing her—the relics of remembrance—had turned antique, too.

"Excuse me, sir, but you're really not supposed to touch the quilt."

St. Claire was startled to find his palm was pressed against the fabric. He hadn't registered the sensation. Embarrassed, he stood and apologized. The woman who'd spoken to him was middle-aged pretty and motherly with a bolt of gray in her corner part.

"I didn't mean to. The whole thing is very beautiful."

"Thank you. It turned out a lot better than we expected, considering that not one of us had touched a needle before."

"You have a child on the quilt then."

"Yes. My daughter." Her voice went rigid with solemnity as she gestured toward a square in the bottom right corner. "You may have to stoop back down to see it. Her face turned out pretty dark when they printed the fabric."

The girl was frizzy-haired, plump but confident in a taut blouse and mini-skirt. St. Claire didn't see much resemblance to the mother; he was thinking of his middle sister, Devlin. She looked just like this at eighteen.

"My husband told me since I laid out the order of the pictures I should have put hers in the middle, somewhere where you could see it. But that seemed sort of selfish. And since the last photo I had of her wasn't all that good, I just thought I'd stick her in the corner, out of the spotlight."

Patty Lee Pruitt 1971-1989

"She's my age," St. Claire said.

"Well, I hope you take it as a compliment if I say you don't look thirty-five."

"That's because I'm only thirty-four. My birthday's coming up."

"Then you're younger than Patty. She had a May birthday. No wonder you still look like a boy."

"My mom says I never grew up."

He knew he looked more like a mess than a boy. Still, the woman was polite enough to laugh. "That's what moms are in the business of saying, I suppose. We were going to do a little presentation, but you see how few flies we're drawing. You're the longest conversation I've had with anyone here tonight. Folks tried to tell me that this wasn't the right place to show off our work. We can't compete with cotton candy and loud music."

"It's not you. There's a boy missing. Everywhere I go I see his face. I'm guessing it's scaring people away—"

"I know all about Chance. I've spent the last two days with his family—his grandmother, that is. This afternoon she asked me point-blank if I thought his picture would end up on our quilt. That was how she put it: 'end up.' I wanted to tell her none of our children just 'ended up' here, but I couldn't, of course. That would've been too selfish. There was really only one thing I could say: 'He won't end up on a quilt because he's okay. They'll find him soon.' It's what she wanted to hear. Nobody wants to hear what we're trying to say with the quilt."

St. Claire looked to the ground. There were things he wanted to hear, too, and because of them he decided he wouldn't tell the woman about A.J. He thought of what Heim had said that morning, about how selfishly he'd behaved this past year. It'd been so long since anybody had told him what he wanted to hear—that A.J. could still be alive—but it didn't seem fair to demand that reassurance when he'd given barely thirty seconds' attention to the last picture of Patty Lee Pruitt.

"I'll be your fly."

"Excuse me?"

"You've drawn me tonight. Do your presentation and let me be your audience. If you knew anything about me, you'd know I'm all the crowd you need."

It came off as more boastful than he meant it. The woman twisted her head, a bit thrown, but still she asked her tent-mates if they were willing, and they were. St. Claire expected them to gather around him to talk informally, but instead the woman directed her friends to pull a folding table up next to the quilt and to line up behind it. He inadvertently took a few steps back when she set a small amplifier onto the table and began adjusting the volume.

"Can you hear me over the music?" The country music had begun again, browbeating its way into their space. "I can talk as loud as I need to. . . ." She looked straight at St. Claire. "Anyway, my name is Beverly Pruitt. I'll tell you about myself later. For now, let me just say that those of us standing up here are members of a special group. In my life I suppose that like a lot of you I could be accused of joining too many groups. I've been a member of the PTA and the church choir and way back in high school I even paid dues to be part of something called the Future Housewives of America. But this group we're part of is one you don't choose to belong to. You're made a member of it when someone takes your child away from you."

Her eyes left him. St. Claire looked over his shoulder to see he was no longer alone. A man with a toddler had stopped to listen.

"Welcome," Mrs. Pruitt greeted them. "We're not here to scare, I promise. We only have stories we want to tell."

St. Claire felt a flush of jealousy. The toddler was straining forward, but the man held him back.

"No matter how much I practice for a night like this, I can't ever keep myself on track, so you'll all have to bear with me. What we want you to know is that there are a lot of people who aren't with us tonight. They're not ready to be here, they haven't come to that point where they're not afraid to talk about what they're feeling for worrying it will upset other people. This is what you do when your husband or wife can't talk to you any more because your house is haunted by memories—*No, wait, please, don't go. . . .*"

The man ignored Mrs. Pruitt, pulling the toddler away, the boy's head twisting over his shoulder. St. Claire realized the child was staring at him, and he felt conspicuous again. Tomorrow he would get a haircut and shave, he decided. It was better to blend in.

"Well," Mrs. Pruitt said to St. Claire, "you see what happens." She had to raise her voice to compete with a surge in the music; the amplifier hardened her words until they clanged like anvil strokes. "All of us here went through these things and that's why we came together—because we know we'll always want to talk about the children we've lost. Our group is called Parents of Murdered Children. Each of us has a story to tell, and that's what we're doing with this quilt. Not every parent whose son or daughter you're looking at could be here tonight, but there are five or six of us, and if we can indulge your patience for just a bit longer, we'd like to take this chance to share our stories. Smitty, you start. . . ."

She handed the microphone to a short cantaloupe of a man who looked at it as if it were a strange medical instrument. "Do I really need this?"

Mrs. Pruitt didn't hesitate: "If you want to be heard, yes."

Uncomfortable, the man wiped his bald head and introduced himself. He was from Noblesville, he said. Then he tapped at a top corner of the quilt. "This is my wife and my daughter. About a week after my mother-in-law took this picture, I came home and found Donna in the living room. I tried to save her but she'd been stabbed too many times. It took a longer to find the baby—"

"Tell them *how* you found your wife," Mrs. Pruitt interrupted. "Tell them how you counted the stab wounds in her chest. You thought your girl had been taken until one of the policemen went to the freezer for ice, and there she was, curled up like she was sleeping."

The man flinched. "Sis," somebody said sternly, but St. Claire was hung up on a different word: who was *them*? He looked over his shoulder again. The crowd flowed steadily past, still chewing corndogs and licking at cones, but now instead of simply ignoring the quilt, several of them gaped. St. Claire didn't the doubt the oddity—a lineup addressing a lone man as if speaking to a crowded auditorium. It didn't do much to settle the strangeness that the lineup and the man were both staring right back at passersby.

"They need to hear this. We deserve to be heard. If Smitty doesn't want to talk, let Lana. Lana, you tell your story."

The red-haired woman who was Missy Tidewater's mother reluctantly took the mic to describe her daughter's murder. She didn't go into much detail: Missy fell in with the wrong boy, the boy owed his dealer money, the dealer decided to teach the kid a lesson, Missy got caught in the crossfire. The story sounded like something from a soap opera; there was more too it, St. Claire knew. There had to be. *Slow down*, he wanted to tell her. *I want*

to know it all, everything. If you knew me you'd know why I'm here—
I am here to listen. . . .

But he didn't open his mouth because he could see how upset the other parents were with Mrs. Pruitt. The more staccato Missy's mom's sentences became, the more the others tamped their stares into the ground as deep as the poles supporting the canopy. Mrs. Pruitt shook her head, her front teeth sunk deep in her lip. The longer she stared at the passing crowd the tighter her eyes became.

Missy's mom finally faltered. "I'm sorry, Sis, but this . . . this just seems . . . *silly.* . . ."

Mrs. Pruitt reached past two other parents to take the microphone. "We're not being silly. We're being ourselves. This is who we are. I'm tired of people assuming we should be over it. Sometimes I get angry with myself, sometimes I think my pain is my pride, but it's not. We speak with an authority of experience that says, 'I have been through this and I want you to hear it.' It's not often we have an audience that's not a captive one. I plan on talking until this man here walks off. And I'll probably keep on talking after he does."

"I'm not walking off," St. Claire mumbled, but he wasn't sure Mrs. Pruitt heard him. She stepped out from behind the table, nearly tugging the amplifier over as the mic cord went taut.

"This is Patty," she said, tapping at the corner picture. "She wasn't outgoing, but she was smart. She had graduated high school and was planning on going to Franklin College. They'd offered her a scholarship. My husband and I were grateful because being farmers we weren't sure how much school we could afford. Neither of us went to college; you didn't have to in our day. I knew when she didn't come home that night the worst that could happen had happened. *I knew*, but we had to find her. That took two days—"

Without warning she held out her hand.

"I promise we will not hurt you—we're only talking. . . ."

Startled, a heavy-set woman who'd stopped hustled away. Mrs. Pruitt shook her head, bitterly.

"It took two days to find her but two months to find out what happened. The sheriff tracked down a day laborer who'd been watching her and her girlfriends dance at the ice-cream parlor that night. They tracked him all the way to Seymour and when they caught him he admitted to what he did. The confession took all of three minutes, less time than it took to murder her. She was on her way home and he cut her off on Greensburg Road right before Smiley's Mill. That's not but two miles from our farm. He took her into a cornfield across from the creek. He took her and then he took her life—that's exactly how he described it. Because he confessed there was no trial. My husband and I wanted one because we wanted some explanation. We wanted to know why our daughter, why Patty. Everybody kept telling us there wasn't any 'why'—this man, they said, was just evil through and through. 'Just' evil. I thought that was too easy. Evil comes from somewhere; it's created by something. Well, for four years after that this man was in prison. His name was Henley Miles. I wrote him letters asking why. He didn't answer. I wrote letters saying I looked forward to seeing him put to death because he was denying me that explanation. I wanted to see him beg for his life. I told him he could at least lie, but even that was too much for him to give. One morning he hung himself from the end of his bedpost—no note, no reason, no nothing. Ever since then I've wished Henley Miles was alive as much as I've wished my daughter was alive. They say that seeing your child's killer put to death is supposed to let you move on, but it doesn't happen that way. . . ."

She stopped again when yet another passerby paused to see what the commotion was about. Mrs. Pruitt started to call out to him, but when their gazes locked, he, too, departed. It left Mrs. Pruitt looking like she was struggling for breath. St. Claire wanted to cheer her on. He wanted to tell her it didn't matter if nobody else understood; he did. He wanted to comfort her by assuring her he appreciated her anger, appreciated how she used it in a way that he didn't seem able. *Anger with an aim.* She wasn't just scaring random sparrows. She hadn't forgotten or let go of her pain. She was doing something with it.

"When your child's killer dies it's just the start of a new chapter, one in a book that can't end, ever. When we started this quilt, it wasn't because we thought it would bring closure. We weren't that naive. We did it because we needed a new way to tell our story, both to ourselves and to you. And once we feel like we can't get any more from this quilt, we'll have to find a new way of saying it, because it's all we have to say. Don't be surprised if you hear from us again."

One of the men in the lineup gently took the mic from her and switched off the amplifier. The rest of the parents swallowed her in a circle, then walked her to a folding chair at the far edge of the canopy. St. Claire thought Mrs. Pruitt had broken down in tears, but she hadn't. She merely sat, arms folded, sullenly enduring Missy Tidewater's mom patting her back as if a few taps of consolation were a mystic cure.

"It's the boy," the man called Smitty stepped up to explain to St. Claire. "It's hit her hard, so close to home and all. . . ."

St. Claire looked one final time to the crowd. He understood now why he didn't belong: there was no home to be had, at least not one where somebody didn't try to sit you down to quiet you. Before Smitty could say more, St. Claire slipped to the sidewall where he could disappear hopping the alley of stakes and shock cords supporting the tents and booths. On his way out St. Claire brushed beside the quilt, close enough for a quick clasp of its dangling edge. He smiled to himself, careful not to let the pleasure show.

This time he felt the calico on his palm.

Striving after wind

An old woman stepped into a kitchen, startled to discover herself someplace other than where she expected to be. "Oh dear," she said, blinking at the unfamiliar territory. "Now remind me where I am."

"You're at Sis's, Grandma."

Sis stood at the sink balancing a mixing bowl across her belly as she beat the powdered lumps from a bag of instant brownie batter. "You should sit down and talk to me. You're walking around like a lost lamb."

Sis was embarrassed to realize she'd raised her voice, even though Ethel—her grandmother's Christian name—heard better than any one hundred and six-year-old had a right to. By way of apology, she set down the bowl to help Ethel take a seat, but the old woman had already begun a tortoise crawl to the table. The running joke in the family was that Grandma Brandywine, stooped and slight, was older than her weight. Chance Birmage, Sis realized, managed barely a twentieth of her century before he disappeared.

"I don't believe I'm lost," the old woman decided as she wrestled a chair bulkier than her own body back from the table.

"Tell me if you need a hand. That's why I'm here."

"Now I don't remember this furniture being so heavy."

Ethel began almost every sentence with *now*, as though she were trying to pinpoint just what moment of time that word referred to. Sis had a hard time believing this was the same woman who'd once embodied her childhood dread, whose displeasure she feared incurring more than all the paddle-wielding schoolteachers and Bible study leaders she'd suffered through. Martha was too young to remember, but back when Sis was a girl their grandmother would erupt at the slightest provocation, take offense at the thinnest hint of disrespect. Sis didn't hold a grudge; she looked back on the weekends her parents sent her to stay at Ethel's farmhouse as more odd than damaging. She could laugh about the time Ethel made her stand forty-five minutes in a closet for forgetting to turn off a hall light, or the winter day she got knocked upside the head by a shoe flung from across the room as she reached for a Christmas figurine on the mantle.

"That's because it's not your furniture. It's mine and Pete's. Yours is out in the barn. There are only two things of yours here, your Victor-Victrola and your rolltop desk. You gave me those both years ago, after Horace went. Do you know where you are now?"

The old woman looked baffled.

"You're at Sis's house. I'm going to tell you that until it sticks. You're not at your place, so if you're expecting Horace to waltz in—well, he's not going to, not today and most likely not tomorrow either."

"Horace?"

Ethel repeated the name to herself. Sis felt bad for mentioning Horace at all, realizing she was unnecessarily testing the old woman. There were questions she had wanted Ethel to answer since she was old enough to understand that her grandmother lived unmarried with a man in an age when that was frowned upon, questions that at this point weren't likely to be answered. It wasn't that Sis never asked; she often prodded the old woman about the family history on days like this when it was her

breathing out the ghost

turn to watch Ethel. What Sis regretted was having not asked sooner, before the dementia softened up the old woman.

"I know you know Horace. Don't be coy now. You were a lot of things but you were never coy. You were ahead of your time. If you'd taken up with Horace fifty years later it wouldn't have been a big deal. Mom and Dad wouldn't have had to go all the way to Greenville to find a minister willing to marry them, and I wouldn't have had boys canceling dates on me. It's a good thing Pete didn't listen to what the preachers said about our family or I'd still be rooming with Mom and Dad. Even worse, I'd be rooming with Martha."

"Oh, yes. Martha. I remember Martha. Beverly and Martha. Those are Clinton's girls."

"That's right. Do you remember Mercer?"

"Mercer? Well, now, Mercer. If I'm not mistaken he was. . . ."

"Mercer was your husband. You lost him to tetanus when he stepped on a nail. First there was Mercer and then there was Horace. One to tetanus and one to cancer. One's been gone almost eighty years and the other forty. Do you remember now?"

It was clear Ethel didn't. Some days when they had this conversation Sis would name the entire family for her. "There was your father. . . . He had the neatest name of any man I ever heard: Esquire. Esquire Parker. You lost him to a train derailment before you ever met Mercer Brandywine. And before you lost Mercer there was a baby that went from influenza. I can't tell you her name because nobody remembers. She was Dad's own sister but it's been so long even he can't recall. You had three more children after that. My dad was the oldest. The other two are gone now, too, but you still have all of us grandchildren. There are eight of us. I'm Beverly and my sister is Martha. And then there are the great-grandchildren. Twelve of those. I know you can't possibly keep them straight because I'm a whole half-century younger than you and I can't."

In reality, she didn't name the great-grandchildren because she dreaded the thought of having to explain who Patty was. She had to do that with enough people; she shouldn't have to with her own family.

"Now who do we have here?"

As Ethel was about to sit a child crawled from under the dining table to claim the old woman's chair. To celebrate her victory, the girl gave an imperial shake of her uncombed cowlick.

"Get up from there right now." Sis shook her stirrer at Tillie, and a dollop of batter splattered on the carpet.

"You spilled some," Tillie pointed out.

Sis set the stirrer in the bowl and wet a dishtowel. "And that doesn't change a thing. You still better hustle from that seat."

The girl reluctantly planted her feet on the carpet. "You can have your chair back, Grandma. I didn't really want it anyway."

"Well, goodness, you are a handsome girl. Now you must be one of Clinton's."

"You always ask me that. You've asked me that a bunch of times already today." Tillie thrust one of the stuffed toys she was carrying in her great-grandmother's direction. "You should ask Charlie Malarkey that."

"Tillie, be nice," Sis admonished. "Grandma, I'm Clinton's daughter. That's twice today now we've gone over this. Tillie's mine."

The old woman wet her wrinkled lips and looked puzzled. "Clinton's daughters can't be old enough to have their own girls. Seems to me they should be children themselves."

"I passed fifty a long time ago. Just like Dad passed eighty, and Martha passed forty. Before you know I'll be sixty. Wow. I'm old now. Way too old to be chasing an eight-year-old, wouldn't you say, Tillie?" She went back to work, smoothing the batter so it filled the corners of the pan evenly. The oven light glowed orange-red; the thing seemed to take forever these days to preheat. She and Pete would need to replace it soon. Along with the furnace and the wallpaper in the guest bath that was slowly twisting back from the wall. Meanwhile, the mix was refusing to flatten. Sis had to remind herself that no one had begged for brownies; they'd finished breakfast just a short time ago, but kitchen work kept Ethel occupied. After the dough cooked and cooled, Sis would help the old woman hold a butter knife steady so she could slice the pan in a checkerboard pattern.

"I bet Grandma doesn't remember Patty."

"Tillie—"

The girl's eyes inflated to the size of silver dollars. From Sis's response Tillie knew she'd said something wrong, even if she didn't know why it was wrong. Ethel was staring blankly at the wall, oblivious.

"In the mudroom, right now." Sis pushed open the door to the back entryway. In addition to several pairs of boots, all caked with muck and dung, the Pruitts' mudroom housed their hot-water heater and an unused toilet that Pete installed back when he could afford to hire out help. Sis sat the girl on the toilet seat, and closed the door behind them. "Why'd you ask that?"

"I don't know."

"It didn't just pop into your head out of nowhere."

Sis couldn't remember a time when she'd ever heard Tillie say Patty's name—the younger daughter had never been told about her older, lost sibling. The girl swung her feet, a sure sign a confession was coming.

"Grandma Dorothy said it."

"What did she say?"

"She said I had an older sister I'd never get to meet. Because she was dead."

"And she just told you this—out of the blue?"

Tillie hesitated, then confessed. "I saw her picture. In grandma's wallet. I was looking in her purse because I wanted to see if she put me or Joey first. And I found this girl's picture, and on the back it said 'To Grandma, from your Patty.' All I did was to ask who Patty was."

"And I take it all Grandma Dorothy did was to tell you. So who did she put first?"

"Joey. My picture was way in back. She even put Grandpa's before me."

"Then that's your punishment for snooping." Sis thought of all the places along the walls of her house where Patty's picture wasn't. "In the future, if you have questions, you ask me, not your grandma. Got that? Now go get your animals picked up. Your dad will be home before long, and he won't be happy seeing them in a heap."

Tillie started back toward the kitchen, relieved to have gotten off the hook. At the door she stopped. "How's come I never knew I had a sister? Even if I'd never get to meet her?"

Sis let her eyes wander as she sought an answer, one that could satisfy her as well as Tillie. She focused on the shelf behind the child—two rows of canned tomatoes, pickles, carrots, and beets. Like the specimen jars she'd seen in her high-school biology classes: pig hooves and rabbit fetuses preserved in pints of formaldehyde. She'd wondered then how many years they'd sat there, and she wondered now how long her own canning had waited in the mudroom to be opened and eaten. Memories were like these abandoned foodstuffs—you sealed them with paraffin in glass, screwed the lid tight, and placed them in an undusted corner—there for you, waiting, but only when you wanted them.

"Go clean up your toys," she told her daughter.

The child blinked a few times before realizing a better answer wasn't coming. Then she spun around and marched off with an exaggerated soldier strut, leaving Sis alone, bare feet on cold concrete.

AN HOUR LATER SHE climbed the hayloft of the old milking barn. She'd just put Joey down for a nap and stationed Tillie in the playroom with paper and crayons at an antique grade-school desk. There was a rocker in the room for Grandma Brandywine, who could keep an eye on the child while the child kept an eye on her. That gave Sis maybe a half-hour to herself before Pete came home for dinner. As wet as the ground was this fall, he'd only be a few minutes before speeding back to his drowning beans. Still, that meant another meal, more time in the kitchen. She should be defrosting the freezer ham in the microwave, but had decided Pete could survive one more day of the leftover roast. In the mudroom she pulled on the red-hooded jersey she kept for winter work. It smelled sharply—a mixture of cut grass, farrowing pen, and dust. She preferred that odor to the bland cleanliness of detergent, and only laundered the jersey a few times a year. It was the smell of the nearly forty years' labor she and Pete had put into their farm.

The loft was the part of the barn they hadn't refinished when Pete took charge of his family's acreage, way back when he and Sis were newly married. They'd borrowed heavily to upgrade the feed troughs and pasteurizing system for the Guernsey herd his father had kept. In Pete's dad's day, dairy farming could turn a reliable dollar, but it really hadn't been profitable since the early eighties, and Pete had long ago sold off the cows and scrapped the mixers and purifiers. For years the stalls and tank room sat ghostly empty until he turned the lower part of the barn into a farrowing pen. The expense of installing a new waste pit was prohibitive, so he'd built six-inch wooden wedge legs for the cages to sit on. He also rigged a mini-sluice to help channel the waste into a pile that could be easily scooped with the shovel attachment on the riding lawn mower. They had argued over keeping pigs so close to the house. Sis complained that a manure smell would permanently fume the porch, but when Pete said they'd get used to it she had no rebuttal: she couldn't say the odor would put an end to any entertaining they might do because they hadn't entertained in seventeen years. Pete promised it was only a temporary arrangement anyway, even though that was three years ago now. He hadn't even pretended to look for financing to build a shed farther back on their land.

In the fall, the cold concrete-block walls contained the stench, so as Sis climbed the worn two-by-four steps, only irregular eruptions of snorting betrayed the hogs' presence. The loft was thick with October dust and crisscrossed with silvery filaments of cobwebs that draped languidly over the high-hanging beams. Bales sat stacked against the western wall, but the plywood flooring was bare except for the occasional pigeon splatter or molted feather. Like many farm families, the Pruitts used their loft mostly for storage these days, saving the bales for chicken bedding. She made her way to the far wall, past a pile of trunks and cartons and picture frames. She lifted a blue tarp covering a settee and sat for a moment staring at the sky through the square cut high in the walls. Autumn was Sis's favorite season; the crispness of the air simplified things, dropping leaves from overcrowded limbs and leveling the fields to flat clarity.

From outside she could hear the far squabble of chickens, and she was reminded of a story her father used to tell when she was little, before Martha was born. Mrs. Finkbeiner, a widow as joylessly German as the sound of her name, lived near Sis's parents' house, just around the crick in the road that went to Shelbyville. The woman was rumored to hurl cornhusks at kids who rode their bikes into her yard and fire her pellet gun at wandering dogs. Once a neighbor even caught her trespassing in his pasture with an armload of saltlicks that she swore he'd stole off her land. But by far the strangest thing she was known for were the chickens said to roost in her guest rooms. As her dad told it, the older Mrs. Finkbeiner got, the easier it was to rely on chickens to cure her infestation troubles. The thought of mice and chickens scurrying across someone's living quarters inspired hours of bad dreams in Sis, who would wake to the stray sound of a passing car or a mewing yard cat, and she'd imagine a strange claw or paw on her chest. Forty-five years later, she knew her father was joshing her, passing off an urban legend as a country truth so she wouldn't wander past the family range line. And it worked. Her parents' farm had seemed a universe unto itself, and anyone who lived outside its solar system of silos had been certifiably alien—whether they roomed with chickens or not.

As she rested on the settee she wondered what tall tales Tillie would remember from her childhood when, years from now, she climbed her own hayloft—if she didn't end up in the city, in a house with a sloped attic that scraped her shoulders. The girl would recall that strange rumor called Patty; the name would flash through her mind, the face she'd only seen once through a transparent slipcase in her grandmother's wallet.

For a moment Sis held her breath and concentrated on the sounds of her world—the flutter of roosting wings, acorns tumbling on the roof, the asthmatic cough of a distant diesel engine. They were fleeting noises, but they wallpapered her life. Yet she'd allowed Patty to be removed from that pattern, taken away from her—twice. For Tillie, that meant a sister twice removed, a doubled absence, a story never substantiated. In decades to come, Patty would be Tillie's Mrs. Finkbeiner.

SHE DIDN'T STAY LONG in the hayloft. She never did. Time alone never quite lived up to its name, for Sis was no sooner by herself than reminders of obligations unsettled her solitude. She was missing the third day of the search for Chance because Grandma Brandywine needed watching; she decided she would take supper to Mrs. Birmage tonight. That would be her service for the day.

On the way down the ladder she saw a rat scuttle across the barn floor. She threw a desiccated cob at it, but her aim was bad and the rat squeezed through a hole in the empty corncrib. She would have to set out the snap traps now, although she didn't like to because it upset Tillie and Joey to see the broken necks and twisted tails—even though they were growing up on a farm, her children weren't accustomed to violence or death. She and Pete hadn't sheltered Patty from any of that, and look what happened.

On the ground she pulled off her gloves and stuffed them in the pockets of the worksmelling jersey. The frump they added to her abdomen made her wonder how absurd a sight she'd been when she was pregnant with Joey at forty-nine. After Patty's murder it had taken her nearly three years before she could even make love with Pete. Intimacy seemed disrespectful to her daughter's memory; her family's lot was to grieve, not to enjoy. Later she realized she and Pete hadn't touched each other because they were both terrified of having more children. It was only when her age made pregnancy seem unlikely that they'd resumed relations, though it was so painful and short that afterward neither could sleep and would end up losing a day's work because they were up drinking coffee at their drop-leaf table at midnight. They didn't talk about their sorrow, of course; their silence was agreement enough. Sex was selfish. Still, they were husband and wife, and real marriages are supposed to be consummated, so twice or thrice a year they consented to the ritual, usually quickly and wordlessly out of duty to the fulfillment that a lifetime together was supposed to bring them. The joke was that for all the rarity of their togetherness Sis ended up conceiving, not once but twice when she should've been undergoing her change. Just another of God's little jokes on her. By the time Tillie and Joey would be old enough to have children, she wouldn't be much younger than Ethel had been when Ethel became a great-grandmother.

She had slid the barn door shut before she saw the unfamiliar truck parked in the driveway. She wondered how it could have snuck up without her hearing the wheels crunch the gravel. Normally she could be in the house with the dishwasher sloshing and the microwave humming and she could still sense an approaching automobile. She felt an instinctive rush of panic—*the kids*—but the house sat silent and drowsy in its usual faded-white fashion, no doors open or ajar. She stepped toward the truck's rear bumper and noticed near-archeological layers of grit and film covering its curves and fenders. She was almost close enough to peer through the windows of the shell when the driver-side door opened and a pair of corduroy legs spilled to the ground.

"Mrs. Pruitt—"

Whoever he was, he was a mess. He was freshly showered and shaved but his cheeks and chin were dotted with blood splotches, as though he'd cleaned himself with hangover eye. His hair was cut so close to the scalp that the splashes of gray looked like mangy bald streaks, and he seemed about two sizes too small for his clothes—his pants hung low off his hips and his Adam's apple bobbed loose in the white sea of his open collar.

"You don't remember me, do you?"

"I'm afraid I don't."

He looked disappointed. "I shouldn't be surprised, I guess. I tried to clean up. I needed the haircut bad—it'd been a while. We met last night, at the street fair." He stuffed his hands deep in his pockets, leaving an oval island of belly exposed in the space between his T-shirt and the gray elastic waistband of what Sis assumed were boxer shorts. "You told me about your daughter. About Patty, I mean. About the picture in the quilt."

"Oh, yes. I remember now."

It was a lie—polite, but a lie nonetheless. She couldn't remember what the stranger in the tent had looked like. She'd long ago grown to ignore the faces of strangers she told her story to.

"My name is Colin St. Claire." His hand came forward; Sis shook it. It was light, frail, far from masculine. She thought of the evaporating bones of old men's hands, so thin that you feared snapping them if you shook too hard.

"Is there something I can do for you?"

"I know this is weird. You're not accustomed to some stranger coming to your home, but. I don't know how to say this. I've been rehearsing this all morning, and here I'm stuttering all over myself. You have to understand, I've been talking to myself for a long time, and when you do that, nothing has to make sense. You ramble and digress because you hope that the roundabout way will eventually deliver you to your point, the gist of what you're feeling, but then you realize all you've got in you are clichés—"

"I'm not sure I follow you, but you're right about one thing: this is strange. If you really heard me speak last night, you know I've had my share of strange in life already, so unless there's something *specific* I can help you with. . . ."

She mapped out a straight dash to the door if this man didn't leave. She would sidestep the frayed right work boot that tapped the ground only inches from her foot. It wouldn't take but a few strides and she could jump the hedge bordering the porch. Pull the screen door with one hand, push the interior door with the other. The door was steel reinforced—Pete had replaced their old hollow entry a year earlier when a few farmhouses on the north side of the county were broken into. Now a thief could kick to his heart's content and do more damage to his foot than to the house.

St. Claire fumbled with his wallet, trying to unfold its flaps. "This is why I'm here."

Between his fingers, a crinkled photograph, its edges wearing away, as if dissolving. The image was of a child, younger than Chance Birmage, younger than Joey. The boy had the curliest hair she'd ever seen. It rose two inches off his head, a dandelion of brown curlicues and kinks.

"I've been looking for him, almost a year now."

She looked at the child and then at the man. There was no doubting the resemblance: they shared the same marble-shaped eyes, the same olive, almost foreign, skin tone. "I—I haven't seen him."

St. Claire closed his eyes and his face tightened with an awkward laugh. "I'm not going door to door." He took the photograph back and tucked the wallet against his abdomen. "I know you're busy, and I'm sorry. I just thought you'd understand."

He lowered his head and began backing away. The movement gratified her. She wanted only to slip inside her home; she was ready to lose herself in wife-work. She wanted to surprise Pete with a plate piled high with Salisbury steak, potatoes, and thick, lumpy gravy.

But she couldn't.

"I'm sorry. I didn't mean to be rude. I'm just not sure how I can help you."

St. Claire held his palm flat against the driver's side window, staring at his reflection. Sis could see her own face against the muddy translucency. Her head was comically shrunken, a flattened pebble on the plateau of her shoulders. His image was just the opposite, his head elongated until his forehead shot out of his skull like boulder jutting from a cliff face. He withdrew his hand from the glass, seemingly fascinated by the shrinking fingers on the pane.

"Have you ever seen yourself on a mirrored surface when you didn't expect it? It's startling because what's there never quite seems to be you—there's always some distortion, some disfiguration that disappoints your sense of who you are. It's different from when you primp at the bathroom mirror, or when guys at the gym grunt at themselves. Those are controlled environments. You convince yourself of what you want to see. When you're caught off guard like this though, you lose your bearings. You wonder if you've been fooling yourself, giving yourself credit for being special in some way you're really not. . . ."

Sis squeezed her gloves in her fists. She knew what he was asking for; she felt the familiar tug of need drawing her toward his anguish. But the past four days had worn her sympathy down to impatience. What frustrated her wasn't the fact that people like this St. Claire told their stories over and over again. It was the lack of an ending for these stories. There was no resolution. Seventeen years later, her own story had yet to conclude. Sis had tried to keep Patty alive through her activism and she had tried to let her go by not speaking of her at home, yet neither effort brought an end to her grief. She felt condemned to suffer a perpetual flu, the ache that drains the muscles' tautness, the flush of fever on the brow. It was her lot.

Sis steeled herself. "Tell me about your son."

HIS STORY SPILLED OUT like yolk from a cracked egg. He told her about the anxiety that came at the sight of an empty car seat, a feeling less about fear than about being embarrassed by overreacting, by letting melodrama get the better of him. How many times had the boy put him through that sensation? He described the Sunday morning he and his wife awoke after a night at a friend's lake cottage to discover the child missing. They searched the cottage and then ran frenzied to the dock, where St. Claire slipped on the mossy planks and fell on his tailbone. They stood at the water's edge for several minutes, watching the bobbing current for a floating tennis shoe or baseball cap. It wasn't until their hosts suggested searching the backside of the property that they found the boy. He'd walked straight up the cottage's driveway and was standing only a foot or so from the road, playing with the metal mailbox flag. They marveled at the good luck and swore they'd be more cautious in the future. But of course in the rush of life their attention slackened, and soon they were again leaving doors unlocked, letting him roam from their sight.

St. Claire described the length of time it took him in the parking lot to call the police. There was a line there; once crossed, it made the fear more real, more palpable. How he'd fumbled at the pay phone—he didn't have a cell that day. Instead of dialing 911 outright he punched the endless digits of his telephone credit card, riding a roller coaster of invisible circuitry before being connected with the local emergency services. Why? Had he hoped that in the silent seconds it took for a human voice to come on the line that the boy would reappear to spare him from having to say aloud what was flashing through his mind?

Then he described what it was like to be a suspect—the interrogations, the veiled accusations, the presumption that anything he said had to be dissected before it could be taken as truth. All this was new to Sis. She was accustomed to her friends in her POMC chapter complaining about the police not looking them in the eye, how they had to harass detectives, assistant DAs, and parole boards into keeping them informed. She thought of By-God Bob Birmage answering the same questions from Dub Ritterbush for four days running now. How easy it was to wish Bob would just bring an end to everyone's anxiety, just as she'd wished her daughter's murderer could settle it all with a confessional paragraph that began *This is why.* . . .

She remembered, too, how applause briefly broke out among the volunteers the second morning they searched for Chance as the rumor spread about Dub picking up a drifter. It was so odd to hear that clapping on the lawn of the Shiloh Baptist Church; it confirmed what Sis suspected about the volunteers–that part of the lure of being there was the unusual entertainment it offered. No, *entertainment* wasn't the right word, too harsh. But there was something definitely play-like about the drama, and the applause betrayed the audience's hope that the beginning, middle, and end would follow each other as if scripted, concisely, without decaying into tedium.

"That was you, wasn't it? The one they found at McCrae's Hill the other day."

"I've been chasing ghosts for almost a year. A tidbit of news comes my way, and I rush after it, hoping to find a kindling of coincidence, but those are very rare. What was this boy's name again? His first name, I mean."

"Chance."

"Right. I read that in the newspaper and thought, *How appropriate.* I knew my time was running out, that something decisive had to happen or it never would. I don't think I can live with that. With nothing decisive happening, I mean." He looked square into her eyes, blinking as if suddenly sensitive to the sunlight. "What do you think possesses parents to give a child that name? What are they thinking?"

"I don't know."

"Maybe it's a recognition of the forces of coincidence. Of happenstance." He sucked wind over his teeth. "I bet I know what people said to you when Patty died."

"She didn't die. She was murdered."

"Of course. There's a difference. I'm guilty of what I'm criticizing. See, for you, it's important to note the difference, to let people know that it was done to her. *To die*, that's an action verb. The subject of the sentence is the agent of the predicate. You don't like it said that way because it negates the truth: she was acted upon. But people don't want to say 'she was murdered' because that's a reminder of how subject we are to randomness, to a sudden convergence of things we can't control."

"You were going to tell me what they said when my daughter was murdered."

He scratched nervously at the top of a hand. "They said it was God's plan."

"And you don't believe that?"

"Belief and acceptance are two different things."

"I don't remember that Sunday school lesson."

"It's true. You can believe a fact and resent it for being true at the same time. I believe in God, I know I do, but that doesn't mean I don't want to talk him out of a few things."

"About your son, you mean."

He nodded, his eyes shut, as if he were dozing off to the intangibility of his desire. "Can I show you something?"

Without waiting for an answer, he shuffled to the back of his truck and twisted the latch to the cab. The door fell back with a creak to reveal a sloppy assortment of debris: an unzipped sleeping bag, plastic grocery bags, Coke cans, a cheap portable radio, and everywhere, cassettes. Some were in their cases, labeled, others littered about. St. Claire reached into the darker interior and fished out a fistful of heavy sketch paper.

"Do you know what these are?" he asked, showing her leaflet after leaflet of inky scrawl. "Don't look at the letters as letters. Look at them as shapes."

To Sis it was less comic than sad: "I still see letters. Letters in search of words."

He arranged four sheets on the truck bed until they spelled a word: *G-O-N-E*. "This is the only part of my old life I've retained. Designing typefaces. A hobby to keep me sane. I used to do it for a living. Well, not actually. It was for slow days, making scripts for special occasions. Mostly it was on the computer, but I liked doing it by hand much better."

"They're very nicely done."

This time she wasn't lying. She didn't have a clue if the stroke marks amounted to anything artistic, but they looked competent. In fact, they seemed to have been sketched by a far steadier hand than the one jittering at the end of the stranger's arm.

"There's a long tradition in type design. Actually two traditions. The first one is patronymic—the designer gives the type his last name, like father to a son. That always struck me as pretentious. The other requires more imagination; it's more artistic. The names come from aesthetic ideals, ideals of beauty, that is. This one, the one I've been working on"—he snatched the E into his hand and held it toward her—"this one I'm naming 'Chance.' You know why?"

She shook her head.

"Because the shortest distance between two points isn't a straight line. It's an accidental intersection of angles. It was by *chance* that a boy named Chance disappeared and brought me here, and it was by *chance* that I happened upon you at the festival. Doesn't it ever frustrate you that the course of our lives is determined by these coincidental occurrences? Don't you wish you could find this boy just so you could say, 'This will not happen on my watch. Not again?'"

"My husband's due home any minute. He's not too fond of folks he doesn't know turning up on him."

St. Claire tossed the paper back in the truck bed and shut the hatch. "I'll go, I promise. I just heard something in your voice last night—something I wish I could hear in my own. It wasn't calm and it wasn't stoic, but it wasn't wild and emotional, either. You were intent."

"Last night was not a good night for me. Showing the quilt unbalanced me. I'm not normally like that, yelling at folks. I wasn't myself."

"You mean you weren't what folks expected you to be. But now you're telling me you're not what I expect you to be. You don't want to be intent, I get it." He looked around. "You've got a farm here to run, a family to take care of. Do you really have a grandmother who's a hundred-plus years? That's what they say about you in Shelbyville—that and Patty. A century is a long time to live. I doubt anyone can make it that far being intent. But just one more thing before I go, though: what's your favorite book of the Bible?"

The question startled Sis. She fumbled to remember what came after Deuteronomy.

"Mine's Ecclesiastes—the preacher, you know." He pinched his eyes shut and began reciting: "I have seen everything that is done under the sun and behold all is vanity and a striving after wind." He blinked and drew the zipper up on his jacket. "I never really understood that line until I looked up the original Hebrew. The word they translate as 'vanity' is the same word for 'vapor' or 'breath'—did you know that? So it's really 'Vapor of vapors.' Life's not a bitch but a breath, and you and me, the things that bond us, the people we've lost, they're nothing but mist, too, exhalations that were always going to disappear."

He yanked open the driver's door and lifted himself inside. "I'm an Old Testament kind of guy. I guess that's why I came here. When I heard you last night, I heard the voice of someone like me, someone who's chasing something ephemeral, something she can't see or name. Now I'm thinking that you're probably more New Testament. Redemption, reconciliation, salvation, all that. Tell your husband I'm very sorry about his daughter."

Without ceremony he cut the truck wheels into a broad arc and disappeared with a gasp of carbon dioxide into the stopple fields dappling the horizon. Sis stared long after he was gone, replaying his words, certain that what she'd just heard had to be the insanest thing ever.

tenderloin

Dickie-Bird Johnson spat into the hollow of his palm, stuffed his wet fist under the waistband of his underwear, and began slicking himself. He used his free hand to draw a cigarette from a half-empty pack, lighting it with a quick snap of his thumb across a matchbox flint. He sucked deep and felt the singe descend through his lungs. As one hand worked a semi-circular motion, the other flipped casually through the pages of a rumpled magazine. Dickie's eyes lingered over the pale human shapes reclining across the pages. The lavishly arched bodies hardly kept his interest anymore. Truth was, smoking gave him more pleasure. He held the smoldering husk a few inches from his face and marveled at how much gratification could come from such a modest thing. *If I could put a pair of lips and arms on you,* he thought, *I'd be the happiest man on earth.*

He returned the cigarette to his mouth where his teeth left a damp impression on the filter wrap. Pretty soon he'd reached the back pages of the magazine, which were full of lurid photos and bold-faced telephone numbers promising instant elation in triple exclamation points. A few weeks earlier, he'd lifted a phone card off a dozing guy at a bar and tried a few of those numbers, just for fun, but the voices on the other end were just sad old twinks with unconvincing falsettos. What a rip.

It didn't take long. When he was finished Dickie-Bird kicked his briefs off his thighs and wiped the jit with them. Then he tossed them in a pile of dirty laundry. He lit another cigarette and sat on a futon mattress, naked except for the tank top that stretched across the prodigious hump of his belly. It was 6 p.m. and he had fifty-three dollars to his name. The carburetor of the converted school bus that served as his residence needed jiggering, and to top it off Dickie felt a little flutter in his chest cavity that he believed was a premonition of a heart attack. And those were the simplest of his problems.

Just a few weeks earlier he'd dodged a bullet when a boy who'd narked on him failed to show up for an interview with a D.A. As Dickie figured it, the kid's parents hit the highway once they realized how long they'd have to hang around a bunch of apple-jacking lawyers. The parents were a pair of dope losers anyway—they'd sell their kids for a quarter bag if given a chance. Dickie did them right befriending their two boys. They were good kids, smart kids who took him seriously when he poked their fingertips with needles and made them take a blood vow not to go spreading their secrets. But one of the boys let him down. But to even it all out, the parents did him a favor, so who knows why things happen the way they do? God works in mysterious ways.

He pulled aside the grimy beach towel that doubled as a curtain for the back bus window. Outside was a picnic table, some empty beer cans, and piles of fallen leaves. Pretty desolate compared to summer when Dickie would wake up to discover bodies right outside the school bus door, slumbering from exhaustion. It was fun spending summers with the Rainbow Family. This past one had been his third—not the best, but good enough. Earlier that June he'd rolled into the Mark Twain National Forest with J.P. and Saxophone Sam—so named because he was forever honking on a battered tenor sax while Dickie drove through Michigan, Indiana, Illinois, and finally

Missouri. Sam had a knack with the ladies. No sooner had they arrived in the woods and set up camp than there was Sammo, every night it seemed with a new one, a blonde one, red one, even a few nasty old blue-haired ones, grunting away while Dickie and J.P. tried to steal some midnight relief from the humidity. *It's the drums*, Sam would say. They were everywhere, pumping away through the jamboxes that the Rainbows lugged on their shoulders. You weren't supposed to have electronic equipment; if you wanted a rhythm to accompany your commune with nature, the Rainbows recommended you bring your own acoustic instruments. But nobody paid attention to the rule, so as you walked along the paths in the thick of the heat you'd come across people gyrating, humping right out in the open to the rump-a-pum-pum. People caked in mud with crazy symbols smeared across their faces and chests. The Rainbows were free with their food and they gave away mounds of pot and mescaline. At night, Dickie sprawled with J.P. across the futon mattress, Saxophone Sam rutting a foot away, his dreams dancing throughout his head to the rhythm of the ever-beating drums.

That was early summer, when times were good. But if Dickie-Bird knew anything, it was that good times always go bad. And summer started going bad when J.P. started bitching about trips to the souvenir shops. *Fuck you and your fuck-fuck-fucking cards. Who the fuck buys Halloween cards in June?* The little bitch was the same way when it came to the post office: *A stamp is a stamp is a fucking stamp already. Let's get the fuck out of here and get some shit. I need some shit, dude. Get your cock out of my ass and get me some shit*—that was how J.P. talked. His favorite expression was, "Fuck a duck, dude." Yes, that was a conversation with J.P.

As if that weren't bad enough, one afternoon Dickie caught the kid licking the gill of some near-albino trout with a tattoo right above her kootchy. In Dickie's own school bus—*his own bus*—bought in Coconut Grove, Florida, for a thousand dollars and outfitted with a countertop sink and a portable refrigerator and a couch and a futon mattress. *Why you got to do me like that?* Dickie-Bird asked.

What? J.P. snapped back. *Am I your nigger? I ship too, you know.*

That had pissed Dickie off. *I treat you good, real good. Three meals a day good.*

J.P. laughed. *Three meals?* And then he laughed. *Three cans a day of Beanee-Weenee is more like it.*

Well, then, Dickie said, *take your busted cherry back to Cass City. See if I care.*

And J.P.: *Don't think I won't, don't think I won't. You see this snow-white twat who's taken such a shine to me? I can stick my dick anywhere I care to and she'll still get me any shit I want. I want some shit, dude.* That should've been the end of it, but J.P. just couldn't let well enough alone. *You big fat stinking slob*, he'd screamed. *Do you know how God awful you reek on a hot summer's day? You your own ty-fuck-fuck-fucking-phoid fog!*

And then he was gone—definitely *not* back to the orphanage outside Cass City that his foster parents ran. J.P.'s adoptive dad had chuckleheads enough to feed. The guy'd bid the boy a fond farewell by giving Dickie-Bird a baseball card he claimed was worth two hundred dollars. *This'll come in handy—handy dandy, if I know you*, he'd said. No, Dickie knew right where ole J.P.'d gone: off with the trout and her tattooed kootchy and J.P.'s cock stuck in her ear probably.

The salt in the wound was that they took the satchel in which Dickie kept his cards and envelopes. *Don't worry, Fatso,* J.P.'s note said. *I'll mail them for you. In the meantime, eat a peach.* For the first week it drove him nuts. Dickie would smoke a joint to sleep, only to have Sam tumble in with his catch of the day. He'd lie there listening to the slapping skin and in his head he couldn't help but picture it, the tattoo. A damn ruby-red heart, split jagged down the middle to commemorate some unspecified pain, riding atop the pudenda like a straw hat. He could hear J.P., too. *Let me mend that heart for you, sugar doll. Let me massage it for you. All I gotta do is stick you with this here cock like I've been stuck all my life by fat stinking slobs like him. Only unlike in my case you're gonna feel good getting fucked because I love you . . .*

So to cure his loneliness Dickie had started drifting down to the Kids Village in the mornings. That was where the Rainbows set up activities for the children. Minor league stuff: a puppet booth, some arts-n-crafts time-fillers, a guy with ukuleles who knew exactly two songs, "Tiptoe through the Tulips" and "Tie a Yellow Ribbon Round the Old Oak Tree." Dickie found his calling there in the village. At first he'd sit on a tree stump and kids would run by and ask to pat his bald head. Pretty soon he started entertaining them with stories he invented. *You see this?* he'd ask, tapping his bare scalp with his middle fingers. *You know why there's no hair? Napalm. From the war.* Tons of kids scampered through the dirt to hear him, boys and girls. After that he put on his black vest and let them pat his jibber-jabber, the doodads and necklaces, pins and dangling thingies he'd hung across the fringe and buckles. One day he was eating a chicken drumstick somebody gave him and a scruffy little princess asked who he was. *I'm the Pied Piper,* Dickie-Bird told her with a grin.

Two boys in particular were his fans, Zachary and Ron Ron. They were seven and nine. Dickie noticed them squatting on their haunches while he reeled adventures off the top of his head, and they were bug-eyed enthusiastic. *Where's you mom and dad?* he asked after noticing them kicking through the underbrush a few paces behind him as he walked home.

Getting high, one said.

They're stoned all the time, the other told him.

You don't smoke, do you?

They shook their heads, as if he'd never speak to them again if they said yes.

Good, Dickie said with a smile. *Don't ever, because if you do, your taliwackers will fall off.*

Back on the bus, they played checkers and talked about video games. When Zak got sleepy Dickie laid him on the couch, and then went to gather firewood with Ron Ron.

This went on for several days, maybe a week. Then one afternoon while Zak napped it finally happened. It just did. He and Ron Ron talked about it, and Ron Ron said okay, and he liked it and for Dickie it felt good to touch and be touched once more.

It went on for a while. Dickie almost never thought about J.P., and when he did, it was with spite. He imagined J.P. dumped off at some trashy bus station, the tattooed kootchy leaving him for a better bone. *Who needs you now? What goes around comes around, you bastard piece of ass.* Dickie would repeat it to himself as Ron Ron snored at Dickie's belly: *That little faggot who thought he was too good to be a faggot was just an orphan piece of ass.* Eat that peach, J.P.

But then the boys failed to show up one morning, and Dickie knew they had talked. If he'd been smart he would have hit the road right then and there, but he found himself unable to leave the forest, hoping either Zak or Ron Ron had merely taken sick. That afternoon he was roasting marshmallows when the adults arrived at his campsite. Four of them. The four horsemen of the apocalypse—that was the first thing to pop into Dickie's mind. Four horsemen, all because of a little horseplay. It was the boys' parents, accompanied by two members of the Shanti Sena, the Rainbows' security troop.

"I wasn't alone with your kids," Dickie'd blurted out. Why, he didn't know—the words just jumped out of his throat, like a retch. Neither the mother nor father cried; they were glassy-eyed and remote, partly from the marijuana and partly from the hassle. The security men took his picture with an instant camera and told him state troopers were on the way. Dickie offered them a marshmallow. When they declined, he asked if they'd prefer a s'more. *Got plenty of graham crackers*, he said, trying to be cool. One of the Shanti Sena was the ukulele player. He went by the name Amazing Ray, and he sat by the fire practicing chords until the cops came. He played on as the troopers searched the bus. Amazing Ray had spiky hair and a rattail that dangled halfway down his back; the braid flipped against his shoulder as he tried to sing. Dickie was watching that rattail flap as the cops found his k.p., the toy box where he kept the cheap freebies from fast-food meals, even the baseball card J.P.'s dad gave him. *Where's the diary?* Fuck if everybody on the goddamn face of the earth didn't ask him that. As he told them to kiss his big fat fucking ass, Dickie knew it'd be quite a while before he stretched out on the futon mattress again.

He tried to fob off a phony name on the cops, one he'd borrowed from a righteous nut case up in Michigan that'd tried to

breathing out the ghost

do him harm. But it didn't work; the cops had his fingerprints in a database for sex offenders. He sat in county jail for three days when an investigator for children and youth services showed up. The guy wouldn't even speak to Dickie. Instead, he took a clipboard out of his briefcase and set it down so Dickie could read the report:

"Complainant noted that on Wednesday or Thursday, July fifth or sixth, in the afternoon at approximately two or three o'clock, Zachary and Ronald Weinmeyer went over to the suspect's bus. Z. was sleeping on a blanket near the bus door, while Mr. Johnson and R. lay on Mr. J's mattress. R. noted that Mr. Johnson pulled his penis out of his pants, then pulled his pants down. After this, R. pulled his penis out and they spent sometime fondling each other. R. reported that Mr. J. ejaculated into his own hand. The following Friday, July the seventh, Z. and R. again visited Mr. J's bus and again Z. slept. Once again, R. laid on the mattress with Mr. J. Mr. J. removed R.'s penis from his underwear and orally copulated him. The following evening R. and Mr. J. became sexually involved, this time Mr. J penetrating R. anally. . . ."

"What do you have to say?" the investigator asked.

"It wasn't like that at all. You make it sound so cold and unloving. He would never use the word *penis*. He would say *thingie*."

This did not humor the man. *Chicken-shit chickenhawk*, that's what he called Dickie.

Dickie shrugged. How *do* you explain it? He didn't try. "I've got a problem. *You*'d call it a problem, I guess."

The investigator wrote on a yellow legal pad. Dickie knew what it said: *Mr. Johnson admits that he has a problem with sexual addiction.* Had he not been sitting in a holding tank, Dickie would have invited the investigator to debate the finer points of "problem." *It is only a problem because you have me here,* Dickie would have told the man if that conversation had taken place. It had not been a problem on those July afternoons. *If you'd been there,* Dickie would say, *you'd see it was quite beautiful and no problem whatsoever. R. was no orphan piece of ass, let me tell you.*

He stayed in the county lockup for three weeks. He was kept in a separate cell from the peddlers and thugs, but he could hear their taunts. *Hey, chickenhooker,* they'd mutter. *Gotchyaself caught in the Tenderloin. Big fat chicken boy. Fingerlickin' good.* The jailers indulged in fat jokes, too. Since Dickie's cell was the last in the hallway, they'd roll the meal cart up to him, shaking their sorry heads, saying, "We run out of the grub, boy. You'll have to do without. But then again, you look like you could do without, dontcha?"

By day, Dickie pondered the litany of clinical, cold-sounding terms that they called charges: *involuntary deviate sexual intercourse, statutory rape, indecent assault.* He marveled over their meaninglessness. If he was guilty of indecent assault, what, pray tell, was a decent one? At night Dickie went to sleep by beating off into a blanket, which he then wadded up and stuffed in the crack between the concrete wall and the mattress. In between day and night, he lay on his back, his hands on his mountainous gut, staring at the ceiling, blank-eyed as a dead man.

Dickie had resigned himself to the tedium when one afternoon, out of the blue, they released him. His court-appointed lawyer—some bucktooth kid with a tree's worth of paper spilling out of his arms—told him that Zak and Ron Ron, along with their parents, had disappeared. The district attorney's office had no choice but to drop the charges. Dickie tried to shake his lawyer's hand, but the guy put his fist behind his back and cocked his buckteeth in contempt: "You're not exactly one for the scrapbook. I got boys of my own." A trooper rode him back to the woods, where Dickie figured he'd get his bus and head back to Michigan. It was almost late summer. He could pick up some cabinetwork in Sinclair County. He hiked a mile back through the red junipers and sycamores. The Rainbows were long gone, except for a few drifting stragglers like himself. He recognized Amazing Ray, strolling the woods, rattail flapping, still strumming his nylon strings as if singing to the flora. Amazing Ray gave him the same look as the lawyer with the big choppers. "Save your breath," Dickie-Bird called out to him. "I'm going."

And he'd planned to keep his word, right up to the minute he wedged open the school bus door and saw the lockbox he kept hidden behind the false cabinet door above the sink splayed on the floor. The lockbox formerly containing nearly nine hundred in twenties, left right there beside a battered tenor sax. Dickie picked up the box, shook it, dropped it, then hurled the saxophone against the bus wall before he found the note on the counter. *Dear D.B. Bet you didn't know you'd gone into the pawn business. But seriously, take care of the sax. I'll be back for it! In the meantime, eat a peach! Sam.*

Dickie had been eating that peach with one hundred and ninety dollars. That was the amount in his pocket when they had carried him off to county. Almost two months later, he was down to fifty-three. And that wasn't even taking into consideration the carburetor. Dickie scratched at the zippered skin behind his scrotum. He was going to have to break down and call his mother to wire him some money. If he could just get back to Sinclair

County, he'd pick up some work and make that nine hundred back in nothing flat.

He was thinking about that when a sense of panic flushed through his bowels, set off by shadows moving outside the windows. He sprang to his feet as the door to his school bus tore open. A surge of wind gripped his arms, and he felt an intense burst of pain around his liver. He fell backwards, his exposed testicles squeezed between his thighs. It was hard to breathe; that coronary flutter he believed was a foreshadowing of a heart attack came and went. He scrambled to focus, but could only see white. It took Dickie a moment to realize a pillowcase had been yanked over his head.

I said not to hit him, dammit.

It was just a pop. Just a pop, wasn't it, Dickie-Bird?

Shut your lid.

Hey—a third voice now—*if you can't control this guy I'm calling the state troopers. I called them once before, and I'll call them once again.*

I can control him. He can't control himself, but I can control him. Hold his legs.

Dickie felt a clutch at his ankles.

You recognize me, D.B.?

It was the first voice.

Get the duct tape on him.

He heard the ripping adhesive and then his legs were bound together. *Get it over with*, Dickie thought. Another rip, no speaking now. Hands grabbed his wrists, the tape mashing the carpal bones into each other. Things were crashing—*his things in his bus.*

No monkey business now, the third voice said. *I didn't put in for monkey business.*

Just let it alone. Jesus, settle down. Now.

The pillowcase was yanked away. Dickie blinked several times to focus his sight. "You're too late. Somebody else got my money first. Hey, wait a minute, who are you guys, anyway?"

There were three of them. One was Amazing Ray, the Shanti Sena. The second paced back and forth in a three-step strut like a skinny bull, his face gnarled in fury, nostrils throbbing. The one who sat on Dickie's chest was short but strong. He had a green ski cap that peaked about four inches above his head, and his arms were thick like corded wood. When he grabbed Dickie's jaw Dickie imagined the vein on his biceps inflating under his windbreaker.

"I can't believe you don't remember me." The strong man spat his words into Dickie's face. His breath was hot and smelled of mint toothpaste. "You've been thinking you're my pen pal, after all."

Dickie thought his teeth would crack from the pressure of the man's grasp. "I don't know what you're talking about," he said, lips bunched into a pucker.

"Say it, Dickie." The man was squeezing harder. "Say my name."

Then it happened. The one who paced stopped pacing long enough to draw his leg back and shoot his foot into the doughy fat that hung above Dickie's thigh.

"Hey now—hey now," Amazing Ray yelled.

The man on Dickie's chest bolted upright and grabbed the kicker. The kicker slapped at the strong man, but the only thing that fell to the floor was the ski cap. The man, his hair mussed by the knock, grabbed the kicker by the collar and with one arcing thrust of his arms he threw the kicker into the dirty laundry pile. "I told you to get cleaned up so you didn't *eff* this up." the man said, his voice larded with disgust. Dickie watched the kicker burrow his way from under the soiled shorts and shirts until the throbbing ache in Dickie's side reminded him why the kicker was on the ground in the first place.

"I've been bruised," Dickie announced.

"No more games." The strong man swung his legs back over Dickie's belly and squatted over his chest. "Say my name. Come on. I know you know me. Say it."

"I'm telling you, friend, I—"

"It was only last February, Dickie. Not eight months ago. You and me. You remember. You filed a complaint on me, lost me my license."

"I did that? Fuck a duck, dude—if I did, I'm so sorry. But last February, I was methed up, bad. I don't remember anything from Columbus Day on last year. It's a total blur."

The man rested his weight down on Dickie's ribs. He looked back at Amazing Ray, who stood at the counter looking like he wished he had a ukulele to pluck. Then the man looked at the kicker, who remained splayed in Dickie's clothes pile, balling and unballing his fists.

"It was his boy, Dickie. I don't care about the license. I do but it's not as important as the boy. Last February you were a cocky little twink. You had a smart answer for every question. But now I'm not asking." He nodded toward the kicker. "You see him as well as I do. He looks like he's been struck by lightning. You know what happens when a tree gets struck by lightning. It's burnt *from the inside out*. That's him, Dickie. From the inside out."

Dickie looked at the man in the laundry pile.

"Say my name," the strong man said.

"You're St. Claire, then?" Dickie asked. The kicker didn't answer. He just stared at Dickie, his chest rising and collapsing with rigid breathing. "You don't look anything like I figured."

"My name," the strong man kept saying. "My name, Dickie." He squeezed Dickie's jaw harder.

"Colin St. Claire." Dickie's tongue was sideways in his mouth. To form words, he had to speak around it. "What kind of pussy name is that, anyway?"

Dickie expected a punch for that, but the man on his chest just squeezed harder. "*My* name, Dickie. Just like you wrote it on all those cards."

"All right, enough already. You know I know your name. You know I do."

Satisfied, the strong man let go. Dickie felt the skin of his face relax and tumble back around his neck.

"Heim-*ster*-hol-*ster*. So you're still spreading rumors about me. I should dig up the dirt on you. I should sue you and him for de*fam*ation of character."

"You'd have to prove you have character." Heim looked at St. Claire, quick, unsteady glimpses, as though he were trying to nail his companion in place with angry hammerhead hits of his eyes. "I'd like to see you do that."

"This isn't right and you know it. Didn't you learn your lesson last time? Now you're gonna make me make trouble for you all over again. Ain't nothing to write a letter, you know."

"No trouble this time, Dickie. Try taking me out and you'll be taking yourself out. File a complaint on me and I'll get J.P. up to Michigan to testify what you did to him all summer. You've messed that kid up bad. He's angry and wants revenge. So does this gentleman accompanying me. If you want me to protect you from him, you better be willing to tell us a few things starting with—"

"I told you last time! I don't know what you're talking about!"

Dickie bucked, trying to tip Heim from his stomach. But Heim dug his kneecaps into Dickie's shoulders and kept his balance.

"Starting with your diary."

"My diary? Jesus—not again! I don't keep a diary. I can't even write. I'm—what do they call it—illiterate."

"Don't crock us. You all keep diaries. It's part of the pathology. Now where."

"I'm telling you—"

Heim looked back at Amazing Ray. "Go water a tree," he said.

The Shanti Sena nodded and disappeared outside. St. Claire was still clenching and unclenching his fists. Heim snapped his fingers and held his palm out. "Give it to me," he told St. Claire. St. Claire stood up and reached around to the back of his oily corduroys. Heim grabbed Dickie by the arm, his other hand still out. "Roll over."

"Hey, wait a minute," Dickie yelled. He tried to resist, but Heim slipped beside Dickie's bulk and yanked him sideways.

"Just like cow tipping," Heim said. The next thing Dickie knew he was face down on the floor, the balls of his taped fists punched into his own diaphragm. "One last time. The diary."

"I swear as Jehovah is my wit—"

Dickie heard two brittle snaps and felt Heim's elbow in his lower spine.

"You always walk around with your two scoops hanging out?"

Dickie became aware of a thin but intense sliver of heat that hung like humidity just below his buttocks, and he thought, *They are burning me. They have come here drunk with their righteous indignation and now they will mutilate me. They will hurt me when I have never hurt anyone. No one, not one.* Dickie started to cry.

"It's just a book of paper. All you have to do is tell us where it is and I won't roast your marshmallows."

Dickie was balling, blubbering full force.

"You're not a man. You won't be able to take the pain. Just think, Dickie. The most sensitive spot of your body. The most vulnerable part. C'mon now. You're not a man. There's no harm giving it up when you're not a man."

"Do it already," St. Claire told him. His voice was high, his words tripping over themselves.

"Sit tight." The heat sharpened. Dickie felt his sphincter tighten. "However bad it is now, it gets worse. They always tell you that pain is never as bad as you imagine it, but that's not the case. Not with a candle lighter, not in this spot."

Dickie heaved hard, tears and mucus from his nose streaming over his lips, into his mouth, coating his front teeth.

"Just think. Less than a half-inch now and you'll be a gelding. But distance is no guarantee with a flame. It shifts and contorts itself, lapping at the oxygen until it strikes something solid—"

Dickie wondered if he wouldn't drown in slobber before the actual scorch shot its way up his nerves. *Righteous indignation,* he thought. *Righteous indignat—*

"Something solid, like you. . . ."

Before Dickie was aware of the pain he heard St. Claire scream "Do it!" and then the sensation rushed from the hind part of his scrotum up through his anus, cooking its way into his bowels. The flame felt like clutching fingers, at once hot and cold, at once a tickle and a pinch.

"Above the sink! In the cabinet!"

The heat at his flanks lifted. He heard footsteps. They must have belonged to St. Claire, because Heim's weight still held him to the floor. The hinge creaked, and a palm slapped at a shelf. Then a caterwaul of glass and silverware as the dirty dishes skidded across the counter top.

"A false wall, behind the false wall. . . ."

St. Claire ripped a plywood slat from the cabinet back and palmed at the pages of a small notebook. Heim rose and reached for the diary.

"You don't want to look. Let me."

Dickie twisted his head to one side, buttering the down half of his face in slobber. Heim and St. Claire were yanking the book back and forth like children fighting over a toy.

"You're violating me. Reading my personal thoughts and feelings."

Heim twisted St. Claire's arm until the diary clattered to the ground. He scooped it up with one lunge and, keeping his back to St. Claire, he shook the notebook open. He read the dates of the entries. *November 12, 13, 16.*

"*You are you're* is apostrophe *re*, Dickie. Not *y-o-u-r.*"

"I said I couldn't write already."

"You're quite the Casanova, huh? Do you know what J.P. said to tell you? He said he keeps a picture of you. For sentimentality's sake. Every time he comes in that girl's dented mouth he makes her spit it out on your face."

"You wouldn't understand! You've never loved! Neither of you. If either of you had ever loved you would not condemn any man's love!"

"Here. November twenty-two." Heim read for a minute. Then he looked up from the notebook, his face white and grim. St. Claire's eyebrows sat high on his forehead in infinite expectation.

"What is it?"

"Nothing. Nothing about A.J."

Dickie saw St. Claire's lips tighten until his skin seemed to disintegrate and his face became a lifeless skull. St. Claire cocked himself back for a moment, his eyes haughty and despairing at the same time, and then, as if flung from a slingshot, he sprang into the air, his arms in front of him, fingers curled tight into his fists. He could have flown across the room on the engine of his ire, too, had Heim not swung his arm around his waist and jerked him backwards. The two bodies stumbled over their intertwined legs until Heim planted his palm on St. Claire's chest and thrust him to the wall. St. Claire was screaming profanities, one atop another until the consonants lost their hard edges and his voice became a single slur of ugliness. The bus door whooshed open and Amazing Ray jumped up the steps. Before he could say anything the racket stopped. It took Dickie a moment to realize why—only when St. Claire began thumbing at the purple stream leaking from his nose was it obvious that Heim had punched his friend square in the center of his face.

"This ends now," Amazing Ray insisted.

"It ends when I say it does." Heim took up the diary again. "Where's the real one, Dickie?"

"What are you talking about now?"

"The real one. This is a fake. I know it." He ripped pages one by one from the binding. "Every entry's in the same pen. *Every* one."

The pages twirled like inebriated butterflies in the stuffy bus air. Dickie watched them cartwheel to his feet.

"If I tell you the truth, will you stop?"

"I will."

"And get me up first. I want to sit up."

"Fair enough."

Heim helped Dickie twist his bulk around. Then he pulled the fat man by the armpits until his blubbery back rested against the wall.

"Now. Talk."

"Okay, just let me get my breath." Dickie inhaled deep. He wished he could smoke. He needed a cigarette. "What was his name again?"

"A.J.," Heim told him.

"That's right. A.J. And where did I see him?"

"You know where."

"No, really, tell me where. There's been so many—you've got to understand. If I had the real diary, I'd know for sure, but I had to lose it, you know. So tell me."

"The Home Depot, that's where, you bloated pig fu—"

Again, St. Claire's words disintegrated into profanity.

"Okay, okay, I remember now." Dickie felt calm all of a sudden, settled, as if he were ready to slip off to a deep soulful sleep. It had been so long since he'd rested well. He thought of Sinclair County and how cool mid-Michigan would be in middle-late October. "A little fellow named A.J. at the Home Depot there in Bay City, right?"

"Come on, Dickie."

"It's clear as twilight." Dickie smiled, his chin wrinkling with pleasure. "A sweet boy he was. He said to me, *Just please don't let it hurt like my Daddy's does.*"

For what seemed an eternity a gray silence overtook the bus. Heim, St. Claire, and Amazing Ray all froze in place. Or if they didn't freeze exactly, Dickie thought, inertia got the better of them. They moved so slow that Dickie wondered if he hadn't been yanked from the here and now and relocated to an alternative dimension, for though his brain raced, the rhythm of the world around him thickened to a molasses drip. He felt as if he sat upon the inner rim of a wheel that appears to spin faster than the circumference of its spokes. *Time is funny like that,* Dickie decided. *It starts and stops and slows without any perceptible measure.* He was still pondering that jerky irregularity when he saw it: a silver blur that hovered in the air like a flying saucer as it left St. Claire's hand. It crawled at first, a slow-blossoming shadow, but then without warning it ignited and rushed straight at Dickie's head. He felt it smash into the knob of his forehead and bounce off his belly, clattering to the floor. Only then could Dickie make out what the object was: his thermos—*his own thermos in his own bus.* Fuck a duck, dude. Dickie was aware of a stream of blood running past his eye down the bridge of his nose, but all else became form without shape, forms losing their shape, everything in front of him dribbling away into a massive blending swatch of darkening blue.

Dammit dammit dammit but Dickie couldn't tell who spoke. He could only register the words as cadence, not as meaning but as a musical phrase that was hoarse-sounding and spitty like the low guttural honks that Saxophone Sam had made during the good part of the summer when Sam's belly's breath rushed past the wet reed through the neck and lungs of his instrument. Dickie couldn't get Sam or J.P. or the good part of the summer out of his mind. He saw them vibrant and within reach and so he chased after them, wanting to shelter them in his arms before they slipped into the murky encroaching twirl that pulsed outward from his split forehead. Because all his energy went to keeping his crumbling attention together Dickie didn't hear that same voice *Colin you bastard catastrophe you've killed him you have you've k—*

AS SOON AS HE saw the blood, St. Claire spilled headlong out of the bus, upsetting an aluminum pyramid of stacked beer cans and scattering the dormant leaves as his wrists hit the turf of the campsite. Before he knew he'd fallen he was upright again, kicking his feet through the tangled vines of wild viburnum and nannyberry bushes. Behind him he could hear Heim screaming his name, yelling for him to stop as he, too, navigated the obstacle course of thorns and cockleburs and scratching branches. St. Claire leaped over the fallen, half-rotted trunk of a swamp willow and tumbled anew into a hidden sinkhole. He felt his left ankle tighten and fronds scratch at his cheeks. He had no sense of distance, only direction. As he dodged a thicket of heather he felt his spine buckle. His legs gave out and as he tried to protect his face as he fell he realized Heim had tackled him. The two of them rolled like lovers down a short ravine until they crashed into a pot-bellied basswood. St. Claire heard Heim grunt from the impact, but the jolt wasn't hard enough to dislodge his grip on St. Claire's collar. He swung an elbow back behind his ear and made contact. This time Heim let go. As St. Claire curled free he saw his friend on one knee with a palm covering his mouth. Heim's once-crisp khakis were splattered with mud and torn leaves. Without speaking St. Claire rose and jogged up the ravine slope. Once on level ground he broke into a sprint, no longer concerned with tripping. He didn't believe he'd ever run so fast before. He didn't know how far he ran before he reached the Suburban parked at the end of a cul-de-sac that led out of the forest. Beside the Suburban was a faded yellow Volkswagen bug that belonged to Amazing Ray. St. Claire squatted at the Suburban's backside and felt under the bumper. He knew Heim kept a spare key there.

He had only lurched forward a few yards when he saw Heim in the rearview mirror, still chasing him. St. Claire sped up, and the figure in the mirror began to shrink.

The last St. Claire saw of him, an enraged Heim was leaping up and down.

He looked like a popcorn kernel trying to avoid boiling in skillet oil.

Dub Ritterbush parked his patrol car along the dirt lane that led to the only Sugar Creek landing in Johnson County. His headlights spread through the deserted pasture separating the dusty road from the creek bank. With a tug of his signal lever, he turned on his high beams. Because it was only early evening, what remained of daylight washed out their intensity, but he kept them on anyway. Night was coming. When it arrived it would do so quickly, like a storm clap, and the land would darken without warning. Dub would keep his eyes trained on the spot his car lights illumined, telling himself he must stay awake and stay alert. For the boy's sake.

He unscrewed the cap of a thermos and poured a dollop of hot coffee. This was his life now: a daybreak interrogation of By-God Bob Birmage, a morning's futile search, a quick sandwich from Subway or Arby's fetched by a deputy, an afternoon of driving and looking, a ten-minute nap in his leather recliner when he came home for the Tupperware dinner that his wife, Cinda, prepared for him, and then back to searching. Dub had come to hate this time of night, knowing when the blackness hardened around him, it would leave him with a sense of impotence. The first night Chance had been missing, he'd slept without resting, thinking that he only had to get to morning and the clear light of day would reveal the child's whereabouts. But then daytime proved just as dim as night, and by the fall of the next evening, Dub knew he'd be awake until the end, until something resolved itself.

He passed the thermos cap to his left hand to feel around on the seat beside him with his right. A deer spot was there. From time to time he would plug the adapter into the cigarette lighter and bathe the autumn land with it. On an average night during an average week—during deer-hunting season in particular—he might be out here combing for teenagers who did this very thing for a joke. It is illegal in Indiana to spotlight deer. The sudden brightness can freeze them until they bolt wildly out of fear, sometimes ending up on the hood of an automobile, broken by a bumper, all for the sake of an adolescent prank. But Dub could justify his using the spot. It was a boy, not an animal, he hoped to spook into visibility.

So Dub sat and watched. He couldn't sleep. Pretty soon, he thought, he would tell himself he wasn't allowed to blink. The world is pregnant with motion, but one shuttered eye can miss its fleeting, can overlook the fleeing. He used his high beams and his deer spot against the dark, not so much to scare up whatever hid in the landscape but to chase away the midnight sense of futility. Dub believed he could do it—that he could settle things, one way or another, if only he could bring enough light to bear. In the meantime, he would have to sit and watch.

When next he remembered to drink from his thermos top, his coffee was cold.

deliberate speed

The first thing Heim did when he saw his Suburban's taillights vanish in the dusk was fall to his knees and vomit. He didn't mean to. The roll down the ravine, compounded with the pumping throb in the neck that the crash into the basswood tree had given him, set off a confusion of sensation that left him reeling. His body had become a giant bolus of pain. Chasing after Colin wasn't the running he trained for; Heim preferred a hard, martial rhythm, a motion that could not, would not be unsteadied. But St. Claire had gotten him into a full-tilt sprint, and that had upset the reserve Heim so carefully cultivated. By the time they'd reached the road, a tearing flash had started shooting from up under his lowest rib, like some invisible hand reaching through his skin to yank the bone clean out. And as Heim had watched St. Claire peel away in his own Suburban—a truck that wasn't even really his, but for all intensive purposes was his *in-laws*, for fuck's sake—he thought for sure that spectral grip would jerk him flat down into the dust and drag him behind the bumper like a rattling tail of tin cans.

He hunched forward on his knees, resting his knuckles on the ground like an offensive lineman waiting for a quarterback to call set. He gulped for air. But then a hot surge shot up his esophagus, and before he could swallow it down, the vomit burst over his tongue. For a second Heim stared disbelievingly at what had come out of him. The odor flushed his nostrils, and several reflexive gags closed his throat. He kicked himself upright and lurched back. Then he spat, but the egg-rot taste wouldn't go. He felt splatter on his hands, too, so he shook his wrists hard, but the crud was caught in the webs of his fingers, and he had to wipe them on the rump of his khakis. "Goddamn," he kept saying, "Goddamn it." He hated vomiting because it was such an involuntary action.

To calm himself, he stared toward the spot, some two hundred yards away, where the road bent right and disappeared behind a thick, stony bluff. It was two miles of unpaved pathway to the nearest county highway, and from there God only knew how far to the nearest town. Heim had no choice but to wait for Amazing Ray. He slipped into the forest's foliage drapery across from the trail that led back to Dickie's camp and only a few feet away from the Shanti Sena's Volkswagen.

One leg went to sleep before Amazing showed up. When Heim heard shoes crunching the matted autumn leaves, he crouched low in the ferns so not to scare the old hippie. Amazing Ray poked his head out of the woods, his stoner paranoia dictating cautious glances to the right and left before he stepped into the open air, swinging the macramé guitar strap that held his ukulele to his back over his shoulder and pressing the instrument protectively to his side. Heim let him get a key into the lock before he jumped out of the woods.

"I don't want nothing doin' with you or your buddy."

"You're going to have to get me out of here. He's got my truck. There's a gun in that glove compartment that I've got to get hold of before something more happens. It's in my wife's name."

"Seems to me that comes under the category of your problem, not mine. If I was you, I wouldn't had a gun anywhere near that nutcase, anyway."

Heim was about to excuse St. Claire once more when he became aware of a certain lightness at his hip. He patted at his side with an open palm and then swore to himself.

"Tell me you've got a phone in that car. I've lost my cell in those woods."

IT TOOK FORTY-FIVE MINUTES to find it. Amazing Ray stayed a dozen paces behind as Heim wandered off the trail to map the swath St. Claire had mowed down during the chase. Holding his own cell, the old hippie dialed and re-dialed Heim's number while Heim kicked through the underbrush.

As they moved deeper into the forest, he tried to talk himself into leaving the cell behind. If he told Stephie he'd lost it, he wouldn't be lying. He could get a replacement on the cheap. But what kept him searching was the fear that some flake—another Amazing Ray sort—would come across it, and there would be a call. An unexpected call from Missouri wasn't outside the realm of possibility, and Heim had a world's worth of contradictory lies to keep ordered. He couldn't afford not to bring every single detail to heel.

Finally, he heard the phone ringing not far from the basswood tree, halfway up the slope of the ravine. Heim cursed himself for not thinking first of that spot. If the basswood could knock the wind out of him, it could knock a cell phone off a belt clip. He located the phone in a bed of fallen wahoo leaves and hit the talk button. *Must be some kind of irreplaceable, huh?* he heard Amazing

Ray say, both through the earpiece and from a few feet away. Heim clicked the phone quiet and stuffed it securely in an inside coat pocket. "Damn right irreplaceable," he said. Then they retraced their steps to the cul-de-sac.

"Give me some privacy for a minute," Heim said when they reached the Volkswagen. He pulled the phone from the pocket as the Shanti Sena answered him: "You take all the privacy you want, pup." Heim hadn't called home since he'd left, and he wasn't going to risk losing the cell again before talking to Stephie. He turned his back to Amazing Ray and the autodial was kicking in when he heard the Volkswagen engine rip into a throttle. He spun around just fast enough to see the wheels spin in place for a second, as if the VW was afraid to take its courage out of neutral, and then the car burst forward, draping Heim in an orange veil of spit dirt.

This time—the second of the day, the second of the damned *hour*, he wasn't going to get left behind. Snapping the phone closed and stowing it in his pants pocket (he wouldn't lose it a second time, either), Heim bolted diagonally to where he knew the forest bed declined down to the next level of switchback road. Unsure how wide the wedge of land he had to cover was, he moved faster than he was thinking—again, no time for his usual kind of running—and was surprised by the sudden down slope.

His feet were so far ahead of his senses, the declivity tripped him before he could adjust his balance. He fell forward, managing to land on one forearm like a batter sliding towards first base, then flipped onto his side and started tumbling horizontally. As he rolled, he remained unaware of the rocks slashing at his palms and the prickers burrowing into his socks—he thought only of the throaty sound of the VW's engine knocking below and towards him.

At the bottom of the slide, one hand by luck—by chance—gripped a loose rock. As he came out of his final spin and stood, he let the velocity carry his arm out from behind his back so the rock careened wildly out of his fist in a desperate, unaimed chuck.

His aim was better than he thought; the rock (it turned out to be a chunk of concrete block) caught the back right hubcap of the Volkswagen. The hubcap shot away from the wheel rim with a clatter. The brake lights burst into red, and the Bug stopped. Amazing Ray came running around the back bumper, his rattail slapping at the top rivet of his spine. He looked from the tire to the dislodged hubcap, trying to figure out why the one split from the other, then saw Heim struggling to rise at the road's edge.

"You get me somewhere that'll rent me a car, you'll never see me again," Heim told him. "Ditch me here and swear to God I'll be so close behind you I'll be the hair on the back of your legs."

Amazing Ray blinked for a second, his face grim with his lack of options. "Door's unlocked," he finally answered. He didn't budge until Heim was securely inside the Bug.

BY THIS POINT THE only thing more shot than Heim's nerves were the Volkswagen's shocks. The junky car seemed to hop from tread mark to bump to sinkhole on the uneven roadway. The awkward motion flushed Heim with a quease that had him gripping the armrest. The blacktop wasn't much better; the county highway grading was so steep that whenever the car rode into a curve he had the sensation of tumbling side over side, again, just as he had twice today, once down the ravine and once down the bluff. But the worst had to be the taste that stuck to his teeth. With nothing

breathing out the ghost

else to do in the car, he took to running his tongue around his mouth, trying to lick away the residual grit of his vomit. The egg-rot flavor seemed to permanently blanch his gums. He kept exhaling short, thick breaths to push the smell away, but it was no good. He was cupped in his own fog.

When they passed a convenience store outside a jerkwater hamlet, Heim told Amazing Ray to pull in. The Volkswagen slid between a pair of gas pumps and a newspaper kiosk streaked with grease. "Give me the keys," he said when Amazing let the bug idle.

"I ain't going nowhere."

Heim leaned over and twisted the key to OFF before yanking it from the ignition switch. "I know."

It was absurdly bright inside the convenience store. The place glowed like a Plexiglas castle. A clerk stood behind a counter, a spray bottle in one hand and a rag in the other. He kept wiping down the same spot beside the cash register, over and over. The clerk was a doughy-faced kid with a weedy moustache and a mullet whose tail dripped out the back of his ball cap. Back in central Michigan when Heim was a teenager, over in affluent Midland they called a mullet a Bay City waterfall.

Heim roamed the aisles until he came to a short stack of overpriced toothpaste. He grabbed a tube, a toothbrush, and a bottle of mouthwash for rinsing. When he dropped his purchases on the counter, the clerk flicked his eyes from the items up to Heim's face and back.

"What's the matter? You recommend a different brand or something?"

His hostility didn't faze the clerk. "We got band-aids and disinfectant, too," the clerk said. Heim was confused until the kid tipped his chin. Heim touched his top lip and felt blood. He stared at the blotch red smearing his fingertips. He couldn't believe he was so detached from himself that he had been bleeding without realizing it.

"I don't want band-aids *or* disinfectant. I want some goddamn toothpaste."

Outside he squirted almost a third of the tube onto the bristles of the toothbrush and then scrubbed at the inside of his mouth. He scraped away in a hard sawing motion that tore his gums and blistered the skin of his tongue. When all he could taste was spearmint, he broke the seal on the mouthwash and gargled. Then he spat the foam on the concrete where it pooled next to a line of propane canisters. As he screwed the top back on the toothpaste, he caught the clerk watching him. The kid immediately went back to wiping down his counter. A few seconds later, Heim saw him squirt a shot of glass cleaner into the air and sniff at the mist.

He returned to the Volkswagen and stuck the key back in the switch. "You weren't gonna tell me I'd busted my lip?"

Amazing Ray was gazing out the windshield. "I figure a man ought to know when his own self is bleeding."

"How far to the nearest airport?"

"We get to I-55, we can swing around the backside of St. Louis to Lambert on 70. That's your best bet for a car. Forty miles, I'd say."

"Then go."

They didn't talk. The silence bothered Heim until they got to the interstate. From there on up to St. Louis, he watched the strange procession of city names: Crystal City, Festus, Herculaneum, Kimmswick. Just beyond Arnold they caught the bypass and went west until they were in the middle of St. Louis's rich suburbs. When they hit I-70, they turned east until the terminal at Lambert Field came into view. Amazing Ray pulled the car to the curb where a lone black porter helped an old lady tag her beat-up luggage.

"You know, if anybody asks me about it, I'm gonna have to tell the truth. You didn't leave me no option on that."

Heim unbuckled his seat belt and let the shoulder restraint shoot back into its retractor. "You do that. And when you're going over all the details with them, you make sure and tell how little it bothered you. How while you were standing there watching, you were wishing the whole time that you had it in you to join in. Because you know you wanted to." He pushed open the door and stepped into another patch of unnaturally lit air. "And thanks for the lift."

Inside the airport, he rode an escalator to the lower level baggage pickup. Just down from the chugging conveyor belts was a thin corridor stuffed with rental-agency stalls. A line three to four deep piled up in front of most of the booths, so he went to the one empty counter. He knew why it was empty; this particular agency had a reputation for being more expensive than the others.

"What cars do you have?" The agent was a large woman with a second chin that flopped over the buttoned collar of her neck. Her hair was frizzed by a bad permanent that made it look as though someone dumped a bowl of brown lettuce over her head. Heim saw the agent checking out his lip.

"I'm sorry, sir, but we're all spoken for until Thursday."

"Really?" He pointed at the back wall of the booth where a panel of slots hung over a block of hooks. Several sets of keys hung from the hooks. "I see five tickets there waiting for pick up.

About twice that many keys. You driving the extras home tonight?"

The agent wet her lips, and dropped her eyes down to the scroll of paper that unspooled next to her computer terminal. "It seems we've had some cancellations. Was there a specific car you were interested in?"

He slipped his wallet from his back pocket. "Like I said, what do you have?"

The agent poked at her paper. "I've got an economy, a mid-size—but no luxuries, I'm afraid."

"I don't want a luxury. How about a truck? You got a truck anywhere on that list?"

"We have *one*. A Dodge."

"Good enough. I'll take it. For a week."

He tossed his driver's license on the counter. But instead of giving the agent his Visa, he kept the card in his palm, staring at the letters that spelled out both his and Stephie's name. Heim had less than a hundred dollars on him now; he'd paid for everything so far—his gas, his food, his nights at the Best Western in Shelbyville—all in cash so there'd be no paper trail. He was meticulous about credit-card receipts, after all. He kept them organized, month by month, so he could check his statements for unauthorized billings. If he'd used his Visa, there'd be all those receipts to explain. Plus, Stephie now cut the family checks. It hadn't been that way until the Dickie-Bird mess, when Heim had fallen into a funk and was late paying insurance on the Suburban. There'd been a cancellation notice and Stephie hit the roof, and took over the check-writing responsibilities, insisting he wasn't reliable anymore. Truth be told, he had been happy to pass on the job; Stephie did all the grocery shopping, after all, and she was

breathing out the ghost

always on him about Trace needing a check for this or that field trip, about Alex needing one for a preschool fundraiser.

But now he regretted relinquishing that authority. There was no way he could put a car rental on the Visa without Stephie getting wise to it. Even if he hid the actual bill—which would show that someone with his card had been to Lambert Field in St. Louis, not to a Kalkaska county hog farm—he couldn't hide the charge itself. The Heims never put more than about fifty dollars a month on their Visa because until recently they could never get under their twelve thousand dollar limit. Not only was the truck going to kick up what they owed by a couple hundred, Visa would raise their interest rate for again exceeding their available credit.

"Would you prefer to charge your truck to a different credit card? We also take—"

"No. Put it on this one."

As her passed her the card, he felt his neck and shoulders rope tight. He'd just kicked a corner brick out on the house of lies he'd built.

EVEN AFTER SIGNING ALL the paperwork, he still had to ride a shuttle bus to the agency lot before he could get to the truck. That meant waiting outside at a stop with a group of crisply dressed business travelers, a set of useless keys pinched in his fist. Amid all the smart suits and leather bags, Heim was aware of how out of place he'd become; people huddled around the stop kept shooting sidelong glances his way, unsettled by his cracked lip and muddied pants. When the shuttle finally arrived, he pushed his way to the front of the group, not caring how rude it made him seem. He took a seat in the back where the dark sheltered him.

During the ride, disembodied voices talked about going home. One man was telling his business partner that he needed to hightail his clothes to the dry cleaner's because he'd hit the lounge at the Sheraton and now his lapels stunk of beer and cigarettes and his wife was a real Assemblies of God type who'd go ballistic if she found out he'd snuck so much as a single drink out of her sight. Heim was tempted to lean up a few seats and tell the guy just how insignificant his little lies were.

The shuttle finally dropped him at the lot. He had to show a security guard his rental agreement before he could get past a tall perimeter fence. Then he followed the numbers on the signs beside the rows of parking spaces until he found one that corresponded to the agent's scrawl on his ticket. It was a late model, glowing clean under the arc lights. After the rides in the Volkswagen and the shuttle bus, it was going to feel good to be behind the wheel, to be in control for a change.

But after only a second of idling, Heim turned the vehicle back off. He rolled down his window and then removed his cell phone from his pocket. He stared at the phone's blank face for a while, trying to get up the nerve to call home. Finally, when he realized he was wasting time, he dialed.

When the line picked up, all he said was *It's me.*

"Hey, stranger." Stephie sounded glad to hear from him. "I guess you've been too busy to call, huh?"

"Yes." There was an awkward silence; Heim wasn't sure what to say next.

"So did Paps's sow come through all right?"

"Yeah, the sow's fine." He regretted calling now. The sound of her voice made her presence in his life suddenly palpable; details from a thousand memories flashed before him, details that he wanted to clutch in his fists so they wouldn't slip again from his awareness. The gold tennis bracelet he'd bought her one Christmas sliding up her forearm as she stretched to yawn. The way she crossed her ankles when she hopped up on a kitchen barstool while talking on the phone. The way her hair fell across the shoulders of a certain turtleneck that he liked to see her wear. These images came to him so vividly, and he wondered, sadly, if it was his guilt, not so much his love, that made them stand out so sharply in contrast to the dull tedium of his longing. He wondered, too, whether Stephie had just as many lies on him.

"So when you coming home?"

"A few more days." A brief silence made her seem more removed than all the actual miles separating them. "Paps's not in good shape, doll. He thinks he's got a malignant mole on his shoulder. Somebody's got to take him to the doctor, get him checked out. But after that, I'll be there. Trust me, I'm so ready to come home. I want to *be* home."

"Okay. A few more days, then."

"Hey—" He didn't want to leave things on a sour note. He knew he didn't deserve a more assertive expression of her affection, but he needed it from her as badly as he needed a shower and clean clothes. "Tell me about the kids. How are the kids?"

"What about them?"

"I don't know—something, anything."

He heard a sigh, and then she was saying, "We don't have the minutes for this, Bob."

It was truer than she knew. Outside of Michigan, his roaming charge doubled to a dollar a minute. But more than that: the call would show up on their cell bill, and it would reveal, irrefutably, that he'd called her from St. Louis. Stephie would see the bill because she wrote the checks now.

"I'll let you go. Just one more thing."

"What?"

"I don't want you to be mad at me."

There was silence again. It wasn't much, but it seemed a century.

"I'm not mad," Stephie finally said. "I just don't understand why you're not where you belong."

WHERE YOU BELONG: HEIM could hear those words, still, as he made his way from the lot to catch a long circular access road that fed him to a highway onramp. Only a four-hour straight line called Illinois separated St. Louis from Indianapolis. He stayed on I-70 East, skipping the northern bypass because he didn't want to veer from that line. Rush hour was over, but the downtown traffic was still thick, and he was held to a slower pace than he would have liked. But then he was out of the city and on the bridge that took him over the Mississippi River. He heard a sharp click as his front wheels went over a girder seam, and he thought of how similar it sounded to the snap of J.P.'s right wrist when it broke. Heim hadn't heard the left one snap. J.P. had been screaming too hard.

Once outside East St. Louis he switched on the radio and scanned the AM stations. He found a tape delay of Jim Rome and kept it there. Heim was a big fan of old Romey; Van Smack's voice was going to make the ride seem uneventful, normal. It was week eight of the NFL season. He thought about how—with any luck—he'd be spending this Sunday's games grilling steaks, goofing with his kids between plays, loving Stephie. It was never that romantic in real life, he knew, but he wanted those things so badly at that moment that it wasn't hard for fantasy to meld into memory. He listened to Rome recite prospects for the weekend's agenda: The Colts were hosting New England. The Bears were off to Philadelphia. The Lions at Tampa Bay. Heim's favorite team, the Packers, were off.

Five miles farther on, he rode a cloverleaf to the bridge that crossed the interstate and turned onto the ramp that would lead him back to St. Louis. But halfway down, he let the truck wheels go onto the shoulder, and parked in a bank of milkweeds.

He sat for a while, his palms slippery wet. *Laugh's on me*, he thought. Today had been just one long slingshot joke of a day, and now here he was, about to launch himself back over space he'd stupidly thought he was through with: back over the Mississippi River, back through downtown St. Louis, back to the southbound interstate that straddled strangely named towns, back to the unevenly graded county highway, back past the jerkwater hamlet where the convenience store clerk sniffed at the mist of his glass cleaner, back to the pockmarked dirt road, past the spot on the buff that he'd fallen down and then, once around the road's bend, to the part of the bluff that he'd scrambled up, back to the cul-de-sac and the trail, back through the forest to Dickie's bus and back inside, back for the Green Bay Packers ski cap that St. Claire had knocked off his head.

Back for the cap he had failed to retrieve when Colin bolted out of the bus and Heim had no choice but to light out after him without time for tidying the details.

He could no more leave that hat than he could leave the phone, but for different reasons. The phone was what tethered him to Stephie, to his kids. Had he lost it, even if he hadn't been calling home regularly, he would have felt cut off from them, cut off from his very life. But the cap—it tethered him to Dickie, for meshed in the underside of its weave were hairs from his own head, and a single one of those hairs contained enough DNA to place Heim in that bus as surely as if he owned it himself. *I might as well have signed my name to the guest book.*

He sat watching the interstate stretch in front of him, feeling puny and weak, insignificant in the order of things. It was impossible for a man to displace a single ounce of air without getting washed backward by a tidal wave of consequences.

But it was a waste of time to worry about time wasted. He looked over his shoulder to make sure the road was clear, then drove the rental truck out of the milkweeds and into the westward flow of traffic. A minute or so later, a car rushed up and blasted past his left side. Heim was tempted to stomp on his pedal, too, but wouldn't let himself. There'd be no more sprinting, no more rushing—that's when things went haywire. Starting now, he would move along in an even-tempered way, in an even-keeled tempo. He would move to that hard, martial rhythm that paved a motion that could not, would not be unsteadied. From here on out, he was going forward with deliberate speed.

To that end, he was happy to discover at least one thing working in his favor: the truck had cruise control.

again, for the first time

Another day, another prayer service. This one, the fifth in just under a week, was a Wednesday-night candlelight vigil sponsored by the Mt. Gilead Baptist Church. Three of the other four had been held at Shiloh Baptist, with an additional service organized by Evangel Presbyterian up in Greenwood, the home church of Chance's maternal grandparents. That one had proved a lackluster affair, staged on the concrete steps of the Jefferson County Courthouse and drawing fewer than twenty frumpy souls who shivered together under a wet, sludgy wind. Chance's mother, who hadn't sat in a pew since high school, didn't even bother to attend.

Nobody in the Birmage family was affiliated with Sis's church, but Mt. Gilead had nevertheless called for its congregation to gather at the base of McCrea's Hill out of sympathy for someone who was: Dub Ritterbush. Or maybe they were doing it because after a week of waiting for news of a resolution, one way or another, they simply felt they needed to *do something*. All day, Sis wondered whether she wasn't to blame for this. What had she and Pete done while Patty was missing, before they found her in the cornfield? They had asked their church to stand with them and unbox the votives.

Which was exactly what she was doing, again, as she stood in the saturated pasture that sloped upward to a rounded hilltop normally populated by a half-dozen grazing Holsteins. As the church members made their way up the slope, she handed each a slender candle stuck in the middle a small paper plate for a wax

193

catch. A few feet away, Sis's father, Clinton, clicked the trigger of a grill lighter. As each wick rippled with light he whispered the same rudimentary safety instructions that he offered every Christmas Eve service, even though there was little in the open air to catch fire. "Hold your candle down low if you're wearing your hair spray," he told the women, most of whose heads were safely protected by scarves and bonnets. "We don't want no fireworks going off." And to the children: "Keep it clear of your face. Them long nose hairs I see'll light right up." A few of the young ones giggled until their parents shushed them into solemnity.

The attendees lined up, the lower halves of their faces glowing. They were a mismatched bunch, some garbed in worksmelling clothes, others in Sunday khakis, their pant legs stuffed into their rubber boots to keep the cuffs clean for next week. For the other services Sis had worn freshly pressed blouses and slacks, but a week's worth of making herself presentable had resulted in little more than a lot of ironing, so now she found herself, in a sweatshirt and denims, staging a quiet, unnoticed protest against the formality of these vespers.

When a sufficient number of church members had arrived, Mt. Gilead's minister called the group to order. Rev. Starke hardly lived up to his name; he was a professionally personable man, one of those modern Baptist preachers who took classes on how to be engaging. He never addressed a crowd without poking his fingers to the beat of his crisply enunciated consonants. In his soundproofed office where he counseled parishioners he was known for rolling his chair out from behind his desk and sitting with his elbows on his knees to display his practiced empathy. Sis knew Rev. Starke was well intentioned, but she missed the days when a preacher was less a counselor or therapist than an instrument, someone who gave voice to God's word. In her childhood she had spent Sunday mornings in an intoxicated state of awe as the old-time traveling evangelists held sanctuaries hostage, stomping on the wood floors, pounding their fists, waving their arms as if in the heat of a fit. They never spoke in anything less than a coyote's yowl. As a girl Sis had known a good deal of showboating went into their delivery, but even so there was no playing tick-tack-toe on the morning bulletin or slipping comic books between the hymnal covers. At any moment those preachers might call you up front and demand that you kneel down before the long steel cross that hung from the rafters. The evangelicals made you afraid of God.

Rev. Starke was a whole different bird. He was always polished and at ease, and he never perspired. His manner was smooth, like a comedian or talk show host. His sermons were full of humorous anecdotes, illustrations from everyday life, references to current sports events. Full of everything but what Sis had craved most in life this past decade and a half— certainty, fixed and unshakable, motionless as Mt. Gilead's unmovable cross.

The preacher stepped to the center of the mourners, coughing twice into his fist, his polite way of taking command and quieting the murmuring crowd. Sis did what the rest did: she stared at her candle's flame, which danced wildly as it gorged itself on the wax.

"Thank you all for coming tonight. I spoke with Brother Dub this afternoon, and he thanks you as well. He hopes you'll understand that with things unresolved as they are he can't be here tonight, and he asks that you continue to pray for little Chance." His voice was low and soothing. Sis thought of how interchangeable it was from Shiloh Baptist's preacher. Then Rev.

Starke loudly inhaled, taking a long dramatic pause that intensified the brittle passing of an October breeze.

Sis felt her father's hand on her back, as much for his own sake as hers. Clinton hadn't attended the vigil for Patty, years back; he had insisted on staying home to take refuge in a routine of chores that had to be done, regardless of how God tried to interfere with them.

"I see most of you are looking at your candles. I understand why. Moments like these are awkward. Because it is incomprehensible to us that a child could simply vanish from our midst, we're afraid to look to each other to provide an answer. We let ourselves assume that if we individually lack that answer our neighbor must as well. Because in my heart I confess to being baffled, I certainly can't count on Harold Purvis here to my right or Joanna Parker down there by the gully to give me some solace. What could they possibly know that I don't? That's what we're saying to ourselves. And so we turn our eyes away from each other to the one thing in our presence that seems alive—this light in front of us that one minute trembles and the next flexes itself, strong and upright.

"I have no problem with you looking into that flame. Fire is among the most holy of our symbols. In Jeremiah we are told that Lord's word is like fire, and from Deuteronomy we know that God is a consuming fire. So as you feel that heat, the burning wax—feel it for what it is: the earthly breath of divinity, here to purify you of all doubt.

"I say this to you because I want you to know there's another kind of fire, a deceitful sort. It's flashy, and it lulls us into despair. When I was in college they taught us a fancy word for it: *Ignis fatuus*—that's Latin for the phony fire. It's the fire of destruction, and it hypnotizes us with the power to render all matter, all substance into nothingness. So as you stare at those candles, think of the fire of the stars and the sun and of the fire that illuminates, not of the fire of ash and dust. Know that the false fire exists, but guard against it. Whatever you do, don't stare at it too long, because it'll invert you, deaden you, twist your soul to a pretzel knot."

He stopped for a moment, taking another deep breath, as though savoring the air. "You need to know about the phony fire because I sense some of you giving in to hopelessness. Those of you thinking the worst, believing that Chance couldn't possibly be with us after a week gone by now, you've allowed that doubt to kindle until, like the flame in your hand, it would scorch you, leaving you with a mark of your own powerlessness. You think we can't protect ourselves against whatever's lurking around us. Well, if that's the case—if you're one of those doubters—you might as well snuff out that candle, because you're allowing yourself to stand in the darkness without hope. I tell you: do not choose to stand in the darkness—choose to stand *up* to it! Don't buy into the idea of randomness! Don't believe in coincidence or accident! All that happens happens for a reason, for the fulfillment of a majestic design that isn't ours to question but to submit to!

"It's your duty not to give in, regardless of what happens. Remember the words of the apostle Paul to the Colossians: 'Parents, do not embitter your children, or they will become discouraged.' Before we pray I want all the young folks here to step to the middle of this gathering ground with me. Come on now, don't be shy, little ones. It's for you as well as Chance that we come here this night."

Slowly the half-dozen children who'd accompanied their parents gathered around Rev. Starke, who stooped and then stretched to gather them in the breadth of his wingspan.

"You grown ups, you look to the faces of these children. When you put them to bed this evening, I want you to kiss their foreheads. I want you to taste the salt of their skin, for that's the essence of innocence. It's your duty to preserve that sweet simplicity! If you whisper one unhoping word, allow yourself to question *even if it's in the silent chamber of your soul*, you steal *their* opportunity to believe as certainly as if you'd put a pillow case over their pretty, sleeping faces."

The children were motionless, eyes inflated with fear at the thought of their mothers and fathers sneaking into their rooms and interrupting their dreams. Rev. Starke reassuringly mussed the hair of one youngster before returning them to their parents with a gentle push of his palms.

"Let us bow our heads. . . ."

The group obeyed, but Sis kept her eyes open and her head locked straight. As Rev. Starke implored the Lord, his tone seemed all wrong to her. He spoke with gentle authority, like an adult trying to reason with a toddler. The crowd was lulled. They had no fear, no sense of danger, of being besieged. She was convinced that Preacher *had* to believe at this late date that something irrevocable had happened to the child. It defied common sense not to. An eight-year-old could not live a week on a creek bank. An eight-year-old could not go a week without being found. Sis felt her father's hand again at the nub of her spine, and she resented it just as she resented being here, being a part of this group and this ritual, staged to reaffirm a faltering communal fiction. Her father's hand was a reminder that she was obliged to share Rev. Starke's unshaken confidence and agree that whatever is is right. As Preacher thanked God for his blessings, Sis squeezed the melting candle until the wax burned the insides of her fingers.

"Amen," the minister finally declared. Heads lifted in unison. "In just a half-moment, we're going to extinguish these candles. And when we do I want you to remember that even though that light is gone from sight, it remains within you. Now I'm going to count to three, and when we hit that three, we'll blow them out— but together now, all right? One—two—three—"

Three dozen people jointly exhaled. Silence accompanied the sudden darkness—but not because nobody knew how to discretely leave McCrea's Hill and slip back into the stream of their busy lives without offending the fact of a boy being gone. The quiet arose because people were wondering to themselves why Sis blew her candle out on the count of two.

"YOU DON'T SEEM YOURSELF tonight," Rev. Starke told her as the crowd dispersed. They stood at the outer edge of the field, Sis balancing her cardboard box on a fencepost. The newly deposited candles were re-hardening, their drippings drying in one gelatinous lump. Now the box would sit in a fellowship hall closet until Christmas—or until the next tragedy, whichever. Out of the corner of her eye she watched her father make small talk with Donnie Gibson, a redheaded farmer whose land lay within walking distance of Mt. Gilead. "Twenty minutes"—his voice rang like a church bell—"I do believe that's a record short one for the reverend."

"How are you holding up?"

"I'm fine. Just a long stretch of days, that's all."

"I'm worried about you. I know this has to hit you harder than the others. I'd half-thought you'd come see me this week. I was tempted to drop by, but. . . ."

"There are more important things than me, Brother Rick. I know that."

"I noticed you didn't like Colossians as the Scripture. What wisdom would you give those who came out tonight?"

"You're quizzing me."

"Maybe you'd say nothing?"

"No, I know that'd be all wrong. I guess maybe I'd go for something a little less—"

"Starry-eyed? Pie in the sky?"

"Now you're choosing my words for me."

"I'm sorry. You'll have to forgive me. You know, in all the years I've stood in a pulpit, I never really knew someone who lost her faith. Most folks, they take it for granted. And I don't mean that in a bad way. They come to church and Sunday school, and they do their home Bible study, but they don't *wrestle* with it. They believe in God in the way they believe that breakfast is the morning meal and supper comes at night."

"You think I'm wrestling."

She didn't ask it as a question. Rev. Starke's stare was dead weight on her shoulders.

"I think you're just about pinned to the mat."

She started to cry. She didn't understand how it began so quickly—she felt nothing, and then her eyes and then her face was wet and flushed. She wiped at her cheeks with her thumbs, afraid Rev. Starke would try to console her. Then she cried harder, wondering when and how she became too hardened for consolation.

"Do you know how many people admire you, Sis? You must understand that. I don't think I've spoken with anyone here who hasn't held you up as a role model. All I ever hear is 'If I'm done wrong I hope I can hold up like that Sis Pruitt's done.' That has to give you some assurance that you've done the right thing."

"But that's it . . . *that's just it.* In the last week, since all this, I've begun to think, to realize really, that I've been dishonest. Not lying, I mean, but not up front or out in the open all these years. Working with my POMC chapter, visiting all those families, making the quilt—it's all been out of anger. And not at whom you might think, either. It's anger at *them,* at the people who come to hold their candles for a few moments—as if that does any good— anger at people like you who think that a verse or two is some kind of salve, anger at God."

"You can't appreciate the good you've done? Good that's come out of that rage?"

"If I could, wouldn't you think at some point that it, this feeling, this bitterness, would stop? I mean, I feel like a dormant volcano. I've kept my marriage intact and I've had two more children. I've allowed people to believe that the lava's cooling, that if I haven't gotten over it—I doubt anybody expects that to happen—but at least I've coped well. But I'm tired of doing the right thing. I'm tired of this churning inside. I'm waiting for a spark to set me off. . . . You know what he says, don't you?"

She gestured toward her father, waiting alone in the truck, Donnie having headed home. His profile was squat and square-chinned. He was in his mid-eighties but had yet to suffer much erosion of old age.

"No telling what old Clinton would say."

"He says I ought to have my own TV show. Like that guy on *America's Most Wanted.* He gets to remind everyone every week that his boy was murdered, and he gets his revenge every Saturday night. Every time he calls one of those fugitives a scumbag, you can see his face light up with righteous pleasure. That's what I want. I want to call someone names, and I want a stage to do it on."

"But with letting go there's peace, too. Isn't seventeen years long enough? Patty knows what you've done for her. She wouldn't begrudge you getting on with your life. She knows you have a responsibility to Tillie and Joey."

Sis shook her head. "It was so easy for the rest of them to let her go. That's why I can't. She was barely in the ground a month before Pete had her room boxed up and in storage. I think he was afraid I'd turn her room into a shrine."

The reverend took hold of her hands. His touch was cold.

"Go home, Sis. Let yourself enjoy your life, your family. Nobody expects more from you than you've already given, not even Patty."

She pulled her hands from his to wipe her face again, this time with her palms. As she lowered her wrists, the minister had her locked in an embrace she didn't want, but she allowed him to pat her back, just as her father had during the vigil. She was thinking of what she wished she had the courage to tell him: *You're only saying there's peace so I'll shut up and keep it to myself. It's been seventeen years and three months and twenty-one days and everybody here thinks the same: when has it been long enough not to hurt?*

Back at the car, Clinton, nonplused, slid his old bones past the stick shift and into the passenger's seat so that she could drive. "He give you a good talking-to?"

"You don't need to be so delicate. I'm not that fragile."

Her father tucked a fingerful of tobacco behind his lower lip, which then bulged as if swollen. "No, I don't reckon anyone'd ever accuse you of being fragile. That wouldn't sit at all."

She started the car. "I'm hungry. You got room with all that chew for some cheesecake? Mom had one in the oven for dessert when I dropped the kids off. There ought to be a slice or two left, if the kids haven't devoured it all."

"I can make room. Might even have some ice cream in the deep freeze. Was it you or Martha that wouldn't eat ice cream without vanilla wafers? "

"That was Martha, Dad. We couldn't afford wafers when it was just me. Come to think of it, we couldn't afford ice cream. We had to make ours out of snow."

"We never had it that rough. You're inventing."

"No, you're just not remembering right. You better work on that. Remember how you used to come home from Smiley's Mill with one cream soda and three straws?"

"It don't hurt to go without sometimes. Maybe your sister'd be more settled if I'd'a brought four straws home when she was small."

"You should've made her eat snow more often, too."

She drove, transfixed by the way her headlights spilled across the asphalt, the long yellow beams bringing into relief the pocks of the asphalt. Through the side windows she saw the low-cut shadows of the recently combined cornstalks. Her father was silent except for the muffled scratch of his down vest on the vinyl car seat as he adjusted his cap. He was always fiddling with it, a nervous gesture developed from long years of tractor driving. Sis found the quiet saddening; it was as if the world has been broken open and drained of meaning, leaving only the opaque blackness, void except for the occasional curls of light that fringed the sky's crust. As the truck gained speed, the curvature of the road seemed to carry the wheels in its own line of flight; Sis realized she could steer with just two fingers. She wasn't tired but she felt lightheaded, removed from the physical immediacy of her motion. What finally engaged her was a butter yellow glow that lingered in a thin mist above the horizon. It was perhaps a mile or two to the northeast, not far from her great aunt Opal's old homestead, which in the four years since Opal's death now had been rented out to six different families. The illumination was too porous to be from a car headlamp or a porch light. It hung just above the horizon, like the fiery embers of some celestial fallout. Had central Indiana been hit by a meteorite?

"You running errands before we get that cheesecake? You missed the turn off."

"Just taking the roundabout, Dad."

As the road bent to accommodate the jut of another field the eerie light intensified. Sis was struck by the soupy, concentrated glow, a mystical combustion. She tried to think of sunshine, of the warmth that brought life to terrestrial shadow. She couldn't remember what it was like to lie in the warmth of a fireplace or a camp fire; all she had felt for years was the furnace blister of her resentment, her desire to strike back. The light was orange now. It bled through the night, seeping around the orchards and homes, the tractor sheds and cattle pens, crowning the land with an unholy halo.

Sis tried to let her thoughts go. They were silly. Nature was neither good nor malevolent—it just was. A dumb, blank thing without morals, without notions of right and wrong. She thought of Rev. Starke's words: *Fire is among the most holy of our symbols.* What is a symbol? It's what we make it be, she told herself. To the nothingness of nature we affix a meaning that isn't really there.

Sis knew that daylight would allow her to take these questions for granted. A milk-gray haze would cover the land; it was a regular feature of the Indiana autumn. There would be rain and then snow, the earth would harden and freeze, and her days would be consumed with making meals, calling meetings, finding diversions for her kids. And then when she least suspected it another night like this would bring to mind the image of a man and a girl wrestling in a cornfield. She would experience the image of Patty garroted with her brassiere as she had throughout these long years—at once with the dead weight of familiarity (again, she would think, here it is *again*) and yet freshly painful, as if it were hitting her for the first time. Always and again, for the first time. This, she realized, was and would be her life.

The glow was no longer in front of the truck. She and her father were nearly parallel to it. Then the corn patch to her right gave way, and the light unveiled itself to her from the cleared plot of an old homestead.

It was fire.

Even though it was twenty yards from the road, Sis was startled enough to brake and swerve in the opposite direction. Clinton fell against her side, grunting heavily. For a second Sis's hands left the steering wheel as she tried to balance herself, then she mashed her foot on the brake petal and the truck jerked to a stop.

A gutted barn crackled in an orange embrace of flame. At a safe distance from the burning wood stood a half-circle of spectators who seemed to stare dumbly at the gyrating fire.

"There's no way it could have touched us," Sis said, as though to reassure her father, and not herself. Clinton struggled to pull himself upright.

She heard a tap at her window and saw Rev. Starke, who had been following not far behind, motioning for her to roll down the window. "Everybody all right?"

"We're fine. Everything's fine."

Some of the spectators jumped the drainage ditch and were running to the truck. Caught between the fire and Sis's headlamps, they looked like demons with misshapen heads, blackened by smoke. Sis had heard stories about strange goings-on in the unassuming countryside—mutilated animals, symbols scratched into the ground, pentagrams fashioned out of charred sticks. She wasn't sure she'd even know these people if it were daylight.

"That's the old Blankenship barn," one of the demons said, approaching her window. She realized that was a helmet parked atop his head and that he and the others wore heavy coats. They were volunteer members of the Marietta fire department. "County inspector says she's gotta come down. Old man Blankenship left some hay in her. Says he wanted her to go out with a big flash."

"He got his wish."

A central timber split and yanked a section of frame to the ground, spitting up a cloud of embers that shower back down like fireworks.

"Kinda beautiful," one fireman said.

"Not quite the word I would use," Preacher said. He leaned into the window, whispering, "*Ignis fatuus, ignis fatuus.*"

Sis closed her eyes. The lids felt heavy, fitted with a coat of iron. When the firemen returned to the barn she started the truck again and waited for her minister's car to pass her. Then she doubled back toward the missed turn, trying to ignore the barn's reflection in the rearview mirror. She found she couldn't help herself, however. There *was* something beautiful in the limber, arching strokes of light. She had to brake suddenly once more when because of her inattention the passenger's side wheels slipped off the pavement.

Her father spoke in a frustrated, parental voice that Sis didn't believe she'd heard in forty years. "You better pull over and let me drive. I'd like to get home alive."

AT HER MOTHER AND father's farm: the first thing she saw stepping into the kitchen was Joey with a crayon stuck sideways in his mouth like the bit of a horse harness. Waxy purple scrawls decorated his belly. A few feet away, Tillie lay prostrate on the carpet scissoring at a sheet of construction paper half her size.

"Neither of you has had a bath yet? I guess grandma's fallen down on the job."

"Bathing children isn't your mother's job," her father snapped. He stood before the open freezer, looking for ice cream, still irritated that she never pulled over to let him drive. Sis decided to let it pass.

"*You,*" she told Joey, "go get your clothes off. You're hitting the tub before we go home. And you"—Tillie pretended to have suddenly gone deaf—"you get the floor in shape."

Neither child budged.

"First one done gets the ice cream," their grandfather offered, scooping servings into tiny plastic bowls. That worked: the children snapped to life.

"I give up." Sis removed her coat and went to the living room, expecting to find her mother playing dominos in front of the television. Instead, a stranger sat stiffly in the good recliner, with her mom relegated to the worn davenport. The two of them shared the uncomfortable look of people who ran out of things to talk about a half-hour earlier.

Sis let out an awkward hello, and the man stood. He was shorter than his beefy command of the recliner would suggest—

only an inch or two taller than Sis herself. His face seemed younger than his presence, too. Sis figured him to be only in his late twenties—a puny number of years, a boy's. Even under a half-week's worth of stubble, his skin looked bright and fresh, undeterred, marred only by a light crease in the corner of his top lip.

"Mrs. Pruitt, I need to speak with you. My name is Robert Heim."

LATER, SEATED AT THE kitchen table, Sis watched Heim eat a generous portion of cheesecake ladled with vanilla ice cream. Declining coffee, he had already downed two glasses of water and was about to ask for a third. Her parents had the children in the back bathroom. From behind the walls Sis could hear water dumping into the tub.

"He talked a lot about you." Heim ate as fast as he chewed, though never at the same time. He struck Sis as someone who worked hard to hone his energy. "You struck him as 'intent'— that's what he kept saying."

"I don't know that means."

"Honestly? I don't either, but the thing you need to understand about Colin is that the more he talks the less sense he makes. I must've heard your name a thousand times. That's why I came here—I mean your home. Your neighbor at the next farm over gave me directions to your folks' here. I was hoping to find my Suburban in either driveway. I don't know where Colin is if he hasn't been to see you."

"I only saw him the two times, like I said. The first I don't really remember, but the second time, he frightened me. That's funny what you say about him talking. He was going a million

breathing out the ghost

miles an hour in my drive, but it wasn't off the cuff. Every word sounded rehearsed, labored over even. I had the feeling he'd been waiting for a long time to say those things—to anyone who'd listen. I couldn't tell you what all he was talking about. I just remember *how* he sounded. It wasn't like music, but it was musical"—she laughed awkwardly— "as if that makes any kind of sense."

"I know what you mean. The first time we ever spoke, over the phone, he went on and on, and then he broke up, or broke down, I mean, sobbing, not crying, and he apologized. He said, 'I've got logorrhea.' I'd never heard that word before. He's wordy, he thinks in words—he sees them laid out on paper as he talks."

Sis refilled Heim's glass, and their hands touched. He swallowed the water in a few long gulps that set his Adam's apple bobbing, then continued. "He told me a long time ago how the words will hit him every once in a while: 'Lost boy.' You think about it, and you can't. 'Too mythic,' he would say. You think of Peter Pan. You think of Oliver Twist and the Artful Dodger. You think of the Lindbergh baby, and before him, little Charley Ross. Do you know that story? I didn't, not until Colin told it to me. That's like him, too. Every formative event in his life, and he goes and reads a book about it. Little Charley Ross—I guess you could call him the first famous lost boy, the original Etan Patz. He was four years old, back in the 1870s I think it was, kidnapped by a couple of grifters. The police screwed up and killed them in a shoot out, and they never found the boy. For the rest of his life, the father would go from town to town to investigate a sighting or to check out someone claiming to be his son. The poor guy never knew there were so many brown-eyed, curly-haired kids around. You know what's really weird? The father's name. His name was Christian. Seriously. It adds a whole parable dimension to the story." He clicked his fingers against his glass. "I think Colin sees himself as that guy. He has to *be* that guy. Like anything less would be abandoning A.J. I've asked him: 'How do you abandon someone who's lost?'"

"What does he say?"

Heim shrugged. "He says I could never understand unless it was my kid. But I think he's wrong. When he first came to me about this case, I didn't want anything to do with it. I'd seen a million movies about lost children. I always thought their appeal was too easy. I mean, they'd take someone and put them through this horrible ordeal. The whole point seemed to be to show how well a person could survive, bloody but unbowed and able to transcend all the agony. I guess that's supposed to be uplifting. I believe in all that faith in human endurance stuff, don't get me wrong. But those stories struck me as self-congratulation, underhandedly sentimental, slightly obscene. But after meeting Colin, I don't think that way. A missing child speaks to something deeper in us, something harder to abide. It's some original loss, an inherited absence we're made to live with. We can't say quite what it is. Just some sense of something missing, something we'll never get back because we never had it, you know?"

Heim brushed his hand across his forehead, as though his head ached from putting his thoughts into words. "Ever since I met Colin and Kimm—that's his wife—I haven't been able to look at my children the same way. I think of every possible way I might lose them. I tell myself I should enjoy every second I'm with them, but I'm too busy thinking it could all vanish if I turn my back. That's what the story of a missing child does to us. We go on in time, but we stop living. I've been trying to give Colin his life back, but in some ways, he's way ahead of me. He doesn't want it anymore because he thinks he never really ever had it."

The water from the bath suddenly stopped; Sis wished Heim would lower his voice, fearing her parents and her children would overhear the conversation. "I think he looks at you to see how he *could* have gone on living, of getting by despite that hole in the soul. You two really couldn't be more opposite. Think about how people suffer, what they do with their suffering. There are two roads. There are people who manage, who cope. Remember those old commercials, those Timex commercials? Silly as it sounds, that's what some do: they *take a licking and keep on ticking*. Whatever happens, they endure, and they find dignity in perseverance. From what I know, that's you. Others—Colin— they see themselves as kamikazes. They think it's nobler to go down in flames."

"Maybe it *is* nobler," Sis said. Maybe perseverance is really just passivity. And if there's dignity, well, I haven't found it yet. Actually, I kind of envy him. There's been so many times that I've been disgusted with myself for 'taking it,' as you say. I'd like to give back as good as I've gotten, too."

She could tell she'd caught Heim off guard. "Yes," he said slowly. "But you have to know what you're fighting against when you fight back. Otherwise, you're just lashing out. And that's usually when the shrapnel hits the bystanders."

Heim didn't blink or avert his eyes; he was everything St. Claire wasn't—solid, steady, machine-like. The only imperfection was that creased lip. The more she looked at it, the more she tried to dissuade herself it wasn't what it looked like: the scab of a fresh split.

"Something happened between the both of you, didn't it? It must have for him to run off with your car and strand you."

"It's better if you don't know about all that. But I've got to find him. I have a few ideas where else he might have gone, but I'd like to leave you my cell phone number. In case he comes back."

Before Sis could fetch pencil and paper, the phone rang. It was Pete, home finally from the bottomland. She turned her back to Heim and stepped into the living room for privacy. She asked politely about his day, feeling guilty for not telling him about this man, just as she had failed to tell him about St. Claire. She assured her husband that she and the kids would be home soon. When she returned to the kitchen, Heim sat with his own cell phone to his head, smiling.

"You reminded me I'd forgotten to call my wife." He closed the lid and slipped it back into his pocket. "I feel horrible. I've had to lie to her about all this, and I'm running out of excuses. I don't know if she could understand why I'm doing this, chasing after Colin like I'm his shadow or something. I started out trying to save him, but now I'm in the position of having to save myself—a piece of myself: my beliefs. Well, you see what happens when get involved with him. You end up doing nothing but talking, talking, talking. . . . If you get me something to write with, I'll be on my way."

He scratched his number on the back of an envelope and then Sis followed him to the porch where she watched him climb into a truck that was too shiny and polished to be anything other than rented. She remained even after his departure, staring past the gray face of a crescent moon. She always seemed to be watching men zoom away toward some hasty horizon—first her father in her childhood and then Pete in her marriage and now St. Claire and Heim. She strained to see some lingering sign of the barn fire, but there wasn't any—the night was just one long strobe of darkness, unfurling.

Sis thought of St. Claire, somewhere out in the pitch black, careening like a planet gone out of its orbit.

She felt heavy in her own motionlessness. She imagined her feet growing through the bottoms of her shoes, her toes burrowing through the concrete of the porch to stretch deep into the layers of alluvium and shale that packed the ground, shoots and rhizomes binding her to this place, this spot. *This is my Midwest,* she thought. *My Indiana, my life. I am just an outgrowth, a stem of something deeper.* She lifted a foot to make sure that it was just a crazy thought in a head that had lately been crammed full of them.

Still—she felt rooted.

in nomine diaboli

Have you ever wondered what would've happened to Ahab had he gotten his whale?

Say that in those last moments of the chase he hadn't got caught in the harpoon line. Say he hadn't been jerked neck first into the wake to become a dangling fob at the end of his own barb. Say he and his madman crew managed a fatal lance that laid his enemy to waste. Imagine the joy that would spread across his scarred face as he danced a jig atop the carcass, his peg leg defiantly wedged in the blowhole. Imagine the wad he'd shoot as he watched the blubber stripped and boiled in the try-pots. What next? How would he get back to the land of the living? He'd head home to Nantucket. To love his wife. To be happy. To raise his boy.

It's a detail little remarked upon, you know, that Ahab had a young son.

Or more apropos of us, to you and me, A.J.: what if he hadn't been bowstrung, but the flying turn still tore astray of its groove. What if the eye-splice knot at the rope's end still shot straight out of the boat so the whale was able to slip away, wounded but not willing to let itself get carved into decorative candles for landlubbers? Imagine the old man's dismay as he sees the thing escape, leaving only a trail of chum swirling in the backwash. How could he return to the land of the living then? He'd row away, go home. He'd brag about his deeds to the old salts in the beer stalls. He'd assure his wife he had straightened out his soul.

At night he'd creep into his son's room and whisper in the boy's ear: *I did it for you.* And yet he'd never be able to just be content. Because if he were, he'd have to be normal.

Could he do that? Once he stood, a mighty speck on an ocean, daring the lightning to strike. Now he'd have to contend with a wife wanting to know why he thinks he's too good to take out the trash. He'd probably end up staring at the sea, misty-eyed, recalling how the anger once gave his life purpose. I hear him saying, "Happiness is like the horizon of calm water days—infinite, awesome, tedious. Where's that razor's edge I used to walk?" That's why the story ends the way it does. It has to. Anything less would disappoint.

At least that's what they'd have us believe. To be alive, really alive, you must bear the burden of being deep. Lug that cross of discontent. Do you know, little man, the first emotion in all of literature? Call it what you will: wrath, rage, ire. *Sing, O goddess, the anger of Achilles, son of Peleus, that brought countless ills upon the Achaeans. Many a brave soul did it send hurrying down to Hades, and many a hero did it yield a prey to dogs and vultures, for so were the counsels of Jove fulfilled from the day on which the son of Atreus, king of men, and great Achilles, first fell out with one another. . . .* That's *The Iliad.* Go look it up. But if the reference is too arcane for you, remember the song with the slinky riff that I used to pluck out on the guitar. The best line in the whole thing: *I wish I was like you—easily amused.* What a devastating putdown for those without the misery to love company. Yes, it was once quite nice to think shallow people had it easy. No needs, no wants, no problems. And that we, by contrast, were special because—why? Because we could never settle, could never compromise. Perpetual disappointment was a sign that the needles of our machinery were more finely tuned. It meant we were *sensitive*. Like a seismometer, we were privy to those faraway vibrations lesser folks could never detect.

But that was then. You know what I think now?

I think the shallowest ones are those who want to believe that they're deep.

Like me.

Oh, yes—and him.

I WISH I COULD tell you what the wormwood and gall was that ate away at your grandfather. He had a job that paid some money. He had a house that threw down a decent patch of shade. He had us. What more was there? He should not have been a blasted man. And yet that's how I remember him, clinging to his discontent in the fierce belief that if he let it go he might cease to exist. Your aunts and uncle and I heaped the weight of our father's melancholy upon ourselves, blaming ourselves. We knew what people said. We could do the math. *He's twenty-seven—with a ten-year-old?* And later: *He's thirty— with a thirteen year old?* We grew up thinking we were living proof that babies shouldn't make babies. At least *I* grew up that way. A moral to a story. In every angry glare, every eruption of *pissitude,* I saw who he blamed. He couldn't look at me as anything but the sum total of what he'd missed out on in life. But I shouldn't hog all the glory. It affected the others, too. Your aunt Cassie can't resist sleeping with nearly every fifty-year-old man she meets because she craves—what's the word she always uses?—oh yes—*approval.*

At some point—I can't say when—I began to believe that the resentment he projected upon us (me) was a sort of inverted vanity. It was the dream of being tragic. Maybe he wished he'd been on one of those missions—just once in his life—where the group leader says, "Boys, some of you won't be coming back." Maybe he wished he'd gone down in a blaze of glory. Whatever.

When I think of him now I think of someone who brooded because he was better at that than at golf, tennis, or softball. Your uncle Robbie can talk all he wants about the chemistry of emotions, about how happiness is a matter of scientifically leveling off the fluids. We all have our theories. Your great-grandmother believes that he off'd himself *though if you think about it, there's damn easier ways than with a myocardial infarction.* Your grandmother once said that a heart attack doesn't result from a broken heart but from a surplus of it. We all have to convince ourselves of something.

I know better. What got him was the goiter—the goiter of egotism.

It's a hereditary condition.

There is a dark, mad mystery in some human hearts, which, sometimes, during the tyranny of the usurper mood, leads them to be all eagerness to cast off the most intense beloved bond, as a hindrance to the attainment of whatever transcendental object that usurper mood so tyrannically suggests. Then the beloved bond seems to hold us to no essential good; lifted to exalted mounts, we can dispense with all the vale; endearments we spurn; kisses are like blisters to us; and forsaking the palpitating forms of love, we emptily embrace the boundless and unbodied air.

Translation: When you have nothing else in life, your problems are your pride.

I suppose I knew it would end up this way. I could feel him growing out my brows, bleeding out my skin. His kisses blistering mine. I could feel me becoming him.

I didn't want to. I wanted my life to toe a line. Your love was the line I wanted to toe.

What did I have when I didn't find you? Nothing but the anger that was my inheritance.

The terrifying thing is to know it was in me even before you were gone.

I tried to talk about it with your mother once. We had a fight about why I pushed you so hard, why I wanted so much from you. It wasn't that she needed an explanation; she wanted me to understand for my own sake, as well as for yours. But the sad fact is that what's dark in you never seems quite so profound when it's brought to light. I realized that as I found myself fumbling my words. They sounded superficial to me–how could they not seem silly to her? Nothing but wind from a bore—self-preoccupied, self-crucified, self-deceived wind. How could I explain to her that what I really wanted was to dissolve until all that remained of me was instinct and intuition, until I was nothing but energy without introspection, motion without mood. I wanted out of *me*.

You can imagine her response. "You should see someone," she said. The idea was horrifying. How common, how jejune. To talk out loud about myself at that point would have meant that I was nothing but the product of the oldest story in the world: *Adam raised a Cain*. I couldn't do it, not even after she flipped through the yellow pages and scheduled me for an appointment–which I skipped. I didn't go because what I had to say would have merely seemed most simple

most ordinary

and therefore

most terrible.

Seek your father and you search for God. Search for your son and you seek what you were never able to be.

If I could go back and relive that conversation with your mother, I would explain myself with a line from a movie I saw once in college. The movie was unintentionally funny, so the line skirts parody, but it still speaks to the relief of absolute emptiness: *I turn my eyes to the inside, and I dig the vacuum.*

And that right there is the problem. When I see myself I don't see anything organic, anything original. I steal my aphorisms from outside sources. My actions pantomime the exploits of others. I'm all imitation, a gloss of a citation. Somewhere along the line I began compiling myself from the excerpts of better men.

That's the difference between your grandfather and me. I couldn't tell you where he got his spleen. He never read, never went to movies. He'd have thought it silly to think of himself as the Ahab of the interstate. But for me, plagiarism was predestination. Words were my peg leg, rubbing raw the wound as surely as the old captain's did. (It's another little remarked upon fact that Ahab's first artificial limb snapped, spearing him in the groin and emasculating him). I believed in words as I believed in gods. I was idolatrous. I could sing pretty about the shapes they made on a page, how their bodies ride certain curves to carry our eyes along a line of print, how their extremities carry the weight of that line.

I believed in the stories told by those lines, too, in the men whose lives I thought I was meant to emulate.

What was it about those men, all those men in all those stories that made me want to be them?

They were fallen because they were doomed to be felled. And they were felled because they couldn't accept that they were fallen.

But that's really horseshit. I know that now.

What I really got from books was the same thing your grandfather got from breaking glasses and punching walls: the belief that you're only truly alive if you're a match strike away from immolation. That's how you figure out that idolatry's real name is Narcissus. I found in the words the truths I wanted to hear. Go before you get old. Burn out before fading away. It's all a grand excuse for interring yourself in your own head. Once you're there, you never have to venture out.

So now I know that the words aren't what I thought they were. They've become empty containers to me, shapes to fill a space. Beyond the slants and serifs—*nada*. Remember that typeface I was calling *Chance*? *Vanity* would have been a better name, or better yet (remember the Hebrew, my boy), *Vapor* or *Breath*—but no matter. Those pages made for a nice confetti shower just past the state line.

The same for the homemade maps charting my season on the line, the clippings, the journals. It's all gone.

Now I know I would like to have read only words that I was certain weren't about me.

I would like to have read books in which I didn't imagine myself the hero.

I would like to have stayed home, where I could wake up and enjoy the mussed bed, the smell of the coffee, the spoon rattling in the throat of the almost-empty jelly jar.

I wish I'd lived an orderly life.

I would like to have loved your mother better.

But that was then. By taking to the road I took an oath. I didn't realize it, but I did. Why stop my cribbing now? *Ego non baptizo te in nomine patris, sed in nomine diaboli.* I baptize you not in the name of God but in the name of the devil. Now there's no more you, and there never was a me. The lives that were ours, the people we thought we were—we're just their ghosts.

I probably had it all assward, anyway. My luck, Dickie probably *didn't* have anything to do with you. But we'll never know.

Ding dong, the Dickie's dead.

There's only one road open for me now. When you can't go back, you can only go forward. There's logic to that if you think about it hard enough.

In the meantime, I have speed to keep me company. The pills are a treat. Something there is to an amphetamine to make you lean and mean. The euphoria, the inflated sense of invulnerability—just the kick in the pants I need to take myself out.

But first thing's first. I've got to find a boy. If not my own, any will do.

what martha said

"And you haven't told Pete *any* of this?"

Sis didn't like the look on her sister's face. Martha sat, a cigarette in one hand and a doll baby's head in the other. Scattered around her feet on the Pruitts' living room floor were the porcelain torsos and limbs that she'd cast in her shop kiln that week.

"I know what you're thinking, and you're wrong."

She stopped tending the heap of folded laundry on the couch long enough to wag her finger. Martha took a drag and held the baby's head up as if it were impaled on her fist. As a child one of her prized toys had been a ventriloquist's dummy, so she often interacted with her dolls as if she were doing a Charlie McCarthy routine.

"Hmm. Two different men in a week and you haven't said a thing to your husband. I don't know. Sounds like trouble to me."

"I know nothing would give you more pleasure than to think there's a problem in my marriage, but you're wrong."

"Oh, come on. Everyone's got problems."

"I know that. I'm talking real ones."

Martha rested her cigarette in the ashtray and began fitting the plastic head to a neck socket. From the guest room she and Sis could both hear their grandmother's shallow, unsteady rest-breathing. Sis was watching Ethel for the day while her parents attended a historical society meeting up in Indianapolis.

"I'm just saying that when you don't tell your spouse everything, you're hiding something. You think Rick ever mentioned the chirpy in his ceramics class? Hell, no. The first I

222

heard of her was when he said they were moving up to Whiteland together. If you don't want to heed the voice of experience, that's all right by me."

"How about we change the subject?"

"I just wonder why this man—what'd you say his name was? St. Cloud?"

"St. Claire."

"I just wonder why he thinks *you*'d know anything about his son."

Sis scooped up a pile of clothes to carry to the kids' bedrooms. "It's not about his son, really. That's what his friend said. He just sees the route we went, me and the others in our POMC chapter—and he wishes he could have gone on that way. You know, moving on, soldiering forth, perseverance. All that."

"Uh-huh. St. Claire. Well, he doesn't sound that saintly to me." She laughed. "St. Claire, coming to bow at the shrine of St. Sis, our lady of perpetual perseverance."

Annoyed, Sis went to Tillie's room and yanked a dresser drawer open. The socks and panties were all a-jumble; the child refused to keep her clothes in the orderly rows that her mother made for her. As she dumped the drawer's contents on the bed and began separating them, she thought about what Martha said. Martha always made snide comments like that, suggesting she resented how people thought of Sis. *St. Sis?* Sis had never lobbied for canonization. She didn't want to be Mother Mary to anyone but her own kids. But Martha insisted on insinuating that Sis had been sanctified by tragedy, as if that were some kind of reward. She was still mad by the time she finished straightening the drawer. The stacks of undies and socks weren't much more orderly than they'd been.

When Sis returned to the living room, Martha had finished assembling the doll. She was bouncing the immobile body on her knee. "That's about half weird what you're doing there," Sis told her sister tartly.

Martha pinched her eyes at her sister, stubbed out the cigarette, and began dressing the doll in a lacy gown she'd sewn herself.

SHORTLY BEFORE LUNCH, PETE called on the two-way. If the weather held and the rain didn't start again, he could finish harvesting the bottomland that night.

"You calling to place a dinner order?"

Sis let out the talk handle, and the Pruitts' kitchen filled with squawking static. It struck her as silly to communicate through a two-way in an age of cell phones, but Pete was adamant that they weren't getting rid of the radio. He'd seen enough changes in farm life, he insisted.

"What you got on the pot?"

"Well, nothing. I just didn't realize how late it was. It's Martha's fault—" She said this jokingly, making a face at her sister through the doorway to the living room—"She's been talking my ear off all morning."

"That don't surprise me none. Well, listen, it's for the best. I'm gonna keep on going instead of breaking to eat. I just heard on the radio we're supposed to dip under thirty tonight. We may even get a snow blanket."

Sis checked the kitchen window. The sky was overcast, but the gray didn't look formidable enough for snow.

"I need you to bring me a sandwich and another thermos out here. You got the time for that?"

6reathing out the ghost

Sis wondered if that remark was supposed to mean something. She decided to let it pass. She was always deciding to let things pass. "I'll be out there in a few," she said, and signed off.

She brewed fresh coffee and heated some ham for a sandwich. After she packed the lunch sack and filled the thermos, she asked Martha to watch Ethel and the kids while she made the short run to the bottomlands. Martha cocked her brow, pretending to be imposed upon, and went back to dressing her doll.

Outside, the temperature was indeed falling; the mini-van door handle had an unexpected bite to it. Heading over a series of sloping roads toward Sugar Creek, a few turns brought her to a partially cleared field where she saw Pete's combine churning through a row of knee-high soybean stalks. As the paddlewheel header spun, it kicked up mud chunks, along with yellow leaves that had dropped from the stalks as the beans ripened in their pods. The combine's smokestack let out steady bellows of black exhaust as the big diesel engine was struggled to keep the machinery moving through the wet land. Through the windows of the glassed-in cab Sis could see Pete gripping the steering wheel with both hands, his body visibly stiff even from a distance. Behind the cab, a long, stovepipe-shaped auger swung loosely; when the two-hundred-bushel bin beneath it to reached capacity, Pete would stop the header from chewing, pull up alongside the grain wagon at the far end of the field, and dump his cargo. Then, he would start back into the rows.

Sis parked the mini-van on the road, afraid that if she pulled into the field her tires would get stuck. Once she stepped off the blacktop, her feet sank. As she tromped through the freshly thrashed muck, she noticed water standing in both the terraces and the combine's tread tracks.

When Pete saw her approaching he cut power to the header and let the combine idle. He stepped onto the cab porch to lower the five-rung step-down lashed to its steel side. When he skipped the final rung to hop to the ground, his toes disappeared in the squish. "You got here fast."

"I aim to please." She handed him the sack and thermos. "Service with a smile, and all that."

His face wrinkled under the beak of his cap. He stuffed the thermos in the pocket of his down jacket and slapped the chaff off his trousers. "You all right?"

"I'm fine. I know you'll be glad when you get all this done. Maybe we could go to Louisville next weekend. We really haven't spent any time together the past week or so."

"That'd be good. We don't have to usher that Sunday service, do we? We can trade with someone." He bit into the sandwich, ham falling out of the bread slices so it dangled at his chin. He pushed it into his mouth with a dirty finger. "How about defrosting some venison for supper tonight? I ought to be done by seven or so."

She hesitated. "I was going to go sit with Mrs. Birmage tonight. Dub asked me to."

He stopped chewing as though a filling had come loose. Then he swallowed. His voice was not only clogged but cold. "You're sticking the kids with your parents too much."

"When am I supposed to stop helping? You tell me, because I don't know. Just give me the date and I'll tell Dub. I'll say, 'Sorry, but my concern has expired. It's time to move on.'"

"I'm only telling you it's about time you think about doing things for your own."

She closed her eyes. "I'll have the venison in the fridge for you. You can warm it up. I was going to make a broccoli-cheese casserole before I went anyway. And for your information, Martha's keeping the kids tonight."

Pete re-wrapped the sandwich and stuffed it back in the sack. "Thanks for the sup." He started back toward his Massey-Ferguson.

"You know, if you're worried about the kids not being home, *you* could pick them up after you're done. All you have to do is give them a bath, get their teeth brushed, and read them a few books so they go to sleep."

"Tomorrow morning I have to haul this load to the elevator and get our money so we can eat the rest of the year. Then I've got to fix the propane gauge on the blower to get the moisture in the silos down, and on top of that, I've got two sows intending to farrow before I'm ready. I'm doing all that tomorrow for *us*. You're staying with those people for *you*."

"That's a funny thing to say considering you were the one who dragged me kicking and screaming to Shiloh Baptist." She felt so angry she thought she could boil the mud swallowing her boots. Something jumped out of her mouth before she could contain her wits. "We're going to have Grandma's party at our house. I just decided."

That stopped him. Pete looked over his shoulder.

"What are you talking about?"

"You're right. I've gone without for too long. I can't keep doing it just because folks might not approve. We'll do the birthday at our place."

"I don't have time for this. We'll talk some night when you can decide you can be home."

This time when he started walking he didn't stop. Sis watched him hoist himself up the ladder and then lock the ladder back in its hold. It hardly seemed worth all the work it took for the conversation they'd had. The engine throttled, sending a fresh blast of exhaust out the combine's top. The header kicked into its spin, its teeth ready to comb the field anew as the machine's boxy frame lurched forward. Sis didn't stay to watch. She'd been through nearly forty harvests with Pete. She knew that for him it was the most satisfying part of farm life because it was the most routine. He found security in that repetitive movement. Each row he reaped was the diameter of a world he didn't have to leave; each wide swing of the combine at the end of that row dug the trenches of its perimeter. But for Sis it was just the opposite. All that back and forth—it made the motion seem nervous and confined, trapped in its own boundaries. She found it boring.

ETHEL SAT ON THE davenport watching Martha work. Tillie and Joey had abandoned their playroom as well to observe their aunt's hobby. The scattered body parts particularly intrigued Joey. When Sis walked into the living room he was holding a pair of porcelain arms to the top of his head, wiggling them like devil horns.

"Blaaaaah," he yelled in an attempt to appear demonic. His tongue was a little too short to make him scary.

"Put those down." Sis picked up a drink cup from the end table. It had left a sticky ring on the wood. "Really, Martha. You've got my living room looking like a mortuary. Don't you think so, Grandma?"

The old woman smiled at the sound of her name, even though she wasn't certain what had been said. "Well, now, I'm not sure about that."

Sis grabbed a washcloth from the kitchen and wiped the ring away.

Martha jammed an outstretched plastic arm in a socket. "I saw this story on the news the other day. About a woman who buried children in her apple orchard." Everyone looked at her. "I don't mean she killed them. Anytime she heard a story about a baby's body found abandoned in a trash bin or in the woods she'd take it and give it a funeral. They call them throwaway babies. There didn't used to be a name for them because nobody ever thought of having a child and pitching it like a sack of sh—"

"Do you mind?" Sis gestured at her own children.

"They really throw away babies?" Tillie was sitting at Martha's feet.

"See what you've done?" Sis tossed the rag into the sink.

"Only really sick people do it," Martha assured her niece. "And mean ones. But this lady felt so bad about it that she spent all her own money so those babies could be buried proper."

"Callie Nevers told me this dead baby joke at Sunday school: What's red and sits in a corner? A baby chewing on a razor blade."

Sis swatted Tillie's arm, hard. The girl leapt to her feet and danced at the pain.

"You stop that and you stop it now." Sis turned to Martha. "Do you see what you've started?"

She went into the kitchen, leaving Tillie to her tizzy. Martha followed. "Are you cracking up? I've never seen you hit one of your kids like that."

Sis yanked a serving of venison from the freezer and began stripping away the butcher paper, which stuck to the meat. "Why don't *you* have a nickname?"

"What?"

Sis parked her hands on her hips. "I've been Sis for fifty-five years. For twelve of them I was Sis before I was even a sister to anybody. You wouldn't know what a responsibility that's been. You've never had a nickname."

"You keep talking like this and you're likely to get a new nickname: Crazy."

"That's funny coming from a forty-year-old who still tells dead-baby jokes."

"I told the story," Martha corrected her. "Tillie told the joke."

"Oh, well, then, never mind." Try as she might, Sis wasn't very good at sarcasm. She blew the air out of her cheeks. "It's just—a few days ago Tillie let it slip about Patty. She knows about Patty, I mean."

"How?"

Sis jabbed the light button on the microwave. The meat was sweating. "Mom had a picture in her wallet. Tillie saw it and asked who Patty was."

"Well, that's mom. She was never much for hoarding secrets. 'Specially when they had good gossip value."

"I didn't tell you this so you could put mom down."

"O-kay. You are wound tight. But you know Tillie was bound to find out at some point. Joey will, too, if Tillie hasn't let it slip already. You were going to have to talk about it someday."

"I'd like to have chosen that day. Actually, Pete should have done the choosing. Taking down Patty's pictures was his doing."

They waited for the buzzer on the microwave to go off. When it did, Sis popped the door open to feel the venison. It was close enough to defrosted. She rinsed off the excess water and patted the meat with a paper towel. Then she took out the flour jar and with a sifter breaded the slices.

"Pete's just a man. You've got to forgive him for that. He doesn't know any better."

The frying pan was already on the stovetop, still crusty from the kids' breakfast eggs. Sis gave the pan a quick wash as Martha went on, not bothering to scrub away the yolk flakes. She melted a tab of butter in it. When she laid the venison in the skillet, it cackled in the grease. One day, she thought, she would start cooking more healthily.

"Maybe Pete did the only thing he could. Maybe his not talking about it, not admitting it to Tillie and Joey—maybe that was the only way he could imagine coming back to this house and living with the ghosts. Like I said, he's a man, and a man's first instinct is to run from his problems. You could have had it a lot worse, too, you know. At least Pete didn't do to you what this St. Claire character did to his wife. I mean, what kind of man leaves a woman to go on a wild-goose chase, even if he is trying to find his son?"

Sis flipped the steaks with a meat fork, standing back to avoid the sputtering grease. She was about to say something—she wasn't sure what—when she heard Tillie laughing wildly. That girl, she thought. Amazing how similar her laughing and crying sounded.

Tillie came running into the room, bouncing on her toes.

"Guess what Grandma said! Guess what Grandma said!"

"Please—calm down."

"Grandma was looking at those dolls and she goes, 'I think it's high time Clinton and Dorothy had a baby.'" The girl giggled again, her eyes bugging. "She's crazy. . . ."

Martha was smiling; there was no way Sis could discipline Tillie with her own aunt chortling at Ethel's expense. Sis gave them both a roll of her eyes, but she wasn't really thinking about her grandmother. She was thinking about Martha's comment.

What kind of man leaves a woman to go on a wild-goose chase? She was wondering how someone who entertained dolls heads could say something so sensible.

WHAT MARTHA SAID WAS still on her mind after the venison had cooled enough to wrap it in foil and refrigerate it. She made the kids' lunches and poured their apple juice, and after they finished eating, she rinsed and dried the plates, returning them to the correct cupboard. As she was putting away the silverware, she was struck by how many times a day she cleaned the little spoon and fork set that Joey ate with. Just a few hours earlier, she'd scrubbed it after breakfast, and in a few hours she'd be doing it all over again. That's what made her think about Martha's little comment. What kind of *man*. Was it really unimaginable that a woman would do what St. Claire had done? I would, she told herself. She tried to think what her and Pete's lives would be like had Patty's body not been found. She couldn't imagine seventeen years of keeping house while waiting for a clue or break in the case. She wouldn't have had Tillie or Joey. She couldn't have celebrated Ethel's birthdays or gone to her parents' for Sunday dinner. She and Pete would never have made love. They might have gone to church, but probably not. She couldn't imagine showering, ironing, gassing up the car to get to Mt. Gilead—all the little things she had to do before the worship service. What would be the point in pretending everything was normal?

Before she knew it she was halfway into making the broccoli-cheese casserole she'd promised Pete. She had sautéed the broccoli and onion and greased the dish and had even opened the can of cream of mushroom soup when she was struck by how lost in her thoughts she'd become. It was almost as if there were two of her—

the normal Sis who did what was expected of her, including spicing the casserole with the ham hocks that Pete liked, and the woman inside her head, the one who took on the outside forces trying to undo her. She unscrewed a large can of Cheez Whiz and began ladling it in the soup with a wooden spoon. The cheese was thick and took some stirring before the unnaturally yellow hunk dissolved, blending with the gray of the creamed mushrooms. She added the broccoli and onion and flattened it all together in the dish. And then, as she used a butter knife to set the pre-heat temperature on the oven, it hit her: the real question wasn't why St. Claire had left home.

The real question was why his wife hadn't gone with him.

AFTER SHE PUT THE casserole in the oven she called Dub's wife and apologized for having to back out of sitting with Mrs. Birmage—a family concern had come up. Then she called Martha into kitchen. "Do me a favor."

"What—I don't have a life? I'm already taking the kids tonight."

"Can you take them now?"

Martha cocked her head again—her favorite gesture. "What are you up to?"

"Just tell me. Yes or no."

"Well, I've got to teach a sculpting class at the shop at three. I can take them with me, but what about Grandma?"

"You can leave her here. She'll be all right. Mom and Dad can come back early to get her. They were going to eat supper up in Indy, but they don't need to be driving on 65 after dark."

"You want me to leave a hundred-year-old woman alone in your house?"

"Mom and Dad leave Grandma when she naps. She'll need a nap this afternoon. If you go at three, she won't even be awake when they come for her."

Martha sighed. "Poor Pete. It's going to break his heart when he finds out."

As always, Sis let it pass.

AT THE GAS STATION at the Franklin exit she filled the gas tank and withdrew thirty dollars from the ATM. As she made her way to the I-69 on-ramp, the weather report came over the radio. "Fahrenheit's falling," the DJ said in a wiseacre voice. "Possible snow tonight, so pull on your long johns." Sis thought: *Here I am heading north, and I didn't even bring a coat.*

She couldn't remember the last time she'd crossed the state line. There was the occasional weekend getaway she and Pete took to Louisville, but that didn't really count—Louisville was only ninety miles away, and it was just over the Kentucky border.

By Indianapolis she was fighting the temptation to turn around. This long a trip demanded advanced planning; there were too many things that could go wrong. Pete might call the Birmages; Martha might forget to have her mom and dad return early from their meeting. But by the turn-off to Muncie she'd fallen into the hypnosis of the road, letting momentum carry her on. She passed the Fairmont exit where the billboard for the James Dean Museum dwarfed a broken-down farmhouse with the old-time tractor rusting in the yard. At Ft. Wayne she stopped and bought a pop. By Angola it was mid-afternoon, and she started eyeing the clock, wondering whether Martha was handling the kids' afternoon crankiness or if Pete was still pouting.

breathing out the ghost

Then she was in Michigan. She went past Kinderhook, Coldwater, Quincey, Tekonsha, and Olivet. The interchanges around Lansing confused her; she accidentally ended up on I-96 heading west toward Grand Rapids. She stopped for gas and to stretch. The attendant gave her directions, and soon she was going toward Bath, Laingsburg, Shiawasseetown, and on up through Flint. By Clio the sky was darkening, and Sis could tell it was cold outside. She turned on the heater and felt the ventilation blow past her shoulders to the empty seats behind her. At Zilwaukee the extension bridge that went over the Saginaw Bay inlet caught her off-guard. At one point the flooring of the bridge was made of grating rather than concrete and as her wheels hummed over the sprocket holes she felt stranded in the altitude, awaiting a fall.

She took the Bay City exit and stopped at the first gas station she saw. There were three St. Claire listings in the local phone book. Colin's was the first. Sis shivered as she wrote the address on her palm. At first she was afraid to ask the way, wary that her accent was too country for this area. The station lady would know she didn't belong here. The woman was kind, however, and pointed to a city map mounted to the wall. Sis bought a coffee out of appreciation.

Bay City wasn't a big town and she needed only a few turns off the main thoroughfare to find the correct street. She trolled slowly, wondering whether a mini-van with out-of-state plates would arouse suspicion in this neighborhood. St. Claire's house was toward the end of the block, tucked back from the street on a corner lot with a fat pine that dropped a needle trail all the way to the sidewalk. In the driveway, a woman was unloading groceries from a Honda Civic.

Sis stopped the van a few houses down, unsure she could actually approach the wife. But then she thought of the four hundred miles she'd just driven, and how much more foolish it would be to return to Franklin for nothing. She swung her purse strap over her shoulder and locked her doors. As she reached the driveway she saw the woman struggling to shut the Honda's trunk lid while holding a gallon of milk in each hand.

Sis apologized out loud and said, "You're Mrs. St. Claire?"

The woman spun, not quickly or in an unbalanced way but startled at the unexpected sound of her name. Sis understood; she'd suffered that same hesitation when St. Claire first approached her. "Do I know you?"

"No, you don't. But—I—I know your husband. And his friend, Mr. Heim."

A look of confusion crossed the woman's face. She seemed to be searching through old papers for an important document she didn't believe was misplaced. Then the confusion hardened into something just short of annoyance. "You've seen him since the last time I have."

Sis remained a few feet outside the garage, not wanting to cause the woman more discomfort. The sun was setting; it threw the square shadow of a basketball hoop on the concrete.

"I can't tell you why I'm here," Sis began. "I came all the way from Indiana. I know what happened to you. I don't know anything else about you or your family except that. That, and that your name is Kimm. I don't know specifically what's become of your son, but I have a sense of what you're feeling. It's been several years, but a man—he strangled my daughter. A few days ago, I was showing a quilt of pictures my friends and I made—we're all parents of murdered children—and Colin saw it. It made him tell me the story."

Kimm had shut her eyes. She was young and very pretty, Sis thought—not at all worn down by what she'd been through. She had light brown hair, and skin the same color as the milk she held. There were freckles across her nose and cheeks that looked like sprinkled ginger. Her fairness made her seem transparent. When Kimm opened her eyes again they were teary. "Is he okay?"

"I don't know. His friend Heim doesn't think so. Something happened to them—I don't know what. But Heim says he's in trouble, that he's a danger to himself."

She set the milk down on the Honda's bumper. One of the jugs tipped and fell to the ground, flattening its side. Kimm stooped to retrieve it, but instead sank to her knees and buried her face in her palms. Sis squatted next to her and did for Kimm what she'd done for many people: she held her.

"Can I help you carry these things in?"

Silently, Kimm rose and went through the garage to a screen door, which she disappeared behind. Sis gathered the milk and followed. The interior of the house was striking, very artistic, the kitchen painted in silken yellow, the living room in darkened peach. Between the candelabra on each mantle end were small, intricately hand-painted boxes, and the walls were adorned with sconces and black-and-white photos that provided a stark contrast to the colors. The photos weren't family pictures, but blurred, abstract images, bordered by sharp blue matting and black frames. It looked like the sort of interior showcased in designer magazines.

As Kimm washed her face at the kitchen sink, Sis put the milk in the refrigerator. "Your house is beautiful. It makes mine looks like a shanty."

"I wish I could take credit for it, but he did all the decorating. He even taught himself framing and did the pictures. We met in art school, you know. It's funny, everybody assumes it's the woman who's responsible for wall hangings and curtain rods and all that. But I was never really interested in those things. I went to college and all, but my only ambition was to be a mom, which I guess means I wasn't ambitious at all."

"Motherhood is the biggest ambition you can have. I never went to college, and I've never regretted it. Being a mom's taught me more than any job I could have gone to. A lot of things I'm not sure I ever wanted to know."

"Most days . . . I just get up and go to work. I didn't work when he was here; I didn't have to. But when he left, I didn't have any way of paying for the house. His middle sister is a lawyer, and she knew some people needing a nanny, so they gave me a job. . . . His mom sends a check every month, but I haven't cashed any in months, not since it hit me he wasn't coming back, and I just couldn't take her money anymore."

"A man copes differently than we do. My husband and I don't ever talk about our daughter; it's as if she never existed, just a figment of the imagination. We don't even have any pictures of her in the house. He took them all down. Does that make sense? In his mind, it's over and done, something he can't change, so rather than remind himself of that powerlessness, he thinks he has the strength to pretend it didn't happen. I think your husband thinks the same thing, but from the opposite side: he can't do nothing." She stopped. "I'm sure I'm not the first person to tell you this."

Kim stood silently for a moment, then seemed to snap to, as if reminded of something. "I'm not a very good host. Would you like something to eat? You must be hungry if you came all the way. Indiana—that's far."

"You don't need to go to any trouble. I just sort of ambushed you like this."

"It's no trouble." Kimm opened the refrigerator and set a cheese ball on the counter. Then she fished the cupboards for some crackers. "This family I work for now—they had a big Oktoberfest party last weekend. They sent me home with all the leftovers."

They sat in the living room, a tray of snacks in front of them. Sis tried to hide her hunger by only nibbling. Kim didn't eat at all. "When I want to feel sorry for myself, I think I'm one of those fishermen's wives—you know, the ones who wait at the windows for a sign of their husband's masthead on the horizon. What do they call those roof decks on the tops of coastal houses?"

"I'm not sure," Sis admitted.

"Is it widow's walk or widow's wharf? But really, I stopped expecting him a long time ago. I knew he'd never find A.J., but I knew he couldn't stop looking. I really don't care about me; it's Neve I worry about. You know, her not knowing—"

"Neve?" Sis asked.

Kimm's face flooded with realization, and she trembled again. "He didn't tell you about her."

"No, no. . . . He did. I just forgot, that's all."

Sis didn't lie very well. Kimm sank onto the couch, staring at the ceiling. "I guess I should have expected *that*, too. I suppose it was too much to believe he was out there feeling guilty, if not for my sake then for hers."

Kimm pointed toward the built-in bookshelf that covered the far wall. Except for a big TV, it was filled with thick, encyclopedia-sized books, some standing upright, others stacked atop each other on their sides. On one stack was modest gold frame. The picture was small, and Sis had to step close to it to make out the faces. She recognized A.J. by the dandelion puff of curly hair. Neve had her father's hair, too. Most of her face was taken up by her grin, one of those wide, uninhibited children's smiles. Sis remembered baby pictures in which Patty had that same expression.

"She's a beautiful girl. So was he." Sis caught herself. "He still is, I'm sure."

Kimm looked the same, except that her hair now grew to her shoulders. It was St. Claire who was virtually unrecognizable. In the picture he was forty pounds heavier, and his hair was neatly trimmed. The real difference was the eyes. That afternoon outside her house—his gaze was milky, distracted, afraid to focus on one point of space for fear that he'd miss something off to the sides. Here he stared straight ahead, his attention fixed. St. Claire looked settled, content, happy.

"The funny thing is that when A.J. was born I think Colin was a little disappointed. He has three sisters, and he was always very protective of them, and I think he wanted that same feeling of needing to be depended upon that he was used to. Don't get me wrong. He never ignored A.J., never. If anything he wanted too much of his attention. And then when Neve came he was always with her, trying to teach her the alphabet before she could even speak. At first I thought he was being one of those Type A personality parents—you know, the kind that drive their kids to be overachievers. But then it started to hit me. If he could teach

breathing out the ghost

them everything he knew, all he could do, they'd be so indebted to him that they could never doubt him, never resent him. I don't know. Maybe I thought about it too much. I just wanted a normal family, you know?"

"I do know." Sis put the frame back on its book stack.

The back door opened, and a there was the thunderous spill of little feet on linoleum. A child raced through the kitchen, yelling for her mother. She stopped dead when she saw Sis.

"Hello," Sis said.

"Come here, baby," Kimm called, motioning with her hands. Neve wiggled her arms free of her backpack straps and jumped belly first onto the cushions, her body thrust forward in an exaggerated swan dive. The girl nestled at Kimm's side.

"How was karate? . . . She takes this kids class. It's the cutest thing you ever saw—all of them in their outfits. Can you say hi to mommy's friend?"

The door slammed again. Now a man stood in the kitchen. He said, "Hey, baby," then saw Sis. Sis looked back at Kimm, who was awaiting her reaction.

"Hey, Steve. This is—"

Sis told him her name, stepping forward to shake his hand. The man was handsome, with a thick but manicured moustache and one of those broad, Victor Mature torsos.

"I should be going. I've got a long drive."

"You're not from around here?" He followed her once she stepped into the kitchen, as if he were a dog protecting his territory.

"No, I'm from Indiana, a township just south of Indianapolis." She felt as if she were lying, though she was only trying to reveal as little as possible. "I was just in town, making a friendly call."

"She knows Colin." Kimm's voice was drained of emotion. The man's eyebrows rose as his body tensed. Kimm set Neve on the floor and told her to take her backpack to her room. As if part of a conspiracy, the girl didn't acknowledge her father's name. She did as told, and disappeared in a hallway past the wall of books.

"Big Man Colin." Steve's sarcasm was heavy, menacing. "How is he these days? He enjoying himself?"

"Stop it, Steve," Kimm snapped.

"I'm sure you're a nice lady and all. But you can tell your friend he doesn't need to send anyone around here anymore. Not that he'd care, but tell him his family's fine. Being taken care of."

"Oh, for Chrissakes—"

Kimm ran out of the room. A door slammed in the hall. When Sis looked again Steve's temples were throbbing to the rhythm of his bluster. It was such a man thing to do, she decided. To flex at even the most slender threat.

"You should go help her. And you shouldn't judge him, or what he thinks he's doing. Not until you've had to live with what he does."

Steve seemed surprised by Sis's strength. "What about her? Hasn't she had to live with a lot?"

"She has, but it's still not something you'll ever understand. She won't stop suffering just because you're here. The wound won't ever heal. Life will go on, but however many favors you do, however you help her out, she's always going to know that parts of her life have gone missing. You can't make her forget that. She shouldn't have to."

She left him there in the kitchen, disarmed and blinking, his big hand gripping the counter. Outside and almost to her car, she heard Kimm behind her in the driveway.

"He's just a good friend."

"It's not my place to say anything. I wouldn't judge you."

"I just couldn't do everything myself, you know? I couldn't work and get her to school and to all the kids' things a girl her age wants to do. . . . He's a buddy of my brother's—they went to high school together. He's a cop. He works the night shift, so he picks her up from school. It was his idea for her to take that karate class. He's a bit of a tough guy, but he's nice enough. He's good to me."

She covered her face, crying full out. "I just needed somebody to be good to me again," Kimm said.

Sis felt she should embrace her once more, but she felt more like a stranger than she had twenty minutes earlier. "It's natural enough. Anybody in your place would have done the same."

"You believe me, don't you? That this isn't the life I wanted?"

"I believe that."

Sis got into her car, leaving Kimm sobbing into her palm. As she drove up the street she felt heavy and complicit. She turned on the street that would take her to the interstate. It was almost dark now, and between the darkness and her own accelerating speed she felt apart from things, even though she was moving through them. She thought of Tillie and Joey and what they were likely up to at Martha's. She looked at the clock on the dashboard. It was ten after six, and that meant it would be after midnight before she would be able to tell herself that she'd never really left her children.

apropos of wet snow

From inside the cab of the combine, Pete watched the reels of the header bat down row after row of soybeans. As the stalks fell backwards, their stems snipped clean by a line of saw teeth on the header's bottom cutter bar, the bean pods scratched against the metal of the machinery, making the sound of a whisking broom on carpet. To Pete, it was a much more pleasing music to work by than corn. Corn pith let off a brittle snap when severed, and the ears rattled as they traveled the intricate system of augers and rotaries that ground the kernels off the cob before spitting the loosened grain into the back holding bin. Whenever he worked a cornfield, Pete turned up the cab's radio so the local farm and weather reports drowned out the persistent thud of the shucking. Threshing soybeans was harder work because the plants grew close to the ground, and the combine might trample rather than harvest them. But the work was more calming as well, a light drizzle as opposed to a hailstorm. In the soy Pete kept the radio off so he could enjoy the soft skitter of his harvest.

He would have enjoyed it more this past week if not for the rain. The land was so muddy that the field mice and ground martins could barely keep ahead of the cutter bar. The combine's wheels churned rather than rolled; Pete had to keep to a relatively slow speed to keep from digging himself under. Rain made the combining more costly, too. A few days earlier before mowing down his first row he'd walked a section of the bottomland for a quick check of his soybeans' moisture. When beans were of a good consistent dryness they rattled in their pods as foot traffic shook them. But Pete's walk hadn't made much noise. He'd gathered a random handful of pods, which he shelled on the hood of his truck. Just as he thought: some of the beans were so bloated the excess water actually collected in the pods. Others were soft and squished easily between his fingers. He even found a few beginning to mold. That meant he had to finish the harvest today. Otherwise the cold could freeze the moisture, hardening and then cracking the beans from the inside out. If that happened, the crop would be a total write off. As was, Pete figured the grain elevator would dock him a good twenty percent off market price.

That bad a hit was enough to make him wish he could sell out and retire. He was fifty-six years old, after all. He knew guys his age that had built up enough of a nest egg to stop working. Most had liquidated back in the Reagan days when crop prices fell and interest rates hit double digits. They'd moved on to jobs in computers or sales, and they'd invested their surpluses wisely enough in the bull market to stock their portfolios with high-yield investments. From time to time Pete caught up with them on the golf course. They owned snazzy sets of designer clubs and didn't worry when the stray ball landed in the drink. Pete never before cared about material possessions, but now he admitted to a surge of envy when he saw those guys strolling around in handsome Ralph Lauren polos and sharp Etonic cleats. One of them, Wayne Langford, sold off his land back in '84. Wayne never did have much common sense when it came to running his operation, and he'd overextended himself badly in the late seventies when inflated land values led to a farm refinancing craze. He had to be hospitalized and doped with anti-depressants when the bank chained his barn doors shut. Pete figured Wayne couldn't be too sad these days, though. The last time Pete saw him, he was tooling around in a forty-thousand dollar SUV.

Whenever he thought about Wayne's reversed fortunes, Pete wondered if he and Sis hadn't been shortsighted in their business approach. For thirty-seven years, they'd taken life a season at a time, cutting back on expenses when times were tight, indulging modestly on a dinner out and a weekend away when they felt flush. Their work hadn't done much more than keep them going, though. The last time Pete balanced the books he and Sis had less than six thousand in handy cash. They drove cars until they fell apart, grew their own vegetables, put off home improvements. For at least ten years Sis had been complaining about the oven not heating up fast enough; for almost as long, Pete had been wishing he could install a farrowing house with an actual waste pit. They could afford small fixer-uppers, but interest payments, equipment upkeep, and insurance always got in the way of their big payoff.

Pete tried to think back to their first year as a couple. He couldn't remember it real well, they were just kids out of high school then, and he knew they'd been too young to map out where their life ought to end up. He'd always followed his father's motto: *There's you and the job in front of you. Get it done, quick but right, and move on.* That sort of thinking, Pete now realized, got you ahead only an inch or two at a time.

He blinked hard, tired from concentrating on the bean rows. Sometimes he wondered whether this particular patch of ground was even worth its bother. He'd been planting it for less than ten years. Before that it had lain fallow because of the high water table. Sugar Creek was only thirty yards away, and the underflow meant the ground maintained a marsh-like sogginess that was good for weeds and sunflowers but nothing that turned a profit.

Since the 1940s, when Pete's dad inherited the acreage from an uncle killed in the war, the Pruitts had used it to pasture cowherds. Pete, however, didn't believe in letting any land go unused. Government set-asides did enough of that, paying farmers not to plant to keep corn and wheat prices steady. A decade earlier he'd calculated the yield per year he'd have to reap to drain the soil and still make a small profit. At a dollar a foot, drainage tiles were an expensive proposition, but Pete figured that with hard work and a little luck he could pull in between three and five thousand a year after expenses—enough to make the effort and investment worthwhile. This season was a basement scraper, however. He'd be lucky if he made a buck off these beans.

As the combine ate its way through the beanstalks, the sky darkened. All day the sun had been stuck behind a horizon-wide barrier of clouds that gave the air a gray sense of oppression. By mid-afternoon the clouds had thickened, now looking like waterlogged cotton balls ready to fall apart. Pete could tell the temperatures were falling from the exhaust floating behind the combine—on a warm day the smoke rose and dispersed quickly, but in cold air it hung to the ground, drifting in patches. Pete didn't like to use the heater in the cab—no matter how you fiddled with the settings it made the cab hot and stuffy. A slight chill was better for work. It braced you. If things got too cold you zipped the jacket higher up around the throat and pulled the earflaps down on the cap.

It was just before supper when the snow finally started. At first it slapped so faintly at the cab window that Pete thought the rain had started again. But then the moisture thickened and crystallized. Soon the flakes were cartwheeling down in a steady-enough stream that Pete had to switch on his wipers. Within a half hour the snow was crusting, making it even harder for him to follow the row lines. As he finished a section near his grain truck he set the combine in idle and lowered the cab ladder. All week his boots had been sloshing in muck. Now when he touched the ground they made the sound of crunching gravel. Pete wasn't sure which he disliked more.

He climbed the plywood-slatted side of his grain truck to untie the canvas flaps of a bundled tarp. Hopping down, he unclamped the metal guide pole he stored along the truck's side. He fished the head through the tarp's toe line and dragged it the length of the tank, covering the beans. As wet as they were, there was no point in packing them in slush.

Back in the cab Pete knew it'd take even longer now to finish the field. Snow was rare in Indiana in late October, but not unheard of. He adjusted the cutter bar's clipping speed so it mowed faster. Beanstalks humped over with snow stooped even closer to the ground, meaning more opportunity for the header to miss them. Pete guided the combine to the end of its present row and then began swinging it sideways to clip the next swath.

As the combine turned he saw a flash of gray shoot through his headlights. A heavy clunk followed. Pete immediately stopped the reels' rotating, figuring a sprinting rabbit had leapt into the chattering saw teeth. He jumped down from the cab again, this time not bothering with the ladder. He'd been up and down so many times already he figured he'd spent more time climbing the rungs than combining. If he'd been combining corn he'd have just kept working. The picker implement that cleared cornfields wouldn't jam up for anything short of a dog or deer. But the header that cultivated beans and wheat was more sensitive; it sat on hydraulic skid plates that were supposed to keep the cutter bar

breathing out the ghost

a few inches above ground. If a rabbit came between the skid plates and the soil, it would stop up the saw teeth so they wouldn't slice the stalks clean through. If that happened, the beans wouldn't end up in the combine throat. They'd just get run over and crushed.

Pete stepped around to the front of the header and peered through the reels. The headlights shot down plenty of illumination, but he couldn't see anything. He walked the width of the cutter bar, checking the skid plates, but then again, nothing. Then, as he was coming back to around to the cab porch, he heard a faint groan from somewhere in the cleared rows. He boosted himself on the fat tread of a combine tire and reached into the tool pail he kept on the porch. He worried that his flashlight batteries might have corroded from all the rain, but when he clicked the switch it threw a healthy yellow beam. He followed the noise to its source a few feet from the side of his right tire.

It was a cat. It rested on its side, breathing heavily, its legs extended in the mud. There was a wide diagonal gash across the abdomen that exposed its innards. Pete could see the lower edge of the rib cage and the bloody, bulbous belly sack, which throbbed shallowly. The cat's eyes were dilated, and it had a distant, resigned expression on its face. He bent farther over, nudging the cranium softly with his toe to check for a collar. The neck was bare. If he'd found tags Pete might have tried to save it, but the lack of a collar meant this was a barnyard cat, not a pet. Pete drew a deep breath and mashed his heel where the animal's head rested.

He cleared his throat and spat over his shoulder. Any other day he wouldn't have thought twice about what he'd done. Farm work was full of humane violence. He had seen squirrels and rabbits cut in two by frisbee-sized disc blades. In the past he'd killed any number of calves and ponies too feeble to survive. In childhood he'd learned to slaughter chickens by yanking off their heads and pigs by shooting them in the temple. Pete had been on the receiving end of that violence, too. Once when he was adjusting the bolts on a plow the hydraulic system failed and the whole undercarriage fell on his chest, pinning him to the ground for three hours until a soil-testing team happened by. Just two years earlier, a good friend asphyxiated when he fell into a corn bin trying to unplug an auger. Pete had been the one to haul out the body, coated in grain dust, up from the sea of kernels. There was enough danger around that you took death for granted. It was natural.

But as Pete's flashlight beam bounced over the land, he caught sight of the snow settling along the terrace slopes. Something in the lumpy contour reminded him of a freshly filled grave, and he thought of Chance Birmage. Pete had kept the boy from his mind all week. The bottomland was his priority because he could do something about it. But now he found himself dragging his beam along the mounds, wondering if the boy— wherever he was—could feel the freezing soil. The image of a grave that he hadn't visited in a long time overtook him: the brass marker, decorated with the flower arrangements that he and Sis used to place at Patty's plot.

He extinguished the light and chastised himself for wasting time. He hoisted himself back up on the cab porch and took his seat behind the steering console. A rev of horsepower shot a gust of smoke out the exhaust. As the header paddles started spinning, Pete put the combine in gear and set about finishing the task in front of him.

ETHEL COULD NOT NAP. She knew someone had tucked her into bed, but she couldn't remember who or why. She knew she was by herself, but she wasn't aware who had left her behind. Most of the time she didn't remember she had granddaughters, much less a great-granddaughter who had been murdered. She could tell you her name, where she came from, and who her sons and daughters were. She could tell you about the child, too—a girl—who'd died of influenza before it could even sleep in a big girl's bed, though she couldn't remember a name. She was aware she'd outlived both her parents and at least two of her adult children.

But ask her to tie these milestones to a specific date—or even ask her her age—and she'd respond with a look of bafflement that made you question whether you knew what you were talking about. Ethel's mind no longer operated according to rules of chronology. She lived fully within random moments of her memory as if nothing had come before and nothing after. Her family often had a hard time determining just where in her own history she was. Yet they learned to tolerate and even forgive her dementia, figuring that if you made it past a hundred, you'd earned your freedom from clocks and calendars. As Sis's father liked to say, Ethel was too old for time.

So as she stayed at Sis's that afternoon, the passing hours didn't trouble her. She had no sense of waiting, and didn't worry that no one had come to fetch her. It never entered her mind that Martha, overwhelmed by the hectic scramble of keeping up with Tillie and Joey, had forgotten to call her parents.

Ethel walks from room to room, touching unfamiliar lampshades and photographs, opening doors and closets, pulling light cords and twisting faucet fixtures—searching for an object or memento to anchor herself. Whenever where she was slipped her mind—and that was often—this was her routine. It doesn't worry or frustrate her because she doesn't know she is doing it. At such moments Ethel's mind is like a blank page in a book. When words come they might take her forward or they might take her back, but in the meantime she has no sense of anything missing.

What catches her attention this time is the Victor-Victrola, which sits in the corner. Details return to her. It's freshly arrived from Indianapolis, where Mercer purchased it for her as an anniversary gift. As long as it took to ship, they should-a got a discount. For what it cost they could-a made an effort to get it to her within the month. She flips open the lid. Inside is the Victrola logo: a brown-eared white dog—Nipper—its head cocked to a horn shaped like a flower blossom. *His Master's Voice* written below.

She opens the double doors of the bottom cabinet where she keeps her 78s filed by title in alphabetical order. This way, she can tell when her children have been messing with her collection. Her favorites are the ones put out by the Gennett folks over in Richmond. She has many of the recordings by Kentucky fiddlers and banjo-janglers like Dick Burnett and Leonard Rutherford, Welby Toomley, Edgar Boaz. Mercer loves Fiddlin' Doc Roberts' version of "Shortenin' Bread." Unlike the other fiddlers whose bows hop and bounce on the strings like feet on hot coals, Doc Roberts rolls out the melody in long, fluid strokes. Ethel also likes the Carter Family, but her favorite is Shortbuckle Roark, a skinny Pineville, Kentucky, boy whose signature song is "I Truly Understand You Love Another Man."

Ethel can't find her Shortbuckle 78, so she puts Fiddlin' Doc on the Victrola's felt-lined turntable and turns the crank. The needle on the platter's shellac surface brings a screech and cackle from the speaker.

The record only plays a few bars of music when Mercer barrels through the front door, bouncing on one foot. He's been told to enter the house through the mudroom; he knows better than to track a fleck of mud on Ethel's rugs when he's been plowing a field.

"Goddamn," he says, collapsing backward in a chair, his leg extended. "Get this boot off me, woman."

Ethel has her hands around the back of his heel before she sees the nail. Only the head is visible; the rest is driven through the sole.

"Got you bad?"

"Clean into." Grime slicks his face. "You gonna have to yank and yank'er hard. It's up there in muscle, feels like."

She slides a footstool under Mercer's calf, squatting in front of him for leverage. He grips the armrests, dusty fingers dirtying the fabric. She tugs. At first he grunts. Then he yells at her for not pulling harder. She jerks, sending him arching up in a spasm of curses. When the boot finally gives way, sliding over the bridge of his foot, blood dribbles onto the floor.

"You best not go staining my rug," she tells him.

"Give a man some caring, will you? Fetch me the salve."

She reaches into the throat of the boot, feeling for the nail's tip. It sticks up through the sole about a half-inch. "Long one like this you must be nicking a nerve."

"Damn well hurts, I know that. Go get me that salve, and bring the gauze and tape with you, too."

She goes to the mudroom where there's a long sink for after-work washing. On the shelf above the sink are their basic medical supplies—cotton balls, scissors, tweezers. When she returns to the living room Mercer is digging the nail out of his boot bottom with a jackknife. When he finally pulls it free Ethel's surprised at how long it is.

"You gonna get you lockjaw with this one," she says.

Mercer screws the top off the salve can. The room fills with a thick, oily odor. "You wishin' me dead for a reason?"

He rubs the gauze across the brown paddy until he can pinch off a buttery chunk in his fingers. When he lifts his foot she sees the puncture, as round as a pencil, just above the ball of his heel. She holds the nail. The tip is wet with blood and along its shaft are small hunks of flesh.

"Need that tape," he tells her as he smears the salve over the wound with the gauze. Then he begins wrapping, covering the entire foot from the ankle to the joints of his toes. Ethel returns to the mudroom and fetches the roll of adhesive. When the bandages are secured Mercer tries to place his weight on his bad foot, but the pain sends him sinking back into the chair.

"Of all the damn times. I'm gonna need a pair of winter socks."

Ethel scurries up the attic hideaway to the boxes that store the winter clothes. She rifles through them until she finds the woolen socks. When she hands it to Mercer he rolls one sock up in the other and stuffs it in the boot. This time when he stands the pain shoots only part way up his tendon.

"I'll take my sup soon as it's ready," he says, limping to the door. "And you'll pardon the mess on the floor. Wasn't meaning to make more work for you."

"When you get sick and die is when you'll be making the work for me."

He is halfway out the door, letting flies buzz into the house.

"As soon as that lunch is ready, now, you come get me. I got my work, you got yours."

And he does his work until the fever and the trouble swallowing get so bad he can't muster the energy to lift himself off the mattress. As he lies silhouetted by sweat she mops his brow and chest. He tries to groan out the names of records he wants her to play, but his mouth is paralyzed. That's all right, though. Ethel knows which ones he likes. "Shortenin' Bread," she tells him. "And 'Billy in the Low Ground'"—another Doc tune—"I'll get you some Fiddlin' Doc. That'll soothe you." She plays the song over and over for him, thinking of how when it was the child had boiled with flu fever Mercer sat in the living room listening to "Billy Low in the Ground." He never came near that baby once it took sick.

That's before the spasms. Once he takes to jerking and stiffening uncontrollably she has no time for memories. All she can do is try to hold him down so he doesn't shake straight off the bed.

"How deep was it?" The Shelbyville doctor is contemptuous of country people. He can't believe someone would be so careless as to step on a nail. *Hicks*, he thinks.

"Mercer said it was an inch or so through."

"Not much I can do. Keep his forehead cool."

"He thought the salve would cure it."

"A salve will close the wound, that's all. It won't get the critters in his blood." He says *critters* with a sharp twang. "They're close to getting a vaccine out. Too bad he couldn't a-waited a little while. Another year at most and maybe I could treat him then, but this . . . this is the worst lockjaw I ever seen. You better get your preacher over here."

Ethel is shaking her head. The doctor can't believe she doesn't cry; he's never known a woman on the verge of being widowed not to wail and shriek. He wonders if she's just too damn dumb to comprehend what'll happen to her when her man goes. The doctor doesn't know she's already lost her father and a child and that those losses already wept her bone dry. All Ethel can think about is the vaccine that's only on the verge of existing. *I'm gonna be mad if he goes and that shot comes out right after. You better not take him from me and then turn around and make a cure 'vailable 'mediately. That ain't fair.*

But that's what happens: by the end of 1927, less than six months after Mercer dies, tetanus is treatable.

The doctor stands on the Brandywine porch looking over the fields that are their farm. His buggy is parked in the yard, the horse pulling against the reins that hold it to the hitching post. Ethel knows he owns a car, but he won't drive it when he calls on country people. He doesn't like his car getting dirty.

"You and the little ones gonna half to scratch it out yourselves. How many acres you got here?"

"Seventy-five."

"Land prices aren't too good right now, but I 'spect you can get enough for what you got here to set you up in town. I been meaning to get me some ground. Maybe we can work up a deal."

"I'm not selling."

When he looks at her, his eyes bug almost as big as the impatient horse's.

"You're going to run seventy-five acres? I could see it if those children was older, but they ain't but tots. How you going to do the fieldwork and keep them on the straight 'n' narrow?"

She doesn't answer. She knows what he's thinking: *That's the pride in you talking. You're people always were too proud.* The doctor scoffs as he goes down the unpainted plank steps and turns his horse toward the roadside. He never does send a bill for treating Mercer. Whether it's because he feels sorry for her or because he figures she's too proud to bother with paying, Ethel never knows.

Darling.

Horace, you know better than to call me that.

You gonna play that tinker box of yours all night long? I know you're wanting to work me to death, but I could'a sworn a man was given the night to sleep by. Them cows ain't gonna let me rest come morning, you know.

Horace doesn't like music, not like Mercer. He complains when he hears the Victrola cranking. When he tries to sing along to the 78s, he shows off an ear as tin as a can. But that's only one way he doesn't resemble Ethel's dead husband. Truth is, you couldn't find two men less alike. Mercer was tall, broad. Had he made it past twenty-nine he'd have grown thick and round as the silos he blocked and mortared with his own hand. Horace is a divining rod by comparison: thin-waisted, thin-haired, thin-skinned. In the barn he looks aghast as Ethel grabs a chicken by the legs, holding it upside down, its flapping wings hurling feathers and scattering dust. She lays the bird on a stool, plants her foot on the neck and with a yank separates the torso from the head. The wings continue to batter until she shoves it into a tub of hot water. Horace is staring at the bird's decapitated head, its beak cracked open slightly. *You want me to do that? That's not my idea of romance.* She says *No romance about it* back to him. She scoops another chicken into her hands and thrusts it at him. *It's your work now. You best learn to do it right.* When Horace tries to clasp the bird's knobby legs, it leaps at his chest and scampers up his face before chuting to the barn floor. In a burst of vengeance, Horace kicks at its tail. *Ain't ever seen it done that way,* Ethel tells him.

Your liking that tune there tells me you ain't as cold as you pretend to be. You like it so much, I tell you what—we'll play it at the wedding. That's right, Ethel. You agree to marry me instead of just lending me half your bed and I'll hop right up behind that organ player and yodel it out for you. That's right, "I Truly Understand You Love Another Man."

Horace is always talking wedding. It slips out his mouth no matter what the conversation. Ethel ignores him. He raises his voice, bangs his fists on the table, threatens to leave. *I can go back to French Lick any time it suits me,* he says. *I have opportunities there. I could'a been a rich man by now, running a business instead of farming your dirt.* She tells him where to find his suitcase. Horace smoothes back his hair. Whenever she ruffles his feathers he takes to combing the few oily strands still on his scalp. *Can't you tell I love you? What more do you want from a man? I know you didn't put Mercer through this monkey business.*

But Mercer didn't have to say he loved her. His presence, his strength, his abilities, they were proof enough. Horace says it so often and with such pleading she can't help but doubt it. She knows that it was the newspaper obituary that brought him to her door. She found a clipped, folded copy of it in his suitcase once. She can see the anaconda way he eyeballs the animals, the land. A pig in the poke is bacon on a breakfast plate to him. The fields are house lots just waiting to be settled. Ethel and Mercer's land is only two miles past the Shelbyville city limits. Horace believes that cities are growing, pushing outward. Anyone owning ground this close to the storefronts could be sitting on a gold mine. After a hard day of trying to show her he's at home in hay and silage Horace jokes about the life they could be leading. *Damn cows got you up at four in the morning. Four a.m.! In French Lick, we could be sleeping in 'til nine.*

Her answer? *You should-a been a country doctor. You could go round telling folks to wait a year before they go to die and then try to buy folk's land out from under them.*

Horace doesn't seem to grasp that he's being beaten at his own game. For Ethel it's a dare she's willing to play for as long as he can stand it. If one morning she awakens and he's gone, she won't worry. There's no shortage of field hands needing work. Most are smart and humble enough to understand that their cologne on her pillow wouldn't make her weak, starry-eyed, malleable. It's his foolishness to think that just because she lets him throw his leg over hers at night he can make claims on her.

I know why you won't marry me. You think you're better than me. Sure. You got your granddaddy's name and money. Them pea-fowls trampin' around your yard—them's your pride flaunting itself up under everybody's nose. I know it was your family not your husband that got you this land. That's what they told me in town. See, they feel sorry for me. They figure it's holier to be the steer than the cash cow. How you like them apples?

Ethel thinks *You dumber than you know, Horace. God brought me you when he realized he'd took from me once too often. He took my daddy before I even knew him, the girl before she could even speak her own name. And now Mercer. He took Mercer from me over som'thing he allowed to be curable not but a year later. How much does He s'pect to take from one person? Y'see, Horace, I've loved and lost, and I'm not losing no more. God brought you to me so's I'd have someone to take it out on. He brought me you 'cause He was 'fraid'a me takin' it out on Him.*

She is playing the Victrola when he comes rushing at her from the roll-top desk she lets him keep in the sitting room. It is his prized possession; he had it shipped from French Lick. Into its many cubbyholes he stuffs the little pieces of paper on which he's jotted his moneymaking schemes. *A restaurant called the Dew Drop Inn. The name alone will attract people.* Whenever he reads them to Ethel, she laughs at the foolishness. *You know how many Dew Drop Inns they got listed in them Indiana travel guides?*

Now he's holding a little tablet of paper up to her face. It's full of hash marks encircled by the names of the month.

You ain't started yet, now have you.

That's nothing you need concerning about.

I'm telling you, I know when you are and when you're not. See? I've been keeping track. All I gotta do is make a little mark a day, one for every one I don't find your woman's things when I burn the refuse. And I should'a started finding them five days ago.

That paper doesn't mean nothing 'cept that you know to count past thirty.

You're such a smart one, ain't you? Making me yank'er out and all. But that's a dumb one on your part, Ethel. Cause I could let slip a part of me and you'd never be none the wiser. And that's what's happened. Yes, ma'am. I got you now. You're mine, and this around here I been sweating out my teeth for—it's mine, too.

Ethel smiles knowingly.

Don't give me that face, woman. That's your 'give-the-dog-the-bone' look. How're you thinking you can carry on like we do and you never end up plump?

I told you, Horace. I've loved and lost and I'm not losing more. You can do to me as you please, but it won't change nothing. They got'm a syrup under the counter at the drug store. All I need's a swig 'n' my insides go empty as I feel. Wasn't it you saying you don't mind them calling you a steer in town? Think about what being a steer means, Horace. It means you got nothing on me. You can't take from someone what she don't care to have.

He seems to wither under his clothes. He looks at her and then at his paper and then balls the paper up in his fist, tossing it to her feet. All those months of making hash marks, reaching twenty-five or twenty-six only to find her discarded rags and having to start counting all over again. When Ethel remains uncowed, he does the only thing he knows to rattle her: he flips up the Victrola needle and snatches Shortbuckle Roark off the turntable. Before she can stop him he chucks it right out the front door. She makes it to the porch just in time to see it splatter into dozens of little shellac pieces. *All right*, she says. *You got me. You got the one last thing. But there's nothing more. Nothing 'tall.*

After that, he disappears. She assumes he goes off to the hayloft, the palace where he hides his imperial pouting. But when she checks the barn later, she finds the hay mounds undisturbed. By day three she wonders if he hasn't made good on that threat to go back to French Lick. But then one morning when she goes to do the milking she finds him already at work in one of the cow stalls, making his usual mess as he tugs at the engorged udders. She lets him be. He takes his breakfast and supper without a word. At night she is combing her hair, preparing for bed, when he finally decides to speak his piece.

I was gonna get you your record back. But dammit if I couldn't find another one.

It's just a bit of song. It don't mean any more to me.

She answers without turning her face from the mirror. Horace breathes shallowly, as if his options have just sat down hard on his chest. When Ethel finishes her hair, she extinguishes the light and slides onto her side of the feather bed. Horace, as always, follows her lead and stretches out at her side, wordlessly.

The next time that they speak of love more than forty years have passed. Ethel and Horace have lived and worked side by side, seen her children off to marriage, seen two of those children die, watched grandchildren grow up and get married and have Ethel's great-grandchildren. But the thing that's supposed to hold two people together exists only in phantom form for them. For Ethel, the ghost is the memory of what was once hers, what she's pledged never to have for fear of losing again; for Horace, it's what he wishes he might've known.

Horace lies in their feather bed, the last day of his life, eaten through with cancer. He calls for Ethel to bring a glass of apple juice.

You know, I did you right my whole life. Don't you think you owe it to me? To tell me just once what you been denying me all these years?

Maybe he's right—maybe he's earned it. Love is just a word, a breath of air like any other, Ethel thinks. She could say it and not mean it and he'd be none the wiser. But even this bit of charity would make her reach for something that's not been there for a long time. *I'd tell you what you wanna hear* Ethel says when she consents to speak *but the satisfaction wouldn't live up to your expectation.*

Horace closes his eyes. He knows what he's known for near forty years—that it's a waste of breath begging kindness from a woman who's pledged herself to being mean. The only thing that's new about it is that he doesn't have any more breath for wasting.

Standing at the Victrola, Ethel looked at again for her Shortbuckle Roark 78, not realizing she'd already remembered why she couldn't find it. She removed each record from the cabinet, reading the label as best she could. The Carter Family, Elmer Boaz, Fiddlin' Doc Roberts. She neatly stacked them one atop the other. The children were always disturbing them. She kept the 78s in alphabetical order so she'd know when they'd been into them. Then the weight of the discs slowly brought back knowledge of their fragility, and she saw again the platter spinning from Horace's hand. *I Truly Understand You Love Another Man.* She saw the 78 shatter, and the pain of that loss came back to her with fresh intensity.

Ethel couldn't quite name everything that had been taken from her, but she knew there'd been a lot—so much that the old resentment that used to consume her when she was strong enough to keep the bitterness fed and fat returned, too. Somewhere in her mind she heard someone that sounded like herself with a question: *What all, what more you plan to take from me?*

Her hand stung. When she looked from the Victrola's cabinet to her fists, she saw she was gripping the broken fragments of a 78. Jagged shards lay on her lap and on the carpet. Was it "Billy Low in the Ground"? She couldn't tell—the label had worn itself illegible—but she recalled how Mercer played that particular song over and over as the flu baby whose name nobody can remember howled its last, how afterward he wanted to hear it in the thick of his own dying. Everything of Ethel's died; everything she valued eventually left her. *Just when I thought I'd done my share of losing, something else gets snatched away from me.*

But then Ethel remembered how she'd steeled herself in the aftermath of Mercer's going, back when she made the vow not to love but to spite: something can't be lost if it's never had. She picked up the topmost platter on the stack she'd made. A simple pinch and it crumbled, cookie-like. As did the next one and the next until she was free of them all.

That's how Pete found her when he returned from the bottomland: palms pricked with stigmata of shellac, stretch pants faintly specked with blood, Ethel had taken to wandering from room to room, touching unfamiliar lampshades and photographs, opening doors and closets, pulling light cords and twisting faucet fixtures. She was unburdening herself of the memories that had hurt her the most.

alibis & lies

The first thing Sis saw when she arrived home was the note under the doorknocker. *At hospital*, it read. Which hospital? Not saying was Pete's way of punishing her.

Back in the van she turned on the mobile and fumbled with the push buttons. Pete answered on the fifth ring. He wouldn't say what was going on; he'd only admit to being at Shelbyville General before bleating a curt *Get out here quick*. Then he hung up without saying good-bye.

Sis retraced her tread marks back through the otherwise undisturbed groundcover until she came to the eastward turnoff that led to the Shelby County line. The midnight quiet that had almost soothed her to sleep on her ride home now seemed eerily vacant, as if taunting her with its emptiness.

When she reached the hospital parking garage, she realized she didn't know who to ask for. She had no way of finding Pete, either, unless she called him again. Then she spotted her father waiting just inside the sliding doors.

"Who's hurt?"

"Your grandma had a little spell. She made a mess of them old records of hers and cut her hands some. Pete got scared and called up an ambulance—for cuts on a hand! But I think old Grandma spooked him. He came in that house and thought he'd run into a walking ghost."

"Why didn't you pick her up?"

He squinted at the question. "Nobody bothered to tell me I was supposed to."

"Martha didn't call you?"

"You know better than to count on your sister for something that important. I wouldn't be leaving your children with her, neither. As hot to trot as she is, they're liable to end up in Tijuana selling coconuts."

Sis decided to agree and blame Martha. That way, she didn't have to blame herself. She knew Pete would do that.

In the elevator she caught her father giving her his disapproving look. "I know what you're thinking. Don't say it."

"I'm not *saying*. But I'll be *listening*. I wanna hear what you got to tell to your husband."

The elevator stopped and the doors opened. Her father pointed down a short hallway, toward a waiting room. She found Pete in a corner chair, staring sullenly into space.

"She okay?"

He wouldn't look at her. "You wanna tell me where you been?"

"Tell me how grandma is and we'll talk."

This brought his eyes to hers. He was about to say something when Sis's dad slipped around them to take a chair. He tugged a folded newspaper from his coat pocket and went to reading while he spoke: "Grandma's going to be all right. If you haven't figured out she's not going anywhere anytime soon you not been paying attention. But we all been living like she's got her wits about her when we know that's not the case. We been selfish, I reckon. We been resisting putting her into a Medicare house because we didn't wanna admit what that meant. She's got more than a hundred years, and we still can't bring ourselves to think or talk about losing her."

breathing out the ghost

Pete and Sis both looked at him. He was either oblivious or indifferent to the attention.

"I think I need to talk to your daughter alone," Pete finally said. This took Sis's dad by surprise. Sis wondered if he had really expected to stick around for the fireworks. Her father refolded the paper, horizontally this time, as though the vertical creases would wear out the fibers. He huffed as he returned to the hall.

"Before you even get going," Pete told his wife, "you ought to know I called the Birmages. Cinda Ritterbush was pretty surprised to hear I didn't know about the family emergency you had to cancel out for." He rocked the chair back against the wall, his chin stuck forward.

"Maybe I was feeling the future. As it turns out, I wasn't lying. We did have an emergency—I just caused it."

"Where did you run off to?" She didn't speak, so Pete had to, again. "You don't think there's a problem when you're hiding something from your husband?"

That made Sis laugh inadvertently. "Martha said that same thing."

"Now I *know* there's a problem if you're taking your sister's advice. She danced all over herself, I'll have you know, while I was trying to find you."

"You're not accusing me of anything, are you?"

"That depends on what you've got to tell me." His fingers drummed his pants leg. "Which, you'll notice, you've yet to do."

"I don't know what to say. . . . I met this man—wait." She laughed harder. The awkwardness between them seemed so unnatural. "That's *not* it. I didn't meet a man like that. He's a stranger. . . ."

She glanced at her husband's profile. His eyes were clamped tight with the anticipation of a prisoner awaiting electrocution. "Christ," he said. Pete almost never swore.

"It's not like that. This isn't *The Bridges of Madison County*." For the third time that day she found herself telling St. Claire's story. She told Pete everything, including the part about Kimm and the widow's wharf where she no longer waited for her husband. "That day at the house he looked like the oldest, saddest man in the world. He's up against something he knows he can't win, but he won't cut and run. And that could've been me. It could've been any of us in the POMC. It could've been *you*."

"So that's what this is all about." He didn't sound relieved. He stood and faced the only decoration in the room: a framed painting of a young boy riding a tractor as if it were a bucking bronco. "I know you believe I never think about her. You've never said it, but I can tell. I'm here to tell you that isn't the case. Plenty of times I wish it were. All this time later, I still don't go anywhere without seeing her. For a long time when I hauled loads up to the grain elevator I'd follow the county line so I didn't have to go down Greensburg Road. Ten miles out of the way, but I thought if I kept out of where they found her she'd stop spooking me. But that didn't work."

"But you took down her pictures . . . the pictures, then her bedroom, then everything we still had, everything we had *left* of her. You took it all and you boxed it up and stuck it in the barn. You weren't the only one she was spooking. We could have talked about it."

He chewed his lips, then shrugged. "I suppose I could have to gone to pieces like this friend of yours, but I did what I thought was best. I sucked it up and toughed it out. I went on. I took care of us."

Sis had closed her eyes. "I never wanted you to fall apart. I always respected the way you kept the farm going. You don't understand. It's not about you. It's about *me*—how I dealt with Patty's going."

"You wish you'd packed up and left?"

"No. The thing is, there've been times when maybe I did. That's what's messing me up. Hearing St. Claire's story, it just sounded—I don't know—heroic. That's a silly, cheap idea. It's all big muscles packed under superhero suits. But I guess I fell for it. It was just so different from how I'd coped. But now I realize what an escape job he's pulled. Under the excuse of *doing something*, he's not done anything. It's the perfect alibi for not having to go on." She stood up, her hands trying to narrow down what her words wouldn't commit to. "You should have seen my face when I saw the little girl he left behind. I felt so foolish because I realized I'd just done the same thing with Tillie and Joey, just on a smaller scale."

"It's not the kids you left behind. It's me. Nothing you just told me couldn't have been told to me earlier. Hell, I'd have probably told you to go, spend a whole day rather than jackrabbit up and back. But you had to hide it all. That's what I don't understand."

"I know. I don't either."

"People been telling me for I don't know how long that I needed to be reining you in on all this running around, making speeches and showing quilts and such—your parents among them. Said you've lived too long within your grief. But I figured you needed those things, so I didn't complain. This morning was the first time in all the years we got between us that I ever told you your place. I never wanted to, and I never had to before because you *made* that place yours. Even with all you've had going on since Patty, I never doubted you wanted to be there. This past week, though—when you were home, your mind wasn't. And all I'm saying is that if you keep imagining you're somewhere else, pretty soon you'll end up there."

Sis was silent. She'd talked non-stop for seventeen years, but now she felt mute. What good were words? She was afraid words would dilute rather than congeal what she was feeling.

When she finally spoke, she said, "You know what? That's the first time I've heard you say her name since I don't know when."

"I say it every day—in my head."

She nodded, wondering if she had a right to ask more than that from him. "You go home and sleep. I'll stay out here with Dad."

Pete pulled his coat around his shoulders. It was still damp and dusty around the arms and shoulders. "I about fell over her when I saw her."

"Patty?"

She said it because she was thinking of something she hadn't remembered in a long time: Pete had been the one to identify her body. He'd gone alone to the Shelbyville morgue. He hadn't wanted Sis to have to go through it.

"Your grandma. Never seen anything so empty looking standing upright. But in the end your dad's right—she'll outlast us all."

He kissed his wife, dutifully and quickly, and left. Sis sat back down, trying to remember how long since they'd been that intimate. Eventually, her father drifted back into the waiting area, pouring himself a cup of coffee that to Sis looked cold even from where she sat. They didn't talk but for a short word or two. Sis drew up a second chair and stretched out so she could sleep.

As she dozed she dreamed. She saw Grandma Brandywine stretched out on a mortician's table, naked, her wrinkled dugs and skin waiting for her final funeral scrubbing. Only instead of coating her face with pancake makeup and fluffing her hair, the mortician was holding a mirror over her open mouth, checking for any lingering sigh of life. The image made no sense and stayed with Sis long after she woke up. Much later it hit her that the mortician in her dream was Ed Surley, who'd prepped Patty for her funeral-parlor viewings. Ed himself had died not long after Patty, which only added to the weirdness.

It was the mirror that bothered Sis the most, though. She'd never seen a body readied for a burial, but she was smart enough to know a mortician didn't have to look for breathing. When she was little she played possum with her father. She would pretend to sleep while he talked about her, poked her, tickled her, anything to bring a smile to her faces. If he couldn't break her concentration by ribbing her, he'd place a pocket mirror beneath her nose. "Now I know you ain't dead," he'd say as he watched her exhaling fog the mirror's surface. When that didn't work, he pinched her nostrils shut, and Sis would explode into gulps and giggles. But when Ed Surley laid his palm over Ethel's face, Ethel remained motionless, her rubbery body as emptied of air as a deflated balloon.

Sis was startled awake by her father's poking finger, which made a hollow thump as it tapped at her clavicle.

"What's the matter? Grandma?"

"Your grandma's fine." His lower lip was plump with morning chew. The waiting room smelled of fresh coffee. "I was making sure *you* hadn't gone and given up the ghost. You ain't moved in hours."

Sis didn't understand how her body could be so still while things in her head were so jumpy.

Bob Birmage spent that night the same way he'd spent the previous six since his son disappeared: drunk. So drunk that he woke up shortly before midnight in his truck bed, iced down like a beer keg. He had passed out before dark a few miles south of his mother's farm, in a field off County Road 800. When he came to, he was covered in snow. It felt like a prank. Here he was, waking up like a human igloo, like fucking Frosty the Snowturd. *Why couldn't I just'a died?* he wondered. *Instead I got to be that guy . . . what was his name? The guy who passed out for twenty years.* Oh well, no matter. It would either be over soon or else it wouldn't. One way would almost be a relief at this point; the other would mean he was a lucky chunk. Bob wasn't sure which was better, to be relieved or lucky.

He rolled his two-hundred-plus pounds over the side of his truck to piss a quart's worth of hobo wine into the snow. Then he headed west on 44 to Franklin. The town was dead dull as usual, but Bob liked it that the body count in the serviceably named Grill Bar on Jefferson Street—his hangout—usually maxed out at four. Of which he was one. He ordered a Jack on the rocks and let the sour mash draw him back into a pleasant state of oblivion. To pass the time he bought five bucks worth of lotto tickets. He borrowed a quarter from barkeep's tip jar to scratch off the gum.

The lotto tickets were a bust. He tore them in half and brushed the pieces on the floor.

"You must be expecting the sheriff again in the morning." The barkeep slipped a cork coaster under Bob's second Jack. "I notice you get yourself loosey-goosey when you're thinking you're about to be hauled in again."

breathing out the ghost

"Fool can't tell when a man's being straight. Hey, turn to *SportsCenter*. I wanna see who's got the pole in Martinsville this weekend."

The keep wiped his hands and began surfing the channels of the bar's TV with a remote control. When he passed wrestling, Bob told him to stop. Wrestling was his passion. The way those pumpkin heads tore into each other was so funny. And the stories—they were damn good. All about honor and revenge. They had the simple clarity of Biblical parables. Bob started telling the keep about the different wrestlers—who'd beaten whom, who'd been a villain but was now a good guy, whom you were supposed to root for. Whenever a large-breasted woman came onscreen, Bob slapped the bar top. "Look at them tomatoes. Jesus. Those girls bend over to tie their shoes, they can't get back up."

The keep looked disgusted as he refilled the whiskey.

"What's your problem? My money not got enough green?"

"Your money's fine, By-God. It's you that's lousy. What are you doing in here, anyway? If you're innocent, you're not exactly acting it. You want to look innocent, get out of here and go try to find your kid."

"Everybody's a judge, ain't they? The minute that kid was born the whole world started telling me I done him wrong. I ruined his life before he got home from the hospital."

The keep jerked the top of the cooler closed. "You shouldn't have made a baby if you're gonna be one yourself. Nothing more precious than a little kid. You know why I work nights? So I can spend my days with my mine—"

Oh, God, Bob thought. *Here it comes.*

"—I could work any shift here I want, you know, but I take this one for just that reason. I should sleep when I get off work but I'd rather be making Lego tanks. See how much I love my kids? My ass stays out of bed 'cause I love them so much."

Bob was scraping his teeth with the tip of his tongue. "Come on over here and let me pin a medal to your chest. By God, every son of a bitch is Father of the Year in his own head."

The keep gave up and started rinsing dirty glasses. Bob returned to his wrestling. But after loading most of his glasses in the dishwasher, the keep stepped back over and blocked Bob's view of the television. "All I'm saying is that if you got something you need to be telling Dub you ought to do it quick. People around here are twisted up over this. They want to find that boy safe, By-God." He leaned into Bob's wide, fuzzy face. "You listening to me, you skunk?"

"The only thing I got to say is move." Bob tapped the side of his glass. "Move and fill her up."

The keep turned his back and started lining up dry glasses on the table behind the bar. When all the glasses were clean, they would form a pyramid six stacks high. Bob felt the syrup begin to sugar over his perception. Occasionally he looked at his watch, calculating how long before the deputies came for him.

He was holding a swallow of whiskey under his tongue when someone joined him at the bar. By this time Bob had gotten his buzz back and probably wouldn't even have noticed this new guy, but when the keep turned to take the guy's order, the guy said, "Stoli. And Chance Birmage's dad."

"He's all yours," the keep replied in disgust.

The man was skinny with a mangy buzz cut that made his head look nicked and stapled. His eyes sat back deep in his head, and he seemed to vibrate to some invisible current of energy. Bob felt like he eyeballed the guy forever. A good drink slowed down time and made you feel as if you were standing over your own shoulder, watching things happen.

"How's it going, bub?"

"Don't think I know you."

"No, you don't. That's true. And I don't know you. But I know what you're going through."

"You do?"

"Sure. Sheriff asks the same questions, you give the same answers. He says he doesn't think you're being honest, you say, 'How's come I have to disprove what's not true?' Am I right?"

"By God, you got it. Finally, some goddamn sympathy for me in all this! It's about time."

The stranger nodded with satisfaction. "Imagine by this point those guys—drilling you day in, day out—they're like dogs trying to catch their own tails, huh?"

"You got that right, too."

"They strap you to the lie detector yet?"

"Fuck no. I won't let them. They can't make me do shit."

"What if they could? Do you think a polygraph would mean anything?"

Bob shook his head. "It wouldn't prove nothing. They rig them puppies to mean whatever it is they want them to. They rig them with the question. I'm an innocent man—I'll say it 'til I'm blue. If they want to know where Chance gone, they need to ask his momma."

The man shot the Stoli, his face twisting at the taste. "She passed her test, though, didn't she? That's the rumor."

Bob shrugged. "I heard'a people training themselves to pass detectors when they're guilty as dogs. Don't mean shit unless you want it to. I may not'a done innocently as concerns certain things in this world, but that don't mean I'm guilty of *everything*."

The man ordered a second Stoli and shot it, too. "I don't disagree. That's the game, isn't it? They want you to question your own reality. They ask you a question, and you give a true answer. But then you hear the needles scratch the graph paper, and you see the man drawing calibration lines, and you think, 'What if this machine calls me a liar?' In the movies it's all neatly girdled in certainty— there's an instrument for detecting lies. *Deus ex machina*—you know what that means? Literally, God out of the machine. Figuratively, it's whatever contrivance or device brings a story to a nice and neat end, like in old Greek plays when an actor playing a god would be lowered into the action from a gear box of pulleys. A polygraph is too neat of a *deux ex machina*. It lets us believe an unresolved mystery can be brought to a close. We want all that mystery and ambiguity wrapped up, don't we? Even if it's a forced resolution, that's better than having to live in suspended animation."

Bob curled his brows at the guy. He'd never heard such a rush of nonsense.

"You ever watch interrogation scenes in those movies?" the stranger was asking. "You could be reading from the Bible and still come up short on the truth-o-meter. Because the game's rigged against you."

St. Claire watched the keep stealing peeks at him. He was pretending to concentrate on the glass he was toweling off, but his eyes kept darting up. "You keep working over that mug and you'll end up with a shot glass."

The keep squinted at the accusation as he set the glass and the towel down. "If you boys want another you better order quick. About to be last call."

St. Claire gave Bob Birmage a friendly slap on the back. "By-God, what say you and me find a more hospitable place to drink?"

"Now I know you're not from around here. If you were, you'd know this is the *only* place to do your drinking."

"Aw, come on. I got a cooler's worth of beer out in my truck that needs floating. We'll just drive around and talk."

A big frown crossed Bob's face. He leaned away from St. Claire, sizing him up—so far he nearly flopped right off of his stool.

"Now why in the hell—" it sounded like *hail*—"would I go somewhere with you? I don't know nothing about you."

St. Claire dropped a ten-dollar bill on the bar, patting it a few times for good measure. "Because you know I know what you're going through."

And he walked out.

Bob pondered his options. It was either going to end or it wasn't, he decided. He rose and followed.

He was out the door before the keep realized he hadn't paid for either of his whiskies.

"So where we going?"

Bob was stuffed in the passenger seat of a Suburban. The driver didn't seem to belong to the car. The car was clean; the dash smelled of Armor-All. The driver was dirty and smelled as if he'd drawn his last bath two days ago.

"I don't know. . . . Hey, let's go to the grain elevator."

"What?"

"You worked there, didn't you? Everybody says it. 'By-God worked at Skelley's, only Skelley's ain't Skelley's anymore. It's an ADM place.' Still, a grain elevator is as good a place as any."

Bob shrugged. He didn't understand half of what the guy said. He talked too fast. "Where's that cooler you promised?"

"Behind the seat."

Bob corkscrewed around, reaching behind his back. He'd never been a fast mover, and he was soon aware that his host had grown impatient with him trying to flip the hatch. Finally, St. Claire took both hands completely off the wheel to knock open the cooler lid himself. "You really would waste your whole life over one damn beer, wouldn't you?"

Bob grabbed the wheel, afraid the truck would veer into one of the squat mailboxes lining Jefferson Street. "You're nuts." He twisted the cap off a bottle. "But I guess me being here makes me a damn nut, too."

"Sure. Hey—you want to see something really nutty?"

Before By-God could answer, St. Claire slapped the lock on the glove box to dig through a thatch of papers. When he yanked his hand out, his fingers were wrapped around a snub-nose .22.

"Jesus Christ! Put that away—I got enough problems without you wiping my nose with that thing."

St. Claire spun the pistol around his finger like a gunslinger. "Siege or besiege?"

"What?"

"Besiege or siege? People think those are synonyms, but they're not. One's a verb and one's a noun, and that means you either do it or it's done to you. You can besiege something, but you can't siege it. You can be besieged, but you can't be sieged."

"You don't put that gun away, I'm gonna bail out this door. And I'll be taking this beer with me."

St. Claire laughed. He tossed the .22 back in the glove box and closed the door. "You're nobody's fool, By-God. You're just a misunderstood man. Let's clear up that misunderstanding. Tell me about your son."

"Aw, not that again. I'm gonna have to go over it all here in the morning."

"I'm not asking about him disappearing. I'm asking about him. Tell me about *him*."

Bob thought. When nothing special popped into his head, he drew a long swallow from the bottle's neck. "He was just a regular kid."

"He *was*? But he's not anymore?"

"What?"

"You said 'he was.' That's the past tense. I hope to God you're not using the past tense when that sheriff's questioning you. That'll get you into trouble."

Bob was trying to decide if he was the butt of a joke.

"Oh, never mind," St. Claire said. "Tell me something specific. Like what you guys did for fun. You play ball with him? Pretend you're the Indian and him a cowboy? I bet at the very least you took him swinging at the playground."

"His mom did all that stuff."

"Yeah? So what'd *you* do with him?"

"I gave him four hundred bucks a month, that's what I did."

"When you were working—"

"Now just a damn minute here." Bob's face was flushed. He was starting to get pissed. "I'll sit with you and drink your beer, but that doesn't mean you get to insult me."

They were outside the city, moving through the interchanges along Highway 31, west of Franklin. The lights from the traffic stops and businesses charged the snow with an electrical vividness.

"I'm not insulting you, friend. I'm just asking questions. If you don't like them, you do the talking."

"Man, what do you want from me?"

"You and Chance, that's all. By-God and Chance. Those aren't synonyms either, now are they? But here, let's try it this way. Why do you think people think you had something to do with his being missing? Besides the polygraph, that is."

"How should I know? I've had my share of chumps telling me how awful an old man I been since he come out the womb. You should've heard that keep back there giving it to me. There been times I think some people get off on what's happened. Makes them feel better about themselves, you know?"

"What *has* happened?"

"What?"

"You just said something happened. If something happened, it must've happened to Chance. I'm asking what happened."

"I'm about tired of your goddamn riddles." By-God took another long drink. "Okay, so yeah—so I've been a bad dad. I'll admit it. It wasn't nothing personal with the boy. I just don't have it in me to give, you know? Me and him, we went belly up. Can't say why."

St. Claire was silent for a short stretch. "That's some deep thinking. It takes a real man to be comfortable with his failings. But that's not it, not it at all, bub. You could've been straight out of *Little House on the Prairie*—all that Michael Landon, gentle-walks-the-ploughman stuff—and they'd still blame you. Trust me on that. No, it goes much deeper. There's a hostility we've got in us as fathers—it's stitched straight into the fabric of our nature. We're made to go missing, you know? We are the empty space. It's the myth of lost origins, the wish fulfillment of orphanhood: we want the freedom from authority while reserving the right to resent that freedom. Try as we might, we're not going to plug that

God-shaped hole because we don't want to. You remember the last words of our buddy Jesus Christ? *Eli eli lamma lamma sabacthani*—'Father, my father, why hast thou forsaken me?' That's me and you, By-God—we're the forsakers."

Bob wasn't following at all. The blank look on his face made St. Claire smile. "I know I'm talking nonsense. I've got logorrhea. You know what that means? It means I shit words. But here's the deal: you think you weren't doing your job for that kid? Well, you weren't—but you *were* fulfilling your fate. Even if you didn't have anything to do with him disappearing, you couldn't have kept him here if you'd tried. Trust me again on that. It was all out of your hands, right from the start. Hey—look here. The grain elevator."

St. Claire stopped the Suburban at the mouth of a gravel lane. In the distance beyond a short thicket of trees were the elevator silos, which dwarfed the squat tin shed that housed the scales that weighed farmers' harvests. A gate closed off the lane, its metal slats glowing in the wet moonlight.

"Why you want to come out here, anyway? You know anything about me you know I got canned by this place. I don't want to be here. Anybody comes along, we'll get hauled in for trespassing."

"I want you to kill me."

Bob wasn't sure he heard right. He asked St. Claire to repeat what he'd said, but St. Claire just went on talking, staring through the windshield to the scales shed.

"The way I figure it, this would be the prime-o spot to dump a body. You could hide someone with my girlish figure in one of those silos and nobody would be any wiser until they filled the train cars. Maybe not even then. Flesh decomposes, an auger can grind bones to powder. Just more foreign matter. Don't the grain companies want some percent of dirt and fine in the kernels, to keep it down to grade? It's almost organic when you think about it. Dust to dust, right?"

"Jesus H. Christ," Bob said desperately.

"See, you're my *deus ex machina.* You're the god who's going to get me out of this story I can't bring to an end. Well, I take that back. Chance is, not you. He's the god, you're the machine, the instrument. So what do you say? The gun's right there. Let's do it. Let's make a pact."

Bob yanked the Suburban door open and slid into the snow, swearing to himself. *Now I've got to walk all the way back.* He'd known all week things would end either in relief or with luck but he hadn't counted on duck-ass crazy. He'd only taken a dozen or so steps through the slush when he felt something pelt him between the shoulder blades. He whipped around just in time to see St. Claire hurl a second snowball his way.

"What's your damn problem?" Bob hopped out of the snowball's path. It hit the grass near his big feet and exploded in a puff.

St. Claire packed a fresh snowball in his bare hands. When the ball was hard, he bounced it in his palm. "You wouldn't be murdering me, you know. I've already off'd myself in a figurative way, but I just can't seem to get the literal part down. I know you know what that feels like. Don't you want out, too? What's stopping us? If I had any sarcasm left in me I'd say that self-destruction's been so much fun, I don't want it to end. But what's your excuse?"

By-God was staring down the long dark road. "I'm gonna have to walk that son of a bitch," he said aloud. When he looked back, St. Claire was squeezing the snowball against his forehead.

The snow began to crumble, chunks dribbling down his chin and chest.

"Seven times in nine months I've been through this. I can still name every one of the children I thought I could find. I can remember every *place* I tried to find them. First there was my son, A.J. St. Claire, in Bay City, Michigan. Then it was Molly Ketchum in Manistee and Denita Burgiss in Alpena and then Stephen Holcomb in Ionia and Amanda Totch in Mt. Pleasant and now your son, Chance, somewhere between Franklin and Shelbyville, Indiana. Each of those kids is here with us right now—their ghosts are, anyway. They'll be your company, walking with you after I go, for as long as you choose to go on. Maybe your son's ghost is one of them—I don't know. What I want you to know is that each time I thought I was chasing a presence that was evil and ugly and that had abandoned us here in this orphanage of an existence, but except for A.J.'s it never turned out to be more than you. It was never more than a father or a stepdad or an uncle or a boyfriend who just snapped. *Just snapped,* that was always the explanation. The clincher is that this is the fourth straight time that the polygraph's been refused. If you were me, you couldn't keep going through it either. There's only one thing left for me. For you, too. Let's curse that mofo and die, big boy."

"Why'd you have to bother me tonight? Jesus. Things been bad enough without all this."

"So you'd know what you have to look forward to. I'm your Ghost of Christmas Future." He dropped his fist to his side and popped what was left of the snowball as if it were a balloon. "What didn't kill me didn't make me stronger, By-God. What didn't kill me just left me standing here, wishing I *had* been killed."

And with that he was gone. Later, Bob would remember actually *feeling* the headlights of the Suburban spilling across his belly, then disappearing as the truck sped away, tires spitting up a trail of mush. He stared at the empty road and then started walking.

As hard as he tried, he couldn't help but think of the names of the children St. Claire had recited. He felt the night crowd tight around him as sure as if those kids' elbows were in his ribs. In his mind he pictured the brown bank of Sugar Creek he'd grown up playing on. He remembered how his boy had always taken off his shoes and socks when he gamboled on that spot, even this late in the fall. *Catch you a cold like that*, the father had warned.

Before too long his boots were soaked through, and the cold had eaten its way up his legs. As he trudged along, he cursed everything he could think of in his life. He didn't care about how it would end; he only wished now that it would. This week had gone on long enough. He tried to push everything out of his head, but words were like the elbows of the spirits jabbing him. The words weren't *relief* and *luck* anymore. The words were *ashes* and *dust*. One to one, the other to the other.

Not a damn soul ever gonna understand, neither, he thought the whole way to the creek.

i'm so tired

Heim was in the middle of his morning jog when his cell phone rang. It was his first run in a week, and it felt good. Days of waiting for St. Claire to turn up had left him with little to show for his time but a bottled sense of frustration, which he'd decided to uncork. He'd come to Indiana with only a few changes of clothes, and among them weren't his running shoes. He had to buy a pair at the local Wal-Mart—a cheap, fifteen-dollar pair that he planned to pitch in the first rest-stop garbage can he passed on his way home.

He hadn't gone to Wal-Mart for sneakers. He'd gone to buy a little cassette player—a cheap one, he hoped—so he could listen to the tapes he'd found in St. Claire's truck. After driving back and forth between Franklin and Shelbyville, scouting for a sign of his stolen Suburban, Heim had decided that turnabout was fair play. He fashioned a homemade slim jim out of a strip of plastic and opened the truck, which St. Claire had abandoned in the Best Western parking lot. Heim didn't know what explanations he expected to find there; he just knew he deserved some. He had a military sense of loyalty, and whenever he felt his betrayed, it kindled resentments he wasn't good at extinguishing. But even more, he needed to hear those tapes because he needed to justify his own actions.

When he discovered the first boxful of cassettes stuffed under the passenger seat, he figured they were as close to a coherent answer as he'd get. Then he opened the back latch of the truck and found the mess St. Claire left behind—unwound cassettes, unmated socks, unopened soda cans, a life undone. Heim picked through the wreckage of Colin's grand mission, gathering the cassettes in an oily pillowcase left wadded in the sleeping bag. The rental truck didn't have a tape player, so he went to Wal-Mart. The shoes, plus the gym shorts and the marked-down hooded sweatshirt he'd also bought—those were impulse purchases. Heim got them in case he felt the need to put some distance between him and St. Claire.

At first, he tried to listen to the cassettes in his motel room, but there were too many distractions. Even with headphones covering his ears, he couldn't shake the racket—the couple bickering in the next room, the grind of the housekeeper's cart as it rolled outside the door, the industrial hum of wires and pipes that the walls couldn't quite absorb. Heim couldn't concentrate on St. Claire's voice, too bound in the loop of normalcy. There was no making sense of Colin that way. So with a pillow he stole from the motel, he climbed in the back cab of St. Claire's rusting truck and spent the entire night there, in the dark, going from tape to tape to tape.

He wanted to go through the cassettes in chronological order because he believed there had to be some logic, some progression to St. Claire's decay. If he could just find that moment when Colin had lost his senses, Heim could carry him back there and gather the man's wits for him. In the early days after leaving home, St. Claire labeled each tape by date, so all Heim had to do was go down the line they formed in the shoebox. The tapes were full of stories, as though Colin were trying to recite for A.J. a lifetime of family gossip and legend that the boy would have grown up hearing if not for a certain day at a certain Home Depot. *Why was it I wanted to be a typographer?* began one. *What was it about the arrangement of words on a page that I loved?* And another: *You should know how I met your mother.* And another: *Let me tell you about the time your grandfather took a sledgehammer to the car.*

But then at some point in the tapes—it was fairly early on, a month or six weeks in—the stories stopped, and the tone changed. It wasn't from the amphetamines; Heim could tell from the start when St. Claire was wound up. He talked about it, for one thing: *This trucker here in the Sioux just sold me twenty blue capsules and now my tongue is twenty blue and I have got it going on, apple pie, going on!* When Colin was high, he sounded like that—crazed words just spilling from him, words in search of ideas, order, meaning. Heim fast-forwarded through most of that nonsense. But even worse was when St. Claire was on the ride down: his voice thickened, his consonants lost their pop, and his thoughts dribbled off into chokes, sighs, and moans.

Pretty soon there wasn't even mention of A.J. anymore. In the early tapes, the boy's name popped up endlessly, thrown into sentences in the most awkward of ways, as if Colin believed that by just saying *A.J. A.J. A.J.* he could hone in on his son. But the boy that had gone was now gone from his father's lips, replaced by some generic *you* Heim couldn't identify. It was clear from those contexts that it wasn't the child, it wasn't Kimm, it wasn't even St. Claire himself, but somebody, something more ambiguous, more menacing: *Why is it that you've done to me what you've done to me, mofo? Why?* And on like that.

The saddest tape was the last one. Heim had stopped listening to a cassette of an obviously lubed Colin choking on a gob's worth of profanities, cussing *you* out. He turned off his player, disgusted, and rolled over on his side to settle the lonely, isolated feeling that crept up on him. Something poked him in the back. It turned out to be St. Claire's own handheld tape recorder. Heim's first thought was of the twenty bucks he could've saved if he'd found it before heading to the Wal-Mart. He slipped the last tape in his own player, rewound, and pushed the play button. His earphones filled with a voice that sounded feeble and drained. St. Claire repeated the same words, again and again, each repetition hardening and slowing the rhythm until his tongue tapped against his teeth like a cracking stick:

> *And I, who loved you once,*
> *Childblind,*
> *Know now*
> *Right worship is defiance.*

Forty minutes of that. Or, rather, several minutes and then disintegration: St. Claire's voice trailing off—he was falling asleep, Heim guessed—and the phrases began to peel away until St. Claire was saying only that last line, several times, and then not even the entire line but its last word: *defiance ... defiance ... de-fi-ance ....* And, after that, not even the whole word but a stray syllable, just *fi ... an ... de...* And then nothing at all, just a shallow swish of air that may have been Colin breathing or just a hiss on the tape itself.

After the tape stopped, Heim clicked off the recorder and crawled out of the truck. By that point, it was just short of dawn, and the moonlight mixed with shadow made the snowfall look blue. Exhausted, Heim carried the pillow up to his room and slept for two hours. When he woke up he knew he needed to jog.

So he ran—a crazy thing to do the morning after a surprise dose of snow when all he had to wear were a pair of flimsy gym shorts and a hooded sweatshirt. But the motion was steadying. As Heim cut from the motel's access road to the zipper of Highway 9 that ran through a patched jacket of tilled fields, he was thinking of how he was going to square things with Stephie. When he called home now, he could tell she was certain that she was being lied to. She kept asking him questions, trying to trip him up on the details: *How many babies did that sow farrow again? What did the doctor say Paps's B.P. was? What was that prescription that the doctor had you fill? How many pills a day does he have to take?* Heim thought he should just go home and tell his wife he'd done what he did for A.J.'s sake. She'd understand it then; she was a mother herself, she'd have to. But by the first quarter mile of his run, he knew that this was just another lie. He couldn't even claim he'd gone after Dickie for St. Claire. He was moved by something bigger and deeper and of his own—a sense of anger, revenge, righteous defiance. Heim knew he had to get that out before he ruined his life. That's why he was out in the snow, his legs pumping like pistons, believing that in the hard chopping of his pace he could burn off whatever impurities had put that unruly tiger in his tank.

He was up to a good clip on the county road, about a seven-minute mile, when the cell phone rang. Heim stooped for a moment to catch his breath before answering. When he clicked the talk button, it only took a few syllables to recognize who was calling.

"I think I've found your friend," Sis Pruitt said.

"Where?" Heim was breathing deeper than he liked. It made him sound anxious.

"In my orchard. How fast can you get here?"

SIS HAD SPOTTED THE Suburban as soon as her father turned the bend at the top of their property line. The truck couldn't be missed, abandoned amid the cluster of apple trees, just short of the grape arbor.

"Whose is that?" Clinton asked as they pulled past the abandoned milk barn.

"I think it's a friend of mine's," she lied. "One of my POMC friends."

"Your friends always park in the middle of your yard?"

"I don't know what's going on." It was the most honest thing she'd heard herself say in a while.

He let his truck idle next to the walkway to the door. "You want me to come in 'til you find out what's happening?"

"You've had a long night. Go get some rest. I'm sure everything's all right."

Inside, she fumbled through her purse for the number Heim left her. She knew the Suburban couldn't have been parked too long. Pete had left early to take his soybeans to the elevator. He'd have seen the car if it'd been there when he left. She didn't want to think what would've happened had Pete been home when St. Claire plowed into the orchard. St. Claire wouldn't have had time to set his emergency brake before Pete would've had him in jail. Or the hospital.

When Heim answered her call, he sounded agitated and out of breath, not at all what Sis expected. She didn't understand why until his rental truck barreled into her drive, and he bounded down from behind the driver's side door in nothing but shorts and a hooded sweatshirt—another dimension of the day's craziness.

"Has he moved at all?"

"I haven't seen him." They stood on the Pruitts' walkway. "I don't know if he's even inside."

"Maybe you better wait here," he told her.

breathing out the ghost

She didn't. She trailed him as he jogged past the porch and the kids' swing set. By the time she caught up with him, he was on his tiptoes, his face cupped to the back window. Heim was still exhaling heavily—his breath left a cloudy stain on the glass. "That's him all right."

When Sis looked, all she could see was a foot thrown over a back seat, a body buried under a heavy flannel hunting jacket. Heim marched around the truck's corner, yanked open the side door, and lifted himself inside, disappearing between the seats. She saw him reach over the passenger seat and flip open the glove compartment. He rifled through it, swore, then slapped the door shut. A second later St. Claire came spilling out of the car, landing face down in the snow. He didn't move.

"Is he okay?"

Heim jumped to the ground, his face red. "He's fine. He's asleep."

"He sleeps pretty sound."

Heim rolled St. Claire onto his back. His mouth fell open, and a pasty tongue rolled from one corner to the other. Heim pulled an eyelid back. The pupil was dilated, distant. Heim let the lid fall.

"This is your brain on drugs . . . but at least he left me a quarter tank of gas."

"Carry him inside. I can make some coffee—for him, I mean. I know all you drink is water."

"I hate bothering you more. I should take him back to the motel, but I can't. The last thing I need is for a maid to catch me dragging his body into the room." Heim stooped over St. Claire again, slapping at his colorless cheeks.

St. Claire stirred slightly, a faint gurgle creaking from his throat. "Thirty-five," he moaned.

"What's he saying?" Sis asked.

Heim scratched at some invisible irritation at the side of his head. "I'm guessing that's how long the speed binge lasted." He grabbed St. Claire's wrist and with a single jerk pulled him up and over his shoulder, hunching from St. Claire's weight. "You sure you don't mind? I'll try and be out of your hair in an hour or so."

Sis rolled her eyes. "Might as well. Things couldn't get any stranger."

She led Heim inside to her living room, where he dumped St. Claire in the recliner. Sis made fresh coffee while Heim tried to shake his friend to life. It took a long time; St. Claire's body was like a deflated bag—there didn't seem to be anything left inside. Slowly the color came back into his skin and his eyes regained focus.

"You know where you are?" Heim asked.

"Hell."

Heim laughed a little. "I wouldn't take that personally," he told Sis. When St. Claire saw Sis, he sat up a bit, trying to straighten himself in the recliner. She thought he was embarrassed, but then realized a different expression was wrinkling his brow and squeezing his eyes—a sort of vanity or pride, a look that said, *Here I am and here I stay.* It wasn't the face she'd seen the day he appeared in her front yard, nor the one in the picture on Kimm's shelf. It looked rehearsed, a pose. St. Claire's elbows were poised on the armrests at sharp angles, his chin resting on his knuckles in a gesture of exuberant brooding. He looked every bit the aristocratic vampire.

"My picture's not sewn on a quilt somewhere is it?"

The comment brought a blush of anger to Sis's cheek. She set her coffee down and pulled a footrest over so she could sit square in front of him. "I don't know you but barely, but you've come into my life in a big way. I'm going to be honest and tell you that you've not been a good influence. What you've been doing—what you've done—is wrong. No way around it. You may think you were trying to fill the hole left by your son's disappearance, but you weren't. Not by a long shot. You just made that empty space bigger for other people."

St. Claire's ears twitched as if maternal sternness was an alien sound.

"Last week you told me I was running after wind, that I was like you—chasing something I couldn't get hold of but couldn't let go. Well, I got my hands on it. Do you know who showed it to me? Your wife. And your daughter. They showed me that it's a lot easier to leave than to be left behind."

Heim almost felt sorry for St. Claire. Sis sounded as if she were disciplining one of her children. But he had been wanting to say the same things, and for a long time. "Come on home, Colin," he said protectively. "Let's *both* go home."

St. Claire's expression hardened even more. He looked at Heim, then switched his glare back to Sis. "Now I know why my ears have been burning the past few days. I can just hear the two of you diagnosing me, dissecting me. I just want to know—who did the autopsy and who did the funeral oration?" When he realized neither Sis nor Heim was going to give him the reaction he wanted, he leaned forward until his face was close to Sis's. "Let me ask *you* something. Can you name all the human faults, all the human sins that there are?"

Sis stayed silent; she wasn't going to play his game.

"You being a good Baptist and all, I'm sure you know. Of course, there's the big seven: anger, lust, sloth, greed, gluttony, envy. What's the other one? Pride, yeah, pride. How could I forget—it goeth before a fall. But tell me this: why isn't *anguish* a sin? Why not disgust, despair, ire, irritation, dog-sick-of-it-tiredness? Why isn't earmarking yourself for annihilation a sin?"

St. Claire and Sis were locked in one of those old-fashioned blinking contests, each trying to outlast the other's stare. When St. Claire faltered, his eyelids fluttering, he twisted his head to one side and balled his face shut. "Giving up, not caring, it's not a sin because it's not asking for forgiveness. It's way past redemption, rehabilitation, whatever the hell it is you two want from me. There aren't any laws governing grief except the law of certain obliteration. I mean—" He blinked again in Sis's face— "my God, doesn't that sound freeing to you?"

Heim squatted beside Sis's footstool. "You're talking nonsense. You need to think about Kimm and Neve, not yourself. How's that for freeing? Step outside of your own misery."

St. Claire laughed. "The old Heimster. Heimster-holster. I wish I'd met you in an earlier life, you know? You could have taught me a lot. You've got this presence, this confidence, this sort of 'don't mess with Texas' thing. No way is anybody going to cut you off at the knees, most of all yourself. You're like those old toys we had as kids—you're the Weeble that wobbles but won't fall down. That's how we're different, so different. . . ." St. Claire shifted suddenly to Sis. "Did he tell you how he lost that detective's license?"

Sis looked at Heim, who for the first time seemed something less than what St. Claire described him as—certain, unshakable. Heim shifted his weight to his other foot, defensively.

"He didn't, did he? See, he comes off very stable. Smooth-oiled and all. Like an engine you'd never guess was capable of misfiring. Come on, man. Tell her how you lost it."

Heim swiveled to his feet, nodding, as if the movement worked the words out. "All right. It's public record. You could find it out easy enough if you wanted to, Mrs. Pruitt. I lost my license last February because I stuck a gun in the mouth of the man I thought took Colin's boy. The guy goes by the name Dickie-Bird, and I was positive he knew where A.J. was. I was thinking about what that kid might have gone through. I wanted this man's diary to prove what I was certain of, and when he wouldn't hand it over I lost control. I drew on Dickie, and I made him hold the barrel between his teeth. I could have fired, too. I wanted to. I had the thing cocked—" He didn't do it consciously, but his forefinger and thumb were stuck out, making the shape of a gun—"but I didn't take it further. Maybe I should have. Dickie filed an assault complaint, and now I'm in another line of work. It's not of my choosing. But it is my doing." He turned back to St. Claire. "You happy now?"

But St. Claire was busy gauging Sis's response.

"You don't approve of that, I'm sure. But you secretly admire it, don't you? I know I did. That's all I've wanted this entire time—to cross that line like Sgt. Heim here did. Kickin' ass and takin' names, isn't that what they call it? To *make* something happen. Sad thing for me, though. You do it the first time, you want to do it again. Isn't that right, Heimster? Go ask By-God Bob. He'll tell you."

Heim's arms dropped to his side. "The Birmage boy's father?"

Sis shifted back, shooting Heim a startled look. "Oh, my God."

"Jesus, Colin. Tell me you—"

St. Claire shook his head. "Everybody knows what happened here, but nobody was doing anything. Seven days of tramping around like you'd just happen onto him. What were the chances of you finding Chance? By-God, By-Chance, By-God, By-Chance, By-God, By-Chance—you weren't going to resolve it. You all knew it, but nobody else would make a move."

Sis rubbed her forehead. "What made you think you could—"

"Don't tell me you don't know." St. Claire jerked forward, as if lurching for her. "You do. I heard it in your voice that night when you were talking about the quilt. I mean, when you spoke, you sounded like you could have pistol-whipped the crowd. You can't tell me you don't want to take somebody—and you *know* who—by the throat and throttle an explanation out of them."

"Maybe I feel that way sometimes, but it's a feeling. I'm not going around attacking people."

A wounded look entered St. Claire's eyes. "Of course not. But I'm a sick man. I've crossed the line, gone to hell in a handbasket, been rode hard and put up wet. I roll that rock to the lip of the cliff and let it fall back over me. I've lashed myself to a boulder with adamantine chains to pick my liver with an eagle's beak. It goes nice with the flint I stabbed in my heart after going around the world only to discover I'm an oasis of horror in a desert of boredom. See? I've the power to kill but not the power to die. I've grown up to find all Gods dead, all wars fought, all faiths in man shaken. I've made a mansion on the hill of this dark night of the soul. I'm Tiresias, throbbing between two lives, suffering all because I went down to the crossroads to give the devil his due. I won't go gently into the dark, dark night because to live outside the law, I've had to be honest. I'd give you everything I've got for a little peace of mind except that, baby, I *was* born to run. Yes, ma'am. I'm that cowboy on the steel horse I ride and I'm wanted dead or alive. And you know what else? Don't you get it?" He leaned forward again. "I've fallen and I don't *want* to get up. I want to be let alone so I can swallow my own spittle."

St. Claire sat back, contempt fattening his features. He stared straight at Sis. "A few days ago I killed this man that Heim had me convinced took my son. I don't regret it. It felt good. I did what Ole Heimster couldn't push himself to do, being the upright Weeble he is. So now it's his turn to admire me. And as for you, can you tell me there's really somewhere for me to go back to? Can I really have this homecoming you two are talking about?"

Heim stepped toward him again.

"Colin, you didn't kill Dickie-Bird. You clocked him good with that thermos. But I went back after you ditched me in the woods. The bus was gone. Dickie had torn out of there."

The brute force that St. Claire had summoned for his tirade dissipated without a trace, as if it'd never existed. He slumped rigidly, his eyes drained, the boastful arch of his back and the haughtiness in his face gone. Under his shirt, his chest seemed to melt. "I can't do anything right."

Sis stood. "I can't believe I'm hearing all this. And in my own house!"

"What would you have me do?" St. Claire stared off into the distance, chewing his lower lip. "I can't go back to being normal."

That made Sis even madder. She slapped her hands on the counter and stiffened, planting her feet on the carpet. "What's normal got to do with anything? Look around this house. Is it normal just because I stayed here, because I kept to its routines? Look at the walls. Do you see anything of my daughter's on them? No. That's what we did—my husband and I—so we could stay here and fool ourselves into thinking we lived normally. We put her away. But she's still here, everywhere I look. I couldn't get away from her if I tried. I've been breathing out her memories for seventeen years. I'll probably *still* be doing it in another fifty. I've got to live with that, all the time, so don't give me that 'being normal' stuff. Normal has nothing to do with it."

St. Claire still stared aimlessly at his feet. She took a breath and calmed herself. "You never began that part of it, trust me. Having to walk rooms where she should be, having to eat with the empty chair at the table, every meal, every day, every year. And you won't until—" She stopped "—Oh, *shit*—"

The profanity surprised both Heim and St. Claire. "What is it?" Heim asked.

Through the window Sis was watching a truck rattle up the gravel drive.

"My husband's home."

She leaned against the wall and closed her eyes until the doorknob twisted and the door kicked open. When Pete saw Heim and St. Claire, he blinked hard and squared his shoulders. Heim stepped forward, tentatively, to shake Pete's hand, but St. Claire remained in the recliner, indifferent.

"These are the men I was telling you about this morning. They've stopped by—unexpectedly."

"I see that." Pete shook Heim's hand. St. Claire finally extended his, too, but the gesture was perfunctory. Pete seemed more offended than if St. Claire had just sat on his thumbs.

"I take it those are your cars out there. Including the one in the middle of my yard."

"We're sorry for that." It was Heim apologizing.

"It was my fault," St. Claire mumbled. "I'll pay for whatever damage I did."

"That's not why I'm here, though I expect there's a good story behind it. But I think you're gonna want to get to the creek. There's sheriff cars galore up there by Smiley's Mill."

For a second, nobody moved, as if resisting time. Then Sis grabbed her coat from one of the stools at the counter, and she led Pete and Heim out the door. Heim had just crossed the threshold when he realized St. Claire was still in the recliner.

"Come on, Colin."

St. Claire didn't move. "I just remembered. Today's my birthday. I'm thirty-five today."

Heim looked to Pete and Sis, embarrassed, and then they all stared at St. Claire, as if what he'd said meant anything to anybody at this moment. When St. Claire finally pushed himself upright, he listed to one side as he followed them to the cars.

bears of a bluer river

The onlookers stood along the eastern bank of the creek where it flowed past Smiley's Mill. A few of the braver ones inched onto the concrete overpass that crossed the slow-swirling water. From there they peered down ten feet at a pair of German shepherds that sniffed, one to a shoreline, at the rocks and craggy vegetation that bordered the lapping current. A detail of sheriff's sedans clogged the market's small parking area. Behind them, along the roadway leading to the little grocery, was a line of haphazardly parked civilian pickups left behind by the crowd as they rushed to see what the dogs had uncovered. By the time Pete and Sis arrived, they had to park more than fifty yards back from the store. Sis checked the rearview mirror to make sure that Heim had kept up with Pete. He and St. Claire had followed in Heim's Suburban.

"You gonna be all right?" Pete asked. Sis was staring a hundred yards past the bridge, past the fork in the road where Greensburg Road veered left toward the interstate. She was looking straight into the field where Patty's body was found.

"I'm fine. Let's just go."

They got out of the car and headed toward the bank.

Behind them, Heim parked the Suburban, clapped his eyes closed, and gripped the steering wheel.

"I need the gun, Colin."

"What gun?"

Heim shook his head. "Whatever you've done here, you've done it to me as surely as you've done it to yourself."

"Whatever's done was never mine to do. It's been done to us."

"That's your excuse for everything now, isn't it? Maybe you're past caring, but you need to hear this. There's an invisible cord tethering you to me. The times I brought you home last fall—that was me jerking you out of the maw into some kind of sanity. Now you've got your hands on the rope and you can help me keep my balance or you can spill me. I don't like you having that power over me. My life would've been so much easier if I had just cut the cord, but I never did. I never could. I knew that if I did I'd be severing something human in both of us. Enough people have cut themselves out of the human chain. Think of Dickie-Bird. He doesn't believe he's tied to anyone else, and look what that's done to him and to everybody he comes across. This is your chance to keep the link. Don't be like Dickie. Give me the gun, and I'll get us out of this however I have to."

St. Claire popped the passenger door open. "Like I said, what gun?"

Heim grabbed his collar and yanked his face close. "You son of a bitch. What about Kimm? What about Neve?"

St. Claire shot his palm out, breaking the grasp with pop to the breastplate. "You don't get it. I know who all I'm bound to. Sometimes you have to sever yourself so you don't drag others down. Never fear: you'll be free of me soon enough." He snaked backwards out of the Suburban.

Heim rubbed the knot at the bottom of his rib cage. When he could inhale without discomfort he stepped down and followed.

Sis and Pete fell into the line along the bank. From there they could see the snorting dogs and the deputies who waded back and forth in the calf-high water, kicking at the mucky bottom with their rubber boots. A few feet from the creek, Dub Ritterbush leaned against a mossy spile and growled into a walkie-talkie. When he saw the crowd watching him he blew the air from his cheeks in annoyance.

"He doesn't look too happy," someone said.

"You blame him?" someone else answered.

"What'd they find?" Pete asked the man beside him—an elderly, grizzled-chinned farmer who smelled of silage and hay.

"Down there—"

Pete and Sis craned past a half-dam of stepping stones that caused the current to swirl and whirlpool. Just past the rocks, flopped unceremoniously in the snow, was what looked to Sis like a beached whale. The shape was hard to make out because it was as white as the ground cover. Then she realized why everything was so white. A sheet had been thrown over something. It didn't take her or Pete long to figure out that something was a body.

"Why do they have dogs down here? They must think there's more to find."

The farmer shrugged. "Best ask him." He nodded down at Dub, who was trying to scale the steep bluff without using his hands. The ground was too wet, however. One foot slid out behind him, and he went forward, his fist disappearing in the mud. One of the deputies had to hand him a knotted rope, which was tied around the fat trunk of a red cedar tree at the top of the bluff.

Sis waited until Dub cleared the slope before cutting out of the line to intercept him. He was inside Smiley's before she caught up. "You know he's here, don't you? You know Chance is here somewhere. . . ."

Dub looked over his shoulder and frowned.

"I can't talk to you, Mrs. Pruitt. You know better than to ask." He turned to the clerk behind the cash register, holding up his soiled hand. "I need a paper towel. You got a roll anywhere?"

The best the clerk could do was a rag. Dub wiped his hand while his walkie-talkie buzzed and chattered. "Who're your friends out there?"

"What do you mean?"

"Them boys standing with your husband. The skinny one's that drifter we brought in last week. The way he and his friend are talking up Pete you'd think you were all long-lost cousins."

"That's By-God on the bank, isn't it? I'm telling you, whatever happened, neither of them had anything to do with it. I know them both. I know what they've been through."

"Really." He tossed the rag onto the clerk's counter. "St. Claire, isn't that the skinny one's name? Did he say anything about what he did to Bob Birmage last night?"

Sis hesitated. "He said he didn't hurt him. I believe that."

"I'm sure you do." His voice was fat with sarcasm. "No, he didn't *hurt* him, but I half-suspect he talked By-God to death. What happened to Bob was likely his own doing. It looks like he was trying to cross the creek. Undoubtedly drunk. From the way he was splayed out, you'd think he must'a slipped and konked his head. Only there's not a bruise to be found on his head. So if he didn't fall down, he laid down. I don't care how drunk a man is: you lay down in forty-degree water, you're gonna feel it. You know what that means? It means he stuck his face in the creek and drowned himself."

"Then what are the dogs doing here?"

"And don't tell me I don't know what all St. Claire's been through. I'm not half the jackass this county thinks I am. I called

Michigan when he first showed himself around here. You know what their state police told me? They said every time a kid goes missing, he turns up on the scene thinking he'll find his son. As if he'll just pull along some curb, and the boy'll be there, waiting to be picked up." Dub's forehead wrinkled. "I can almost admire that in a man. Fact is, the more time goes on I wonder if I'm not becoming like him—chasing after this or that rumor, tracking down clues that don't add up. By-God wasn't going to confess to anything, least of all where the boy is."

The walkie-talkie burst alive with a shot of static. Dub listened and then barked back an answer. Sis knew they'd found something on the bank—the men were speaking in code. "I better get down there. I suspect I'll need someone to be with Chance's momma and Mrs. Birmage later."

"Pete and I will do it. The both of us."

He nodded with as much appreciation as he could muster and then clipped the walkie-talkie back to his side and went out the door. Sis stayed a distance behind him. She watched as he gripped the rope and lowered himself down the bluff. Then she ran toward the bluff's edge, a sudden flush of heat pressing on her. The coming noon was bringing a thaw to the morning freeze; her feet kicked up a wake of slush.

The crowd was moving along the bank, away from Smiley's toward an abandoned lot on the other side of the street that served as a makeshift junkyard where locals dumped their bowed lumber, concrete blocks, old, burnt-out trash barrels. As Sis passed the rusted shell of a dishwasher, its door left gaping for foraging squirrels and raccoons, she spotted Pete's coat among the tightly packed shoulders. When she joined the procession, she felt the electrical jolt of its apprehension.

"There—over there," Pete said as she brushed against his shoulder. He held his step and pulled her to his other side so she was closer to the bluff. Down by the bank a trio of deputies huddled over a thicket of weeds, one of the dogs rubbing its snout in the brush. Across the creek the deputy and the other dog were motionless at the waterline, watching like the rest of the onlookers. Dub came jogging along the bank, his arms swinging at his hips, moving faster than Sis had ever seen him move. He consulted with his men for a moment, then motioned toward the overpass. Another officer ran over with a shovel and started stabbing at the ground. The crowd tightened as people jockeyed for position. Sis stuffed a hand in Pete's coat pocket so they wouldn't get separated.

As the officer dug, the German shepherd's tail twitched in agitation, and the deputy holding its leash had to wrap the restraint around the width of his hand to keep the animal steadied. The deputy threw the shovel aside, and the men fell forward onto their knees, their hands scooping up the broken ground. Just as suddenly, they stopped. Sis felt their air grow leaden. No one in the crowd spoke. No one moved.

The men on the bank drew away from the hole. Their shoulders were slumped, their heads hanging without relief, as though defeated.

When Dub turned, the onlookers could see he held something draped over a stick. He looked up to the crowd, his face drained and colorless except for the gray pallor of perseverance. He held the stick forward like a sword so those above could see what they'd uncovered.

It was a child's sock.

Dub looked at it, then at the crowd. "That's the all of it," he said. "That's everything that's here." Dub dropped the sock into a transparent evidence bag and then chucked the stick aside.

As Sis heard the resulting mumbles and groans, it came over her that they'd been brought to this moment of resolution for nothing. It didn't matter if By-God was dead now. The absence, the missing—it would be with them the rest of the day, tomorrow, the ones that followed.

"Let's get out of here," Pete whispered. Except no one was sure where to go, what to do next. The crowd began to thin into small, loitering clusters. Nobody wanted to leave, convinced that something more had to be coming, that an end to this story was near. Sis stared at the shallow hole beside the abandoned shovel, wondering what more the men might have unearthed if they'd just kept digging.

Then, from the back of the crowd, came a low, unholy moan. As its pitch and volume heightened the onlookers twisted around, searching for the source. It was St. Claire. He was standing knees bent, hunched forward, like a defensive tackle waiting for a running back to barrel at him, his arms stretched straight in front of him. His neck vibrated as his moan grew to a breathless scream. He seemed to be trying to exorcize something from deep inside his soul, as if one long blast of spirit would launch it right out of his rictus.

Then Sis saw the barrel of the pistol poking out of his fists; it was so short and stubby, it was easy to mistake it for nothing more than a bruised thumb. St. Claire had the gun pointed at himself, his hands twitching, his face concentrated on his hands, as if he hoped that shaking would do what he didn't seem able to: pull the trigger.

Before anyone could move or scream or respond in anyway, Heim flew through the space between them, legs out, slicing the air with the fluid movement of a circus acrobat. The weight knocked St. Claire back, had him staggering for balance. There was no way St. Claire could stay upright; every muscle in Heim's body contracted as he threw himself forward, tipping them both to the ground. To Sis's, their falling seemed to take forever, not because there was anything slow or graceless in Heim's tackle, but because Sis was waiting for the inevitable.

When it finally came, it didn't sound anything like what she'd anticipated. She'd spent her whole life on a farm, after all, and she was used to the deep thunder, the volcanic boom that could splinter the sky quiet of a cold morning hunt. This was just a brittle snap, no worse than a rusty hammer dropping on echoing concrete.

Nevertheless, the bullet's firing set the world in motion, and the entire crowd broke into a run to surround the two men who lay on the ground—the one, Heim, on his back, rolling from side to side as one hand grabbed at his left hamstrings and the other clutched his kneecap, a thick fluid like red motor oil bubbling through the fingers of both; the other, St. Claire, dumped face down at a crooked angle, not moving, his body bunched in a pulped heap.

escaped to tell

She understood now why her father couldn't hug her.

Or, rather, she thought she understood, although she was afraid to put it into words for fear of it sounding too crazy. That's because it was a memory inspired by a line in—of all things—a book. A book that should've been just a lame spread of last words in what had been a dry saltine of an assigned reading, a stupid story taught in a stupid class that she didn't care about anyway *because who can care about fucking books when there's a real world to deal with, ya know?* Yet there it was, italicized in a typeface that read as rat-a-tat-tat as her father sounded whenever she focused hard out of love and tried to make sense of his sputtering:

The devious cruising Rachel, in her retracing her search after her missing children, found only another orphan.

The keywords, of course, were the middle and final ones, *missing children* and *orphan*, the first because there was a secret in her family nobody talked about anymore, the brother she'd had but whom she'd never really known and whose name was so rarely spoken all this time after the fact that she wondered if sometimes those around her didn't forget that name if not actually forget the boy himself, not forgetting out of sadness or anger or anything like that but forgetting out of the humdrumness of routine. She'd grown up hearing people say her father's problem was that he couldn't let go, couldn't move on. Forgetting was something you had to do, she supposed, though she herself had nothing really to forget because nobody would tell her stories even when she begged. If she dared to say, "O Mother Mine I want to know it's not fair not to I have a right you can't keep it from me it's part of my life too," her marme would squeeze her fists and try not to cry and answer back, "Please don't make me what's over is done even if we don't know what's over or what was done and maybe someday I can tell you but not today just someday when you're older and it doesn't hurt so bad. It can't always hurt, can it?" And then Neve who hated crying because it seemed it was the only emotion her mother had in her when the subject of the past came up would plant her feet and cock back like a rooster and snap back with, "I'll find him you'll see I'll be the one and then maybe this family of ours won't be so crazy-weird with people tiptoeing around wheezing out ghosts embarrassed by the mention of my father's name. . . ."

Finding her brother had been a secret fantasy of hers since she understood the meaning of his missing. She wasn't allowed to talk about it. Her stepfather didn't approve. He spanked her once when she had to write and illustrate an original picture book for a school project. *Nancy Drew and the Case of the Lost Boy*, she'd called it. That was when she was ten years old and now she was sixteen. That was the story she wrote because that was the story she had to tell, and look what it got her: trouble. That's what books were good for, she thought.

And now she'd almost gotten in trouble over this book. Reading those last words again she thought she knew now why O Mother Mine had gone through her backpack after she left it hanging off a dining-room chair. Leaving it lying around the house was something Neve was usually careful not to do because it was the only way to avoid her mother going through it and the inevitable question she was always getting grilled with when nothing was found: "You've been seeing him, haven't you? Don't lie, I know you have." Sometimes Neve roostered back at this, too. She would say, "Stop with the third degree already. It's not even the third degree anymore. You've passed fourth and you're moving on to fifth." Only she couldn't smart back this time because the sight of her mother shaking a shitty, cover-torn paperback at her threw Neve for such a loop. "Why else would you have this book if you aren't talking to him?" Marme kept saying. It wasn't until Neve showed her the stamp on the inside cover that read PROPERTY OF BAY CITY PUBLIC SCHOOLS that her mother was persuaded. Persuaded but not relieved. "Just don't tell Steve, don't tell him what you're reading," she pleaded. "If he thinks you're sneaking off to see your father there'll be holy hell to pay for you and me both." It made Neve so angry she had something on the tip of her tongue she was going to let fly until she saw the pain scorched in her mother's face and she recognized what she really wanted to lash out at was bigger than her mother and her stepfather. What she wanted to lash out were the things that had broken her father. Only she didn't know exactly what those things were—nobody would tell her the story.

"You were no Rachel. If you had been you'd have tried to find my brother. You'd never have given up looking."

That's what she felt but could never say to her mother.

So instead she told herself that someday she would be the one to find him. Maybe a sister can't rightly be a Rachel, but she would solve the case of the lost boy whose name she sometimes forgot because she wasn't allowed to mention him. Yes, Neve would.

IN THE MEANTIME, THERE was that other word: *orphan*. It made her think of her father because he always seemed so alone. Who would he have if not for her? Certainly not O Mother Mine. Seeing that word printed so close to other letters that spelled out the denied facts defining her existence—*missing children— search—found* she remembered her first awareness that her mother had abandoned her brother. Neve was a child then; she remembered because she was wearing her karate uniform the day they took her to visit him at the hospital. She couldn't remember why he was there; she only knew she was excited because it had been a long time since she'd seen him. She guessed he'd been sick because he was always having moods and spells and fits that embarrassed everyone but her. Neve could remember Marme's resistance to even *seeing* her father. She could feel it as she swung between her mother's and her grandmother's hands across a marble plaza that led to a thick door that wouldn't open without buzzing a buzzer. There was a guard and a man in a white lab coat that she now decided must have been a doctor. She couldn't begin to remember what he said, but her mother's words were as fresh to her as if they'd been said when Neve was on the shaking end of that shitty paperback: "I can't go back to him after all this. I can't take him back. It's been too much."

Neve didn't know what was meant by that; she figured it had to do with the missing boy but it was just another fragment in mosaic of a story she wasn't allowed to piece together. She remembered how she'd had to yank her mother down the shiny hallway to her father's room. He looked so alone, sunk in a chair. She'd done what now, in retrospect, seemed the absolutely natural thing for a six-year-old girl to do: she crawled into his lap and nestled her head to his chest. Yes, that was only natural for a child who'd not been allowed to see her father for so long, but the clamor it created wasn't. O Mother Mine had yelled, "No, not yet come back this is all too fast for me," and then her father's mother and sisters started yelling at Marme until the doctor shushed them all.

By that time Neve had tuned out the racket. She was listening to her father's heartbeat, which she hadn't heard for so long. She was also waiting for him to wrap her in his arms. She thought it must have been the clamor that kept him from doing it; she remembered how he gripped the arms of his chair, nervously, as if the two of them were about to shoot off for a ride in a roller coaster. Then, slowly one hand rose. She was waiting to feel its safety, only she never did, at least not quite the way she wanted to. His hand rose but just as she was about to be clasped to his chest he returned the hand to the chair arm, squeezing it until his veins and knuckles bulged. Neve did the only absolutely natural thing for a six-year-old: she took her father's hand for him and wrapped herself up in the hug he couldn't give.

Now she knew the reason he couldn't do it without her help. It was all in the book: he was an orphan. Everybody was in the process of abandoning him that day because he couldn't be normal. Neve understood completely. How can you hold somebody when you're so afraid they'll disappear from your life? She imagined how he must've held her brother fiercely once. That was why he hadn't touched her, and it was okay. She had made up for it that day, she had made up for it since, and she would make up for it in the future. The next time she snuck out to visit him she would do what she always did for him. She would sit and listen and reassure him that the things he said weren't crazy. He deserved at least one person to do that for him. She would say, "Tell me," when he asked if she knew why he'd once wanted to be a typographer. She would say, "Never—I want to know," when he

breathing out the ghost

wondered for the umpteenth time if he'd ever told her about the time her grandfather took a sledgehammer to the car. She would say, "I would like that—but only if we can do it together," when he asked if she'd like to meet the oldest person in the United States. "She's almost one hundred and seventeen now, believe it or not. Would you like to meet her? I could arrange it. I almost met her myself once, back when she was only a hundred and six. . . ."

Someday, Neve hoped, her father would say, "You should know about your brother," but even if that didn't happen the next time there was always the visit after that and the next still.

Until then, she would show her father that he wasn't an orphan. It would be her way of telling him she would be the one to find the lost boy. Nancy Drew was on the case. She would climb into his lap and listen to his heart beating and when he was too afraid to hug her for fear of losing her she would do exactly what she remembered doing that day at the hospital: she would wrap herself in his trembling arm, and she would kick and scream again when they came to tear her away.

Only this time, she said under breath, I won't let go. I won't.

bunting

On the day of Grandma Brandywine's birthday party, one of Pete's sows farrowed. Sis and the kids stood beside the pen while Pete hunched down over the huffing pig, his boots crunching the fresh bed of maternity straw. As he patted the thick belly, he grabbed the little corkscrew of a tail with his other hand, pulling it back to expose the vulnerable slit between the sow's legs.

"Keep your eyes on door number one here," he told his children. Joey's fingers gripped the wire screen covering the front of the pen, his nose poking through one of the squares, his eyes wide. Tillie was another story. She buried her face in the denim of her mother's hip, voicing her displeasure with a series of melodramatic *ughs*.

"You need to be watching this," Sis told her. "Won't be too long and you can help your dad with the hogs."

"I'm not getting anywhere near those ugly things." The little girl spoke with defiant prissiness.

"You will if I say you are," Pete said, not harshly. "Nothing scary about it, is there, Joseph?"

Too engrossed by the mystery unfolding past the pig's underside, the younger child didn't respond. Sis patted Tillie's back until she remembered she didn't like people consoling her that way. "This isn't even the best part. Wait until it's time to castrate the boys. I wasn't much older than you when I was helping your grandpa with that. You know what castrating means?"

"Nope. And I don't want to."

Sis caught Pete's eye, and they laughed at the girl's squeamishness.

"I think I'll save up and get me a few farrowing crates." Pete stood and swung his legs over the wood slats along the pen's side, joining his family. "You know why, wild child? Every once in a while Ma Hog here ends up squishing one of her piglets when she moves around. With a crate, the bars constrict her wiggle room." He elbowed Sis while talking to Tillie. "Can you imagine that? A momma crushing her own baby. Maybe we should stop letting you sleep in our bed. You never know, you might wake up flattened one morning."

"I don't think that's very funny."

"Come now. Don't be such a girl. Your mom here never wanted to be a girl, did you, honey?"

Sis gave him a look. "You really want me to answer that?"

He shot her a dry kiss. "I'm just kidding."

Before Sis could answer, Joey shouted, his hand extended through the fence. "Look!" As the sow moaned, a shot of cream came out its bloody hind. The fat lips covering the birth canal quivered and slowly split. Then, without warning, the first baby slipped onto the bedding. It was small and slick, as if dipped in pancake batter.

"Start counting," Pete told the kids. Joey reeled off a *one* but was too fascinated by the birthing process to keep track as a quintet of babies burped out of the sow's womb. Tillie let out a yell and looked away. But then she heard her little brother giggling, and she snuck a peek. The freshly born pigs were piling atop each other as they instinctively scrambled for teats. They wriggled and kicked, climbing their mother's thighs before sliding down her belly toward the parallel rows of flopping udders. The kids laughed especially hard as one wrinkled waif went the wrong direction and began nosing for teats along the sow's back. When it realized its error, it scampered clockwise around its momma's head and then dove into the mass of sucklings gathered at her abdomen.

"Believe it or not," Pete explained, "They're not just drinking; they're chewing. Those babies have some mean teeth on them already. That's why I'll have to snip their tails here in a minute. They'll eat them right off each other otherwise."

Tillie whipped around upon hearing that news. "I'm *not* watching that!"

Pete and Sis laughed again. Sis thought about telling Tillie how pigs, being cannibals, would eat their sicker, weaker siblings, but she decided that information would be too disturbing. "You come on inside with me," Sis told her. "We've got balloons to blow up for Grandma's party. You staying out here with your dad, Joey?"

The boy nodded. He was watching his father pour a big bottle of iodine into a bucket. Pete took a pair of snub-nosed pliers off a shelf and began clicking the handles together with exaggerated malice. "Anybody who doesn't wanna see some tail-clippin' better get going." He lifted himself back into the pig pen, the bucket and pliers in hand. Tillie only had to see him grab one of the babies by its hind legs before she went screaming out of the barn. Pete laughed while he threaded the tail into the pliers' teeth and squeezed. The piglet flinched and squalled until it realized it'd let go of the teat it'd been sucking on. Immediately, it slapped its head back into the slurping mass, groping for the nipple. Once it found it, the piglet resumed gulping without further thought to the incident.

Pete winked at his son as he grabbed the next one. "See, no pain in life if you don't think about it."

From the door of the barn, Sis watched her husband snip another curlicue. "I've got to do my hair and get my bath. Don't you two take too long. Folks'll be here in about an hour, and you both need to get cleaned up."

She didn't wait for their response. She went into the house and set Tillie to work stacking paper cups for the guests. Then she went into the bathroom and removed the box of Revlon from the cabinet behind the mirror. She wet her hair and then squeezed the dye into her fading black, careful to comb the gray bolt along her forehead over her eyes. As she dragged the applicator behind the streak she remembered how, the first day Chance had gone missing, the little boy at Shiloh Baptist had called her Rogue, after one of the X-Men. *Rogue is the superhero sponge,* she remembered somebody explaining. *She soaks the energy straight out of people.* That could be good because it allowed you to absorb other people's pain, but it had bad consequences, too. Rogue could hurt people just by touching them.

The more Sis stared at her gray bolt, the humbler she felt. The streak was a sign of her vanity, not any special power she wielded. She had let it remain visible so people would remember what she had suffered rather than what she had survived.

With the Revlon was almost gone, she combed the bolt back into the rest of her hair and hastily blackened it, too.

She let the dye set and then rinsed her hair in the sink, careful to avoid her reflection in the mirror. Then she ran her bath. She closed the door, waiting for the tub to fill before she undressed. Stream rose and coated the window, the moisture forming droplets that streaked down the pane like tears.

Sis got into the tub, hiding her nakedness under foamy mountains of bubble bath. She casually passed the soap across her chest and legs, but mainly she wanted to feel the water's scald. She was dreading the birthday party. Grandma Brandywine was three days out of the hospital and disoriented by the old folks' home on Miller Street that Sis's parents had selected for her. The old woman couldn't remember breaking her 78s or nicking her palms. All she knew was that the bandages that wrapped her hands were thick as boxing gloves. Sis had suggested that they have the party at the nursing home itself to spare Ethel further confusion, but Sis's mother wouldn't hear of it. Obediently, Sis had spent the preceding days readying her own house.

She was sitting in the tub with her chin on her knees when the door opened and Pete entered the bathroom. He was stripped down to his T-shirt and jeans, which made him look scrawny. Sis couldn't understand how he stayed so skinny in the thick of middle age. He closed the door and sat on the wet edge of the tub behind her.

"Can I help you with something?" she asked over her shoulder.

"Gonna bother you if we have a few minutes to ourselves?"

She faced the tile in front of her. In spots, the grout was dark with mildew, and she could see stretches of soapy film greasing the wall. No matter how hard she tried to keep the farmhouse clean, the imperfections leapt out at her. "I don't mind, but I'm thinking about our kids, who'd probably like some lunch here before long, and about our families, who'll be calling for their cake and ice cream."

Pete's hand splashed into the water. His fingers brushed her bottom side as he fished for the washcloth. When he found it, he squeezed the soapy excess across her shoulder blades and began rubbing. Sis grabbed the edge of the tub with her right hand and twisted around.

"Pete Pruitt!" She held a schoolmarm finger up at him, "Never once in forty years have you washed my back, and I don't expect you to start now. What's gotten into you?"

His face creased with a slight, sad smile. He let go of the washcloth and sat down on the carpet so he faced her. It was a second before Sis realized what he'd pulled out of his back pocket: the kitchen cordless.

"Were you gonna tell me your friend called?"

"I didn't figure I had to—not the way you been checking the caller ID your every spare minute."

"Then maybe you can tell me what you and your friend talked about."

A convenient lie came to mind, but she thought of everything Martha had said about dishonesty, and she kept it to herself. "It was the first I'd heard from him since last week, I promise."

"That wasn't my question."

"He said that the good news is the physical therapist thinks he can be up and running again in about six months. The bad news is he doesn't know if he can patch it up with his wife. She wasn't too happy with all his lies."

"I can understand that part of it," Pete said, fingers drumming the tub. His voice was dry. Sis nodded guiltily, knowing it'd be a while before he would forgive her her dishonesty.

"And your other friend?"

She leaned back, resting against the tub's end, her legs fully extended. The bubbles were dissolving. Soon she'd be exposed to him. "Heim couldn't really say. St. Claire is like Humpty-Dumpty, I suppose. Did they ever manage to put him back together again?"

Sis could still see him lying there on the ground across from Smiley's Mill. St. Claire's body really had looked vacated—and relaxed, too, as if at peace. But then Pete had turned him over, and they found him squeezing at his stomach, his face pinched in a sweaty grimace. There were two ambulances that morning. One patched the holes where St. Claire's bullet tore through the back of Heim's left leg and exited out his knee cap, shattering it. The other raced St. Claire up to Indianapolis to retrieve that same bullet from his abdomen. Nobody could believe a bullet from a mouse gun of a .22 could do such damage.

Before Heim was taken to Shelbyville General, he gave Kimm's number to Sis, and she had called Michigan with the bad news. Hours later Sis sat in the waiting room with the abandoned wife as well as St. Claire's mother, Barbara, who had driven down from Bay City. Sis couldn't get over how young Colin's mother looked—she was younger than Sis herself.

When the surgery was over and the anesthesia had worn off, Kimm had been led into the IC unit to see him. She'd come out not a minute or two later, crying. "Goddamn him," she'd whispered to Sis. "You know what he said to me—the first thing he's said to me in a year? 'I went for the heart and got the spleen.' That's the only thing he could say after all he's put us through."

So Sis had held Kimm until she could cry herself out. Barbara comforted her, too, patting her back, not making excuses for her son but just listening as Kimm vented her anger and sadness. A little while later, the women passed the time by talking about their children. They traded stories—not the bad things they'd been through, just a little worksong of memories that made them all laugh and, for a bit, let them forget the circumstances. A few days later, when he was stable, St. Claire had been released from the hospital. Kimm and his mother drove him home.

"It's probably not good for her to go back to him. She needs help herself. They've got him in a hospital up there—a psychiatric place. They're treating him, I guess, trying to get him on his feet, to make him care."

"I guess if shooting a hole in yourself don't do it, nothing will. What do you think'll happen to him?"

"I don't know. I really don't. He could have done himself in, long before that gun even. But he didn't. That should tell him something about himself. I guess it all depends on whether he can accept what's out of his hands, even if he doesn't want to. Then he'll do what we've been doing, what Dub and the Birmages are having to learn. To live with it. If he can. That's it, I guess. I mean, what other choice is there, really?"

Pete didn't say anything, and Sis felt guilty again for the silence.

"Mr. Heim wanted to know if it was all right for him to give our number to this lawyer of his. He asked if I wouldn't mind putting in a good word for him, if necessary. He'd gotten himself in trouble over that man they thought took St. Claire's boy, and he's afraid they may yank his probation. He wasn't supposed to be around any guns, he said. I told him I would do whatever I could—whatever *we* could, that is." She thought for a second. "He's the one I feel for the most in this, you know. It wasn't his fight, but he believed he could make it right, that he could bring things to a heel for St. Claire. That should count for something."

She raised her eyes to find Pete staring at her. "What?"

His jaw was buckled, as though he wasn't sure he should say what he was going to. "I'm just wondering if there's anything else you want to tell me."

"Anything else?"

He nodded, faintly. Then it hit her what he meant.

"You've got to be kidding." She was laughing. "I mean, for the love of God, Pete. Really. He was Patty's age."

"And the other one?"

She wrinkled her face at the absurdity. "Boy, you think I've been having a real wing-ding around here, dontcha?"

"I'm just asking what I'm needing to know for sure."

There was something charming about his insecurity, which Sis had never before seen. "What I'm needing—" she told him "—is a towel."

Pete obliged. He held a towel from the rack on the backdoor open for her as she stepped out of the water, tucking it around her chest. She dried herself discretely, Pete watching her all the while, and then slipped into her bathrobe, her back to him. "Why don't you go check on the kids," she finally said.

After he left Sis dried her hair and applied her makeup. In the bedroom she laid the outfit she planned to wear on the bed and plugged in the iron to press it. While she waited for the iron to warm, she went to the kitchen to fix a quick lunch for the kids. Tillie and Joey were already at the table, drinking chocolate milk. Pete scooped the first of a stack of grilled cheese sandwiches from a skillet hissing with melted butter. "Tillie, you get those cups out?"

"Yes, Mom."

Sis passed into the living room to check one last time on the preparations. The card table was up and draped in a crepe paper cloth. The napkins were laid out in a neat line, with the plates and

breathing out the ghost

plastic forks beside them. The stacked cups looked like a rocket fuselage waiting for launch. The punch bowl was ready, too, lacking only the cream soda Martha was bringing. Most of the table was taken up by the cake box and the stacks of birthday candles beside it. Sis's mom was insisting that they put all one hundred and seven candles on this year's cake. It seemed an absurd demand to Sis. After they pulled out the candles to do the slicing, the frosting would look bullet-riddled.

As Sis turned back toward the kitchen something on the corner wall caught her eye. Above the roll-top desk that once belonged to Horace Hinckle was a frame draped in bunting. The photo was one Sis hadn't seen in a long time. Her first thought was of how much she disliked it. The high-piled hair, the blue-checkered dress, the neon-starred backdrop—they all dated the image. They froze that face to a spot of time Sis felt eternally tied to, no matter how many years intervened or how farther along in life she was forced to move. How sad, she thought, that something that should have been forgotten, buried in bureau drawer with other mementos, would become a family relic, a rune to be consulted whenever they needed to certify their memories and confirm that this person, their child, had indeed existed among them, if only once.

It was Patty's high-school graduation picture.

Sis was wondering how she could take down that bunting without hurting her husband's feelings when she felt Pete step alongside of her, a dishtowel thrown over his shoulder. "I don't want you telling me I hung it crooked, either," he said, and he slipped his arms around her waist, pulling her tight to his chest.

Sis closed her eyes, trusting her balance to the security of his embrace. "Have the kids seen it?"

"I don't know. But they will."

"And then?"

"And then we tell them the truth."

"That simple?"

He let her go. "That simple."

A WHILE LATER SHE was blowing up balloons in the kitchen, tying them together in clusters that they would string like decorative blossoms throughout the house. Tillie and Joey were playing in the living room, her with her cache of beanie babies, him with a toy Tonka truck.

Without warning, Sis heard Tillie say, "I know who that girl is." Joey didn't seem interested. His car wheels made a growling noise as he rolled them across the carpet threads. "That's my sister."

That caught the boy's attention.

"You don't have a sister. You *are* a sister."

"That is too my sister. And yours. But we'll never know her because she's dead."

"No, that's not so—"

"Uh-huh. You can ask mom. Ask her, Joey. Go ahead."

The boy started to speak.

"Wait. I'll ask her for you. Mom—Mom—Mom!"

In the kitchen, Sis took a deep breath, steeling herself in order to tell the story.

Once again.

Spider

There was a boy on a playground. He hung upside down from the monkey bars until the blood rushed to his head and his brain tingled. When he let himself down, he ran to the slide, but the cold did something funny to the metal that took away its slipperiness. The boy had to grip the side rails and jerk himself to the ground. Next he climbed the rope net that hung from the log fortress. Built into the play fortress was another, shorter slide, as well as a tire swing, a fireman's pole, and overhead bars. The boy jumped and gripped the nearest bar, but his muscles weren't strong enough for him to make it across the gravel moat, so he dropped down and climbed among the spiles and support beams. Out of boredom he walked to the swings and started chucking pebbles at a tall block of concrete carved and painted to look like Swiss cheese. When he tired of that he put himself in the lowest hanging swing, wrapping his arms around the chains as he kicked up a little dirt cloud by shuffling his feet. He was sitting there when the man walked up.

Kinda cold to be out here alone, don't you think?

The boy shrugged. This was the fattest man the boy had ever seen. A blue bump above one eyebrow disappeared under his green ski cap.

Where's your mom 'n' dad?

The boy pointed behind him. Beyond the softball diamond, its untended grass growing into the base lanes, was a semi-circle of houses. They were all white with black trim. Their back patios

325

were cluttered with a rummage-sale array of grills, bikes, planters, and plastic swimming pools. There was nobody around, though.

Your mom 'n' dad live in one of them?

My mom does.

Oh yeah? Where's your dad? You don't have one?

The boy shook his head.

Hey, that's like me. I got a mom but no dad. See that place over there? The one with the school bus? He pointed in the opposite direction, toward the street that fronted the playground. Among the houses was one with a squat plank veranda. In the gravel drive was a long yellow bus, cheap curtains strung across the windows. On the veranda was a woman in a rocking chair. She was bundled up in a coat with a Scotch blanket folded over her knees. She seemed to be looking above the playground to some faraway point in the sky. *That's my mom there.* The fat man waved at the bobbing figure, but the woman just kept rocking.

The boy looked at the man. *What's wrong with your head?*

The man put his palm over the discolored lump above his eye. Then he pulled the knit cap low over his brow so the boy could read the word that ran sideways next to a big gold G: PACKERS. The man seemed to be trying to hide the bump, but it was too late. The boy had been so transfixed by the circular crust of blood and the bruised swelling that surrounded it.

I've been to war, the man said. *These guys, my enemies, they tried to kill me. But the Lord doesn't shine favorably on those who just think they're righteous. I was too smart for them, in other words, and I snuck myself home. Nothing I love more than being home." His hand fell away from the wound. "Hey—how's come your mom's not out here watching you like mine is?*

She's in the house.

Yeah? Really? Doing what? I mean, why's she not playing with you?

The boy tipped himself back in the swing so his legs stuck straight out.

She has to clean. She can do it better with me not there.

Did she say that? That's a heck of a thing for her to tell you. The man laughed again. He sat in the swing beside the boy. His weight stretched the rubber seat and made the chain links groan. *You like to swing?*

The boy was gliding back and forth, not very high. *Sure.*

Yeah, me, too. You like to spider?

I don't know what that is.

That's just when you swing two at a time in each other's laps. Your legs, my legs—together they look like spider legs. That's why they call it spidering. Come here and let me show you. It's fun. You can look at these things. He jangled the metal pins hanging on his vest. *You know what this stuff's called? Jibber-jabber. Now tell me that's not a funny name. I saw you checking them out a minute ago. It's okay. You're allowed to touch them.*

The boy was still swinging.

Here— The man leaned over and caught the boy with his arm. The fingers of his opposite hand held out one of the pins. *Take a touch. Go ahead.*

The boy reached out and pinched at the dangling object.

See? That was pretty cool, huh? Now—how about spidering with me?

I don't want to.

Yeah, sure you do. You just think you don't because you don't know how fun it can be. My mom over there, she's got her eye on us both. We won't get into trouble with her around. You come over and we'll spider and then you can go to the post office with me. Do you like stamps? I have to mail a letter to a friend. You can help me pick out a stamp for him. Now come here.

The man raised the boy by the armpits and set him on his lap so the boy straddled the man's hips. Over the man's shoulder the boy could see his home. The windows were dark and there was no sign of life. The wind came along and lifted the dirt of the softball lanes into a cloud that made his house shiver like a dream.

See? It's fun, isn't it? Yes, I bet you're a good boy. And you should stay that way. Because you know what happens to bad boys?

The boy didn't say anything.

Their taliwackers fall off. The man laughed to himself. *Hey, what's your name, anyway?*

The boy told him.

That's it? Really? That's a pretty good name. Better than mine. You know what mine is?

The boy could feel the man's breath on his neck. *No.*

It's Dickie. Isn't that the silliest name you ever heard of? It's almost dirty if you think about it hard enough.

The boy felt the man rear back, his legs straightening so the seat lifted in the air. Then the man kicked his feet off the gravel, and the two of them rode out the arc of the swing. They didn't climb very high that first time, so on their descent the man paddled his feet backward on the ground, tipping the swing to a steeper angle. When they again flew forward, the man leaned back and pumped his calves in the air to build speed. The effort made him grunt like a horse, but a few rounds of kicking raised the seat to a good, scary altitude. Slowly, the boy grew aware of two different sensations. The forward motion made his stomach contract and left him feeling as if he'd left a part of himself hanging in the air behind his body. Then there was the backward glide, which pulled him into the man's chest, shrouding him in the intimate odor of leather, skin, body hair—all of these things close and touchable but too unfamiliar to give a sense of safety. As the pair rose and swooped back, over and over, the boy clutched tight at the armholes of the man's vest. Whenever he felt his hind end slipping from the man's lap, he stretched out his feet, trying to lock his ankles around the stranger's waist. The man's hips were too wide, however, and the boy was left grasping and dangling, waiting for whatever kind of fall might be coming.